PRAISE FOR ROSANNA CHIOFALO AND *BELLA FORTUNA*

"Like a gondolier navigating the canals of Venice, Rosanna Chiofalo takes you on a magical ride filled with family and friends, love and loss, heartbreak and happiness. *Bella Fortuna* is a warm glimpse into Italian-American life."
—Holly Chamberlin, author of *Last Summer*

"Chiofalo, a first-generation Italian-American whose parents emigrated from Sicily in the 1960s, brings the Italian immigrant community and neighborhoods richly to life."
—*Publishers Weekly*

"Skillfully crafted . . . sure to pull the reader into the love of family and the sights and senses of romance in Venice."
—*Metrowest Daily News*

"From the streets of New York to the canals of Venice, Rosanna Chiofalo creates a warm and lively story the reader won't want to see end. Valentine DeLuca is a heroine with intelligence, heart, and courage, the kind of person every woman wants for a dear friend. Time spent with her is a sheer joy."
—Mary Carter, author of *Three Months in Florence*

"A warm tribute to her heritage, the book brings to life colorful scenes from her past as a first-generation Italian American."
—*Astoria Times/Jackson Heights Times*

Books by Rosanna Chiofalo

BELLA FORTUNA

CARISSIMA

Published by Kensington Publishing Corporation

# *Carissima*

## ROSANNA CHIOFALO

KENSINGTON BOOKS
www.kensingtonbooks.com

KENSINGTON BOOKS are published by

Kensington Publishing Corp.
119 West 40th Street
New York, NY 10018

All Kensington titles, imprints, and distributed lines are available at special quantity discounts for bulk purchases for sales promotion, premiums, fund-raising, and educational or institutional use.

Special book excerpts or customized printings can also be created to fit specific needs. For details, write or phone the office of the Kensington Special Sales Manager: Kensington Publishing Corp., 119 West 40th Street, New York, NY 10018. Attn. Special Sales Department. Phone: 1-800-221-2647.

Kensington and the K logo Reg. U.S. Pat. & TM Off.

ISBN-13: 978-0-7582-7504-2
ISBN-10: 0-7582-7504-8
First Kensington Trade Paperback Printing: September 2013

eISBN-13: 978-0-7582-9159-2
eISBN-10: 0-7582-9159-0
First Kensington Electronic Edition: September 2013

10  9  8  7  6  5  4  3  2  1

Printed in the United States of America

*For my sister Angela.*
*And always for Ed.*

# PROLOGUE

# Francesca

You have no doubt heard of me. If not by my Christian name, then most certainly by the names that the media has labeled me with: *La Sposa Pazza, Carissima, Donna Fortunata,* and *Dolci Labbra.* Of them all, my favorite is *Carissima,* Dearest One.

You would have to be a fool not to realize why *Carissima* is my favorite. Who would not want to be known as Dearest One, especially if you are a famous movie star as I am? My fans' respect and adoration mean everything to me. And whenever one of them calls out, *"Carissima,"* I feel his or her love.

As for the other names, I do not care for them. Although everyone believes I have it all—fame, fortune, beauty—I am far from *la donna fortunata,* or lucky lady.

*Si, si.* I can hear your outrage right now. "What? You do not consider yourself lucky? You are a legend! A gorgeous Italian silverscreen star and one of the richest women in the world. Many would kill to have your life!"

*È vero.* I do have all this and more. But as for what really matters—family, friends, love—I have nothing.

The last name I especially detest. *Dolci Labbra,* or Sweet Lips, reminds me of a pornographic film. With their full, pouty shape, my lips have been voted perfect time and time again. Of course I am flattered to have received this praise, but I do not want to be

known as Sweet Lips. And I am not the only one who has inter-
preted this name in such a way. I have had crude men make remarks that refer to the female reproductive organ. It infuriates me
that I am associated with this name. And even though *Playboy* magazine begged me many times to pose in the nude, I never did. I am
a *real* actress, not one of these bimbos who have no talent nowa-
days and become famous because of their looks, most of which are
plastic, or because of a disgusting sex tape they have intentionally
created.

As for *La Sposa Pazza,* who would want to be known as The
Crazy Bride, especially when I have never walked down the aisle?
*La Sposa Pazza* was the name of my first film—and the film that
made me a star. In fact, all of my nicknames—*Dolci Labbra, Donna
Fortunata, Carissima*—were names of my films.

In *La Sposa Pazza,* I play a woman in her early twenties who has
no trouble finding men who want to marry her. But each time my
character is moments away from exchanging her wedding vows,
she runs away. In the movie, my character, Rosa Bianca, who has
been cursed with a name that means "white rose" in Italian, becomes engaged three times. But she loves romance and dating and
knows once she gets married, she will no longer have the glamorous life of a bachelorette.

Again, the irony that my own life would mirror the movie I am
most known for has not escaped me or the paparazzi. For like Rosa
Bianca, I have become engaged several times—five, to be exact—
but have never gotten married. But unlike Rosa Bianca, I never even
made it to my wedding, I am relieved to say. At least I had enough
good sense to realize that my doubts about each of my fiancés were
enough to break off the engagements well before I made it to the
altar.

The subsequent movies all have a wedding theme. In *Carissima,*
I play a poor Italian woman who is turned into a movie star after
she meets a famous American movie director. But on the morning
of her wedding, after she has put on her gown and is ready to leave
for the church, my character receives word that her fiancé has been
killed in a car accident. After this movie's release, my fans and the
paparazzi would chant, *"Carissima, Carissima!"* whenever I appeared
in public.

Audiences arrived at movie theaters in the hundreds on the opening night of *Donna Fortunata* to see if my character would finally find luck in love and get married. My character is a schoolteacher from Capri who meets a Greek shipping tycoon. The tycoon spoils my character and buys her lavish jewelry and furs and takes her to the most expensive restaurants. He proposes in a tiny boat in Capri's famed Blue Grotto. Audiences watched nervously during the wedding ceremony scene on the beautiful Greek island of Santorini. Once my character said "I do," the audience broke out in raucous applause and whistles. The movie ends with a close-up of me kissing my on-screen groom.

After *Donna Fortunata,* all the media wanted to know was when I would be getting married. At this point, I had already broken off my two previous engagements, and the media wasted no time in christening me with the nickname *La Sposa Pazza.* The ugly rumors began surfacing as to why my previous two engagements had not worked out, and of course, the blame always lay completely with me.

By the time *Dolci Labbra* was released, I was engaged to my third fiancé. The movie is a departure from my previous wedding-themed films, and as a result, it did not do as well at the box office. But I am convinced it was that abominable title! Instead of featuring an innocent single woman who is getting married, *Dolci Labbra* is about a widow who seduces rich men with her expert kisses and lovemaking but then kills them. Apart from the title, I had been happy to play a different character from those of my last movies. Though the film did not make the box office sales of my earlier pictures, it sealed my reputation as "the Bombshell of the Mediterranean." Ah, I forgot to add this nickname to the others!

There are many shots in this movie of my back. I had not understood during the filming why the director kept asking me to turn around. I had sworn they were giving me dresses smaller than my size eight, and sure enough when I checked, the garment labels were missing. It was not until I had watched the premiere that I finally understood. The director had been shooting my derrière, which looked even curvier in the tight dresses they were giving me. Though critics had panned the movie's plot, everyone commented on my derrière. And from that moment on, the paparazzi took photos of my derrière, once even while I sunbathed nude on what I thought was a highly secured estate in Lake Como.

It has been fifteen years since I was in a movie. And as I said earlier, I was engaged to be married five times, but never did make it to the altar. At least Rosa Bianca had the thrill of walking down the aisle each of the times she was engaged. I have spent the past ten years as a recluse, which has also added to the belief that I truly am "The Crazy Bride." (Although after my fifth engagement was broken, the media began labeling me with the title *"celibe per sempre,"* or "single forever.") Now, after a decade, my hibernation is over. I am coming out of hiding to travel to America. *Chissà?* Who knows? Maybe people do not care about me anymore. But they say Francesca Donata is a legend—and legends never die.

As for my name preference, I ask to be called "Signorina Donata." Of course, I do not expect the media to be so formal with me. I simply desire that they call me "Francesca Donata." But it is too late for that. The nicknames the media has dubbed me with are part of my legend and what has contributed to my fame. Only family and close friends call me "Francesca."

*"Signorina"* is the Italian title given to a young woman who is not married. It is the equivalent of "Miss," while *"signora"* is the title given to a married woman or a widow and is the equivalent to "Mrs." Since I have never married, I am technically a *"signorina."* But most people think of a young woman as a *"signorina"* and an old woman as *"signora."*

I know it is ridiculous that I insist everyone call me *"signorina"* rather than *"signora"* even though I am in my fifties. However absurd my request is, I do not care. After all, why should I be called something I am not? Again, I am an unmarried woman, and as such, that makes me a *"signorina."*

# ❧ 1 ❧

# Pia

Since I was a baby, the sound of the ocean's waves crashing against the shoreline has lulled me to sleep. We live in the idyllic seaside town of Carlsbad, California. I love the beach and never thought I could see myself moving away. But that was before, when my younger sister Erica was still alive.

Erica and I had spent most of our childhood playing on the beach. But since her death, I've avoided it as much as possible. My father insists on still having the occasional picnic here, which I don't understand because we're not that happy family unit anymore. We're fractured now.

Whenever we have one of these picnics, my father refuses to let me stay home. So we go through the motions. I can tell my mother and brother aren't into it either. We play along for my father's sake. Maybe continuing this one family tradition is his only hope of holding on to some sense of normalcy. But we all know our family will never be normal again.

So here I am, alone on the beach. I need to walk the shoreline one last time. For I have no idea if I'll ever come back. Hell, I can't even stand to be in my home state. Everything reminds me of my sister. And when the memories return, my panic attacks take over, leaving me gasping for air and desperate to escape.

Erica died when I was twenty-one, the summer before my senior year of college. I'd been too distraught to go back to school until three years after her death. Though I'd started to pick up the pieces of my life when I finally felt ready to return to college, I'm far from healed. It's a tough pill for me to swallow since I'm now twenty-five years old and had always envisioned myself having my act together by this age. And just in case I've deluded myself into thinking that I am fine, the panic attacks are a reminder that I still haven't come to terms with losing my sister. As I stare out at the waves, her voice calls out to me. I want to push the memory out of my mind as I've become accustomed to doing, but for some reason today, I don't.

"Pia! Pia! Wait up for me!" Erica struggled to keep up with me as I ran along the shore, trying not to lose sight of the seal we'd spotted swimming in the ocean. I ignored Erica, too intent on chasing the seal.

"Look! Look!" I was startled to hear Erica's voice just a few feet behind me. Her little legs had managed to catch up to me. I looked to where she was pointing. Another seal was swimming from the west, coming to meet the first one we'd seen. The first seal screeched an ear-piercing greeting to its mate, which soon returned the call. Then they began diving in and out of the water several times before they swam farther out into the ocean. We watched them until their glistening bodies melted into the waves.

"I wish I were a seal," Erica said in a tiny voice. I turned to look at her.

"Why would you want to be a seal? You hate getting wet!" I laughed and patted Erica's arm playfully.

"Well, if I were a seal and that's all I was used to, then I wouldn't mind getting wet." Though she was eight years old, she often managed to surprise my family with her perceptive comments.

"Has anyone ever told you how smart you are?"

"Yeah." Erica said this in a very matter-of-fact way and shrugged her shoulders like it was no big deal. Only children can get away with such conceit.

"So, you still haven't told me why you want to be a seal."

"I wish I could swim as far out as they do and see the bottom of the ocean. It's a whole other world. I want to know what they see."

"You can take scuba lessons when you're older."

"What's scuba?"

"You wear a special costume and a mask with a breathing tank attached that allows you to breathe under water. Kyle has a book on scuba diving. I'll show you the pictures in it later."

"Let's go home now. I want to see what a scuba looks like." Erica placed her hand in mine and began leading me back toward our house. I looked out toward the horizon, hoping to see the seals again, but there was no sign of them.

We saw the seals three more times over the next five years, but afterward, we never saw them again. Other residents had told us they'd seen a seal here and there, but Erica and I kept missing them. I remember how magical it felt that first day we saw that seal flipping in the ocean, the sunlight reflecting off its slick, gleaming skin.

Tears are rolling down my cheeks as I stare out into the ocean that my sister had loved so much and that in the end had taken her life. Erica had been swimming when she drowned. It had been a tremendous shock. Of all the ways she could've died, drowning would not have even made the list. I'm still baffled. She'd been a strong swimmer and had even been on the diving team in high school. A few people on the beach had seen Erica waving her arms in distress. A surf instructor who had been giving lessons swam out and brought her lifeless body back to shore. A doctor jogging on the beach had tried to resuscitate her with CPR, but it was too late. The sole explanation my family and I could think of was that she had swum out too far and had lost her energy.

It was so unfair. Erica had been two years younger than me. We were really tight, even though we couldn't have been more opposite. Unlike me, she had been outgoing and popular. Her extracurricular activities had included the photography and art club, diving team, student council, and yearbook committee. Painting was her passion. She loved to paint landscapes, especially the ocean.

We were so close that I'd chosen to stay in California and commute to college rather than go away and be apart from Erica. We'd even attended the same school, University of California, San Diego. We had made a pact that she would transfer and go to art school in

New York after I graduated from UCSD. We were going to get our own apartment and take the Big Apple by storm. We couldn't wait. Now I was headed to New York—alone.

I've wanted to be a writer since I was a kid and had fantasized of going to New York City to work on a magazine. But I'd never intended on making it permanent. Erica and I had loved California too much to permanently relocate. We'd just wanted to get some solid experience before we returned home and started our own magazine. Erica was going to handle the more artistic elements— planning the layout, taking the photographs—while I worked primarily on the editorial side.

Part of me feels good that I've decided to carry through on the plans that Erica and I had. But it's taken me three years to realize that if an afterlife does exist and Erica can see me, she'd be upset that I didn't follow through on our dream. But then there's a part of me that just can't help but be incredibly sad that she's not here to share this experience with me. I'm scared. When Erica was alive, by my side, I'd felt invincible. We'd often completed each other's thoughts, and whenever we collaborated on a project, the synergy couldn't be beat.

In the fall, when I had applied to several magazines for internships, I had begged God to let me land one of them. I could only think about finally escaping California and all of the memories. But now that I'm really headed to New York, the anxiety of failing has set in. I know I've placed this enormous amount of pressure on myself. But how can I not? I have to succeed in New York—for if I fail at this internship and never go through with starting my own magazine, I'll have let Erica down.

In April, I had two Skype interviews with magazines in New York. I found out a month later that I'd gotten the internship at *Profile* magazine.

*Profile* features interviews with everyone from celebrities to high-powered CEOs and politicians to fascinating everyday people. Unlike the trashy rag mags, *Profile* is *the* magazine Hollywood stars long to be in. Receiving an interview with *Profile* means you have arrived.

I'm happy to have landed such a prestigious internship, and I hope it'll distract me from the pain of losing my sister. My father has tried to convince me to stay. I feel guilty that I'm leaving my parents, especially my mother, who's retreated into her own world since Erica died and barely speaks to any of us. I wonder if she'll even notice that I'm gone. My brother Kyle lives near my parents and will be around to keep an eye on both of them. Though Kyle wasn't an Italian name that honored my parents' heritage, my father had always loved it and decided it would be fitting for his first-born. Kyle is thirty years old and works as a civil engineer. I know I can rely on my brother to take care of my parents until I come back—that is, if I ever return. I can't think about the far distant future right now. I want to focus solely on the present and my burgeoning career as a writer.

With this last thought, I say good-bye to the beach that I've seen almost every day of my life, ready to begin a new chapter in New York City.

## ✌ 2 ✌

# Francesca

"Espresso, *signora?*"
"*Signorina, per favore.*"
"*Ahh! Signorina Donata. Mi scusi! Io non l'avevo riconosciuta. Ti adoro molto.*"
"*Grazie, grazie. Si, un* espresso."

The Alitalia flight attendant's hands shake as she pours my cup of espresso. Naturally, I am pleased that she recognized me, but I am still piqued that she called me *"signora"* instead of *"signorina."*

The flight attendant places my cup of espresso on my table, then nods her head and walks away, rolling her cart to the next passenger. We still have not taken off. Glancing out my window, I see five other planes waiting in front of mine. Because of inclement weather, my flight to New York has been delayed by three hours. It is ten a.m. My flight was supposed to have departed at seven a.m. The passengers began complaining after an hour, asking to be taxied back to the terminal instead of sitting on a plane in the baking sun. The crew decided to bribe everyone with refreshments.

"Excuse me, passengers. We apologize again for the delay. We have just received word that we will be able to take off in about ten minutes."

Sighing deeply, I return my attention to the letter I was reading before the flight attendant interrupted me.

*Francesca,*
*I need your assistance with a delicate matter and*
*am asking you to come to New York. I would rather*
*not get into the details in this letter. If you must*
*know more before coming, we can talk on the phone.*
*If you choose not to come, of course I will respect*
*your wishes and not ask you again. All I ask is that*
*you please do let me know either way what your*
*decision is.*
*A presto,*
*Lorenzo*

"Passengers, please return to your seats and fasten your seat belts. We've been cleared for takeoff."

The flight attendant's voice interrupts me. But it is not like this is the first time I am reading the letter. In fact, I have read it four times, hoping to decipher more of its vague message. Folding the letter, I place it in my purse. It has been years since I have traveled on a commercial flight. But of course, my days of flying on a private jet are over. At least none of the passengers in my first-class cabin have bothered me. A few took a second glance, but that was it. My star is beginning to fade—at least in Italy. I suppose I have myself to blame since I stayed out of the limelight for so long. But I was tired. I needed to rest and contemplate.

Peering out my window, I see we are still low enough that I can make out the sand formations that form the island of Sicily. Of course it is another beautiful summer day on the island. Even from my elevated height, I can see the sun shimmering over Sicily's deep azure waters. Mount Etna looms in the distance, adding to the surreal panorama. After living for more than a decade in Rome, I had had enough of city life and ached to return to my home. My villa in Taormina, Sicily, has been a much-needed balm for me. But my cravings to be loved by the world have not died altogether.

On this trip to New York, my focus will be on someone who once was very special to me and whose affection I lost. This will perhaps be my greatest role: reclaiming that love.

## ❦ 3 ❧

# Pia

I haven't been to New York since I was eleven. My first and only trip to the Big Apple had left a deep impression, and though I'd always wanted to return, it just never seemed like the right time. My aunt had offered to pick me up at the airport, but I'd refused. She doesn't drive, and there's no need for her to go to all that trouble of taking a cab to the airport. As my taxi pulls up in front of Zia Antoniella's bakery, my heart tugs a bit as my first memory of entering my aunt's shop with my mother and sister flashes through my mind.

The scent of the freshly baked goods immediately mesmerized me as my mouth watered; I longed to try one of the brightly colored pastries and cookies that greeted me from behind their display cases. Zia Antoniella wasted no time in plopping into Erica's and my hands two fat, chocolate-covered cannoli. I'd never tasted anything like it. Although I felt full halfway through eating my cannoli, I still finished it. My mother looked at me and patted my cheek. *"È molto delizioso, giusto?"*

I nodded my head. Every day Zia Antoniella introduced Erica and me to a new Italian pastry: *sfogliatelle, pasticiotti, baba rums.* For a child who loved sweets, this was like going to a magical kingdom where everything tasted good and you could have it all. Erica's favorites were the rainbow-colored cookies. My favorites were the cannoli and the S-shaped biscotti flavored with anise extract. My mother restricted how much candy and cake we could have at home in California, but for some reason here in New York she let us eat any dessert we wanted.

Remembering this first trip to New York, I suddenly realize why my mother had been so lenient. She'd wanted Erica and me to try the food from her country that wasn't readily available on the West Coast. My mother had wanted us to know something of the culture she'd left behind in Italy when she married my father and moved to the United States.

My mother is from Abruzzo, and my father is from Messina, Sicily. Named Lidia, my mother is the youngest of four children— all girls. Zia Antoniella is the oldest. My father, Bruno, had been born in the United States, but his parents had only emigrated from Messina after they got married. He and my mother met when he took a Perillo tour of Italy and visited Abruzzo.

Tears sting my eyes as I get out of the cab. Will the mother I once knew ever return? I've already lost a sister, but since Erica's death, it also has felt like I've lost my mother.

I pay my cab fare and inhale deeply as I roll my luggage to the entrance of Antoniella's Bakery. Zia's business and her home are in Astoria, Queens, which is about a fifteen-minute subway ride from midtown Manhattan. Before I walk in, I strain my neck to see if Zia Antoniella is behind the sales counter. She's nowhere in sight. Maybe she stayed home today? But no, this is Zia, who hardly ever takes a sick day from her business. The woman loves to work.

A young girl, wearing an apron with the embroidered words "Antoniella's Bakery," is bringing a cup of cappuccino to one of the seated patrons. I glance once more toward the sales counter and see a shock of frizzy hair sticking up and moving from side to side. Zia!

Erica and I had stopped calling her Zia Antoniella after our first day of visiting her when we were kids. It was too long for us to say without getting tongue twisted, so she simply went by "Zia." We also preferred the Italian word for "aunt" over its English counterpart since *"zia"* sounded whimsical to a child's ears.

Sure enough, Zia soon comes around the corner of her pastry display case as she mops the floor feverishly, her head bobbing along with the mop's movements. I take after my mother and Zia with my honey-blond hair. But after decades of dyeing her hair, Zia no longer has the same lustrous golden-blond hue from her youth. Now her hair is more of a dark blond, sapped of all its moisture and resembling matted tumbleweeds rolling in the desert.

I attempt to enter the shop quietly, but the wind chimes hanging above the door jangle loudly, interrupting Zia's mad dance with her mop. She looks up.

Erica's eyes stare back at me. My heart pounds feverishly. I try smiling at Zia, but I can't breathe. *Oh no. Not now. Quick! Think!* What is it the doctor told me? Imagine a peaceful place. The image that surfaces is me eating that heavenly piece of pastry when I'd first walked into Zia's bakery as a little girl. I focus on how sweet the cannoli cream had been and how it had made me feel comforted. My heart rate begins to slow down.

Luckily for me, Zia doesn't notice anything is wrong.

"Pia!" she screams, dropping her mop and rushing over.

She embraces me, which is awkward since her head comes to my chest. My 5'9" frame towers over her. It's as if I'm being hugged by a dwarf. The blond hair is the only trait my mother shares with her sister. I have my mother's and grandfather's tall frame. Erica had inherited Zia's and my Nonna Graziella's petite stature. They're both 4'11", although Zia might be two inches shorter now with her hunched-over back.

*"Bella! Bella!"* Zia strokes my right cheek with the back of her hand. "How long have you been wearing glasses?"

"Since I turned eighteen, so that's what? Seven years now?"

"Why don't you wear contacts?"

"I like how glasses look."

"Hmmm."

"What? You don't like them, Zia?"

"No, no. They're very nice. It's just you are young. You shouldn't be hiding behind those glasses. You have such beautiful eyes. They look smaller with the glasses on."

Leave it to Zia to make a girl feel good. I'd learned a long time ago not to take what people say so personally. I'm sure in Zia's eyes she thinks she's helping me rather than hurting me with this advice. I've always followed my own style, and I'm not about to change because my old-fashioned Italian aunt wants me to. I love my eyeglasses, which have a tortoiseshell frame and a slightly square shape. They are the perfect complement to my blond hair.

"Thank you, Zia. But I really like the glasses."

"Ahhh. We still have the whole summer for me to change your mind." Zia winks and then brushes my sideswept ponytail behind my shoulder—another action that reminds me of my sister, who hated it when I wore my ponytail to the front.

I try not to look into Zia's eyes, but I can't help it. I'm drawn to them. As a kid, I had never noticed any resemblance between Erica and my aunt. Now all I see is my sister in Zia.

Erica's hair had been medium brown with flecks of natural red highlights—much darker than my hair or Zia's hair, even. But she had the same deep chocolate brown eyes that Zia has. My aunt even has dimples on either side of her cheeks as Erica had. If Zia dyed her hair darker, she'd be Erica's twin. I'm now curious to see a photo of Zia when she was younger.

If I'd realized how much they looked alike, maybe I wouldn't have chosen to stay here for the summer. Then again, where would I have gone? My guilt over leaving my parents had prevented me from asking them for any money for rent. Of course, my father had given me some money as a farewell gift before I left, but it's nowhere near enough to pay for the exorbitant rents New York City is known for.

"Sit down, Pia. You must be tired from your long plane ride. You look a little pale. Let me bring you a cup of espresso. That will revive you in no time. Oh, and of course a cannoli and some anise biscotti."

"You remembered." I smile at Zia, who is no doubt trying to impress me.

"*Si, si.* You forget that every year for Christmas since you and Erica first visited, I have sent your favorite desserts to you in California."

At the mention of Erica's name, my smile disappears. Zia quickly realizes her mistake and walks over to me.

"Ahhh, *mia cara.* I'm sorry, my dear." She hugs me. "I still refuse to believe our little Erica is gone. And I can't forgive myself for not flying out for her funeral."

Zia had gallbladder surgery just two days before Erica died. She was in no shape to travel. She'd called my mother repeatedly over the two weeks following Erica's death, always weeping hysterically into the phone. I don't know how my mother managed to take her calls every time when she'd been ready to collapse herself from the load of her youngest child's death.

As I hear Zia's voice choking up, I brace myself for the tsunami of tears I'm expecting will erupt any second. But surprisingly, she dabs at the corners of her eyes with her apron and is fine. Unlike my family and me, she seems to have come to grips with Erica's death. Or maybe she's all cried out? I, on the other hand, have only been able to cry a few times. I keep my emotions locked up, too fearful of what will happen if I give them permission to flow freely. I don't want to travel to that dark place my mother has chosen to go to. Or worse, I don't know what I'll do if I let myself fully deal with losing Erica. No wonder I'm having panic attacks. My doctor has tried to convince me to see a shrink. But I'm not ready. For if I talk about Erica, I run the risk of completely losing it. I've lost so much already. I can't lose any more. Besides, I'm convinced focusing on my writing career will heal me.

"Here you go." Zia places a demitasse cup of espresso in front of me. She even remembers that I like my coffee sweet as she adds milk and four teaspoons of sugar.

I sip the espresso, and she's right. I feel a zing of energy. My stomach growls, reminding me I haven't eaten anything since breakfast. I take a bite out of the cannoli.

"Ohhhh! These don't disappoint, Zia!"

"Of course not! Did you think because I'm getting old that my talent for baking would diminish?" Zia frowns.

"No, no! I'm just saying a cannoli never disappoints. You know I think you're a master baker!"

Zia relaxes at my praise. I'd almost forgotten about her flashes of mercurial temper. My mother has always told me how Zia was prone to fits of irritability even as a little girl. Maybe that's why she never married?

"I'm going to let Megan lock up tonight." She gestures with her head over to the girl I'd seen waitressing the café tables earlier. "Megan! Come here. I want to introduce you to my niece."

Megan must be no more than nineteen or twenty, with jet-black hair that's cut in a chic bob. Long bangs reach down to her thick, dark eyelashes. Her porcelain-white complexion is dotted with freckles, but they don't detract from her beauty. Her most stunning features are her eyes. They're different colors. From what I've read, only a small percentage of the population has this trait. One eye is hazel and the other's violet. I try not to stare as she shakes my hand.

"You guys don't look like you're related."

Unlike me, Megan doesn't even try to hide the fact that she's staring. Or maybe it's harder for her to conceal with those large, different-colored eyes that travel from my neckline all the way down to my feet and back up to my neckline. She's now gawking at my crystal-studded and ruffled peasant blouse. Everyone always compliments me on it. I'm not a slave to fashion, but I do have a weakness for ultra-feminine pretty blouses. In contrast to my fancy tops, I'm rarely seen out of my jeans or khakis. I also love wearing lace-up boots, though with the heat in California I was often forced to trade them in for flip-flops. With my tall frame, I rarely wear heels. I still don't get how tall women wear stilettos, since I'm always trying to hide my height. Impossible, I know, but I still try.

"My niece and I have the same hair color. Well, my hair is darker now, but when I was young, it was just like Pia's. We also have the same personality," Zia snaps at Megan. No doubt Megan's blunt assessment unnerves her.

I doubt we have the same personality, but I know better than to disagree with Zia, so I just nod my head.

"So, Pia, your aunt tells me you're a writer?"

"Yes, well, I'm trying to be."

"She's going to be working for a big magazine in Manhattan! Tell her, Pia." Leave it to Zia to put me in an uncomfortable position. My face flushes slightly.

"It's just an internship." There I go again, undercutting myself—a pesky trait of mine.

"Where?" Megan clearly seems interested.

*"Profile,"* I practically whisper, staring into my cup as I add another teaspoon of sugar, which my espresso clearly does not need.

"Get out! That's one of my favorite magazines! The photo layouts they do are awesome. I don't really care about the stories, though. I'm not a fan of celebrities, but *Profile*'s photographers do stand-up work all the way." Now Megan is really looking at me with respect.

"You like photography?" I can't help but think of Erica and her love of photography.

"Yeah. I'm studying at Parsons. I have one more year to go."

"I'd love to see your photos sometime."

"Sure, that'd be cool. You know where to find me. Let me know when you're all settled. We can go grab a beer, and I'll bring my portfolio. I know a couple of other writers I should introduce you to."

"Okay, that sounds good." I return Megan's smile before she goes to help two customers who have just walked into the bakery. I notice her brightly colored red-plaid tights, which she has cleverly paired with a brown shirtdress that reaches only halfway down her thighs. Over her dress, she wears an embroidered Antoniella's Bakery apron—the only uniform Zia requires of her employees. I do a double-take as I notice her platform lace-up boots. How does she stand up all day in those? I'm also surprised that Zia hasn't objected to Megan's super-short dress and ridiculously high boots. Or maybe she has protested, but Megan's chosen to ignore her? She seems like the kind of girl who follows few rules.

Zia, who had gone into the kitchen while Megan and I were chatting, is back. She hands me a big bakery box. "I packed up a few biscotti and pastries for you to have at home."

"Oh. Great. Thanks," I say with little enthusiasm. I take the box, which feels like it's filled to the brim. My twenty-six-inch waist is no doubt going to expand while I stay with Zia over the summer. But I don't want to disappoint her by turning away the sweets, and of course there's her trademark wrath I'd like to avoid at all costs.

Zia and I leave the bakery and walk S-L-O-W-L-Y. I know she's older, but it's still amazing just how slowly she is walking. Of course, all the shopkeepers who are out sweeping their sidewalks or talking to their deliverymen take the time to say hello to Zia, who repeats to each and every one of them, "This is my sister's daughter, Pia. *Si, si,* the one all the way out in California."

Granted, California is on the other side of the country, but it amuses me how everyone has to make a point of asking "All the way out in California?" You'd think I had flown in from China. Maybe this is the New Yorker insularity I've always heard about. They expect the rest of the country to be like New York and can't imagine living anywhere else.

We finally turn onto 35th Street, where Zia lives. I mentally note how much longer it's going to take for us to reach her home. Zia points out the row houses and reminds me which of her neighbors live where, forgetting that I most likely won't remember them since I'd been so young when I first met them. She's about to point out a lemon-colored house when she quickly drops her index finger as if she's been burned and whispers, "Beady Eyes! They're *always* out." For some reason, she sounds really angered by this fact.

I strain my neck a little to see whom she's talking about and am startled to notice two heads turned toward us as their weasel-shaped eyes lock onto ours with great intensity. Their necks lean well past the driveway gate they're standing behind. They don't seem to care that we notice they're ogling us. Suddenly, a third head pops into view—a massive German shepherd. He, too, stares at us. How bizarre! No wonder Zia is so mad. I want to laugh at the freakish scene before me, but the ultra-serious expressions on their faces intimidate me. I glance away, which doesn't help because I can feel their penetrating gazes.

"Hello, Mr. and Mrs. Hoffman."

"Hello, Antoniella."

The German shepherd barks in greeting and lowers himself back onto the ground, satisfied that it's not a stranger passing his house. He doesn't seem to care that he's never seen me before.

"*Ciao,* Gus." Zia walks over to Gus, patting him on the head. He licks her hand and then looks away as he hears voices coming down the street. Gus's ears twitch as he raises himself back up and perches his paws onto the gate.

I wait for Zia to introduce me to the Hoffmans, but she doesn't. They don't seem to mind since, like their dog, their attention has been directed to the voices that are approaching.

After we pass them, I ask Zia, "Why didn't you introduce me?"

"I don't like them. That's why. And I don't want them knowing my business. Besides, I'm sure everyone has heard that my niece from California is coming to stay with me for the summer. Why should I pretend they don't know when they do nothing but stand in front of their house all day, snooping on everybody? And the way they stare at you! That's how they earned their nickname 'Beady Eyes.' They think they are better than the rest of us. Ahhh!!!" Zia shakes her fist in their direction, but now we're well out of Beady Eyes's sight.

"You seem to like the dog."

"*Si, si.* Gus is different."

"But he stares at everyone, too, just like his owners."

"What does he know? He's just a dog. He's only copying their bad behavior."

I smile to myself at Zia's rationale. She's funny.

We're almost to the end of the street when I see a small crowd of people standing in front of an elaborate Italianate-style house.

"What is going on at the Mussolini Mansion?" Zia quickens her pace, much to my surprise. All it takes is a bit of drama to make her walk faster.

"The Mussolini Mansion?"

"Signora Tesca owns that house. She's rich and a little strange, but a very nice person. But she doesn't tell you much about herself. All I know is that she is a widow with a grown son who hardly ever comes to visit. *Povera!* People are always gossiping about her." Zia shakes her head and makes a little "tsk, tsk" noise with her lips. "The poor soul."

"You still haven't told me why you call her house the Mussolini Mansion?"

"Ah! *Si, si.* She has a villa in Rome that is across the street from where the Italian dictator Mussolini used to live. She's very proud of this and has told several of the neighbors about it. *Pazza!*" Zia points to her head. In a flash, she has gone from feeling sorry for Signora Tesca to calling her crazy.

"Who would be proud to have a house across the street from a dictator? Maybe if it were Sophia Loren's house or Marcello Mastroianni's, but Mussolini? Signora Tesca must've been a Fascist."

She whispers the word "Fascist" as if we're still living in World War II times and Zia is afraid her notorious allegiance will be discovered.

Though I majored in journalism, I also took several art history courses, including Roman Art and Architecture. I learned about Villa Torlonia, which Mussolini had rented from the Torlonia family. From the 1920s to 1943, the villa was Mussolini's state residence. Now Villa Torlonia is a museum open to the public. I was impressed that Signora Tesca owned a villa across the street from this lavish estate.

"All of the neighbors call her house the Mussolini Mansion. Of course Signora Tesca does not know this. Look at it. It is the biggest, fanciest house on Thirty-Fifth Street." With a nod of her head, Zia gestures toward the house.

She's right. The Mussolini Mansion has no place among the cookie cutter row houses that line 35th Street and most of the blocks in Astoria. Calling it a mansion is a misnomer since the house is far from one, especially when you look at some of the McMansions that have become the norm of the twenty-first century in some suburbs. It is a beautiful residence despite its standing out like a sore thumb. I can't help but wonder if the rest of the neighbors are also a little jealous of Signora Tesca's home and wealth. I suspect even Zia is envious.

Unlike the other semi-attached houses on the street, the Mussolini Mansion is completely detached. The two-story structure is built in the Italianate architectural style, featuring a flat roof and a small tower that's reminiscent of the campaniles or belvederes seen in many of the more imposing buildings in Italy. The house is flanked by classical cornices and tall, angled bay windows. I can make out heavy drapery behind all of the windows, which I can't help thinking is a shame since none of the natural light is entering the home. An elaborate wrought-iron gate wraps majestically around the house, but its beauty is marred by the overgrown grass behind it and the abundance of violet and white daisies leaning forward well past the gate, as if they're begging to be picked by passersby. From the countless petals that are strewn on the ground below, I can tell many people have plucked the daisies.

I look toward the backyard, which is clearly visible from the street, and I'm startled to see several stony white faces staring back at me. Marble Greco-Roman statues surround the small yard. A statue of a woman wearing an off-the-shoulder tunic and holding a small platter makes me laugh. Someone has placed an empty can of Budweiser on the platter. It would be easy to jump the low wrought-iron gate. I wouldn't be surprised if trespassers are the norm in Signora Tesca's yard. When you call this much attention to your property in a working-class neighborhood, the temptation to explore it is too great. A few broken columns lie on the ground, and even the sculptures that are intact look cracked from years of being exposed to the elements. Unfortunately, the overgrown grass and old statues detract a bit from the elegance of the Mussolini Mansion.

We finally reach the small crowd standing in front of Signora Tesca's home. They're straining their necks as if they even have a chance to catch a glimpse behind the heavily draped windows. A few of the neighbors are leaning over the gate, trying to see up the driveway.

*"Che cosa è successo?"* Zia asks a man, who's wearing a long-shoreman's cap and is nervously picking his teeth with a toothpick, what all the fuss is about in front of the Mussolini Mansion.

Instead of answering Zia's question, the man looks over to me and begins checking me out from head to toe, but his eyes never reach past my cleavage. I cross my arms over my chest, blocking his view. He quickly averts his gaze and clears his throat for a good long minute. I step back a few feet, afraid the gunk he's been picking at between his teeth might come flying out and hit me in the face.

"Is this your niece who came all the way over from California, Antoniella?"

I mentally roll my eyes at the mention of the far-flung land of my home state.

*"Si,* she just flew in today. Pia, do you remember Paulie Parlatone from when you first visited? He used to bring you and Erica lollipops?"

I look at Paulie as he returns my stare. This time his eyes don't wander from my face.

"I'm sorry. I don't. That was such a long time ago."

"Bahhh! Don't sweat it!" Paulie waves his hand dismissively. "You were a kid. I wouldn't expect you to remember. Where's your sister?"

The color drains from my face, and I return my gaze to the statue of the woman holding the platter with the Budweiser can. It's eerie how the statues look as if they're staring directly at me. I hear Zia mutter under her breath, *"Stupido!"* but it's not too low to escape Paulie's hearing.

He suddenly remembers, slapping his forehead. "I'm so sorry, Pia. I forgot about Erica. I mean, I didn't forget—it's just it has been so many years since I saw the two of you together. Ughhh . . . I'm sorry. I'm sorry for your loss."

I glance back at Paulie, who's now the one staring at the statues in Signora Tesca's yard. He's resumed picking at his teeth, scraping away nervously with the tiny stick.

"Thank you," is all I can manage to say.

"So, did something happen to Signora Tesca?" Zia deftly changes the subject before Paulie can stick his foot in his mouth once more.

"Nothing. But you're not going to believe in a million years who is in her house."

"Who?"

"Francesca Donata!"

Zia lets out a loud laugh. *"That's* what all the fuss is about? *Scemo! La verità, la verità per favore."* She continues laughing so hard, wiping tears from her eyes.

"I *am* telling you the truth. Ciggy saw Francesca Donata get out of that Maserati that's parked in the driveway and enter the house with three men. They must've been her bodyguards."

"Ciggy! Bah! Don't tell me you all are taking the word of that *ubriaco!* Did you ask him how many drinks he'd had yet?" Zia shakes her head. "Come on!"

Ciggy is one of the neighbors on 35th Street I do remember meeting when I visited Zia as a kid. He was hard to forget. He came into Antoniella's Bakery every day with a big fat cigar always perched between his lips. He would make faces, causing my sister and me to laugh so hard. His bald, shiny head and boisterous voice only made him funnier in our eyes. He had a bulldog named

Grumpy who was just as ugly as Ciggy, but Erica and I loved petting him and secretly feeding him cookies whenever Zia wasn't looking. This was news to me now that he drank. Besides his visits to the bakery and Anthony's Salumeria for his favorite heroes filled with *prosciutto, capicollo,* provolone cheese, and roasted red peppers, he was seen every day planted on his front stoop, smoking his cigars (hence his nickname of Ciggy). I don't even know what his real name is. Grumpy was always lying by Ciggy's feet in a comatose state, no doubt from all the cigar smoke fumes he was inhaling. Ciggy was such a permanent fixture on his stoop that when people walked by and didn't see him in his usual spot, they rang his bell to make sure he hadn't died. Everyone knew his routine, which only consisted of going to Zia's bakery and Anthony's deli as soon as they opened at eight a.m., returning home to eat outside on his porch, taking Grumpy for his late morning walk at eleven a.m., and then reading his newspaper until dinnertime. Dinner was the only meal he ate indoors. As soon as he was done with it, he returned to his stoop. Some nights, he even slept there.

"You are all fools if you believe Ciggy! A big movie star like Francesca Donata would never be caught dead here! Manhattan, yes. Astoria, no!"

"Maybe it was just someone who looked like Francesca Donata," I chime in. Like Zia, I'm also skeptical that Ciggy has seen Francesca Donata. Zia's right. Italian silver-screen star Francesca Donata is in the Olympian hall of movie gods like Sophia Loren, Liz Taylor, Ava Gardner, and Brigitte Bardot. She'd been the Angelina Jolie of her day, and I can never in a million years see Brangelina coming to Astoria except if they were filming a movie, which actually does happen on occasion since the Kaufman Studios are nearby in Astoria. But I'm sure once the day's filming is over, Angelina and Brad Pitt take off to Manhattan to stay somewhere trendy like the Hotel Gansevoort in the Meatpacking District.

"I admit, I didn't believe it either when Ciggy first told me, but he saw Francesca early in the morning when he was going to your bakery, Antoniella, to buy his espresso. You know he's had little, if anything, to drink that early in the morning when he first wakes up."

"Paulie, don't be stupid! I'm sure he has a shot of whiskey before he makes his way over to my bakery. I never told anyone this because I don't like to gossip, and if you repeat this, Paulie, I'll come after you." Zia makes a popular Italian gesture with her index finger, running it across her neck to indicate she'll slice Paulie's throat if he betrays her.

Paulie holds his hands up. "Calm down, Antoniella. You know I don't like gossip either."

"Hmmm!" Zia looks at him, knowing he's probably the one who's told the rest of the neighbors gathered in front of Signora Tesca's house that Ciggy had spotted Francesca Donata. I'm surprised she's decided to trust him with a secret she doesn't want repeated. Then again, everyone knows Zia is a woman of her word, especially when her wrath has been invoked.

"Whenever Ciggy comes into the bakery, he takes out those little liquor bottles they give you on the airplane and pours the liquor into his espresso."

"A lot of men like a few drops of sambuca in their espresso. So do I, and I'm not a drunk!" Now Paulie is the one laughing and shaking his head at Zia as if she's overreacting.

"It wasn't just a few drops. He emptied *both* bottles into his cup of espresso. He always asks me to just fill the demitasse cup halfway. And sometimes he even asks for two cups of espresso."

Paulie lets out a low whistle. "His drinking must be getting worse. Okay, I give you that. Maybe he was seeing things. And why would Francesca Donata be visiting Signora Tesca, who doesn't seem like the celebrity type even with all her money."

"Paulie, you're finally starting to sound smart. There is no way Francesca Donata knows a mouse like Signora Tesca."

But just as Zia says this, a woman in the crowd yells out, "It's her! It's her! I saw her peek from behind the drapes on the second floor."

"I saw her, too!" several of the other neighbors yell out. Everyone is now staring up at the windows on the second story. But of course, no one is there.

"*Pazzi!* You're all crazy! Come on, Pia." Zia stomps off.

I follow Zia, but I can't help glancing at the window that supposedly Francesca Donata had looked out from. How cool would that be if the Italian movie star really is here in Astoria?

\* \* \*

As I step off the elevator at *Profile*'s offices, celebrities who have graced the magazine's covers greet me: George Clooney, Bono, Hillary Clinton, Michelle Obama, Paul McCartney, and others. Today is the first day of my internship. Though I keep telling my heart to stop its frantic racing, it's not working. Besides my jitters, I'm also really excited. I'm finally going to get a glimpse into the magazine world I've dreamed of being a part of for so long. I take a deep breath before I push open the glass doors that lead to the reception area.

The décor is swanky and ultra modern. Leather chairs in hues of deep plum and silver circle a cube-shaped glass coffee table. Even the receptionist's desk is made out of glass. More framed *Profile* covers adorn the walls. I wait for the receptionist to look up and acknowledge my presence, but she doesn't. After about two minutes, I finally speak up. "Excuse me, I'm—"

"Andrew! These packages need to be taken to Susan." The receptionist's head finally shoots up as she yells at a young man racing by. He can't be older than maybe twenty-three.

"Don't ask *me* to do it!" Andrew looks completely disgusted, as if she's just asked him to clean the toilets.

"Andrew! She's been waiting for these packages all morning. She'll have my head if she finds out they've been sitting here. I've called you twice about them already."

Andrew stops dead in his tracks. He makes his way slowly over to the receptionist and gets really close to her face as he says, "I'm no longer an editorial assistant. I'm sure you got the office memo announcing my promotion. If you're so worried, why don't *you* take them to her? You are a receptionist, after all."

"Who the fuck do you think you are, you spoiled brat!"

"I'm a contributing editor. *That's* who I am." Andrew smirks, then makes eye contact with me as he quickly sizes me up from head to toe before walking away. I can't help but wonder if I've passed his approval test. Something tells me I haven't.

"Can you believe that?" The receptionist finally addresses me. "Why, the nerve! I've been working for this company a lot longer than he has. Who the hell does *he* fuckin' think he is?"

Clearly, the contributing editor, I fantasize saying to her, but I remain silent even though I'm ready to laugh at the absurdity of it all. I'm also freaked out by what I've just witnessed, but I'm not sure what horrifies me more—the receptionist's cursing in a professional environment or Andrew's arrogance and lack of respect.

"Hello. I'm Pia Santore. I'm reporting for my first day of my internship. Colin Cohen told me to ask for him when I arrived."

The receptionist, who looks to be in her late fifties, with shoulder-length, raven-colored hair and thick, though impeccably groomed, eyebrows, puts on the reading glasses that are attached to a long, crystal-studded chain she's wearing around her neck.

"Leah . . . Leah," she keeps repeating as her finger follows a list of names on her clipboard.

"It's Pia, ma'am, with a 'P' as in 'Peter.'"

"Whad-ya say?"

"Pia. P-I-A."

"No, no, I heard that. You called me 'ma'am.' How old do you think I am? I'm not old enough for you to be calling me 'ma'am.' Get that straight and we'll get along." She lowers her gaze back to her clipboard, resuming her search for my name.

"Oh. I'm sorry."

"Pia. Here you are. Okay, have a seat. I'll ring him."

I walk over to the plum and silver chairs and decide to sit in a plum one, feeling foolish that I actually mulled for a second which color I would choose as if I were a five-year-old child.

"Yes, yes. I'll tell her, Col."

*Col?* Not Mr. Cohen or even his full name. I'd heard that the creative industries were more informal, but I never imagined them to be this casual.

"You'd better make yourself comfortable, honey. He's in the editorial meeting, and Lord knows those can go on forever."

Now I feel like telling her not to call me "honey" and "we'll get along just fine," but that's the least of my problems at the moment. I try to conceal the disappointment in my voice as I simply murmur, "Okay, thank you."

The knot that's been in my shoulder since I woke up is twisting even tighter. But now in addition to my anxiety I'm feeling something else: irritation. Granted, I know I'm just an intern, the lowest man on the totem pole here, but still. What would it have taken for Colin Cohen to interrupt his meeting for five minutes and take me to the cubicle where I'll be sitting? Or even to have his assistant do it?

Well, if I'm going to be waiting a while, I might as well make myself as comfortable as possible.

"Excuse me?"

The receptionist looks up at me, clearly annoyed, and holds up her index finger. She begins speaking into the creamy-colored headset, which looks more like a headband holding her dark locks in place.

"Yes, sir. I'll transfer you immediately to Mr. Cohen's line."

Huh? I thought he was in the editorial meeting? Obviously, Colin—or Col—was blowing me off. The receptionist hangs up and looks at me as if she's telepathically communicating with me.

"Is there a restroom I can use?" I ask her.

"Behind that wall, make a sharp left."

My two-inch stacked-heel pumps click-clack noisily on the shiny black marble tiles. Beyoncé's "Single Ladies" is streaming through invisible speakers in the restroom. I'm surprised they don't also have music in the reception area. Maybe it's too hard for the receptionist to hear her calls? I can imagine her making a stink about it. Then again, as Andrew put it, she's just a receptionist, so they probably wouldn't take her seriously.

I check my makeup in the mirror and am relieved to see it's still in place. Normally, I wear little makeup—just a deep nude lip gloss by L'Oréal, Nars's Outlaw blush, which gives my cheeks that dewy, rosy look, and under-eye concealer. But today I decided to lightly line my eyes in a smoky gray pencil and wear mascara. It has to be a very special occasion for me to wear eye shadow. The last time I wore shadow was at my high school prom. The bun I had pulled my hair tightly into earlier this morning is already loosening, so I take out the bobby pins and begin winding my waist-length hair back into the coil I had it in. Two women storm through the door, giggling loudly. At the sight of me, they both stop laughing and blatantly stare.

I pretend not to notice and keep my back turned toward them. Though my makeup hasn't run, I take out my compact and lightly pat my nose, hoping their fascination with me will soon wear off and they'll go into the stalls. But instead they stand over the sinks as one of them brushes her hair and the other applies lip gloss. I can still feel their eyes on me.

I turn around and walk past them, but the one applying lip gloss says, "Are you here for an interview?"

Vanilla blond highlights are streaked through her dark brown hair, which is ironed super straight. She's almost as tall as me. Like Andrew, she too sizes me up from head to toe. I glance sideways at her friend, who's staring at my sensible two-inch Nine West black pumps that go with my black pants suit. I'm wearing a sky-blue button-down shirt and a pearl choker Erica and my mother gave me for my sixteenth birthday. Suddenly, it hits me why Lip Gloss Chick thinks I'm interviewing. I'm wearing the typical interview outfit— the "safe black suit" one can't go wrong with. They're dressed *nothing* like me.

Lip Gloss Chick is squeezed into a super-tight mini pencil skirt. Her four-inch nude stilettos make her legs, which are bare, look even longer. A sleeveless wrap top with a plunging neckline reveals her more-than-ample bosom. Bangle bracelets loop around her right arm, and on her left, a chunky gold watch gleams in the fluorescent lights. There's no way she bought that from the watch guy selling knockoff Rolexes at the corner.

Her friend looks Indian American. She, too, has super-straight hair, and her sideswept bangs reach to her thick eyelashes. A ruched emerald-green dress hugs her sleek, box-shaped body. A size zero, I'm guessing without a doubt. Her cheekbones stand out in her face, and her wrists are just as painfully thin. She takes off her shoes and massages the big toe of her right foot. I notice the signature Christian Louboutin red soles of her stilettos, which look even higher than Lip Gloss Chick's heels.

"No, I'm not here for an interview. I'm actually interning for the summer."

"That's what we thought, but we weren't sure since you don't look as young as most of the interns do." Lip Gloss Chick locks eyes with Louboutin Chick, and they both smile.

"I'm actually twenty-five." Oh, great! Why did I just tell them my age?

"Twenty-five? And you're interning?" Louboutin Chick asks me, not even attempting to conceal her disgust.

"It's a long story," is all I offer. It's none of their damn business why I am interning only now in my mid-twenties.

Lip Gloss Chick raises her brows at Louboutin. They finally stop staring at me and go back to applying their makeup and brushing their hair.

I'm not sure what to do next. All I want is to escape, but since I'm going to see these women in the office on a regular basis, I figure I should make an attempt at being social. "I'm Pia Santore," I say, extending my hand.

Lip Gloss Chick looks at my hand as if I have swine flu or some other ghastly contagious illness. She then hunches her shoulders, holding up her lip gloss bottle and wand, and says, "Sorry! My hands are kind of full at the moment."

Right on cue, Louboutin Chick flips her head over and begins brushing her hair.

This has to be one of the worst feelings in the world, being left hanging with my hand extended in midair. I draw it back and say, "It was nice to meet you," and quickly make my exit.

As the door swings shut, I can hear their high-pitched laughter. They couldn't even wait a few seconds more to be sure I was out of earshot—not like they cared. I'm sure they wanted me to hear. "Freaks!" I mutter under my breath.

So far in the half hour that I've been at *Profile,* I haven't been left with the best impression. Maybe this is all a mistake?

I walk back into the reception area, where a man wearing a black sports jacket and denim jeans with chocolate-brown leather boots is pacing back and forth. He glances at his watch and checks the time against the clock that's hanging on a parapet near the reception desk. The click-clack of my heels diverts his attention toward me.

"Pia Santore?"

"Yes."

"Oh, there you are. I thought you were never going to come out of that restroom."

I frown, knowing I wasn't gone for more than five minutes.

He holds out his hand. "I'm Colin Cohen, senior editor. But of course you know that already."

He notices the surprise in my face.

"I know I look different from when we Skype'ed. My stylist has been on my case about updating my look."

First, I'm shocked that he actually introduced himself to me and shook my hand. The receptionist hadn't even bothered telling me her name. Second, he has shaved off most of his long, tousled locks that had given him what I thought was the perfect "editor look" when I interviewed with him via Skype. Now only a superfine haze of reddish stubble can be detected. His beard is also gone, making him look much younger, hence, my not recognizing him.

"Hi. Nice to meet you."

"I'm out an assistant today, and I'm more crazed than usual. Follow me."

At 6'5", he's quite tall. I walk quickly, but with his long stride I can't keep up with him.

"You'll be sitting in this cube. I know it's a bit messy, but you'll only be here for the summer, so there's no sense in wasting time cleaning it up."

A bit messy is a huge understatement. Piles and piles of past issues of *Profile* wrap their way around the cubicle. There are even two piles on the floor near my chair. Stacks of papers are crammed next to the magazines. Not an inch of free space is visible on the desk. Post-it notes are stuck all around the computer's monitor and the cabinets that hang above the cube. Coffee stains are splattered on the keyboard and even on the back of the Mac's monitor.

"So, why don't you get yourself settled and look through these page proofs. You'll be the last person proofing them, so just make sure all the previous correx were made and that there aren't any other glaring errors anyone else missed. I need to run back into the editorial meeting. I'll circle back with you after it's over. Sound good?"

"Sure."

"Great, great. I can tell already you're going to work out just fine." With a nod of his head, he bolts off back toward the reception area.

My heart sinks as I take in once more my surroundings. I'm a notorious neat freak. Having this much clutter just unnerves me. I sigh as I struggle to push the stacks of magazines that cover the floor, trying vainly to add some space to my suffocating quarters. But the stacks won't budge. Something's blocking them. I bend over, peering behind them. An old Dell computer stands behind the magazines. It's hopeless.

I begin perusing through the proofs Colin has left for me, asking myself repeatedly, "What the hell did I get myself into?" So much for my glamorous internship.

Though I've always heard the first week of a job is the most brutal, I had never imagined it could be this bad. I'm on the N subway, making my way back to Zia's house after another long day at *Profile*. Thank God it's Friday. My bones ache and the knots in my right shoulder are tangling themselves even tighter together as I hold on to the overhead bar on the subway. I'm still not used to all the walking and standing one does in New York City—and I don't know how long it will take for me to get accustomed to the subway.

Don't get me wrong. I'm not your typical spoiled California blonde who's used to her creature comforts. But living in New York City definitely demands a lot from you. The crowds alone test one's patience regularly. Then there's all the waiting you do. Whether it's for the subway, for a seat at a restaurant, or for traffic to clear, waiting is the norm here.

People's superior attitudes are a whole other beast, but I'm used to that, having lived so close to L.A., where acting phony is actually considered a desirable trait. Though I had often hung out in L.A. with my friends, I'd never developed a liking for it. I'd always been grateful we lived in Carlsbad, a suburb of San Diego, where people are more down-to-earth. I've only been at my internship for a few days, but it's quickly become apparent that people at *Profile* take themselves way too seriously and suffer from the same conceited affliction people in La La Land suffer from. But in L.A., the superficiality and arrogance are much worse than what I've encountered so far at *Profile* or on the streets of Manhattan. At least in the Big Apple, there's variety and not everyone is dressed the same or has their locks dyed the same shade.

"Lexington Avenue and Fifty-Ninth Street," the subway conductor's voice booms overhead. I look at the people surrounding me. From affluent Upper West Side women toting their Prada handbags to restaurant workers and students, all walks of life are represented on the subway. Initially, I had wished my parents were rich so that they could have given me the money to rent an apartment in Manhattan for the summer. Who doesn't want to live in Manhattan? But after spending eight hours, five days a week, trying vainly to fit in with my status-conscious coworkers and order the right trendy cocktail of the moment on the two nights I've been invited to go to happy hour, it's nice to escape to Astoria and be around real people.

"Queensboro Plaza!"

Just as quickly as the car empties, it becomes full again with the teeming crowds who are on the platform. I'm about to take a seat that's become available at the other end of the car when a young woman jumps in front of me and drops into the seat. I'm momentarily thrown off-balance. I shoot her a dirty look, but she averts her eyes, acting as if she hasn't even seen me. I can see why so many New Yorkers get into confrontations with people. The stressful conditions of living in the largest city in the country with a population of eight million people make it easy to lose your cool and blow up at your neighbor. But just when I'm wondering why people can be so rude here, I'm pleasantly surprised.

"Excuse me, miss? Would you like to sit down?" An elderly man rises from his seat. Obviously he's witnessed the hijacking of my seat.

"No, thank you." I smile reassuringly, but the man still gets up and pats my arm imploringly to sit down.

"Go ahead. I'm getting off soon anyway."

I feel awkward taking his seat since he obviously needs it more than me, but I also sense that he'll be offended if I don't take it.

"Thank you very much."

"My pleasure. Chivalry isn't dead anymore." He winks at me.

"That's kind of you. Thank you again, sir."

"You're not from around here, are you?"

"It's that obvious?" I laugh.

"A little. Nothing to be ashamed of, though. Before you know it, you'll blend in, and soon you'll be the one jumping like a panther into someone else's seat." He glances over his shoulder at the young woman who's stolen my seat. She's listening to her iPod and flipping through the pages of *Cosmo*. I can't help but notice one of its glaring storylines: "Give Him His Best Orgasm Ever!"

Yeah, New Yorkers do get a bad rap from the rest of the country. But like my elderly knight in shining armor has just proven, there are also plenty of other New Yorkers who are kind and willing to help a stranger in need.

My stop finally arrives—Ditmars Boulevard—the last one on the N line. I descend the stairs of the "el," as New Yorkers refer to train tracks that are elevated above the street as opposed to those underground. As I make my way up Ditmars Boulevard, the aromas from several restaurants reach my nose. Pizza Palace is at the corner, an establishment that has been in the neighborhood for three decades now. I remember coming here a few times with Erica when we visited as kids.

My stomach is growling. I'm tempted to buy a slice to take home for dinner, but I don't dare. Zia insists on cooking dinner for me every night. She won't even let me eat leftovers. Of course, Zia's thrifty nature doesn't allow her to waste the leftovers by throwing them out. She eats the leftovers herself for lunch.

The steam coming from the souvlaki stand on 36th Street engulfs me in its scent of juicy lamb and sweet herbs. This is the toughest of all the foods to resist on Ditmars, especially since a second souvlaki stand is just two corners away from the first one. Though I've had Greek food in California since I'd first visited Astoria as a child, it's never measured up. Zia can't stand Greek food and had seemed miffed whenever my mother had bought Erica and me souvlaki sticks or gyros. "Why aren't you feeding them your own food? Italian is no longer good enough for you?" Zia would ask my mother critically. It was as if my mother had defected to Greece and was rejecting her Italian citizenship and heritage. My mother just ignored her. I've always been in awe of how my mother can avoid conflict so easily simply by refusing to defend herself. Erica was the same way. I, on the other hand, take after my father and am always ready with a sharp retort of my own if necessary.

With the largest Greek American population in the United States, Astoria is known as Little Greece. Gyro shops and souvlaki stands are a dime a dozen. Owners of Greek restaurants and specialty food shops sport the blue and white flag of their motherland proudly in their storefront windows, even if it's just a small flag. A few restaurants paint their interiors in blue and white, again in homage to their native country.

As I approach the second souvlaki stand, the temptation becomes unbearable. I've been waiting all these years since I was a child to return to Astoria to eat souvlaki again. Just one stick. That shouldn't ruin my appetite, and I can eat it on the street as everyone else does. Zia won't have to know.

I glance in the direction of Antoniella's Bakery, making sure Zia isn't sweeping out front or even checking to see if I'm making my way back from the subway station as she has done already on two evenings. The coast is clear. Of course, there's a line at the souvlaki stand. The woman roasting the sticks is alone, but she has her multitasking skills down to a tee as she turns over the souvlaki, takes money from customers, and keeps the line moving along. I keep glancing toward the bakery, nervous that Zia will come out at any moment. Finally, it's my turn.

"Hello. How may I help you?" The souvlaki vendor smiles.

"Hi. I'd like one souvlaki stick."

"With lemon?"

"Yes, please."

"Bread?"

"Yes, thank you."

"I've never seen you in the neighborhood before. Did you just move here?"

"I'm staying with my aunt for the summer. I just flew in this past weekend."

"Who is your aunt?"

I hesitate for a moment, fearful that the souvlaki vendor will run into Zia and tell her of my betrayal of Italian food. It's no use. I have to tell her the truth. She'll find out soon enough who I am, especially since her stand is just a block away from the bakery.

"Antoniella."

"From the bakery?"

I nod my head.

"My name is Ella. I hope you enjoy your summer in Astoria."

"Thank you. My name is Pia."

Ella wraps my souvlaki in foil with one hand as another hand whips open a brown paper bag.

I hold up my hand. "You don't need to wrap it up. I'll be eating it here on the street."

"As you wish, but take one home to Antoniella. On the house. If Antoniella knew you were here and I didn't give you a souvlaki for her, she'd be mad."

"Really?" I can't hide my surprise. Since when has Zia started eating souvlakis? I'll have to tease her about it. So maybe then she won't mind that I'm eating one? I can say I was feeling faint and didn't think I'd make it home in time. I know. That's lame. Her house is only two blocks away.

I eat my souvlaki as I walk toward Zia's home. There's no sense in hiding it since I have a second souvlaki for Zia. I can't eat both. Well, I could, but then I'd have no room left for any food that Zia has cooked. And *that* would really infuriate her.

As I pass the bakery, I peer into the window to check if Zia is still there. I don't spot her. Megan and another salesgirl are behind the counter, chatting. Megan sees me and waves. I wave back. I want to go in and talk to her, but I'm really not in the mood to possibly have to defend my choice in buying a souvlaki if Zia hasn't gone home yet. So I keep walking. Zia takes a break in the middle of the afternoon and goes home to cook. This way all she has to do when she gets home at night is reheat the food—in a pot on the stove, of course. Zia would never use a microwave for anything. She doesn't even own one.

The few times I've talked to Megan, I've found myself really liking her. So far, she's the only person around my age I've met who seems real; she isn't trying to be anything but herself. I think about the inane conversations I've had so far with my coworkers at *Profile*. It's going to be a *long* summer.

Thinking about my internship is bringing back the knot I felt in my shoulder on the subway. All Colin has had me do this week is proofread. Oh, I almost forgot the few business e-mails I had to draft for him. Maybe he's just easing me in before he gives me an actual writing or editing assignment? It is after all just my first week. But I remember the stories from my college friends who had interned and complained that they were treated like nothing more than secretaries and given work that had no substance to it. Internships are supposed to be instructive; they're supposed to give you an idea of the field so you'll know if it's a career path you want to pursue after graduating from college. But of course that's what the ideal, cloistered university world has you believe. Now that I'm in the real world, I see it's far from that way.

I savor every bite of the marinated lamb melting on my tongue. Before I know it, I'm down to the last piece of meat on my stick and halfway down the block. The crowd in front of the Mussolini Mansion is still there, as it has been ever since the day of my arrival in Astoria. When I walk to the subway station in the morning, only a few people are waiting. But by the evening, there's always a larger crowd. And it's growing every day. It amazes me how much people are fascinated by celebrities, that they can do nothing better with their time than just wait idly for the chance at a glimpse of their beloved star.

I've been walking by every night without stopping. Zia was probably right that whoever Ciggy saw was not Francesca Donata. But for some reason tonight, my curiosity gets the better of me. I wonder if any new developments have occurred.

I notice a woman whom I've seen at Zia's bakery every morning this week—Olivia DeLuca. Olivia owns the bridal boutique Sposa Rosa that is just a few doors down from Antoniella's Bakery. I walk over to her and tap her shoulder. Olivia jumps as if Francesca Donata is the one tapping her shoulder. She relaxes when she sees me. "Oh, Pia. You startled me."

"I'm sorry, Signora DeLuca. I didn't know how else to get your attention. You seemed really preoccupied." Then again, all of the neighbors standing there appear distracted, their gazes locked on Signora Tesca's home as if they possess X-ray vision and can see right through the bricks.

"Please, Pia. Call me Olivia. Everyone else does."

I feel weird calling a woman who could be my mother by her first name. That's not the way my parents brought me up. Everyone is either Mr. or Mrs., *signore* or *signora* if they're Italian. I just nod my head at Olivia's request. It will take some getting used to.

"So, any luck? Have you spotted *La Sposa Pazza?*"

"She's not crazy, Pia. That poor woman. Imagine coming close to getting married and having it not work out five times! Why must everyone always blame the woman? Because men are saints? Ha!" Olivia flicks the back of her hand under her throat—a famous Sicilian gesture of telling someone to go screw themselves. I laugh really hard. I haven't seen anyone do that since I was a child and witnessed my father making the gesture.

"See, you agree with me, *vero?*" Olivia nods her head emphatically.

"So, you're a big fan of *La Sposa*—I mean Francesca Donata." I quickly correct myself. My sixth sense tells me Olivia is probably also prone to mercurial mood swings like Zia.

"Yes. I've loved her since her first movie. She's a *paesana*. How can I not?"

"Francesca Donata is Sicilian? I thought she was from Rome."

"She moved to Rome after she was discovered and still lives there. But she is from Sicily. She even owns a villa in Taormina, which is not far from Messina, where I am from."

"I guess there haven't been more sightings of her, huh?"

"Oh, I'm sorry, Pia. I never answered your question. Beady Eyes *saw* her!"

Zia was right. All the neighbors did call Mr. and Mrs. Hoffman Beady Eyes behind their backs.

"Both of them saw Francesca Donata?"

"No, it was just Mr. Beady Eyes. He was opening his blinds at around ten this morning when he saw Francesca come out from the back with her bodyguards and quickly get into her Maserati. He ran out onto his stoop even though he was still in his pajamas, but of course the car had already gone down the street. He then rang all of our doorbells to tell us. We have been waiting all this time for her to return, but still no sign."

"What? You've all been standing here since ten a.m.? It's past six in the evening now!"

"Well, I've gone back and forth to my shop. I haven't waited the entire time here, but I heard Paulie hasn't left."

I look over to where Paulie Parlatone is standing. He's still wearing the same longshoreman's cap he had on the other day when I met him. Of course, his signature accessory—his toothpick—is sticking out of his mouth as he twirls it from left to right. He's average height, around 5'8", and very slim. He wears his trousers a little on the baggy side. His Members Only black jacket almost makes him look slick, if it weren't for the fact that the jackets haven't been in style since the eighties. His hands are inside his jacket's pockets, and I can tell they're curled into fists by the way his knuckles protrude through the fabric. Though it's June, we're having unseasonably chilly weather this week, and the temperature has only gone up to the high fifties today. I notice a few of the other older men are also wearing Members Only jackets.

Over dinner the other night, I had asked Zia about Paulie.

"THAT one!" Zia huffed. I was beginning to wonder if there was anyone on the block she did like. "His name says it all."

"What do you mean?"

"Parlatone. His last name. *'Parla'* means 'talk,' and *Dio mio,* can he talk! We were lucky the other night, Pia, that he didn't chew our ears off. He was too preoccupied with seeing if Francesca Donata was really in Signora Tesca's home. When he sees you on the street, or even when he comes into the bakery, he can talk for up to an hour, sometimes more! He knows I'm busy, but that doesn't stop him. He waits until I am done with a customer, and then he always remembers exactly where he left off in the discussion. The neighbors have a secret nickname for him too—*'Il Sindaco.'*" Zia dipped her Italian bread into the bowl of minestrone soup she'd cooked.

I tried to remember my high school Italian to figure out what *sindaco* meant. Mayor? No, that couldn't be right, but I decided to give it a shot. "Does *'sindaco'* mean 'mayor'?"

"*Brava!* Yes, it means 'mayor.' We call Paulie that because he knows everyone's business in Astoria, and if he doesn't know someone's business, he makes it his business. And just like a mayor, he also tries to solve people's problems."

"How so?"

"He has the nerve of dropping in on people in their homes. *Cretino!* Poo!" Zia imitated spitting. "*Cafone!* That's what he also is—a boor with no manners. When he sees a problem in someone's home, he offers advice. I suppose he thinks he's helping, but all he does is make these people suffer with humiliation. Who wants him to see their dirty laundry? And then they know once he sees it, he'll waste no time in airing it to the entire neighborhood." Zia ripped off a huge hunk of bread with her hands and chewed it anxiously. To say she looked angry was a huge understatement. I couldn't help wondering if Paulie had seen some of her dirty laundry and exposed it to the public. But I was too afraid to ask.

A cry from the crowd snaps me out of my thoughts. It's Mrs. Beady Eyes. She's yelling, "She's here! She's here!" and is pointing at a shiny black Maserati that's slowly pulling up in front of the Mussolini Mansion. The windows are lightly tinted, but I'm able to make out a woman wearing a silk scarf over her head, seated in the back. Now my heart is racing. Could it really be her?

The Maserati stops. The small crowd, which totals about twelve people, begins getting hysterical when the driver gets out of the car.

"Signora Tesca's driver," Olivia DeLuca whispers to me. Zia had told me that Signora Tesca was rich, but I'm still surprised she's rich enough to have her own personal driver.

The crowd inches closer to the car, but amazingly does not swarm it, leaving enough room should Francesca step out of the car. I find it interesting that their manners are replacing their baser instincts to get close up to their beloved celebrity.

The passenger-side door swings open. A beefy bodyguard-looking type steps out, holding a black satin drape. The driver comes around the car and helps the bodyguard unfold the drape. Then they stand on either end of the Maserati and hold the drape up, covering the rear passenger door. Two other bodyguards, even beefier than the first, get out from the opposite rear passenger door and start waving the crowd away. The neighbors have no choice but to back up as they strain their necks to see over the bodyguards' shoulders.

Something shiny catches my peripheral vision. I look to my left and spot a pair of pointy-toed, red patent-leather shoes sticking out from beneath the black drape the bodyguards hold. The dainty shoes tap-tap quickly along with the hurried movements of the bodyguards. It's the most bizarre sight I've ever seen.

The crowd goes wild, screaming several of the names she's known by as well as other made-up ones. *"Carissima! Sposa Pazza! Bella Donna!"*

Olivia breaks out in Italian, *"È davvero lei! È davvero lei!"*

My Italian high school lessons are coming in handy as my brain translates what Olivia says. "It's really her!"

Suddenly, Paulie's voice booms over the rest of the crowd, "*Carissima!* I love you! I love you, *Carissima!*" And again, just in case his voice hasn't already pierced her ears, "I *L-UH-UH-UH-V* you!"

A few of the neighbors clap their hands and jump up and down as if their favorite football team has won the Super Bowl. Olivia is wiping tears from her eyes and saying over and over, "I can't believe it! I can't believe it!"

I'm amazed by the reaction celebrities elicit in people. Though I'm nowhere near as overcome as everyone else, I can't help feeling the excitement pulsing through me. You'd think I'd be used to seeing celebrities since I'm from southern California. I have seen a few of today's stars like Jennifer Aniston, Pink, Hugh Jackman, and a few others. But I've never seen one of the silver-screen legends. I don't know why, but to me, silver-screen stars seem to exude a different kind of aura from the younger generation of stars.

What am I thinking? I need to take a photo—even if it's just of Francesca's feet. I take out my iPhone, quickly set it to the camera mode, and begin snapping away at Francesca's pumps. The driver opens the gate that leads to the back of the Mussolini Mansion. One of the bodyguards ushering Francesca through the gate drops his end of the drape, and for a few seconds the star's back is exposed to the crowd. The scarf I had seen through the Maserati's tinted windows is a red and white Gucci silk scarf. Francesca is wearing a tight pencil skirt in an ivory hue that complements her bronzed skin. Though her face is hidden, and I'm sure she has to be wearing sunglasses to further hide her identity, there's no doubt that the woman is indeed *La Sposa Pazza.* For her snug skirt shows off one of Francesca's signature traits—a trait that has received as much recognition as her movies and beauty have: her well-shaped derrière.

I continue snapping away with my camera, feeling like a pervert taking photos of a woman's ass. But almost as soon as Francesca's derrière comes into view, it disappears again in the darkness of the drape that her bodyguards have now wrapped around her back.

"Whoo-whoo!" Ciggy whistles in a low, husky voice. "Did you

get a load of that, Paulie?" Ciggy's raspy voice, no doubt from smoking too many cigars, just makes him sound more like a creepy sexual predator.

"Of course I did! You think I would've missed a fine work of art like that?" Paulie slaps Ciggy hard on the back, causing him to cough, as they snicker.

Paulie has taken his toothpick out from between his lips and is waving it around dramatically in the air, probably flicking the crud that was recently dislodged from his teeth onto everyone, and says, "Pia, you can tell your aunt that we were right all along! We know for certain now that Francesca Donata is here. We all saw her backside. And no woman in the world possesses what Francesca has!" He flourishes the toothpick one last time before popping it back into his mouth.

I take a good two steps back should he decide to begin waving his wand again. At least he'd been polite enough when addressing me to say "backside" as opposed to the cruder "ass." But soon I hear him, Ciggy, and a few of the other men bandy around the word "ass" several times. I'm sure they'll all be dreaming about Francesca's well-endowed butt tonight. I shiver at the thought and quickly erase the image.

*"Fanno schifo!* Disgusting old men!" Olivia is by my side again, her eyebrows joined furiously together. She looks like she's going to throttle Paulie and his cronies.

"Are you happy you saw her, Olivia?" I hope to distract her from whatever punishment she is no doubt doling out in her mind for the old men.

"Yes and no. I will not be satisfied until I see her face."

"You don't think that was her?"

*"Si, si.* It was her. As Paulie pointed out, no one has a *culo* like that in the world!" Olivia laughs at her use of the Italian word for "ass." I laugh with her, glad to see that she has a sense of humor after all.

"I'm going to close up the shop, have some dinner, and then I'll come back out. But I have a feeling she won't be going out again since it's late. But what else am I going to do? This is better than watching *La Reina del Sur.*"

My *zia* also watches *La Reina del Sur.* Though *La Reina del Sur* is a Spanish soap opera on the Telemundo channel, many of the older Italian women also love to watch it. Since Spanish is so similar to Italian, they're able to understand most of the soap.

"I should get going, too. Zia is probably wondering why I'm so late for dinner. I'm surprised she hasn't come out looking for me."

"Come back, Pia. We'll keep each other company." Olivia smiles warmly at me. I don't know why she needs my company since I've already heard a few of the other neighbors saying they're also going to continue staking out the Mussolini Mansion.

"Maybe I will. Thank you." I wave to Olivia as she leaves for her shop.

My stomach grumbles. I guess it needs more than the souvlaki I devoured earlier. At least now I can eat the huge dinner Zia has cooked. Sighing, I think about all the pounds that I'll definitely pack on over the summer living with my aunt. Between her large home-cooked meals and the sweets from the bakery she brings home every night, I don't stand a chance.

I glance one last time over my shoulder at the Mussolini Mansion as I walk down the block. One neighbor points to the balconette in the Italianate-style house and actually says, "Maybe she'll come out there later and wave to us?"

I roll my eyes. These people are living in a fantasy world.

My thoughts return to my photos. Pulling my iPhone out of my purse, I scan through the few pics I shot. A crazy idea enters my mind. No, it's too ridiculous. He won't go for it. Then again . . . isn't that how success comes about? From taking chances no matter how far-flung they might seem?

I quicken my pace to Zia's house, feeling more confident in what I need to do next.

# ❦ 4 ❦

# Francesca

I cannot believe it. They still care—about *me!* Even after all these years, the excitement that comes from being recognized and adored is just as thrilling as when I was first discovered at sixteen years old. True, it is just a small crowd in front of Giuliana's home, but give it time. Word will soon spread that Italian silver-screen star Francesca Donata—*La Sposa Pazza*—is here in Astoria.

Surely, no one will believe it at first. They will all wonder why a legendary actress chose to visit a working-class neighborhood in the borough of Queens no less. Manhattan is where they would expect to find me. I can just hear the rumors now: "She really *is* crazy. What is she thinking? The world hasn't heard from her in ten years, and *this* is where she chooses to make her grand return—Astoria?"

I can't help but silently laugh to myself. After all the gossip that has been spread about me over the years, I have developed a tortoise shell. Instead of the ugly rumors hurting me as they did when I was young, I find them amusing now. And trust me. Not caring is a monumental accomplishment for an Italian. *Fare la bella figura* is everything to Italians.

*Fare la bella figura* is the equivalent to what you Americans call "saving face" or making a good impression. In Italian culture, you strive to make a good impression in everything you do in life, whether it is being hospitable to a guest in your home, exhibiting the finest manners at all times, throwing the best wedding for your daughter, attending the funerals of everyone you know, looking impeccable—the list is endless. And as an Italian, you avoid at all costs *fare la brutta figura*—making a bad impression or "losing face."

But I will not lie. I wish I could say I do not care at all anymore about *la bella figura*. Where my appearance is concerned, I still work hard to look my best, though it is getting harder as I get older. I cannot control the signs of aging that are slowly but surely taking over my face and body. Well, between you and me, I have had cosmetic injections to erase fine lines, but I refuse to do anything more than that. The monsters some women have turned themselves into as a result of being slaves to cosmetic surgery are more reprehensible to me than wrinkles. But no matter how old I live to be, I will always wear nothing but designer clothes. My favorite designers are Gucci and Prada. I even like a few of Ralph Lauren's designs on the rare occasion I wear more casual clothes. But that is very rare. I am from the generation in which people actually enjoyed getting dressed up and looking their best.

As for the scandals in my life—some of which are public knowledge; others are not—I have committed *la brutta figura* one time too many to care anymore what others think of me as a person. That is the double-edged sword of celebrity. You want everyone to recognize your face and name, but the sad irony is the public only knows what the media feeds them. I will not pretend, like some of my peers have, that the media has told nothing but lies. Some of it is true.

And I do still care very much that people have not forgotten about me. If it was not for trying to protect Giuliana's privacy, I would have stepped proudly out of the car and waved to my adoring fans. Unlike other stars who do not want to be bothered by the fans who catapulted them to fame, I would have signed autographs for everyone who asked. I would even have talked to them. That is one thing the world has always loved about me—how I would ask my fans about their families and lives. I take a genuine interest in them. Of course, as a star, I have very little, if anything, in common with them. But I value the power of making that personal connection with my fans.

I had hoped to keep my visit here a secret. Giuliana does not need a circus in front of her house, especially since she has led a very private life. No one even knows her connection to me. Though my bodyguards tried to conceal me, it was a pathetic attempt. I feel horrible for admitting this—even to myself—but I am glad they did not succeed. I have spent most of my life in the spotlight, and like a drug, I need the rush that fame gives me. After the ten years I spent as a recluse, I had hoped that I would have lost my insatiable desire to be loved by the public. But what can I say? I am weak.

The door to the upstairs sitting room squeaks open, startling me out of my thoughts.

"Meow!"

A long-haired white cat rushes over to me, no trepidation that it has never laid eyes on me before. Even the cat senses my star power.

"Look at you! *Sei bella! Bella!*"

As if thanking me, the cat yelps a softer "meow" and rubs up against my legs, leaving a dusting of fine white hairs clinging to my sheer black hosiery.

I bend over and pick her up. "*Come ti chiami?* Eh?"

The cat purrs into my ear. Her breath warms my neck. I did not even know that Giuliana owned a cat. Then again, why would I? We have barely spoken over the past two decades, and most of our communication has been through letters. This saddens me—the idea that we don't really know each other anymore. Once, Giuliana claimed she knew *exactly* what she needed to know about me. I suppose she was right. I close my eyes, going back to a time when Giuliana and I had been as inseparable as the moon and the sky. But my mind forces the memory out as tears spring to my eyes. It is too painful to go down that road. Though soon, my visit here will inevitably force me to travel down that path I have worked so hard to avoid.

## ❧ 5 ❧

# Pia

By the time I have dinner with Zia and help her clean up, it's already ten o'clock. Zia's not too happy to hear that I'm going for a short walk this late. Of course, she knows she has nothing to worry about since people are seen walking on Ditmars until all hours of the night, and Astoria is considered one of the safest neighborhoods in New York City. I don't want to tell her that I'm really going to the Mussolini Mansion in hopes of spotting Francesca Donata again—though the likelihood of that is slim. Francesca has probably retired for the evening. I've always wanted to use that phrase "retired for the evening." It feels like a fitting phrase to use for a silver-screen legend like Francesca Donata. Anyway, I'm beginning to go stir-crazy after hanging out with Zia almost every weeknight of my stay here so far. Besides, if I'm going to carry out the idea that sprang in my mind earlier, I must be diligent and stake out Signora Tesca's home whenever I have the chance. That's what a good journalist does.

I know my idea will probably be dismissed by Colin Cohen. But I have to at least try—even if it means suffering humiliation when everyone at *Profile* finds out about it. I can just hear some of their voices now: "All these newbie interns think they have a great idea that will seal their future careers with us. They're all the same! This isn't the movies, where you have a great idea and you go from being a nobody to somebody in the blink of an eye!"

Inhaling deeply, I focus on pushing every negative thought out of my mind. I imagine myself getting a few photos of Francesca Donata, going to Colin, and proposing to him that I can interview the silver-screen legend for an article in *Profile*—an article that *I* will write. The photos will convince him I'm not bluffing. Besides, the press is sure to soon get wind of her being here in Astoria, and Colin will then know I am telling the truth. All he'll have to do is confirm my address with human resources, and he'll see Zia's address is on the same street where Francesca is staying. But I know it won't be that easy, especially convincing him to let me write the story instead of a more seasoned member of *Profile's* editorial staff.

The fear starts invading every cell of my body again. What am I thinking? It's a huge stretch entertaining the idea that Colin is going to let an intern, and one who's been on the job no more than a week, interview a world-famous movie star, no less have her write the story.

I sigh once again—my signature trait. I sigh all the time, whether I'm upset or stressed out or just want to take a deep breath. It runs in my family on my father's side. People always ask me, "What's the matter?" after hearing one of my drawn-out sighs. In this case, the sigh is related to anxiety. My father has always taught me to follow my instincts no matter how farfetched they might seem. So here I am on my way to the Mussolini Mansion to stake out the house, along with the other obsessed neighbors on the block, in hopes of snapping a photo of The Crazy Bride that will convince my internship supervisor to let me do a story on the legend. Opportunity's knocking—though I'm not sure if it's opportunity that will bring me acclaim or shame.

I know I am a good writer. My confidence isn't lacking in that area. But Colin really has no idea how good a writer I am. After this past week that I've spent typing up business correspondence and proofreading countless pages, I'm beginning to wonder if Colin actually read the essay I'd been required to write for *Profile's* internship application. My college's guidance counselor had told me that the weight of the application rested on the essay and my writing skills, which made sense since I was applying to be an editorial intern at a magazine. So when I learned that I'd landed the competitive internship at *Profile,* I felt like I had arrived where my writing was concerned. This was validation that I was a talented writer.

But harsh reality has set in over the course of the past few days, as it becomes more apparent that Colin wants a secretary rather than an editorial intern whom he can mentor. I'd even gone to him this morning and asked him if he needed help with editing any of the stories.

"Pia. Relax. You've been here what? All of two days?"

"Five days."

He'd waved his hand in the air as if it didn't matter whether it was two or five.

"Anyway, this is your first week. You need to learn and do everything that's involved in getting this magazine printed and to the stands. There's more to being a good magazine editor than just writing and editing. Trust me. You'll get your writing and editing experience while on this internship. You'll be here the whole summer. There's time."

I had apologized, which only elicited another one of Colin's annoying, dismissive waves. He waves a lot even when he's explaining a project to me. It's almost as if to say, "And so on; you know what I mean." He waves his hand high up in the air, circling it in a frenzied, quick motion like an orchestral conductor.

Maybe I'm just jumping the gun and worrying prematurely? Like Colin said, I've only been at the internship for a week. But then again, I can't ignore what my instincts are telling me, and they're screaming, "You're not going to get any *real* editorial experience here!"

Even if Colin lets me writes a short piece on the star's coming to Astoria, I'd be happy with that. I'm not expecting him to let me do a feature-length story. I just have to give it my best shot.

I join the crowd in front of Signora Tesca's home, feeling a bit foolish that I've now become one of the gawkers. A few of the neighbors keep walking over to the driveway, just in case Francesca is hanging out in the backyard. This is ridiculous. I can see why Zia was so irritated on that first day when we came upon "the stockers," as she calls them. Of course, she means "the stalkers," but with her Italian accent it sounds more like "stockers." That's why I didn't tell Zia my true motive for coming out tonight. She would've lectured me and told me not to be so *"stupida"*—her favorite insult and the quality she tolerates the least in people.

I don't see Olivia DeLuca even though she'd said she would be coming back out. Maybe she's too tired after closing up her bridal boutique and making dinner. Paulie Parlatone is the only neighbor left of the crowd that's slowly diminishing as one by one they give up their watch and return home. Only the Mayor of 35th Street and I remain of "the stalkers." Though I'm wearing a loose cardigan that conceals my breasts, not that they're hard to hide at their B-cup measurement, I still cross my arms protectively over my chest as Paulie approaches me.

"It's just you and me, Pia." Paulie tips his longshoreman's cap toward me and winks. Normally the sight of an old man winking at me would give me the creeps, but I can tell it's a benign gesture. Unlike the day we first met, Paulie's eyes don't wander down the length of my body. He manages to keep his gaze locked with mine.

"I can't believe I'm out here." I shake my head and start thinking maybe I'll head back home to Zia's as well.

"You're curious. Nothing wrong with that. Human nature. We're all fascinated by the lives of the rich and famous. But I have to tell you, I keep thinking I'm going to wake up and laugh so hard at this bizarre dream I'm having. I mean, come on! Francesca Donata in Astoria *and* in the Mussolini Mansion of all places! Ha!" Paulie slaps his forehead, as if by doing so he will be awakened from this twisted dream.

I laugh along with him. "Yeah, it is pretty weird. But I guess if Francesca had to visit, she picked the right house on the block. This is the fanciest one. And Signora Tesca does have money."

"That's true, although you'd never know it by the way that woman dresses. I've seen her wear the same two dresses in all the years that I've lived here—a navy blue polyester dress and a dark brown one. That's it! Oh, sometimes she has slacks. But she hardly ever comes out in the winter when it gets cold, so you don't see her in the pants too often."

"How do you think they know each other?"

"That's a riddle if there ever was one." Paulie lets out a low whistle. "We were all talking about it earlier. Ciggy said they had to have known each other when Signora Tesca lived in Italy before she came to America. That was a good thirty years ago. Someone said maybe they were childhood friends. But that don't sound right. I stopped being friends with the kids from my childhood when I started working in high school. I didn't have time for school and friends. Ahhh! That was a different time, too. You were focused on getting ahead in life and making sure you had a good paying job. It's not like that now. All you young people care about are friends, friends, friends. And what's this whole Facebook thing about anyway? How can you be friends with someone through a computer screen, for crying out loud?" Paulie slaps his forehead again.

My ears are beginning to ring. Zia's right that in addition to being the Mayor of 35th Street and sticking his nose in everyone's business, Paulie can talk forever. I try reining him in and back on the topic of Francesca.

"So, any other guesses as to how Signora Tesca knows Francesca?"

"Torpedo Tits thinks they're cousins! Oh, I'm sorry. Excuse me, where are my manners. I mean Betsy Offenheimer. Everyone calls her by the name I first used." Paulie clears his throat and mutters in a low voice. "You'll see why when you meet her if you haven't yet."

I don't know who Paulie's talking about, but then an image of a woman I'd seen earlier with enormous, pointed breasts comes to mind. Her breasts had been difficult not to notice. They were cocked far out of her chest like machine guns. But more troubling than her very large breasts was the type of bra she no doubt had to be wearing. For only one of those Playtex bras that harkened back to the fifties could give her breasts that pointed "torpedo" look. In fact, everything about Betsy Offenheimer screamed, "I belong in the fifties." She wore black cat-shaped eyeglasses that were attached to a long string of crystal pearls. And her white hair was tightly wound in a roller set. In one hand, she held a glossy black cane with a cat's head molded out of the top of it. The cat's eyes were glittering rhinestones. In her other hand, she held a leash that was attached to her black poodle's collar. Obviously, she liked the color black. I had only seen her poodle from the back, but I do remember it had this odd habit of leaning its head from side to side as if it were trying to listen for something.

"I think I know who you're talking about. She has a black poodle?"

"Yup, that's Torpedo—I mean Betsy. Betsy and Mitzy."

Interesting. Mitzy's name almost rhymed with her own.

"She never goes anywhere without Mitzy, but that's because she's afraid of leaving her alone."

"Why is she afraid of leaving her dog alone?"

"Didn't you notice Mitzy's eyes? She's blind." Paulie shudders. "It scares the crap out of me every time I look at that dog's eyes by mistake. I try to avoid them at all costs, but sometimes I'm rounding the corner and then BAM! Those milky white eyes are staring right up at me. She looks like a zombie dog! Ugghhh!" Paulie shudders again.

Now I understand why the dog's head kept tilting from side to side when I saw her. She'd been trying to listen, since she has to rely on her sense of hearing to compensate for her lack of sight. My heart aches a bit for Mitzy. No wonder Torpedo Tits is afraid to leave her alone. Great! Now I'm calling Betsy "Torpedo Tits," too.

"Why does Betsy think Signora Tesca and Francesca are cousins? Or is she just purely taking a guess?"

"You ask a lot of questions, Pia! I like that. You remind me of me." Paulie gives me the once-over look that he gave me when we first met. It's my turn now to shudder.

"Just curious. That's all. Just like everyone else."

"Hold on! Antoniella mentioned to me that you are working for a magazine and like to write. That's it!" He snaps his fingers and wags his index finger at me. "You want to be a journalist! No wonder all the questions. Bingo! I'm right, aren't I?"

Paulie looks really pleased with himself. I want to lie just so I won't have to give him the satisfaction that he's right. But there's the chance Zia will blab, as she was telling everyone else in Astoria how I'm going to be a famous journalist someday.

"I'm interning at a magazine. I would like to write for a magazine and hopefully start my own down the road. But I have a lot to learn until then."

"You'll get there; you'll get there." Paulie pats my shoulder as if we're now the best of friends. "Wow! What amazing luck this is for you! You come visit your aunt right when none other than Francesca Donata is visiting! This is fate, kid! Maybe she'll grant you an interview."

Maybe Paulie's right. We do think a lot alike. It's scary to even entertain that thought. But I'm not going to let him in on my secret mission.

"I'm just a fan, Paulie. It would be nice to get a couple of photos of her. Nothing more. Why would a big star like Francesca Donata give an interview to an intern?" I give a high-pitched laugh; it surprises me how convincing it sounds.

"Ahhh! You're selling yourself short, kid. See, this is what I mean about your generation. No ambition. No desire to take a risk. If you fail, you fail. What do you got to lose? You'll be right where you started. But if you succeed, the world is yours."

Paulie has a point. There's more to this guy than just being a nosy, crass talker who often rubs people the wrong way.

Paulie yawns, not bothering to cover his mouth. "I don't want to leave you here all alone, Pia, but I've been standing here since Beady Eyes woke me up with the news that he spotted Francesca. I've only taken breaks to use the john and buy myself a couple of heroes at Anthony's Salumeria to eat while I waited for Francesca to come out."

I can't believe he's eaten his meals here. Again, I marvel at the strange behavior stars bring out in their fans.

"It's okay, Paulie. I'll be fine. I might just take a few photos of the house. I love architecture, and it is an interesting house. Who knows? Maybe I'll get lucky and spot Francesca behind a window." I smile at Paulie.

"Hey! You never know. No one in a million years would've guessed that a movie star would be here on Thirty-Fifth Street in Astoria, Queens. Gotta believe. Gotta believe. Good night!" Paulie tips his cap at me in farewell and crosses the street. I watch him as he walks slowly toward his house, which is opposite Ciggy's. He's whistling softly, and his hands are buried deep in the pockets of his trousers. He never did answer my question as to why Torpedo Tits believes Signora Tesca and Francesca Donata are cousins. He goes off on so many tangents that it's hard to get him to return to the initial topic at hand. I'm sure it's nothing more than pure conjecture on Betsy's part. I don't think they're cousins or even remotely related. From what I've heard from everyone, the two women are worlds apart—not that cousins often have a lot in common. Still, it just doesn't feel right. My guess is that they are friends, maybe not childhood friends, but friends nonetheless.

I pull out my iPhone and begin snapping a few shots of the Mussolini Mansion. If I'm lucky enough to get photos of Francesca, people will want to see where she's staying, too. As soon as I'm done, I'm heading back home. I'm not as crazed as Francesca's admirers to stand here for hours on end. Besides, it is getting late, and I know Zia will worry if I'm out too long.

Having taken ten shots of the Mussolini Mansion from all angles, I'm ready to leave. I start to walk away when a thought occurs to me. This would be the perfect moment for Francesca to leave, now that everyone has gone home. I look over my shoulder up toward a second-story window that's lit.

Oh, this is insane! I start to walk away again, but only take two steps. A good journalist is a persistent one. Hadn't my journalism professors drilled that into me repeatedly? I give an extra-long sigh. If I hope to become a real journalist, I need to learn how to tough it out. I can't give up this quickly.

I tiptoe quietly over to the left side of the house, opposite from the driveway. I crouch behind a rhododendron bush. If Francesca is waiting for the crowd to completely disperse, she isn't going to exit the house with me standing blatantly in view.

After about five minutes, my thighs begin to ache. At least I'm getting a good workout if nothing else.

Suddenly, I hear a door swing shut. I quickly check my iPhone to make sure it's still set to the camera mode and prepare to take a photo, lifting my arms slightly above the rhododendron bush. I can hear footsteps hurriedly making their way to the end of the driveway. My heart races. This might be my defining moment—the moment that will either make my career or leave me forever in the trenches of proofreading and typing mind-numbing business correspondence.

I whisper, "Please, God. Please, let me get a shot of Francesca. If not tonight, then—"

I hold my breath as the gate squeaks open and then shut. A shadow comes into view, and without waiting to make sure I'm getting a clear shot, I touch the camera button on my phone's screen. As soon as the flash goes off, I stand up, not caring anymore if Francesca or her bodyguards see me snapping away.

"What the hell?"

Got it! But just as soon as I think this, I realize that's not a woman's voice that I've just heard. And the figure is now making its way toward me. It's dim since one of the streetlamps has gone out. But it isn't too dark for me to detect a man—a very handsome man who looks to be in his mid-twenties. The expression on his face tells me I'm in big trouble.

"What are you doing hiding there like that? What do you want?"

I hold up my hands. "I'm sorry."

"Oh! Right. I should've known. You were hoping I was Francesca."

"I just wanted one photo of her. But you're right. I shouldn't be here. I'll just go now. I'm sorry if I startled you." I turn around and walk as fast as I ever have in my life.

"Hold up! You don't have to go. I'm sorry if I lost my temper with you. It's just that we've all been on edge with her here."

I keep walking until I hear his last sentence and freeze in my tracks. He's acknowledging that Francesca is indeed in the house—not that I need his confirmation. I, along with the other neighbors, have seen her famous ass. That's proof enough.

I turn around and slowly walk back to him, not wanting to seem like a star-crazed groupie.

"May I ask why she's here? I know it's none of my business, but—"

"You're right; it's none of your business." He's smiling now instead of looking like he is going to throttle me.

"I'm sorry. It's just that everyone is naturally curious as to why Francesca Donata came to Astoria. Is there some light you can shed? Anything at all?"

"You sound like a reporter. If it weren't for the fact that you were going to take a photo of Francesca with your iPhone, I'd be convinced you're paparazzi."

"I'm not a reporter. I'm just a fan hoping to get a photo of her. Like I said, it's not every day that we have a star here."

"Well, I'm sorry to disappoint you. Really. I am. But you're wasting your time. You're not going to get your photo of Francesca tonight. In fact, it'll be next to impossible for you to get a photo of her while she's here."

"So this will be an extended visit for her?"

"Are you sure you're not a reporter? What's your name, by the way?"

"What's yours?" I can't hide the smirk on my face.

"Oh, so now we're playing that game, huh?" His smile deepens, showing off the most amazing dimples I've ever seen on anyone.

"I think my aunt is waiting outside her house. Yes, I can make her out waving to me. I should get going." I wave back to an imaginary Zia, standing on my toes as I strain my neck to get a better view of her. I hope this will show him that Zia's house is quite far down the block and it's not so easy to spot, so he won't know I'm lying if he follows my gaze. Luckily for me, he doesn't look to see if Zia is really standing there.

"Okay, you win. My name is Gregory. Gregory Hewson."

He got me. How could I walk away now without looking rude? I return my attention to him.

"Nice to meet you. I'm Pia Santore." I hold out my hand as he wraps his around mine, giving it a firm shake.

"That's a beautiful name. I don't think I've ever met another Pia. I can see why."

He continues holding my hand. It's unnerving me a bit, but I can't deny I also like the way my hand feels in his. Finally, he lets go.

"I don't want to keep your aunt waiting. Do you live with her?"

"Just for the summer. I actually live in California."

"So I'll be seeing more of you." Gregory gives me a salute as he makes his way toward a beat-up Honda Civic that's parked in front of the Mussolini Mansion.

"Can you just answer one question about Francesca?"

"Ahhh. The fascination once again. Okay, one question just for you, Pia Santore." Turning around, Gregory leans against his Honda and holds out his arms as if to say, "Give it to me. I'm ready."

A dozen questions run through my mind. How do I pick just one? I have to choose the question that's weighing most on everyone's mind.

"What is Francesca's connection to Signora Tesca?"

Gregory smiles. He slyly glances over at the Mussolini Mansion and back at me.

"Pia, if I could, I would give you whatever you desire." His gaze wanders lazily from my eyes down the length of my body. "But I'm sorry to say *that* is the one question I am not at liberty to answer. Good night, Pia." He turns around and walks over to the driver's side of the car, opening the door; much to my amazement, he hasn't even locked it. Who leaves their car unlocked on a New York City street? Then again, the Honda is pretty beat-up. He probably doesn't care if someone steals it.

I can't help noticing how good Gregory looks in his jeans that seem to have strategically placed tears and paint splatters all over them. And his tush is perfectly outlined in them. Suddenly, as if reading my thoughts, Gregory looks up one last time before getting into his car and catches me in the act of checking his butt out. My cheeks flame hot, and there's no concealing it as Gregory shoots a shy smile in my direction. Waving, he finally gets into his car and drives off. I can't believe I actually linger until he pulls away from the curb. Then I realize with horror another thought. Once he gets down the block, he's going to see there's no middle-aged woman waiting for me.

## 6

# Francesca

"There's no need for you to stay." Giuliana adds two sugar cubes to her espresso, keeping her back turned toward me.

"Giuliana, I want to be here. Please. After everything that has happened. Can we not finally put the past behind us and—"

"And what? Be the close friends we were when we were girls?" Giuliana finally faces me. I can see the anger still blazing in her eyes as it did over thirty years ago. But this time sadness also fills her eyes.

"We can try. I know it will not ever be the way it was then, but it would be better than carrying this weight that only gets heavier as we get older."

"You're only here because he wrote to you."

"Giuliana, you know I tried to be a part of your life before, but you would not have it. You refused to bury the past."

"That's not true, Francesca. I've sent you letters. Besides, I thought it was better that we did not see each other. It would've been too complicated." Giuliana makes her way over to the Queen Anne couch with her demitasse cup of espresso in one hand and her cane in the other.

I want to go help her, but I know that will just anger her more. It is difficult seeing her becoming an old woman. She is only fifty-eight, but appears much older. I am fifty-five, but have been told I can pass for still being in my late forties. Though we were inseparable as young girls, we grew up to be very different women. Giuliana has never been vain like me or cared about wearing the finest designer clothes or having the latest fashionable hairstyle. She is thrifty even though I have given her plenty of money over the years. Every time I send her a check, I am surprised she does not return it. But I know why she keeps the money—even if it is from me, someone she detests.

"Thank you for those letters. They meant the world to me." My eyes meet Giuliana's. She nods her head and looks away.

"You are right. It would have been too complicated if we had seen each other." I raise my cup to my lips and take a sip of the scalding espresso, which stings less than Giuliana's evident dislike of me.

"I'm not heartless. I did what I thought was best." Giuliana clutches an ivory lace handkerchief tightly in her hand. Though her eyes fill with tears, she doesn't dab at them with her handkerchief.

"Giuliana, I have never thought you were heartless. If anything, you should be accusing me of that. After all, I did choose my acting career." I blush at the memory of the day when I had admitted to her that acting was my greatest love. But that had been no secret to her. Giuliana had always known me best.

"You were young—and famous. That alone changes someone immeasurably."

I detect a hint of compassion in Giuliana's voice, but at the same time, I cannot help but feel she is also judging me for the choices I have made in my life. But I am not mad at her, nor was I ever. She has every right to feel the way she does toward me.

"I needed to see you and tell you that I want to make things right between us. If you really want me to leave, Giuliana, I will. It is your home, and I must respect your wishes."

"Eh."

I used to tease Giuliana mercilessly about this grunt she gave whenever she was halfheartedly agreeing to something. And no matter how hard she tried to refrain from doing it, she simply could not. I resist the urge to smile. As I get older, I now find myself making the same grunt. If only Giuliana knew. Hopefully, I will not slip in front of her.

"Francesca, I have a confession to make. I asked Lorenzo to write to you."

"*Davvero!* You are playing with me or how do you Americans call it, 'kidding'? You are kidding me."

"*È vero,* Francesca."

"Why did you ask Lorenzo to write to me? And now here you are saying you do not need me to stay."

"You know why. It's for my son. For when . . ." Giuliana's voice cracks. Her hand that is holding her cup of espresso trembles, spilling some of it onto her lap. I get up and pat her dress with a napkin.

"*Sto bene.* I'm fine." Giuliana holds up her hand. "*Grazie.*"

I wipe the espresso that has spilled onto the hardwood floor. Though the household cleaning staff is meticulous, I can still see a few fine white hairs from Giuliana's cat's coat on the floor. Suddenly, the cat comes from behind the couch. She sniffs the floor and then looks up at me, yelping "meow" repeatedly.

"Mewsette, *vieni qui.*" Giuliana pats the seat beside her on the couch. But Mewsette ignores her and rubs her legs against mine. This angers Giuliana.

"Mewsette, *vieni! Vieni!*" Mewsette finally looks at Giuliana, twisting her left ear as if she is trying to get a better signal in hearing her mistress. But she remains next to me.

I pick up Mewsette and drop her off by Giuliana. Reluctantly, she lowers herself onto the couch, but stares at me.

"She likes you—of course." Giuliana's voice drips with bitterness. I pretend not to hear her as I pour myself a second cup of espresso.

Maybe I should leave? It is apparent that Giuliana still harbors much resentment toward me.

"If you will excuse me, I am going to call my travel agent and see when she can book the next flight back to Italy."

I head for the French doors.

"*Aspetti!* Didn't you hear what I just told you? I wanted you to come. I'm sorry if my demeanor has not been warmer. Yes, we have a lot of bad blood between us, but that's not the only reason my temperament is brusque. Some days, the pain is worse than others, and this morning is one of my worst days yet."

I can feel tears threatening to pool my eyes, but I know the last thing Giuliana wants or needs is my sympathy. So I force the tears back.

"If I stay, you must allow me to do whatever I can to make you more comfortable. I know you have hired help, but I want to make myself useful."

Giuliana flicks her fingers up in the air as if she is swatting a fly away. "I'm not an invalid—yet at least. And as you said, I have hired help for that. I don't want you fawning all over me. But I suppose you can read to me. My eyesight has gotten worse, plus I get too tired sitting up for long periods of time to read. I've missed my books." She gestures toward the floor-to-ceiling bookshelves that completely encircle the library where we are currently taking our morning espresso. How did I almost forget Giuliana's love of reading? She used to steal moments away from her chores, hiding from our parents, so that she could read her beloved books.

"I would love to read to you. I have actually been reading more these past few years."

"Yes, I've read about your hibernation in the papers. You really stayed at home in Taormina? Weren't you traveling the world as you love to do? Even though you were no longer in the spotlight, I could not picture you languishing away behind closed doors the way I have most of my life."

Do I detect a hint of regret in Giuliana's voice? Guilt washes over me as it often does when I think about her.

"I only traveled to Rome a few times. But that was it. So why do we not start now—that is, if you are feeling up to it. If you would rather rest, I can read to you later."

"No, now is fine. My pills are finally taking effect." Using both of her hands, Giuliana lifts her legs one at a time onto the couch and adjusts the throw pillows behind her head as she reclines fully back.

I walk over to one of the stacks. "Which book would you like me to read?"

"I've always wanted to read *Rebecca*. It's on the shelf closest to the doors. They're lined up alphabetically by the authors' last names. Daphne—"

"Du Maurier. I know. I have read *Rebecca*."

"You have? Oh, maybe you would rather read something else then." Giuliana's voice betrays a hint of disappointment.

"No, no. *Rebecca* is fine. It is one of my favorite books. I have always wanted to read it again."

I peruse the shelves. Part of me is surprised that Giuliana has not read every title in this library. It seems fitting to read *Rebecca* here. Though Giuliana's house is beautiful, there is also a heavy, melancholy air. And those marble statues in the garden are absolutely eerie. Not even my villas in Italy have any. True, many wealthy people adorn their properties with classical sculptures, and a few are stunning. But the weathered and cracked figures in Giuliana's yard have lost any aesthetic beauty they might have once had.

Mewsette is still by Giuliana's side, but now she rests her head on her mistress's belly, dozing peacefully. Initially, I wonder why Giuliana chose to give her a French name rather than an Italian one. We don't even know French. But then I remember a cartoon. No, it was not a cartoon, but an animated movie. *Gay Purr-ee*! That was the title. It was about cats, and the star was a white feline named "Mewsette." Tears enter my eyes. Giuliana and I saw this movie when we were girls and fell in love with it.

I compose myself before Giuliana notices and sit down in the chair opposite her. How strange to be here with her after all these years. Can we finally come to some sort of understanding after so many decades of hostility and estrangement? Will I get to know once again the girl who used to be my closest confidante? Staying with Giuliana makes me realize just how much I have missed her. This is my chance—my last chance—to finally make things right between us.

I open the leather-bound cover of *Rebecca* and begin reading. But it is difficult for me to focus on the words—for I am too elated that my sister and I are finally reunited.

## 7

# Pia

I'm walking up the block, on my way to the subway station to begin my third grueling week at *Profile*. I can't help but note the difference in my feelings from the first day that I was headed to my internship. I'd been excited and couldn't wait to get to the office. Now, dread fills me every morning as I anticipate another mind-numbing day spent proofing stories I wish I'd had some part in writing—hell, even researching. I'll take research over proofing and typing up Colin's memos and letters while he spends most of his time holed up in yet another meeting. How do these senior editors and executives get anything done when they're too busy discussing how they're going to execute their plans?

I had the privilege of attending the weekly editorial concept meeting last week. I say "privilege" because it's rare that editorial assistants and interns are given permission to attend editorial concept meetings—at least at *Profile*. One rule everyone mentioned to me my first week is that the magazine does things differently from other magazines, and they're quite proud of it. If anyone ever dares to bring up that procedures were done a certain way at a magazine where they worked previously, Colin or one of the other senior editors often replies with, "We're *Profile*. We have our *own* rules." The "own" is always given much emphasis. I've heard Colin say this at least six times in the couple of weeks that I've been there. I mentally roll my eyes whenever hearing it.

Last Thursday, Colin must've felt the daggers I'd been shooting into his back as he dropped off yet another round of pages that needed proofing. After taking a few steps, he'd suddenly stopped and asked me if I wanted to attend the editorial concept meeting.

"I'd love to!" I'd responded, much to my embarrassment.

The eagerness displayed in my voice had been too apparent, for Colin smiled as if he were God and had answered my prayers. A few interesting ideas came up at the meeting for possible articles in addition to which celebrities they should interview next. But a lot of the ideas were shot down by either Colin or Madeline Drabinski, *Profile*'s art critic.

Madeline spends a good part of her work day sashaying through *Profile*'s corridors. Apparently, Madeline had been a runway model in her native Poland; hence, the sashaying. I guess once you're trained to do the catwalk you never forget it, kind of like riding a bicycle. Her hips rock from side to side as she steps one leg in front of the other quite dramatically. If it weren't for the iPad she's always holding, I'm sure her hands would be poised on her hips.

Madeline has to be six feet without her Louboutin stilettos. And I have yet to see her wearing the same pair of Louboutins. That goes for her designer handbags, too. Every day she sports a new bag that complements perfectly her clothing ensemble. Her hair, which is a brilliant shade of penny red with blond streaks, hangs all the way down to her tush. She could benefit from shearing a good two to three inches. For her hair length makes her look freakishly taller. Then again, the four-inch heels don't help either.

She has to be in her mid-forties, and though she looks pretty good for her age thanks to the numerous Restylane and Botox injections that everyone rumors she's had as frequently as her meals, the telltale signs of her true age are apparent in her wrinkled neck and décolletage. The latter is covered in numerous sunspots and moles.

I've made eye contact with Madeline a few times when encountering her in the corridors. She never returns my smile or greeting, so I've given up on saying hello. I can't understand how she got the job at *Profile* given her modeling background. None of the editorial assistants or associate editors I've asked knows if she'd been in magazines before coming to *Profile* or if she had any sort of publishing experience. Our guesses are that she got the job through one of her fashion contacts. Though Madeline is intimidating, she's also intriguing.

I turn my attention to the crowd in front of the Mussolini Mansion, which seems to have grown threefold since the previous day. Francesca Donata has now been in Astoria for two weeks. News of her visit finally leaked to the press a few days ago. All the major networks are doing regular segments on her, and they always end with the same question: "What has brought silver-screen legend Francesca Donata to Astoria? Is it really her?"

Though the residents of 35th Street are convinced, the media hasn't been so quick to believe based just on our seeing her backside. Still, it's enough to bring out a few paparazzi, who are now staked out in front of Signora Tesca's along with the neighbors and other fans. As I near Signora Tesca's house, the neighbors surround the paparazzi. They're talking over one another, asking the paparazzi questions.

"They're related?" reaches my ears from a few neighbors who stand on the outside of the ring containing the paparazzi.

My ears prick up as I slowly register what I'm hearing.

"There's no way! They *can't* be sisters!" Olivia DeLuca shakes her head in disbelief.

So this is why Francesca Donata is here. She's visiting her sister—Signora Tesca.

"How could we not have known?" Torpedo Tits—I mean, Betsy Offenheimer—sounds mad.

"Signora Tesca has lived on our block for decades, and she's never breathed a word that she even had a sister—no less a famous one! I can't believe it! I tell you. You think you know the people you've lived with for all these years." Betsy's pointed breasts are heaving repeatedly as she takes several sighs. Her dog Mitzy seems jittery from all the commotion and is taking a few steps backward, tugging on her leash to try and signal to Betsy that she wants to leave.

"We all have our secrets, Betsy. I'm sure you have a skeleton in your cupboard." Olivia has a faraway look in her eyes.

"You mean 'closet,'" Betsy corrects Olivia.

"Closet, cupboard—same thing! You know what I mean." Olivia looks at me, tilting her head slightly toward Betsy and then pointing with her index finger to her temple. And as if I'm dense and can't get what she's saying, she mouths the word "crazy" to me.

"Crazy" seems to be the popular insult Italian American middle-aged and old women love to hurl at someone they're mad at. If I'm to believe Zia's frequent barbs of *"pazza"* or "crazy," the entire neighborhood of Astoria belongs in an insane asylum.

"You paparazzi are just looking for your sensational story. Show me proof that they're sisters because you sure as hell can't tell from looking at them. I mean, come on! One is hot, and the other is . . . well, the other is . . . different, let's say." Ciggy's voice booms out. I can't make him out in the thick crowd surrounding the paparazzi, but I see the smoke from his cigar swirling in the air as its odor burns my nostrils.

"She's plain as vanilla!" Paulie bellows out.

I cringe, hoping that Signora Tesca isn't standing behind one of the heavily draped windows, listening to everything.

"So I guess it's safe to say the sisters don't resemble each other at all? Not even a little bit if you think about it?" I ask Olivia, who seems to be taking my question seriously as she ponders for a few seconds before responding.

"No, they look nothing alike, Pia. I'm trying to think if maybe their mannerisms are similar, but I just can't see it. They truly are like salt and pepper."

"Which one is the salt and which one is the pepper?"

"Signora Tesca is the salt with her fairer complexion and copper-red hair. Her eyes resemble a weasel's and are light brown. She is very thin and has a slightly rounded upper back and shoulders. Signora Tesca often looks like a man when she walks because she keeps her hands clasped behind her back and takes slow, very careful movements. It's as if she thinks she's going to break a bone just from walking. There is something very delicate and fragile about her. Like her daisies."

"Her daisies?" I ask, completely confused.

"Yes, the daisies in her front lawn? Don't tell me you haven't noticed. They're overgrown, and people walking by, mostly kids, often pick them. No matter how many times her housekeeper sweeps the sidewalk, within a day at the most, daisy petals cover the ground again. They're her favorite flower. She told me this once."

Of course. I almost forgot the overgrowth of purple and white daisies that fill the front lawn of the Mussolini Mansion. The daisies themselves are beautiful, but the green weeds surrounding them and reaching over the gate are an eyesore along with the strewn petals on the sidewalk. Even if none of the passersby pick the flowers, they eventually shed their petals.

"For as long as I've known Signora Tesca I've only seen her wear two dresses—a navy-blue polyester dress and a brown one. They are similar to the dresses that were in fashion in the seventies. Her hair is cut in a sharp pixie style, and you can tell she doesn't pay much to have her hair done even though she's rich. *Povera!* The poor woman." Olivia tears up a bit before she continues. "She lives a rather lonely life, and her sole child—a son—visits only occasionally. People are mean and have speculated that the sight of his mother probably scares him off. Signora Tesca is very quiet, but she has a pure heart. I will never forget how good she was to my daughter Valentina. We were all surprised when Signora Tesca came to me and told me we could hold Valentina's bridal shower at her house. She was very fond of my daughter. You have to see the beautiful antique aquamarine brooch she gave to Valentina to wear on her wedding day. Signora Tesca even insisted Valentina keep it."

"She does sound like a good person." I'm mad at the callous remarks some of the neighbors like Ciggy are making about Signora Tesca right in front of her home.

"On the other hand, Francesca Donata is the pepper—not just with her darker, more exotic looks, but even with her fiery, aggressive personality. But I am just going by what I have seen and read about her. Naturally, Francesca loves the spotlight. That's no surprise. And her . . . how do you young people call it now? Diva?"

"Yes, diva."

"Her diva personality is well-known to the public." Olivia shrugs her shoulders. "All I can guess is that maybe they're half or even stepsisters. That would explain why they look nothing alike. Francesca has a perfect hourglass shape. Her bust and her derrière became famous all over the world in the seventies. The fashion experts of the time said hers was the perfect figure every woman should be so lucky to have. And of course her emerald green eyes helped to make her beauty famous. Who could forget those eyes that stand out so much with her wavy chocolate brown hair? Men were said to go crazy when she made direct eye contact with them. People said it was her cat's eyes that bewitched men."

I can't help noticing the deep admiration and love in Olivia's voice for her idol. Strange how people can get so caught up with a celebrity whom they know absolutely nothing about. The positive traits of a star are all fans ever talk about. Even when Olivia mentioned Francesca's diva-like personality, she didn't dwell on it. She was too absorbed in Francesca's beauty and charisma that have won her the legions of followers she has.

An SUV comes screeching down the road and slams to a stop, diverting everyone's attention away from the group of paparazzi. Two men who look like they're also paparazzi get out of the SUV.

"We got it!" One of the men holds up a sheet of paper with a gold embossed seal on it.

The other paparazzi who have been talking to the neighbors run over, quickly taking snapshots of the official-looking document. One of the paparazzi who had been talking to Ciggy looks over to him and says, "So you wanted proof? Here you got it. A marriage certificate belonging to Signora Tesca, whose maiden name is none other than Scalini—the same as Francesca's real last name."

"Let me see that," Ciggy snaps, hating to be wrong. "How do I know you guys didn't just forge this? You rag mags are known for doing sleazy crap like that."

"Oh, it's real. Someone straight from the Italian consulate was able to help us out with this."

Torpedo Tits starts her rant again. "Why didn't Signora Tesca tell us? I don't understand. Why all the secrecy?"

Torpedo Tits is right. Why all the secrecy, indeed?

My journalistic instincts kick in once again. There's a story here; something much deeper is going on beneath the surface. I can feel it. Somehow, I have to find a way to score an interview with the star herself. Ha! I really am deluding myself. It's one thing to believe that there is a slim chance Colin will let me do a small piece on Francesca's coming to town, but to think that I can get a world-

renowned movie star to grant me an interview is ridiculous. And as
Olivia had put it, Francesca is known for her diva personality. In
other words, she could be a major B-I-T-C-H.

I say good-bye to Olivia and pick up my pace, realizing if I don't
get to the subway station soon, I'll be late to work. My mind won't
stop tumbling though. And then bingo! An idea comes to me. If
only I can run into Gregory Hewson again. He knows Francesca.
He is my ticket to gaining access to the star. But he seems just as
tough to crack as Francesca no doubt must be. I have to give it a
shot. Even if I don't succeed in convincing Colin to do a story on
Francesca, I still need to interview her and write the article. Some
other magazine would surely want the interview. Hell! That's how
I'll hook Colin. Francesca hasn't given an interview in ten years.
This would be her first interview since stepping back into the spotlight—well, if you can call being spotted in Astoria the spotlight.
Colin hates nothing more than losing out to another magazine when
a celebrity is being interviewed for the first time or when there's
some other event that constitutes a first for the luminary.

Running up the stairs of the elevated N train, I jump onto the
subway train that's about to depart from the platform. I nab one of
the empty two-seaters adjacent to the subway car's window and sit
down. Taking my Kindle out of my oversized hobo bag, I try to
focus on my reading. Currently, I'm reading *The Thorn Birds*. But I
can't stop thinking of Francesca—and all that she could mean for
me and my career.

## 8

# Francesca

Rubies, sapphires, emeralds, diamonds, pearls . . . I love them all. On the night of the premiere of *La Sposa Pazza*—my acting debut—my director gave me my first gift of jewelry: a stunning emerald choker with matching teardrop emerald earrings. They were the perfect complement to my black taffeta Gucci gown, and the emeralds brought out the green of my eyes. From that day forward, my long affair with jewels began.

Over four decades, I have amassed quite a large collection of jewelry. And wherever I travel, many of my jewels come also, forcing me to hire an extra bodyguard and take out a hefty insurance policy for my precious gems. Since I had been unsure of how long my stay in Astoria would be, I packed most of my jewelry. Though my days of going to premieres and parties are long over, I like to wear my jewels even when my plans consist of nothing more than staying indoors.

I am staring at my vast collection, trying to decide which piece fits my mood for today and matches my outfit, when there is a knock at the door.

Frustrated over being disturbed, I open the door and snap at the maid.

"*Si*, Angelica?" I ask in a clearly annoyed tone.

"Excuse me, Signora Donata."

"It is Signorina Donata. How many times do I need to remind you, Angelica?"

"I'm sorry, Signorina Donata, but this package arrived for you."

She holds out in the palm of her hand a royal-blue velvet box that is tied with an elaborate pink satin ribbon. There is no mistaking the contents of the package. I am dumbfounded.

"There must be some mistake. This must be for Signora Tesca."

"No, no. The messenger said it was for you, Signorina Donata. There is even an envelope with your name on it." The maid takes out of her apron pocket an envelope on which my name is written boldly in script.

"*Grazie,* Angelica."

"*Prego,* Signorina Donata."

I nod my head, letting her know that is all and she can take leave of me. She quickly walks away, her footsteps making no sound in her rubber-soled maid's shoes. Who could this gift be from? My heart is racing, as I anticipate what awaits me inside the beautiful velvet box. I am torn as I pull at the fluffy bow, hating that I must undo it and ruin the perfect shape. The bow comes apart easily. I slowly open the lid of the box and gasp. A sapphire and diamond bangle bracelet greets me. It is one of the most exquisite pieces of jewelry I have ever laid my eyes on.

I waste no time in lifting the bracelet gingerly out of the box and sliding my wrist through it. Ironically, I am wearing a blue sheath today that matches the bracelet perfectly. Staring at myself in my armoire's mirrors, I cannot take my eyes off the glistening jewels. Ten minutes elapse before I realize I still have no idea who would give me such a lavish gift. Finally tearing myself away from the armoire, I pick up the envelope and immediately smell a light jasmine fragrance. How thoughtful—and romantic! This is simply too much. Smiling, I feel giddy like a schoolgirl—for it has been ages since someone has surprised me in such a fashion.

Opening the envelope carefully, I pull out a pale green sheet of stationery. The note is written in elegant cursive similar to the type that was used for my name on the face of the envelope.

"*I gioielli perfetti per la donna perfetta.*"

"The perfect jewels for the perfect woman," I read aloud.

How lovely! But there is no signature. It must be from one of my fans—a very wealthy fan. How can I think that this bracelet is from someone who wants to romance me? I try to ignore the disappointment I feel.

"*Stupida!*" I whisper to myself.

I stare at myself once more in the armoire's mirrors, but this time instead of focusing on the glittering sapphires and diamonds adorning my wrist, I only see my flaws—the faint but discernible crow's feet around my eyes, the rings that circle my neck, the slight hollowing of my cheekbones.

"*Sei vecchia!*"

I am too old to be seduced. The gift must be from some obsessed fan who remembers me from before old age paid me a visit. But still. Someone cares enough to send me such an extravagant gift. I walk over to my vanity table and pick up the velvet box. On the inside, underneath its lid, there is just the outline of a diamond, but in the center—where the jeweler's name would have been imprinted—it is blank. Turning the box over, I inspect its underside, but there is no indication as to which jewelry store this bracelet came from.

I shrug my shoulders. Jewelry is jewelry, and I'll accept it no matter what. My spirits have been lifted considerably from receiving new jewels. Though I am happy Giuliana seems to finally want a relationship with me, my stay here has been quite difficult. She is very different from the young girl who ran with me through the sunflower fields behind our house in Sicily. I close my eyes. If only I could go back and change everything that happened between us.

Fighting back the tidal wave of pain threatening to surface, I twirl my bracelet around my arm. The sapphires glisten darkly, and the light from the overhead chandelier reflects off the diamonds' facets. It has been a long six months since I bought any jewels for myself. Usually, I treat myself every other month.

My bedroom door opens a few inches, startling me.

"Meow!"

"Mewsette! *Sei cattiva! Si, si!* You are a very, very bad cat. But that is all right. You just wanted to be with me, *vero?*" I laugh softly as Mewsette looks up at me, pleading to be petted.

Bending down, I stroke her lustrous white coat. I hold out my free arm, showing off my new prize.

*"Ti piaci? È bello, vero?"*

Mewsette purrs lazily in agreement. She has good taste just like my secret admirer.

# 9

# Pia

It's a hot, muggy Saturday morning. At nine a.m., the temperature has already climbed up to eighty degrees, and forecasters are predicting triple digits for today. A week has gone by since the news that Signora Tesca and Francesca Donata are sisters first broke. Though I've been hanging out with the other stalkers in front of the Mussolini Mansion every night, I still haven't spotted Francesca or Gregory Hewson. Three weeks have now passed since the star was first spotted arriving in Astoria. I can tell the crowd is getting restless, too, but most of them, especially the old-timers on the block, have nothing better to do. If they were not hanging out in front of Signora Tesca's house, then they would be on some other neighbor's stoop, gossiping. So it might as well be here where there's a chance they can finally see their idol—hopefully her front side this time.

I'm beginning to feel lame. Megan has invited me several times to hang out with a few of her artist friends who live in Hunters Point—the up-and-coming trendy neighborhood in Long Island City, which is about a twenty-minute car ride from Ditmars Boulevard. I am curious to explore more of what New York City has to offer and to make friends, but I have to stay focused on my goal for coming here. Scoring an interview with Francesca will be the only way I'll get real journalism experience, since it's becoming more apparent every day that's not going to happen at *Profile*.

I can't stop yawning. The two cups of espresso I had with Zia this morning aren't doing the job of waking me up. Deciding to give my vigil a break, I head over to the bakery to get an iced cappuccino.

Delivery trucks line Ditmars Boulevard. A few early risers are already making their way out of Trade Fair supermarket with their groceries. Most of them are senior citizens. A trio of old Greek ladies is chatting in front of the Hellenic Imports grocery store as they wait for its doors to open. An elderly couple argues in Sicilian as the wife pushes her empty shopping cart. The husband makes gestures with his hands and waves them in his wife's face, but she manages to keep her stony gaze straight ahead while throwing insults right back at him. I laugh silently to myself.

Whenever I pass Sposa Rosa, the bridal boutique Olivia DeLuca owns with her daughters, I love to see which gowns are currently displayed. I usually just glance as I walk by, but the image hanging in the front window today stops me in my tracks. It's a poster from Francesca Donata's first movie, *La Sposa Pazza,* featuring a stunning, very young Francesca in the wedding gown her character Rosa Bianca wore the third time she walked down the aisle. But of course, like the previous two times Rosa Bianca tried to get married, she got cold feet and ran out of the church. The dress on display is an almost exact replica of the gown in the poster.

I know that Sposa Rosa's specialty is designing and sewing couture knockoff wedding gowns, but I had no idea how closely their creations resemble the original, pricier designs. Now with the image on the poster displayed next to the knockoff, I'm rendered speechless. This dress is truly a labor of love. The third gown Rosa Bianca wears in *La Sposa Pazza* is the most elaborate of the three dresses. It had been a brilliant move on the director's part because when audiences saw the gown, they assumed the director had saved the best dress for last and that this would be the wedding scene in which Rosa finally tied the knot.

Newspapers had reported that the women in the audiences cried when Rosa ran away after her third attempt at getting married. The audiences kept repeating, "Such a shame! That gorgeous gown was wasted!"

Apparently, a few reputable bridal shops in Milan and Rome during the seventies had knockoffs of all three wedding gowns from the movie, thinking they'd be a huge hit. But most brides-to-be had shunned the dresses, believing they were bad luck and would either ruin their weddings or their marriages. I'm surprised that Olivia, who no doubt must be superstitious like many other Italian women, would replicate one of the gowns from *La Sposa Pazza*. Surely, she knows what happened in Italy.

I can't pull myself away from the ballroom gown, whose cathedral train swirls out to either side of the display window. From bodice to train, the dress is covered in the most exquisite lace I've ever laid eyes on.

In the original gown, the lace on the bodice had been sewn onto a sheer panel of organza, and it was strategically placed so that tantalizing glimpses of Francesca's skin and perfect hourglass shape were revealed. In the knockoff gown, the only differences are that it doesn't have the high neckline and long sleeves. Instead, it's been modernized to give upon first glance the appearance of a sleeveless lace dress. But once the bride comes into closer view, one can see the slightly scooped organza neckline, which features a delicate lace trim—the same lace that covers the bodice and skirt. The sleeves are three-quarters length. Unlike on the original dress, they're simply covered in organza with the exception of a thin vine of lace that wraps around the sleeves' edges.

"You like it?"

I hadn't noticed Olivia observing me from the entrance of her shop.

"Yes. It's breathtaking. Olivia, did you sew this dress or was it one of your daughters?"

"Do you think I'd let my daughters work on the dress that my favorite movie star wore?"

"That's true. How could I forget how much you love Francesca Donata?" I wink at Olivia and laugh.

"I only put it up on display this morning. We'll see how it sells." Olivia's face shines with the glow that comes from feeling proud of one's own work.

"But, Olivia, Francesca has only been in town for a few weeks. You couldn't have made this dress in such a short amount of time." I suddenly realize I'm choosing the wrong words. "I'm sorry. I didn't mean any offense. It's just that I've heard how long it can take to make wedding gowns."

Olivia pats my shoulder. "It's okay, Pia. I knew what you meant. And you are right. There is no way anyone could've sewn this dress by hand—or even with a sewing machine—and been done in a few weeks. I'm good, but I don't want to go into the grave just yet. Actually, I started this dress about six months before Francesca even came to town."

"Really? How ironic."

"No. It was not irony. It was fate! It was meant to be that I finally created this dress and that Francesca came here just as I was almost done sewing it."

Just as I'd suspected, Olivia is superstitious.

"But, Olivia, aren't you concerned people will worry that the dress will bring them bad luck since it's a copy of one of the dresses the cursed Rosa Bianca wore in *La Sposa Pazza?* You heard what happened with those other knockoff dresses in the seventies?"

"*Si, si.* But most young brides today don't even know about that movie or how women refused to buy those dresses out of fear of bad luck. I'm surprised you do. But just in case any of my young clients' grandmothers tell them what happened, I've taken care of that all by changing the dress slightly. You did notice it's not an exact replica of the original gown?"

"I did. That was smart of you, not just for the bad luck, but also this dress feels more modern."

"Would you like to try it on?" Olivia's eyes are gleaming.

"Oh no! I couldn't. Besides, I'm not even engaged."

"It's never too early to start thinking about the wedding dress you'll want."

"I don't even have a boyfriend. I can't. But thank you."

"Pia, it's okay. I would love to see how the dress looks on you."

I pause for a few seconds. A large part of me is actually tempted. I've never been one of those girls who has fantasized about her fairy-tale wedding since the age of five. But something about this dress is calling to me. *Stop!* Reason shouts at me. What is the matter with me? I refuse to try on a wedding dress when I don't even have a boyfriend. Besides, I don't even know if I ever want to get married.

"I'm sorry, Olivia. But I really can't right now. I'm meeting a friend at Zia's bakery." I look at my watch. "Oh, wow! I'm actually already late. But thank you so much. That's sweet of you."

"That's a pity. I think that dress would've looked perfect on you. Some other time. Eh?"

I can't help but feel that Olivia knows I'm lying, but she doesn't seem cross with me. I nod my head, still not wanting to commit myself verbally. Olivia runs into her shop at the sound of her phone ringing. I'm amazed by how loud she has the ringer set.

I take one last look at Olivia's masterpiece. Maybe I should've tried it on, since it might be my only chance at ever wearing a wedding dress.

Shaking these crazy thoughts out of my mind, I continue to Zia's bakery. There's a long line of patrons waiting to buy their Saturday morning biscotti, Danish, and doughnuts. Even though the bakery features Italian sweets, Zia is clever enough to also include other popular treats. My stomach grumbles, reminding me that I haven't had any breakfast this morning. Fortunately, since I know the owner, I don't have to wait on line. I go to the kitchen, where Giovanni, the head pastry chef, is pulling out trays of just baked almond *biscotti*.

"Good morning, Giovanni."

"Hi, Pia. How are you?"

"I'm fine. Thanks. How are you?"

"Can't complain. Want a few *biscotti?*"

"Please."

Giovanni takes a sheet of wax tissue, which the bakery employees use when handling the pastries, and pulls off two giant *biscotti*. One would've been enough, but I've learned quickly not to refuse and just accept what's being offered. These New Yorkers can be mighty persistent.

"Thank you."

Giovanni smiles. "Anytime."

I return to the front of the bakery. Zia and Tommy, a teenage boy she's just hired, are juggling the morning crowd.

"Zia, do you want any help?"

"I might have said 'yes' about fifteen minutes ago, but the line is getting shorter now. But thank you. Go enjoy your *biscotti*. Megan is at one of the tables with her friends."

I strain my neck over to where Zia indicates. Megan is seated at a corner table with two guys whose backs are turned toward me. Great. She's probably going to try twisting my arm again to join them, since this is the day she and her friends are planning on going to MoMA PS1, the modern art museum in Long Island City. Megan is the only person I've confided in about my goal to try and interview Francesca Donata. She hasn't made me feel like a complete idiot for even entertaining such an idea. Instead, she's been nothing but supportive and knows this is the reason why I haven't hung out with her yet.

Walking over to the huge Lavazza machine, I decide to have an espresso *macchiato* instead of the iced cappuccino I'd originally planned on getting. Zia introduced me to espresso *macchiato* the morning after my arrival. Adding a drop of milk turns an ordinary espresso into an espresso *"macchiato"* or "stained" espresso. Just a drop of milk is enough to take away some of the espresso's bitterness. As the machine sprays my espresso, I bend down to the small refrigerator behind the sales counter and take out a quart of skim milk. Standing back up, I almost jump out of my skin.

Gregory Hewson is at the sales counter, holding his chin in his hand and smiling at me.

"Sorry. Didn't mean to scare you."

"You didn't scare me. You . . . startled me a bit."

"How are you?"

"Good. Thanks. You?"

"Fantastic, now."

Normally, I would mentally roll my eyes at such an obvious pickup line, but for some reason, I can't help but feel flattered.

"Are you visiting Francesca?"

"Ahhh, the obsession still lasts." Gregory rolls his eyes, but I can tell he's just feigning exasperation.

"It's not an obsession. I'm just . . . an admirer."

"Yeah, you keep saying you're a fan, but my gut's telling me you're lying. Why would you lie to a face like this?" Gregory pouts his lips and opens his eyes wide, much like an innocent boy. I can't help but laugh.

"Let me help you with that." Gregory takes my demitasse cup of espresso *macchiato* from me. "Just tell me where you'd like to sit."

"That table in the corner where the girl with the jet-black hair is sitting."

"Oh, so you were planning on joining me? I'm flattered."

I look at him, confused. I notice that Megan's now only sitting with one of the guys I saw her with earlier. Then it hits me that the other guy was Gregory. I can't believe I didn't recognize him. Well, it was dark the last time I saw him.

"You know Megan?"

"Yup. And apparently you do, too. She's told me all about you." Gregory's smug face says it all. And though he's hot as hell, I can't help but want to slap him right now. It wasn't just his gut feeling telling him I was lying to him about being a fan of Francesca's. He knows I'm a writer if, as he says, Megan has told him everything about me. Anger quickly seeps in. How dare Megan? Did she also tell him my plan of wanting to score an interview with Francesca?

"Hey, Pia! Great to see you here. I see you've already met Gregory."

Plastering on my best phony smile, I force myself to sound cheery. "Yes, we've met. Hasn't Gregory told you we actually met a few weeks ago?"

Megan is stunned.

"No! He didn't." She playfully swats Gregory's arm.

"Yeah, it's no big deal. We ran into each other on her street the other night."

No big deal, huh? The arrogance. But it's my turn to turn the tables on him.

"He was coming out of Signora Tesca's house—the same day everyone spotted Francesca Donata."

"What?!" Megan and her other friend cry out.

Now Gregory looks flabbergasted and even mad. Pangs of regret immediately wash over me. Why isn't this feeling as good as I thought it would?

"Gregory, you're holding out on us? What were you doing there?

Did you see Francesca Donata?" Megan's shiny bob is swinging back and forth with each animated movement of her head.

"Yeah, Greg. What's the deal?" Megan's friend seems just as amazed that Gregory's been keeping this secret from them.

"Hi. I'm Pia." I extend my hand to the friend.

"Oh, sorry, Pia. This is Paul." Megan gestures toward Paul with her thumb, a quirky trademark of hers. Whereas most people use their index finger to point, Megan always uses her thumb, much the way a hitchhiker would.

Paul shakes my hand. He has faint paint stains on his palm. He's sporting what I call a trendy nerd look and is wearing straight-leg jeans with the cuffs turned up, scuffed black oxford shoes, and a plaid button-down shirt. His black-rimmed eyeglasses are a throwback to glasses that were in fashion during the fifties. Paul's sandy brown hair is shaved close to the nape of his neck, but the top is cut in chunky, spiky pieces that are combed in different directions—a popular style many guys in their twenties are now getting. Even Gregory's hair is cut the same way, but his is a little longer than Paul's.

I can't help noticing how Gregory's hair is almost as black as Megan's and thinking that they match. They'd make a good couple. Suddenly, at this thought, jealousy courses through my veins. What is the matter with me today? First, I find myself fantasizing about wearing the knockoff bridal gown in Sposa Rosa's window, and now I'm acting possessive over a guy I've only seen twice. I mentally shake my head. For all I know, Gregory might be Megan's boyfriend.

"So come on, Gregory, out with it." Megan won't let the subject of why he was at Signora Tesca's house drop. I'm thrilled since I'll finally find out what his connection is to Francesca.

"It's really no big deal, guys. And I'd rather not talk about it if you don't mind." Gregory is drinking American coffee, as Zia likes to call it, out of an oversized teacup that almost completely conceals his face.

Gently, I say to Gregory, "You're among friends. We won't repeat your secret."

Gregory glances up from his cup, surprise registering on his face. Hell, I'm even surprised by how sugary-sweet my voice sounds. But I'm not faking it. I never repeat a friend's secret. I'm one of the most loyal friends someone can have.

Gregory lets out a long sigh, sinking into his chair. He places his hands inside his jeans pockets. "Okay. But you guys must swear not to tell anyone. I don't need that mob that's outside of Signora Tesca's house to harass me. I'm already dreading my next visit there because I don't know how I'm going to throw them off."

"Your *next* visit?" I all but scream.

Gregory shoots a frown in my direction. I need to cool it or I'll ruin my chances of befriending him. Again, I'm convinced he's my only ticket to gaining access to Francesca.

"We've got your back, Greg. We swear not to tell anyone." Paul makes a fist and holds it up in the air. Gregory curls his own fist and bumps it with Paul's.

"Yeah, we swear, too." Megan crosses her heart with her hand, which looks very girly and silly compared to Paul and Gregory's guy code. She nods her head toward me, but I refuse to cross my heart.

"I give you my word I won't repeat your secret." I lock eyes with Gregory to show him how serious I am. That's the only visual proof of allegiance he needs from me. He seems satisfied as he holds my gaze a moment longer and then clears his throat.

"I know Francesca Donata."

I can't help but detect a faint smile on his face. He knows exactly what he's doing. He plans on drawing this out for maximum suspense.

"You do?" Gullible Megan has fallen prey already.

"Yeah."

The three of us wait for him to continue. But he doesn't. He takes another sip of his coffee and then takes a bite out of his chocolate-dipped walnut biscotti. He chews slowly. The gleam in his eyes gives away that he's clearly enjoying his little game. Refusing to play into it, I just wait patiently. In fact, I decide to get up at that moment.

Yawning as if bored, I say, "I've got to get going. It was nice meeting you, Paul."

My own game works. Gregory immediately places his hand over mine. "Wait! You haven't heard how I know Francesca."

A million tiny volts of electricity shoot up my arm at the contact of his warm hand over mine. It's even worse than when he shook my hand that first night we met.

"Sorry. I really need to leave. Bye, Megan. Paul." I turn and walk away.

I step out into the hot, muggy air and have almost reached the corner when I hear Gregory shout, "Wait up!"

I glance over my shoulder and see Gregory running to catch up with me. Trying to ignore the happiness I'm currently feeling, I put on my best poker face. That's my first rule: *Never let a guy you like know exactly how you're feeling.* So does this mean I *like* Gregory? My body is screaming a resounding "yes!" But my mind is still trying to be heard with its cautionary "no!"

"Do you mind if I walk with you for a little bit, Pia?"

I shrug my shoulders, hoping this will convey my indifference. "If that's what you want."

"I'm sorry about what happened back there. I was being obnoxious."

I'm taken aback. He knows I figured out his game. Cute *and* smart.

"Look, Gregory. It's obvious for whatever reason that you don't want to reveal your secret relationship to Francesca. I should respect that. I'm sorry for pushing you."

Oh, boy! I've got it bad. That's my second rule: *Never apologize to a guy until—and only while—you're in a committed relationship with him.* Always, always, always let him think he's at fault. I'm suddenly feeling very vulnerable.

*Shut your mouth! Do not say anything more than "yes" or "no,"* I mentally scream at myself.

"No need to apologize, Pia."

See, even Gregory knows the rules.

Instead of heading back to the Mussolini Mansion, I just keep walking on Ditmars Boulevard. I pray he doesn't ask me where I'm going. We're silent for the next block, and then he begins talking.

"My father used to paint portraits of Francesca."

My ears perk up at this news, but I remain quiet, waiting patiently for him to continue.

"I've known Francesca since I was a boy. My father sometimes used to take me with him when he painted her portrait. My parents and I lived in Rome until I was five. Then we came to New York."

"I guess you were too young to remember any Italian?"

"I do know Italian, but only because my parents didn't want me to forget it, so they enrolled me in Italian-language school. Every Saturday morning, I took Italian lessons at a parochial school in my neighborhood. I actually grew up in Astoria, but on the other side of Astoria Boulevard, closer to Thirtieth Avenue."

"You still live there now?"

"No. My parents moved down to Florida last year. My father has severe arthritis. He and my mother couldn't take the cold winters in New York anymore. I live in Long Island City, close to Jackson Avenue. We actually moved to Long Island City when I was in high school. I live in my parents' house."

I add two and two. His father had been an artist, and Gregory now lives in Long Island City. Then I remember the paint splatters I'd seen on his jeans the first night we met. Paul's hands had been stained with paint, too. Gregory and Paul are the artist friends Megan's always talking about.

"So you're an artist just like your father?"

Gregory smiles. "Well, not exactly like my father. We have different styles of painting, but yeah, I'm an artist."

"My sister Erica was an artist." I can't disguise the sadness that enters my voice.

"Was? Let me guess. Good sense entered her head, and she's found herself a profession that won't leave her poor or drive her crazy."

"No, that's not it." I force a smile, but Gregory's picked up on my sad tone.

"I seem to have hit on a nerve. I'll drop it."

"Erica passed away a few years ago."

"I'm so sorry, Pia." Gregory places his hand on my shoulder.

"That's okay. You had no idea. But thank you."

"What medium did she work in?"

"She was mostly a landscape painter, but she wanted to learn more. Not too long before her accident, she was taking an interest in portraits. You and she would've had painting in common." I manage to give a small laugh, but I'm not fooling Gregory. He sees through my attempt at trying to keep the conversation light.

"I've never lost someone close to me. I can't even begin to imagine what you've been through and are going through."

"She was supposed to come to New York with me. While I did my internship, she was going to attend art school. I put off coming here for a few years. I didn't think I could do it without her."

"I'm glad you decided to come."

"Thanks."

We're silent for a few minutes. I'm amazed at how in sync Gregory seems to be with my thoughts. It's as if he's psychic, and he knows I need some time after the heavy discussion. He doesn't even ask me what kind of accident Erica had. I'm grateful for that. I don't think I can handle rehashing the ugly details of her death right now. The little I've said is the most I've said to anyone about Erica's death since it happened. Out of my peripheral vision, I see that he's staring at me intensely. For some reason, I decide to turn my head and meet his gaze, but he quickly glances away. I'm surprised to see his face flush. This is different from the overly confident Gregory I'd seen earlier and on the night we met.

"So I got a call from Francesca before she came to Astoria. Francesca has remained good friends with my father even though it's been years since he painted a portrait of her. She knows that I've followed in my father's footsteps and wants me to paint another portrait of her. That's why I was at her sister's house the night we ran into each other."

"Are you going to paint it?"

"I'm hesitant. I don't paint as well as my father did. I left my portfolio with her. She liked what she saw and immediately asked me when I could start. I told her I needed to think about it."

"But Gregory, this could be the opportunity of a lifetime! This could *make* your career! If it were me, I'd jump at the chance without a second thought!"

"Yeah, I know that already." Gregory laughs.

I realize how I must sound—like some opportunistic vulture. I'm embarrassed.

"I'm crazy, I guess. Most people *would* jump on this since in the art world opportunities are few and far between. I don't know what's holding me back." After a couple of seconds, Gregory adds, "Maybe I do."

He's afraid. He thinks he's not good enough. As a writer, I can relate. Every creative person must go through a period of insecurity.

"You're just as good as your father."

"Thanks for the blind vote of confidence." Gregory laughs. "You've never even seen my work."

"But Francesca has, and if she made you an offer right after seeing your portfolio, she has no doubts you're just as good as your father."

"I know I'm good. It's just my style is different than my father's, and I don't want to disappoint her."

"True. I've heard about her temper."

"No, that's not it."

"You're not trying to tell me she's as sweet as an angel!"

"Pia, don't believe everything you hear in the media. Yes, there's no denying she can have a temper and is . . . How do I put this?"

"A bitch?"

"That's harsh. No, I was going to say difficult. The reason I don't want to disappoint her is that she's been good to my family over the years."

"Really?"

"Yes, really. Everyone has his or her good points and bad."

"That's true. I'm sorry."

"I don't know her extremely well. But I do know there is more to her. I actually have a meeting with her tonight to give her my answer."

"Can't you just call her?"

"That would be disrespectful, especially since she is a family friend. And in the Italian culture—"

"Respect is everything. I've heard of *la bella figura*."

Gregory laughs. "Yes, making a good impression is paramount to every Italian. Francesca is one of the smartest women I've ever met. Even if I had suggested calling her to give her my answer, she would've still insisted I visit her. This way if my answer is 'no,' she can change my mind in person. A fact that the media has gotten right about her is that she's very persuasive. I mean, look at her."

The jealousy is back but threefold this time. I'm also feeling very irritated. I *am* losing it. I'm jealous of a fifty-something washed-up actress. But that's just it. Francesca is far from washed up. I haven't seen what her face looks like in the ten years she spent as a recluse, but she's definitely kept that body in shape from what I saw of her backside.

I can't resist asking. "So she's still beautiful?"

"Yes. It's not the same face from her youth, of course. There are a few wrinkles, but just a few. I can say unequivocally she is one of the most beautiful women I've ever seen."

Boy, he's really rubbing it in. What does he see in me? I'm not being conceited by thinking he's attracted to me. He's given off the signals to me loud and clear. But I can't be any more different from Francesca. I don't possess her voluptuous figure. My figure is leaner. While my breasts aren't small, they're nowhere near the C or D cup Francesca's are. And of course, I'm fair while she has the sultry, olive Mediterranean complexion. There should be a photograph of Francesca next to the word "sexy" in the dictionary. Every cell in her body exudes sex appeal.

"So, what's your answer going to be?"

"I'll probably say 'yes.' "

"You're meeting with her tonight and you still don't know?"

"I'm a spontaneous person. It's hard for me to make up my mind far in advance." Gregory shrugs his shoulders. "I'll let you know after my appointment what I decide." He winks at me. The playful Gregory is back.

We're nearing the small shopping center on Ditmars and 48th Street. I realize this is the perfect place to take my departure from Gregory, since it'll look like I did have errands to run when I ran out on him and the others at the bakery.

"I'm heading to a few stores across the street."

"I'll join you. That is if you don't mind."

I don't mind, but since I'm lying I have to think quickly of what to buy. There's a supermarket, so I decide to pick up a few groceries for Zia.

"Enough about me. You said you were here for an internship. I do remember Megan's mentioning to Paul and me this morning before we saw you that you were working at *Profile*. Right?"

I nod my head.

"So you *are* a journalist!"

"Trying to be." I smirk.

"That's cool."

"I came to New York to get experience working on a magazine. I love to write, and my ultimate goal is to start my own magazine someday. But lately, I'm having my doubts."

"Glad to hear I'm not the only tortured artist."

"No, you're not!" I laugh.

"Why are you having your doubts?"

"I don't have any doubts that I want to still pursue writing and my dream of having my own magazine. But I'm doubtful I'm getting any real experience at this internship."

"Ahhh! It's all crystal clear now."

"What is?"

"Your fascination with Francesca."

I start feeling anxious. It was one thing to confide in Megan about my far-flung idea of getting an interview with Francesca, but I'm afraid of Gregory mocking me. Why didn't I think of this when I hoped he'd be my ticket to Francesca? I'd have to let him in on my secret after all. But now that I'm here face-to-face with him, I'm terrified.

"You're hoping to talk to her, aren't you?"

I nod my head and let out an exasperated sigh. "Guilty as charged. It's ridiculous, I know."

We're at the Berry Fresh Farm supermarket. I try to pull out a shopping cart, but it's stuck.

"Here, let me." Gregory comes over and with one firm pull, dislodges the cart for me.

"Let me be your driver." He steers the cart toward the supermarket's entrance. I giggle. The sound startles me. I haven't heard myself giggle this way since John Esteves pinned a corsage to my dress and accidentally stabbed me with the pin before we went to our prom. I know. That wasn't really a giggle moment, but I was crazy about John even though it didn't amount to anything more than just a few dates. Though I'm twenty-five years old, I've never had a serious boyfriend.

"Which aisle first?"

"Dairy."

That's a safe bet. People almost always need milk or eggs. Zia's refrigerator looks like it's always stocked, but I'm in a bind now. I don't give much more thought to whether or not she really needs what I'm picking up.

I open up the carton of eggs to make sure none are cracked. I'm shivering so hard I'm afraid I'm going to drop the slightly cracked egg I just picked up to switch with an intact egg from another carton.

Gregory wraps his arm around me. His body warmth quickly melts my goose bumps.

"Better?" He's grinning from ear to ear. I disentangle myself from him.

"Thanks, but I'm okay." I can't meet his eyes. I know my face must be the color of the apples we're now passing as we make our way to the produce department. I pick up a carton of strawberries before heading over to the cashier.

I pay for the groceries, and of course, Gregory insists on carrying both bags. He waits for me to exit the supermarket first. He's in full chivalrous mode now.

"So, getting back to our discussion from earlier, I don't think it's ridiculous that you want to talk to Francesca."

"You're just saying that to make me feel better."

"No. I think it shows that you have guts and ambition. If you interview Francesca, that could really help you in your writing aspirations."

I nod my head. "You get it. But I should just leave her alone. She's probably through with giving interviews, especially since so many of the ones she gave over the years portrayed her very harshly. No wonder she's stayed out of the limelight for the past decade."

"I can put in a good word for you."

My heart skips a beat. This is just what I've been hoping for. But I don't want Gregory to think I'm using him. I wouldn't have cared what he thought before, but now I do. I'm committing the one transgression my journalism teachers warned against: *Don't let emotions rule over good judgment.*

*It's okay,* I silently tell myself. *He wants to help you.*

I hesitate before saying, "Oh, I'm not sure about this. You hardly know me. I can't expect you to help me out this way."

"It would be my pleasure."

"Aren't you worried I'm going to say something to her that will tick her off, and then she'll be mad at you for recommending me?"

"I trust my instincts, and they're telling me this is right. I can feel it."

"I can't ask you to do this for me. If you feel compelled on your own, do it, but I don't feel comfortable asking you for this huge favor."

"Say no more."

Gregory is smiling. I can see the idea of helping me is making him happy.

"Thanks. I owe you."

"And I know just how you can make it up to me."

"Already? You don't waste time." I shake my head. "So what's my penalty?"

"Hang out with me tomorrow night."

He's asking me out on a date? Why am I surprised? The chemistry between us has been unmistakable. I need to tread carefully. Bartering his scoring an interview with Francesca for a date with me doesn't seem wise. Then again, what's the harm? My tendency to overanalyze every situation can get out of control. There's no denying I like him. And I haven't had a date since before Erica died.

"I'd have to get home early. It's a Sunday night, and I work the next morning."

"Let's move it up then to the afternoon. We'll have lunch and then there are a couple of places I want to show you. I'll take you home right after dinner."

He wants to hang with me for most of the day? I'm speechless, which he takes as my assent.

"I'll pick you up at twelve-thirty. Sound good? I can swing by your aunt's or if you want we can meet at her bakery. It's up to you."

"My aunt's is fine."

"Great!"

We turn onto 35th Street. I don't want Zia seeing him with me.

I'm not ready for the barrage of questions she'll no doubt have. I'll be better prepared for her interrogation when I tell her about my date over dinner. I just need a few hours to myself to absorb that I have a date tomorrow.

"Thanks, but I can manage with the bags to my aunt's house."

"Don't sweat it. I'm not in a rush to be anywhere."

I remain quiet until we reach Zia's house. "Thanks, Gregory. I can take the bags into the house."

As he hands the bags over to me, he hesitates before he pulls away. For a moment, I think he's going to kiss me, but as soon as the thought enters my mind, he steps back a few feet.

"So I'll pick you up at twelve-thirty." He pulls out of his front jeans pocket his cell phone. "Can I get your number?"

I recite the numbers to my cell.

"I'll send you a text so you have my number, too, just in case an emergency arises and you need to cancel. But don't get any ideas!" Gregory waves his index finger at me.

"I'll see you tomorrow. Good luck with Francesca tonight."

"Thanks, Pia. Have a nice day."

I turn around as I insert my key into Zia's front door.

"Hey, Pia. Would it be okay if . . ." Gregory's voice trails off. I look over my shoulder.

"Would it be okay if I called you tonight? Just to let you know how things went with Francesca. I might need someone to talk to, especially if I do turn her down. You know, I'll need someone to make me feel better about possibly squandering an opportunity of a lifetime."

"Sure. I guess that would be okay."

Gregory's face lights up. "I'll talk to you then."

I step into Zia's house, anxious to set the heavy bags down on the kitchen table. As I make my way back to the foyer to shut the front door, I catch a glimpse of myself in the mirror on the wall and see a sight I haven't seen in years. I look happy. But the moment I realize this, the happiness is replaced by guilt. How can I be excited and go out on a date when my younger sister won't ever have the chance to feel joy again or fall in love?

I slam the front door shut as I mentally chide myself for accepting Gregory's date. My phone beeps. I pull it out of the small messenger bag that's still slung over my shoulder. It's a text from Gregory:

NOW YOU HAVE MY NUMBER. LOOKING FORWARD TO TALKING TO YOU TONIGHT. GREGORY.

I save Gregory's number before deleting the text and return to the kitchen to put the groceries away. I'll have to figure out what to do about Gregory later. I don't have the energy for it now. But try as hard as I do to put him out of my thoughts, all I can think about is tomorrow and where he's planning on taking me. That is, if I decide to keep the date.

# ❦ 10 ❦

# Francesca

"How many gifts have you received now?" Giuliana is sitting across from me at the table in the morning room, where she likes to take her breakfast. She is making a feeble attempt at eating her two *biscotti*. I let her nibble on the *biscotti* and pretend not to notice that she's hardly making a dent. Her appetite seems to be diminishing every day.

"This is the fifth present." I stare at yet another royal-blue velvet jewelry box that Angelica brought in just as we were sitting down. My hopes of keeping the anonymous gifts a secret from Giuliana completely faded when she answered the door herself the last two times the packages were delivered. Although she has three servants, she still likes to do a few of her own chores.

"Why are you waiting? Open it. I know you are dying to see which jewels he's chosen this time." Giuliana has looked forward to the mysterious gifts more than I have. Initially, I'd been afraid they would make her jealous, but if she's been feeling envious, she's hidden it rather well.

"Normally, I would agree with you, Giuliana, but this is beginning to alarm me." Oh, I am a fool! Why did I say that? My sister does not need to be stressed out right now.

"Since when has an admirer alarmed you, Francesca? You've had countless admirers for decades now. I would think you would be thrilled that at your age you still have them—or one in this case." Giuliana's faint smile reassures me she is only teasing.

"I have never had an admirer remain anonymous after two gifts or letters. I am afraid this might be a deranged stalker. And I am staying in your home. I have disrupted your privacy, and God knows I might be placing you in harm's way. I must leave now. You should come with me to Sicily. Please, Giuliana." I am so upset that I cannot eat or drink. I get up and pace the room. Of course, Mewsette is up in an instant and follows me. The cat has become my lady-in-waiting.

"Francesca, stop being so dramatic! This isn't one of your films. *Si, si,* receiving five pieces of extraordinary jewelry in a week isn't normal life either, but come on! Do you really think there is an insane wealthy person out there who wants to harm you or me? I know you celebrities have stalkers and have to be careful, but this is Astoria. I've lived here a long time. We have honest, hardworking people. You have nothing to worry about." Giuliana starts laughing, but soon a fit of coughing erupts instead.

I pour a glass of water from the pitcher on the table and hand it to Giuliana. Once her coughing has subsided, I say, "Giuliana, I do not doubt you have honest, good people here, but this is still New York City—the largest city in the country—with hundreds of *pazzi* . . ." I point to my head, giving her the signal for crazy people.

"And you think you will be safe in Sicily?" Giuliana shakes her cane at me. "Help me up."

I walk over and place my hand under her arm to assist in lifting her. It takes a few seconds for Giuliana to feel steady on her feet. I stay by her side as she takes a few steps forward.

"Take me out to the terrace. Oh, that's right. You can't be seen." Giuliana's voice drips with sarcasm. Although she has been kind to me, and I can tell our relationship is beginning to mend, she still cannot resist mocking me and my celebrity status.

"Let me call Carlo and Angelica. They can take you out there and sit with you if you want some fresh air." I turn to leave, but she grabs my arm.

"And disappoint your loyal followers who have been waiting for days to see your face only to see my sickly one? They'll probably think it's you and that you've come here to convalesce. Ha!" Giuliana laughs so hard that tears fill her eyes. Fortunately, there is a settee nearby that she lowers herself onto before she slips.

"*Si! È vero!* I can see the tabloids now. Italian movie star loses her beauty!" Now I am laughing to the point of tears. Then suddenly, the horror hits me as I realize what I have said. "*Scusi, Giuliana. Volevo dire che—*"

"*Non ti preoccupare.*" Giuliana holds up her hand, letting me know it is okay.

"I am sorry. I just meant—"

"*Basta!*" Giuliana's voice booms loudly. I am surprised she even has the energy to scream. "There is no need for you to lie. You think I do not know I've lost what little beauty I once had?"

"Little beauty? You were—and still are—one of the most beautiful women I know."

"Stop patronizing me! *You* were always the beautiful one, *not* me!" Giuliana is still screaming as she points her index finger repeatedly to her chest. "I was the plain sister. Plain—a nice way of saying '*brutta*' or 'ugly.' When we were young children, people were more attracted to you. It was always you who was the center of attention. Never me." The warm, friendly tone Giuliana had earlier has now been replaced with the resentful tone I've grown accustomed to since we had our falling-out as teenagers.

"Even my own cat prefers you to me." She stares at Mewsette, who is lying over my feet, waiting for me to rub her belly. Giuliana's eyes are full of hurt that her loyal feline companion has also betrayed her.

It is useless for me to say anything since it seems whatever I say just angers my sister more. I pull my feet out from under Mewsette and walk back to the table. Giuliana's cane taps the floor behind me as she struggles to get to her feet. Of course, I want to help her, but she will just lash out at me once again. Her pride demands it. After what feels like an eternity, I hear the floorboards creak under Giuliana's weight as she hobbles out of the room. And just in case her previous shouting did not deliver its point, she slams the door shut.

Rubbing my throbbing temples, I can feel a headache coming on. I shut my eyes tightly, forcing back the tears that have surfaced.

Giuliana will never forgive me. The only reason she is tolerating my stay here is because of Lorenzo, who has yet to pay a visit since I have arrived. True, he is finishing up a research trip in Greece, but his mother needs him now. She should be his number one priority, not his career. Still, he did write to me, asking me to come. His love for his mother was clearly evident in his letter.

A new wave of pain shoots through my heart as I am reminded once again that I will never know what it is like to have the love of a child reciprocated. Sighing, I turn my attention again to the unopened gift from my secret admirer. Anger seeps into me. "You started this. Who are you?"

Mewsette jumps up into my lap, troubled that I am talking to myself.

I have a bad habit whenever I receive a gift. Instead of opening the card first, I rush to unwrap the present. I am much like a child this way, impatient to discover what my surprise is. But this time, I open the envelope first, hoping that my secret admirer will finally reveal himself to me. What makes me so sure the gifts are from a man? Well, that would be a first if they were from a woman. Until proven wrong, I will assume they are from a man.

*"Spero che ogni regalo è stato per la vostra soddisfazione."*

Strange. The previous notes were all specifically tied to the jewels and my beauty. In this note, he is just expressing hope that the gifts have been to my liking. Hmmm . . . It is almost as if he wants a response from me. But how can I do that if I do not know who is giving the gifts or even which jeweler they have come from?

I must unravel this mystery. A week has passed since I received my first gift, and in just seven days, four more have arrived.

*"Mi scusi,* Signorina Donata." Angelica enters the morning room and begins clearing Giuliana's hardly eaten breakfast.

"Angelica, how many jewelry stores are in Astoria?"

"I don't know about all of Astoria, but on Ditmars Boulevard, there are three. Steinway Street has many more, but a lot of them are smaller, cheaper stores."

"I see. Do you shop at any of these jewelers?"

Angelica seems surprised that I have asked her this question. She quickly places the breakfast dishes onto a tray.

"Not often. But two of the jewelry shops on Ditmars are my favorites when I want to treat myself to something nice." Angelica tilts her head slightly, showing me the princess-cut diamond studs in her ears.

"*Sono belli!* So you have a weakness for jewelry, too?" I smile at Angelica. Again, she looks surprised—not that I blame her. I have been rather harsh with her. Unfortunately, I have come to discover that you cannot befriend your help or else they will walk all over you. Besides, they appreciate discipline.

"Yes, but I don't own anything as extravagant as you do, Signorina Donata."

"Maybe you can help me. I have been receiving gifts from the same jewelry shop—at least I think they are from the same jeweler since the boxes all look the same. But the name of the shop is not imprinted inside the box, and it appears the giver of the gifts wants to remain anonymous for some reason."

"Ahhh! A secret admirer! How romantic!" Angelica's eyes open wide. She actually reminds me of Rosa Bianca, the character I played in *La Sposa Pazza,* who was more in love with the notion of love rather than any of her three fiancés. The director of the movie had worked hard with me to get me to convey that "dreamy, hopeless look" as he called it. To me, the expression just looked like I was very confused and did not have a brain.

"Well, I do not know how romantic or crazy this person is, and I think it is time I find out who has been sending me these gifts. Maybe you would recognize the jewelry box if it is from one of the stores you regularly shop at?"

"I can take a look." Angelica is staring at the box I received this morning, which I have not opened yet. I can see she is waiting with bated breath to see the dazzling contents.

I pick up the box and untie the bow. This box is the largest one I have received. My guess is that it is a choker or a long strand of pearls. I cannot help but glance at Angelica out of my peripheral vision. She has her left arm wrapped around her waist, and her right hand, which is curled into a fist, is resting against her chin. She keeps tapping the fist to her chin. I thought I was in love with jewelry! This girl reminds me of a drug addict who cannot wait to get her next . . . how do the Americans call it? Stash? I stroke the top of the velvet box, taking my time opening it. This is sadistic of me, I know, but I relish every moment of anxiety I am giving Angelica.

"Such a lush, soft box! I just love the way velvet feels. *Vero?*"

Angelica merely nods her head. She refuses to take her eyes away from the box even for a moment. I slowly, very slowly, begin to lift the lid. Angelica lowers her head, straining to see the jewels resting inside their velvet case.

"Oh!!!" Angelica and I both gasp simultaneously. Once again, I am stunned at the brilliant gems shimmering before me. It is a diamond choker in the shape of a vine. Two tiers of diamonds encircle the choker, and then two of the vines branch down.

"It is the most beautiful piece of jewelry I have ever seen, Signora Donata!"

I am so enthralled with the choker that I let slide Angelica's calling me *"signora"* instead of *"signorina."*

"Can you please help me put it on?"

"Of course!" Angelica's hands shake as I hand her the choker.

"Please, be careful." I cannot believe I'm letting her hold my precious jewels, especially since she is quivering like a leaf. But I must see the choker on me immediately.

"It is gorgeous on you! Come look in the mirror."

I walk over to the small coffee table in front of the settee that Giuliana was seated on earlier. The coffee table has a mirrored surface. I bend over and am amazed at how the jewels have transformed me. I swear they have taken a good five to ten years off my appearance.

"This is just too much. Who is giving me these extravagant gifts? I must find out. The box." I remember Angelica was going to look at the box to see if she could determine which jeweler it came from. Angelica hurries over to the dining table and picks up the box. As I had with the first gift, she inspects all angles of it.

"Do you have any idea which jeweler uses this style box?" My voice sounds desperate.

"I'm afraid it's not a unique box. The two jewelers I go to on Ditmars do not use these blue velvet boxes. They use black. For Christmas and Valentine's Day, they use red. This is Astoria, not

Tiffany's, where you can always count on the same blue box." Angelica shrugs her shoulders.

"What about the ribbon? Every time I have received a gift, the box has been tied with this pale pink ribbon."

"I have always bought my jewelry from the two shops on Ditmars. I've never received the jewelry as a gift, so I would not know how they wrap it. I'm sorry." Angelica looks embarrassed that no one has ever given her a gift of jewelry. How sad, I cannot help thinking. She has lovely features. How is it that no one has noticed?

"That is fine. Do not worry about it. Can you leave me alone now? I would like to finish my espresso before I run a few errands."

"Errands? You are going out?" Angelica sounds dismayed.

"Yes. I do go out, you know. I am not the hermit you have read about in the tabloids."

"I'm sorry, Signora—"

"Signorina! How many times do I need to remind you and the rest of the staff here?"

Angelica glances down at the floor. The nervous mouse from earlier is back. For a few moments, her personality had come through when she had told me about her love of jewelry. I instantly regret my irate tone with her, but I do not apologize.

"I am sorry, Signorina Donata. I didn't mean to offend you by acting surprised that you are going out. It's just I was worried with all the people outside and the paparazzi." Angelica picks up the tray she was placing the breakfast dishes onto earlier and quickly exits the morning room.

I remove the choker and place it carefully back into its case. Though I would love to wear the piece all day, it is much too elaborate to wear on the streets of Astoria. My search for my secret admirer must start somewhere, so I will head over to the jewelers Angelica mentioned. I walk into my bedroom and open up my armoire's doors. I take off the hat hook a long, auburn-haired wig that I wear when I want to fully disguise myself. Then, I pull out a pair of gabardine trousers, followed by a gray spring coat. It is too warm to wear the coat, but I have to hide this cursed derrière I have or else people will recognize me as they did the other day when my bodyguards did such a poor job of covering me with that stupid drape.

I begin getting dressed, but after I put on the trousers that have become too tight for me, I decide I am tired of hiding. So what if the paparazzi and the crowd that has been camped out for weeks now follow me. This is the attention I sought when I was a teenage girl, before I became famous. I have worked hard to acquire these loyal fans. My behavior of hibernating in Giuliana's house and not even waving to my fans from my window is bound to alienate them soon. As I mentioned earlier, I used to talk to my fans. I always made time for them. That was part of my allure.

Walking back to my armoire, I choose a white linen pencil skirt with a matching cropped jacket. Underneath the jacket, I wear a black, scooped, sleeveless tank that shows off a hint of my cleavage. I open my jewelry box that sits on my dresser and take out the sapphire and diamond bracelet my secret admirer gave me. I decide to also wear teardrop sapphire earrings that were a present from my second fiancé. Pulling open my night table drawer, I reach for my large, round Dior sunglasses. Then I take out the pins that are holding my chignon in place. Instead of using a brush, I rake my fingers through my hair so that the strands have a sexy, tousled look. Glancing one last time at myself in the mirror, I leave to face my adoring fans.

The cries are music to my ears, as are the repeated shouts of "Francesca! Francesca! FRAN-CES-CA!" Of course, my nicknames vie with my Christian name: *"Carissima! La Sposa Pazza! Dolci Labbra!"* Mostly the men, of course, are calling me *"Dolci Labbra,"* and for emphasis, they are touching their fingers to their lips and blowing kisses in my direction. I am in a good mood today. For not even hearing my most detested moniker, *"Dolci Labbra,"* bothers me.

My pulse quickens, and I feel energized. How could I have hidden from the world and my devotees for ten years? How could I have shut the door on all of this? Whoever says they hate all the attention that stardom brings is lying. Naturally, celebrities grow to hate the invasion of privacy, but on the other hand, their need for receiving recognition and love from the public is what motivated them to choose a career in the limelight.

Nothing beats this feeling for me—not even making love. When my loyal fans are throwing themselves at me and professing their love, I feel so alive. Even now with the swell of the crowd pushing up against me, I am enthralled. I have never been afraid of being trampled or hurt although there have been times when I received a few bruises and scratches.

My bodyguards are having a difficult time keeping the crowd back. They looked at me with hatred when I informed them this morning that I would be going out and that I refused to be cloaked with that ridiculous fabric they had wrapped around me a couple of weeks ago. I do not pity them. After all, they earn a generous salary.

"Francesca, are you ready to tell the world what has brought you to Astoria?" An obcse, bald reporter from Fox 5 News shoves a microphone into my face. Soon, several other mikes are thrust toward me. My bodyguards push a few of the microphones away and insert themselves as best they can between the reporters and me. I hold up my hand, signaling to them that it is okay.

"She's going to speak!" resonates through the crowd. "Shhhh! Shhhh!"

The bodyguards wave their arms, motioning to the crowd to step back. Edgardo, my bodyguard who has been with me since I first became famous, screams at the top of his voice, "Give her some space so she can talk."

The crowd obeys Edgardo's request and moves back a few feet. I trust Edgardo with my life, and he has been one of my most loyal employees. But he, too, shot daggers into me when he learned of my plans to walk around town.

"Hello, everyone."

"*Ciao, Carissima!*" A man wearing a longshoreman's cap and holding a toothpick in the air calls out to me. He then places two of his fingers in his mouth and belts out a low whistle, which is soon followed by more. Cheers erupt from the men.

Edgardo towers over the crowd and yells, "Cut it out if you want to hear the lady speak." He crosses his arms in front of his chest, indicating he means business if the crowd steps out of line again. A few of the women's voices reach my ears as they implore the men to stop whistling and remain quiet so that I can speak. Once I am satisfied that the crowd has calmed down, I smile slowly, and then, with a grand flourish, I whip off my sunglasses, shaking my hair out as I do so. This is too much for the men, who resume the catcalls and whistles, indifferent to Edgardo, who is waving his arms about as if he is going to throttle them. I step forward and place my hand on Edgardo's shoulder and whisper to him to relax. My words have always had a calming effect on him. He stands to my side, not fully letting down his guard.

"*Grazie!* Thank you! Thank you to all of you. I cannot tell you how much your love and support mean to me. You are all wonderful, special people."

"We love you, Francesca!"

"And I love you!" I point with my index finger to the woman who has just said this. She is definitely a fan from when I was first discovered, since I can tell she is still wearing a bra that gives her breasts a pointed look. Her cat-shaped eyeglasses and tightly wound curls also indicate that she has not evolved far from the fifties. She holds a black poodle to her chest that has milky white eyes and is shaking from the commotion around it.

"I love you, too, Francesca!"

"Me too!"

"*Ti voglio bene con tutto mio cuore!*"

I wave to each of the people who profess their love to me. Each time, I am certain to make eye contact with them. The crowd inches closer to me as a few people at the front hold out their hands, imploring me to shake them. I begin to do so, but soon Edgardo and my other bodyguards push the crowd back once more.

Camera flashes are going off like fireworks. My audience seems to have forgotten that I wanted to talk and starts chanting, "*Carissima! Carissima! Carissima!*"

"Francesca, look this way, please!" A paparazzo snaps my photo, but not before I've given him my best pose. After he shoots my picture, he says, "You still got it, baby!"

"*Carissima,* over here!" Another paparazzo begs me to turn toward him. This time, I look nonchalantly over my shoulder as if I am caught unaware. A strand of my wavy hair falls over my eye as if on cue, giving me a seductive look.

"Sexy *sirena!* That's what you are," a man with a cigar shouts out to me.

"Hey, that's your new nickname, Francesca—Sexy Siren!" one of the paparazzi calls out.

My own publicist could not have planned a better press event. I can see the headlines of the rag mags tomorrow heralding my return: "Sexy *Sirena* Is Back!"

I toss my head back and laugh. A motion in my peripheral vision catches my eye. The heavy drapery from one of the second-story windows of Giuliana's house has been pushed back. My heart freezes. It is Giuliana. She is staring right at me. She looks absolutely livid—and another emotion flashes across her face. I suddenly seem to hear just how loud the crowd is. What is the matter with me? I had wanted to avoid all of this for her sake. But like a drug addict, my need for attention and love from a multitude of strangers has overwhelmed my good sense.

I lean over and whisper into Edgardo's ear, "Please, get me out of here."

Edgardo gestures toward the other bodyguards, using a secret signal to alert them that we plan on making a quick getaway. Several of my bodyguards work the crowd, creating a distraction as Edgardo and another bodyguard quickly usher me to my rented Maserati in the backyard.

"I guess you've changed your mind about taking a *stroll* along Ditmars Boulevard?" Edgardo cannot mask the sarcasm in his voice as my driver pulls out of the driveway.

"I would still like to visit the jewelry shops on Ditmars Boulevard, but I cannot walk there now with this crowd. I would never be able to lose them. Please drive to the shops, but take a diversion first."

"You mean a 'detour.' " Edgardo cannot resist another snarky comment. I know he is absolutely furious that I refused to take his suggestion of sneaking out of Giuliana's house to avoid the paparazzi and fans camped out front.

"I am sorry, Edgardo. I am simply tired of hiding all the time."

"You are not sorry, Francesca. This is me you're talking to. Remember? I know you were itching to get some attention. Tell it like it is."

"Can you blame me? I have been away from all of this for so long."

"That was your choice. Remember, Francesca?"

"Of course, but I still missed it."

Edgardo shakes his head. "I will never fully understand you. I thought you were through with this nonsense? I thought you wanted to spend the rest of your days in your villa in Sicily and live a quiet, normal life finally. The Francesca I just saw in front of those reporters and people looked like the old Francesca I used to know who could never get enough of fame."

"I did—do—want a quiet life from here on out. But being famous will always be a part of me. I am not saying I want to return to making movies and attending parties every night, but having my fans and the public take an interest in me is still important. Is that so wrong?"

Edgardo pats my knee. "If that's what makes you happy. I don't know. It's your life, I guess."

I pretend to look out the window. Out of my peripheral vision, I see Edgardo is staring at me. There is pity in his eyes. And I hate nothing more than being pitied. Though Edgardo has known me a very long time, and I treat him differently than the rest of my workers, he too is not immune to my lashings.

"Stop pitying me. If there is anyone who is to be pitied it is you. When are you going to find yourself a real woman to look after rather than spending all of your waking time protecting a celebrity?" I turn and meet his gaze head-on, narrowing my eyes so as to give him my most evil stare. And as always, it unnerves him. His pity turns to pain first, then scorn. He lifts up the lapel of his suit jacket and talks into his walkie-talkie, communicating to the other bodyguards in the car behind us that we'll be driving onto the Grand Central Parkway for a diversion.

Sometimes I think Edgardo is in love with me, and that is why he has not found a woman to marry. How pathetic! And he has the nerve to feel sorry for me.

After driving on the Grand Central Parkway for fifteen minutes,

Edgardo feels confident that no one is following us. We make our way back to Astoria. He instructs the driver to park on a quiet residential street, off Ditmars Boulevard.

"I'll make the inquiries at the jewelers." Edgardo places his hand on the car latch, but I immediately grab his arm.

"I am coming with you."

"Oh no, you're not! Haven't you had enough attention for one day? I don't need another mob like the one in front of your sister's house. Please, Francesca! Listen to me for once."

"It will be fine, Edgardo. I will just place this scarf over my head." I pull out of my Prada handbag a black silk Chanel scarf. "No one will recognize me with the scarf and sunglasses."

"Everyone will recognize that body of yours as they did a few weeks ago when they saw just your backside." Edgardo is scanning my figure with his eyes.

His face is filled with respect and awe. Like all men, Edgardo is weak when it comes to a woman's physique. Although he has never crossed the boundaries with me, he falls prey to my sexual charms. After knotting my scarf beneath my chin, I lean over and begin talking softly to Edgardo, telling him I need to get out and walk or else my legs will stiffen from the lack of exercise I have had cooped up in Giuliana's house. With one hand, I rub the back of my calf as if it is very sore, outlining the muscles toned thanks to my daily exercise regimen. Edgardo's eyes quickly dart to my leg. As I am leaning into Edgardo, I thrust out my bosom. My scooped tank top affords Edgardo with a more than generous view of my décolletage. Ever so lightly, I nudge my breast into his arm so that he does not realize the motion is intentional. Immediately, Edgardo's eyes travel up my body and rest on my cleavage.

I silently congratulate myself. My new nickname of Sexy *Sirena* is well deserved.

"I promise, Edgardo. I will behave. You can do all the talking. I will just remain silent by your side like your dutiful wife." I give Edgardo's thigh a playful squeeze and smile.

He jumps away from my touch as if it is molten fire. Clearly, I have unsettled him.

"Okay, but if you open that mouth and give away your true identity, you'll have hell to pay later." Edgardo waves his index finger at me, but I detect a twinkle in his eyes. Yes, the man is clearly quite taken with me.

I motion with my fingers as if I am zipping my lips.

Edgardo holds open the car door as I step out. Once again, I catch him checking out my legs. I silently thank God that at fifty-five years old, my body still wreaks havoc with men's libidos.

I hook my arm around Edgardo's enormous bicep and click-clack away in my Gucci pumps to the first jewelry store we see, Gina's Gems. I am turned off by the name of the store. If it were not for the marble exterior of the shop along with the pricey Rolexes and high-end designer jewelry in the display window, I might have avoided stepping foot inside.

My other bodyguards remain at a distance, not wanting to alert anyone that there is a star among their fold. But none of the pedestrians give me a second look. I stare at the sidewalk to further avoid recognition. Though I would not admit it to Edgardo, I too am uncertain my scarf and sunglasses will do the trick of concealing my identity.

There is only one saleswoman behind the counter, and her hopeful look at the idea of having a prospective customer vanishes as soon as Edgardo inquires about the jewelry box he has taken from his suit jacket's breast pocket. I gave him the smallest box I had received, which had contained an opal ring surrounded by three clusters of pave diamonds.

"No, I'm sorry. That box is not from my shop. I always use either black or red boxes."

The saleswoman barely looks at me.

"Do you know if any of the other jewelers on Ditmars use this type of box?" Edgardo asks her.

I can tell he wants to know just as much as I do the identity of my secret admirer. There is no doubt he is jealous. But as my bodyguard, his number one priority is to protect me. If there is a deranged stalker out there, he wants to know and catch him. I had wanted to keep the gifts a secret, and it was amazing that none of my bodyguards had intercepted the packages when they were delivered to Giuliana's house. But my wanting to investigate the jewelers in town forced me to tell Edgardo about the gifts. Of course, he was stark raving mad that I had not told him sooner about them.

Then, he blasted the other bodyguards for not doing a better job of inspecting all the packages that arrived at Giuliana's home.

"I'm sorry. I don't. It gets quite competitive since there are just three jewelers on Ditmars. I try to avoid the other jewelry shop owners as much as possible. They're not very nice."

"So you own this store? You're Gina?" I forget my vow of silence.

Edgardo stares at me in horror as we both wait for the saleswoman to recognize my voice, but she does not.

"Yes, I'm Gina. I've had my business for five years now."

"So, you are the sole owner? Your husband or another family member does not own it with you?"

Edgardo elbows me lightly, signaling me to shut up.

"I am the sole owner. My husband is a police officer and has no interest in the shop. My parents passed away many years ago, and I am an only child."

Something about the woman makes me feel sorry for her. Suddenly, I realize how I can make her day. I show her my sapphire and diamond bracelet.

"Do you have a sapphire ring that would go with this?"

Her eyes light up. "I have several. They're in the case at the back of the store. I'll be right back. Don't go anywhere."

Her desperation momentarily saddens me. Why do I care about this stranger? Though she is married, there is a loneliness about her that I know all too well.

"What are you doing? We're going home after this, and that's that. I don't want to hear any more arguments from you," Edgardo whispers. He pulls out a handkerchief from his pants pocket and begins wiping his brow, which is sweating profusely. I am really making him work for his money today.

I hold up my hands in surrender, but I know we are not going home after this. He can survive two more jewelry store visits.

I purchase an oval-shaped sapphire ring with two diamond baguettes on either side. Gina is so happy that she shakes my hand and asks me what my name is, but Edgardo quickly answers for me: "Christine." I do not know if Gina believes him with my Italian accent.

We finally leave Gina's Gems. Once outside, Edgardo takes my elbow, leading me toward where the car is parked. I manage to break free of his embrace and quickly walk ahead of him and on to the next shop. Edgardo runs after me.

"You are giving me a heart attack today! What did I say back there?"

"Relax, Edgardo. If anyone is going to get me discovered, it is you. 'Christine!' Really?" I huff in exasperation.

"I'm following you, but only because I don't want to make a scene on the street. People are looking at us." Edgardo's gaze nervously scans the pedestrians making their way along Ditmars.

"Nobody is looking at me. We just have two more stores to go to. It will only take ten minutes."

"As long as you don't decide to shop in them."

"That poor woman needed a sale. I felt bad for her. And I needed a sapphire ring to match my new bracelet. It was business, pure and simple."

"Since when do you feel bad for anyone?" Edgardo smirks, but once he notices that his words have stung me he wipes the grin from his face. "I'm sorry."

"You are forgetting all of my rules, Edgardo. First, I catch you pitying me today, and now you are apologizing to me."

"Francesca's Rules. How can I forget? Rule number one: *Never pity her.* Rule number two: *Never apologize no matter how rude I've been.* Rule number three: *Never say 'no' to her.*"

"Just abide by my rules, Edgardo, and we will be, how do you say it? A-okay?"

"A-okay." Edgardo's voice sounds resigned.

The next jewelry store's name sounds tackier than the first—Forever Gold. There are three salespeople helping a floor full of customers. This visit lasts no more than five minutes since the shop is so busy, and the salesclerk answering Edgardo's questions is impatient to get back to his customers.

The jewelry is not as high-end as the jewelry from Gina's Gems and as a result is more affordable. No wonder business is slow at Gina's. A salesclerk tells a patron that most of their jewelry is imported from Italy. But when I overhear a few of the prices and see the inferior pieces, I have my doubts that the merchandise is imported from Italy.

I let Edgardo inquire about the box and remain silent this time to prevent further angering him. We have no luck at Forever Gold either since the salesclerk tells Edgardo that they have never used this style of box. He suggests we try Castello Jewelry or one of the jewelry shops on Steinway Street. He also reminds us that even if a local jeweler uses such a box that is no guarantee the jewelry came from that particular store. Sometimes people, especially men who are giving gifts to women, want to give the impression that the jewelry they bought is from a more expensive retailer than where they actually bought the piece. I am troubled when I hear this. Could it be my admirer is trying to pass himself off as being wealthier than he is?

Castello Jewelry is across the street from Forever Gold. Finally, a jewelry shop with a lovely name! When we walk into the shop, my eyes are immediately drawn to several exquisite pieces that are displayed prominently on top of the display cases. I regret having bought the sapphire ring at Gina's Gems. I cannot pull myself away from a ruby and diamond necklace with three tiers and a matching bracelet and earrings. I am about to ask the man behind the counter how much the entire set is when Edgardo asks for me.

The salesman is smiling at me and looks straight at me when he answers Edgardo's question. "This set normally is $10,000, but I'm trying to clear out some old merchandise to bring in new pieces. I can give it to you for half price."

"$5,000 for all of these pieces? That would be as if I am robbing you!"

Edgardo gives me a stern look to remind me that I was supposed to remain silent.

"Your accent is beautiful. Italian, I gather?" the salesclerk asks.

"Swiss, actually," Edgardo quickly responds.

"Ahhh, Swiss! So you speak Italian and maybe French? Or is it German?"

*"Français, s'il vous plaît!"* I cannot resist answering playfully. I have about had it with Edgardo for one day, and as I told him earlier, I am tired of hiding. So what if the salesman recognizes me.

The man laughs. "Unfortunately, I have forgotten the French I studied in school many years ago except for a few phrases. So shall I wrap the jewelry for you? If you do not want the entire set, that's fine."

"No, no! Of course I want the set! They are absolutely stunning." I stare lovingly at the jewels.

"Perhaps you'd like to remove your sunglasses so you can get a better view of them?" The man motions as if he is about to take off my glasses. Edgardo quickly waves his hand away, shocking the salesclerk.

"I'm sorry. I did not mean to be so abrupt. It's just that my wife had cataract surgery a couple of days ago, and she cannot remove the glasses. She forgets sometimes."

I cannot believe the silly lies Edgardo is coming up with.

"Oh no, of course! I understand. My apologies. I had no idea."

"Please wrap the jewels. I will take them. I can tell even through my sunglasses that they are perfect!"

"As you wish, *mademoiselle*." The salesclerk bows his head toward me. He removes the ruby set from its display case and places the jewels in a large box. Edgardo and I take note of the box and look at each other, disappointed when we see it is made of black leather.

"Are all of your boxes the same? Do you carry any velvet ones?" Edgardo asks, trying to appear nonchalant.

"Yes. Since I first opened the business, these have always been our boxes. I have never deviated from this style."

"So you are the owner?" I ask.

Edgardo has given up on giving me stern glances, realizing it is useless.

"Yes, my name is Rocco Vecchio." Rocco shakes my hand.

I introduce myself. "Nice to meet you, Rocco. My name is Christine."

I smile from ear to ear, looking at Edgardo, who is doing his best to ignore me.

Rocco then shakes Edgardo's hand. Much to my surprise, Edgardo doesn't come up with an alias.

Rocco begins wrapping the jewelry box, but Edgardo stops him. "That won't be necessary, but thank you. We'll just take the case as it is." He then looks at his watch. "We're running late and need to go if we're going to meet everyone on time."

I nod my head. "It was nice to meet you, Rocco. You have a beautiful shop."

"Please, Christine. Come back anytime you wish."

"I just might do that. I did not have a chance to look at all of your jewelry."

"Good-bye, Mr. Vecchio." Edgardo holds up his hand in greeting and with his free hand prods me forward.

"Please, Rocco. Everyone calls me 'Rocco'."

"*Ciao,* Rocco."

"*Au revoir, mademoiselle.*"

Hmmm. That's the second time he's called me *"mademoiselle"* as opposed to *"madame,"* which would have been appropriate since Edgardo and I are acting as if we're married. Then again, Rocco did say he had not taken French since he was in school. He probably forgot what the correct title should be.

We take a few steps, then Edgardo stops. "Just one more question if you don't mind, Mr. Vecchio?"

"Of course not."

Edgardo lifts my arm, showing my sapphire and diamond bracelet to Rocco.

"Have you ever carried such a piece here or even seen it at one of the jewelry shops in town?"

"My, what an exquisite bracelet! No, I'm sorry to say I have never carried anything quite like that. I would remember if I had. It was a gift, I presume?"

"And why do you think that?"

Edgardo is not thinking clearly today. It appears obvious to me why Rocco would assume my bracelet was a gift since we are asking whether he has ever carried the bracelet in his shop and what type of boxes he uses. It is apparent we are trying to locate the buyer of the bracelet and that it was given to me as a gift.

"Why would you want to know if I ever carried it if you and your wife had bought the bracelet yourselves?" Rocco shrugs his shoulders.

Edgardo looks slightly embarrassed. He nods his head. "Yes. Yes. I am sorry."

Rocco holds up his hands. "No need. You're not the first people to inquire if their jewelry was purchased here."

"Really?" I cannot help but ask.

"Yes, really. People, usually romantics, still love to surprise their loved ones by playing the part of secret admirer."

I am surprised. Romance and chivalry have seemed long dead to me. I cannot believe that I am being wooed again in my mid-fifties. Instead of obsessing over who is my secret admirer, I should enjoy it. Most women do not find themselves in this situation at this stage in their lives.

"Thank you, Mr. Vecchio. You've been very helpful. We won't take up more of your time." Edgardo places his hand in mine as if we really are a married couple and walks away. He has never taken such liberties with me before. I am too stunned to protest.

We are almost out of the shop when I stop to admire an intricate gold-filigree bracelet that is in one of the display cases near the exit.

"Come on, Francesca. Haven't you bought enough for one day?" Edgardo whispers to me.

"You can never buy enough jewelry," I snap back at Edgardo.

"Excuse me, Miss Donata?"

I look up and am face-to-face with a pretty, blond woman.

"I'm sorry, miss, you're mistaken." Edgardo leads me away.

"Please, Miss Donata. I just have a quick question for you, and then I won't bother you."

I pull free from Edgardo's grip and almost lose my balance in my heels.

"Would you like an autograph?" I whisper to her, glancing toward the back of the shop to where Rocco is on the phone and staring at me. Does he now realize who I am? Has he heard this woman say my name? Why am I whispering since I told Edgardo earlier I do not care if any of these jewelry shop owners recognize me?

"No, no, thank you. I don't want an autograph. I . . . I . . . ahh, my name is Pia Santore. I live on your sister's street—well, just for the summer. I'm staying with my aunt. She knows your sister. Her name is Antoniella. Maybe your sister has mentioned her to you?"

I shake my head "no." Giuliana has not told me much, if anything, about her life in Astoria. I am even shocked she knows the neighbors and that she might have friends. She has always been quite the loner except for when we were the best of friends, I think sadly to myself.

"I work for *Profile* magazine. And I was wondering if there was any chance you might be interested in doing an interview with me?"

A reporter? She looks to be in her twenties. She must not have much experience. I cannot let some child interview me. I have always been very careful about whom I grant interviews to. Reporters and editors have a way of distorting the facts even when I have been careful and screened the questions before the interview.

"I am flattered, but I no longer do interviews. Thank you for asking. If you would please excuse me, I must be on my way."

"But, Francesca, everyone is waiting to hear what your plans are."

"Is that right?" I turn around.

"Yes. I heard you were talking earlier to your fans who have been camped out in front of Signora Tesca's home. Everyone is disappointed you didn't say more. Everyone is dying to know if you're going to make another movie."

"I do not believe you, my child. I made it very clear to the world that I was retiring from acting ten years ago." I begin to walk away, but the girl is persistent.

"It's the truth, Francesca. I'm sorry. I mean Mrs. Donata."

"*Miss* Donata."

"I'm sorry. I had it right the first time." The girl smiles at me.

She is getting desperate and is resorting to humor. I can remember when I was that young and desperate, but instead of giving her a break, I snap, "If you are going to make it in the dog-eat-cat world of journalism, you had better get it right *every* time, my child."

I pat her shoulder as if that will lessen the sting of my words and finally leave the shop with Edgardo.

"You sure didn't let her off easily." Edgardo blows a low whistle.

"When do I ever?"

"True. But she's just a kid."

"Kid? She has to be in her twenties."

"That's a kid to old folks like you and me."

"She must learn. You think everyone was nice to me before I made it? If she is going to succeed, she needs to develop a thick shell. She will thank me years from now. I did her a favor."

"Sure, if that's how you want to see it, Francesca."

"What is that supposed to mean?"

"Whatever makes *you* feel better."

"I tell the truth, Edgardo. You know that."

"Forget I said anything. I've had my share of battles with you for today."

We return to the Maserati without anyone else recognizing me. I am a little disappointed since I had hoped more people besides that young reporter would have recognized me. After all, my scarf and sunglasses do not conceal much. As we drive along Ditmars, I finally can begin to understand what compelled my sister to stay in this town. There is a certain charm in the markets and shops that line the boulevard. Many people seem to know each other as they stop to chat.

I close my eyes, pretending I am falling asleep. Although Giuliana lives a few blocks away, Edgardo has instructed the driver to get back onto the Grand Central to once again divert anyone who might have noticed me getting into the car. I think he is overreacting, but I do not protest. The drive will give me some time to myself before returning to the house.

Edgardo's words still plague me. He thinks I am a bitch, as the Americans say. I mentally shrug my shoulders. That is not the worst insult I have received. It does not matter. I have my legions of adoring fans as was evidenced today. I suddenly remember Giuliana when she saw me reveling in my fame. I will never forget that look of disgust on her face. She is repulsed by her own sister. The tears silently fall down my cheeks. Edgardo is right. I am a bitch. For only a bitch would have betrayed her sister the way I did all those years ago.

# ❦ 11 ❧

# Pia

I've totally blown it. I can't believe I approached Francesca when I saw her walk into Castello Jewelry. I should have just waited for Gregory to talk to her. He's not going to be able to put in a good word for me now.

All night, I've been sure to keep my cell phone by my side as I try to watch TV. Normally, I'm not waiting by a phone when a guy I like tells me he's going to call. But in this case, I just want to know if Gregory has broached the subject of me with Francesca.

"My child . . . my child," keeps ringing in my ears. Francesca was so condescending toward me. I should have given her a dose of her own obnoxious behavior right back and pointed out to her that the phrase is not "in this dog-eat-cat world," but rather "dog-eat-dog world." But I'd been too intimidated.

She's your typical spoiled celebrity who thinks just because she had a successful acting career she can treat everyone else like crap. To hell with her! Yeah, right. Who am I kidding? I wish I could blow her off the way she blew me off, but unfortunately, I want this interview and the chance to prove to Colin—or Col—that I have what it takes to be a good journalist.

My phone suddenly rings. Gregory's name appears on the screen. Before I realize what I'm doing, I answer the call after the first ring.

"Hey, Pia! You were waiting for my call, I see." He laughs.

I shut my eyes tightly in disbelief that I answered the phone after only the first ring. Then anger supersedes my humiliation. Did he really have to point out my faux pas to me? I decide to lie.

"Get over yourself, Gregory."

"Whoa! Whoa! I was just teasing you. I know you have better things to do than wait for my call."

He really doesn't have a way with words sometimes. But I decide to drop it before this snowballs into an avalanche. Mustering all my strength to keep my tone light, I ask, "So, what was your decision? Did you grant the queen her wish?"

Gregory laughs. "You're in a bad mood! Hostility is just oozing out of you. What happened?"

"I'm sorry. You're right. I am in a bad mood. I shouldn't be taking it out on you though. Please, tell me how your meeting with Francesca went."

"Only if you promise to tell me afterward what's going on with you."

Gregory has redeemed himself from his earlier transgression.

"Okay. Now tell me what you decided. Are you going to paint Francesca's portrait?"

"Yes, I am."

"Now had you decided you were going to do it before you went to see her or did she persuade you to do it?"

Gregory laughs. "Guilty as charged."

"So, I guess her tricks of persuasion have worked once again."

"Yeah, I guess so. But the truth is even when I told myself I wasn't going to do it, there was a tiny, niggling voice telling me maybe I should. So it's not like she had to work hard to change my mind."

*Work hard? What did she do to him?* My thoughts are getting carried away. The envy I felt when Gregory and I were at the supermarket and he was going on about Francesca's beauty returns.

"So, how exactly did she change your mind?" I try to sound nonchalant.

"She just convinced me."

My heart starts racing. Something doesn't sound right. Did he sleep with her?

"Yes, but *how?* What did she say to persuade you to paint her portrait?"

"It's not so much what she said."

Oh my God! Something did happen between them.

"Gregory, why do I get the feeling you're holding back?"

"Huh? What are you talking about?"

"Oh, now you're going to play dumb."

"What would I be holding back? If I wanted to hold anything back, I wouldn't have even confided in you about this whole Francesca stuff."

"Okay, go on. You were saying it wasn't so much what she said that convinced you to paint her portrait. Then what was it?"

"You've got to promise me not to tell anyone this. I don't want it to get out. She'd never forgive me, and I wouldn't be able to forgive myself for hurting her."

"I promise." My pulse quickens again as I wait to hear him admit he slept with her. Isn't that what starving artists who are trying to get ahead do?

"It was just the dejected look on her face when I told her 'no' initially."

I breathe a sigh of relief.

Grégory goes on. "She looked really sad."

"She didn't actually persuade you? You just felt bad?"

"Well, I didn't change my mind right away. I was trying to stick to my guns no matter how disappointed she looked. Francesca didn't ask me flat out to change my mind. She asked me if I wanted another drink, and then she started making small talk. She asked about my parents. We talked about when I was a kid and how my father and I would visit her so he could paint her portraits. She then said what a shame it would be that I could not continue the legacy my father had left me. And shortly afterward, I told her I'd do it."

"Francesca disarmed you by bringing up the warm memories you and your family shared with her. Subconsciously, she knew you would be reminded of all that she's done for your family, so in essence she guilted you. Wow! She's good, I hand her that."

"I'm not so sure she was being that devious, Pia."

"Come on, Gregory. You've said how persuasive she can be. She's clever. She knew that it would be harder to convince you to change your mind if she just asked you bluntly to do so. She also wanted you to think it was more your idea. The line she used about continuing your father's legacy was what hooked you."

"Yeah, I guess there's some truth to what you are saying, but I don't think she's intentionally trying to be malicious."

"Maybe not malicious, but definitely manipulative."

"It's not the end of the world that I'm painting her portrait."

"Are you trying to convince me or yourself of that?"

"You, of course."

"I don't need convincing, Gregory. Remember, I'm the one who told you this was the opportunity of a lifetime and could open up doors for you as an artist. But if it's not what you really want to do, then you should respect your own wishes. You shouldn't be painting Francesca's portrait out of some sense of obligation toward her for what she's done for your family or because you feel sorry for her."

Gregory breathes deeply into the phone. "You're right. You're right. But I told her I'd do it so now I have to. I can't back out."

"Why not?"

"I don't give my word and then go back on it."

Gregory seems to set a very high bar of morals for himself. That's honorable, and I can't begrudge him for that. I just wish he didn't have such a conscience where Francesca is concerned. After what I witnessed in my first encounter with her, I don't think she deserves it.

"It'll be fine, Gregory. Besides, I'm sure she'll be paying you generously."

"Yes, I can always use the money, especially now that I've . . ."

"You've what?"

"Ahhh . . . Shoot! I was just going to say especially now that I've met you."

I'm moved, but also a bit troubled. As if reading my thoughts, Gregory says, "Sorry. I don't mean to sound presumptuous. That's why I stopped mid-sentence as soon as I realized what I was about to say."

"Don't sweat it."

"So, I haven't sent you running back to California for dear life?"

"Oh, it would take a lot for me to go back home."

How can I admit to him that I don't even miss home? I'm ashamed to even admit to myself that I haven't missed my parents yet. It's not that I hated being around them. They just reminded me too much of Erica. Everything in California screams Erica.

I decide to change the subject. "I doubt you had a chance to ask Francesca about doing the interview with me?"

"I didn't forget, but it didn't feel like the right time to bring it up. My first appointment to begin painting her portrait is next week. I'll definitely ask her then."

"I'm not so sure you should bother anymore, Gregory."

"Who's squandering the opportunity of a lifetime now?"

"Francesca is why I'm in such a bad mood."

"How so?"

"I approached her today."

"What?"

"I'm sorry. I probably—no, I know—I ruined everything. I doubt she'll even listen to you when you ask her if I can interview her."

"Pia, what happened exactly?"

"I had just dropped off some dry cleaning when I saw her in Castello Jewelry. I thought I was imagining it, but even with her sunglasses and the scarf she was wearing on her head, there was no mistaking her. I'm surprised more people didn't notice and mob her. Anyway, she was staring at some jewelry in one of the display cases even though she had a bag from Castello as well as one from Gina's Gems."

"Yup, that sounds like Francesca. She's a total sucker for jewelry."

"Well, I think the whole world knows that. When have we seen her without stunning jewels?"

"True."

"So I worked up the nerve to go over, introduce myself, and ask her if she'd be interested in doing an interview with me."

"And I take it that didn't fly well with her?"

"Francesca wasn't rude immediately. She told me she was flattered, but she no longer gives interviews. Naturally, I was persistent."

"Naturally. You are a journalist after all."

"I'm not a journalist yet."

"Pia, in order to become what you want . . ."

"I have to see it and believe it. Yes, yes, I've heard of that woo-woo New Age philosophy."

"I was going to say, 'In order to become what you want, you have to already think of yourself as being what you want to be.' "

"That's not much different from what I said."

"As I was saying, you need to start introducing yourself as a journalist or reporter or whatever it is you want to be."

"Okay, I hear you, Gregory. Getting back to my story, I was persistent and told her that the crowd outside of her sister's house was upset that she hadn't talked to them more this morning."

"She talked to them?"

"Yes, haven't you heard? It was on *Access Hollywood* and *Extra* tonight."

"I don't watch much TV."

"I told her that her fans were wondering when she'd be making her next movie. She didn't believe me and became very condescending. She called me 'my child' twice. Then she went ballistic because I accidentally called her 'Mrs. Donata' instead of 'Miss Donata.' And she told me that if I hoped to make it in the 'dog-eat-cat world of journalism' I'd better get it right every time."

"Ouch! You did screw up royally."

"Geez! Thanks!"

"I'm sorry, Pia. I know you're already beating yourself up over this, but it doesn't mean she won't grant you the interview after I talk to her."

"You really think you have that much pull over her? I know you're confident that you can score this interview for me, but she just seems like the type of person who does what she wants, regardless of others' feelings. She's used to the universe bowing down and giving her whatever she wants."

"Let me talk to her, Pia. But you're going to have to stop judging her before you've even met her. Aren't journalists supposed to remain unbiased?"

"Look, I appreciate your help. But I'd understand if you don't feel comfortable asking if she'll do the interview, especially in light of my disastrous run-in with her."

"It's fine. I don't think what happened between you two was that bad. I'm sure in your eyes it seemed horrible, but you have to remember Francesca can act like that with many people. She has to protect herself."

"I hadn't thought of that. That does make sense, I guess."

Gregory is right. As a journalist, I have to keep my personal opinions out of the equation. Maybe I was judging her without giving her a fair chance.

"Okay. Thanks, Gregory."

"So, are you ready for our upcoming date? I can't wait to show you some of my favorite places in New York City."

"I'm looking forward to it. I haven't had a chance to explore much since I got here."

"You're going to love it. Trust me."

I remember how I was thinking of possibly canceling the date, but I can't now. He still wants to help me get my interview with Francesca.

*Haven't you punished yourself enough?* I hear a tiny voice inside my head. *It's not your fault Erica died.*

But it is. And I have to live with that for the rest of my life.


"You look beautiful, Pia," Zia keeps repeating as she stares at me in wonder.

"*Grazie,* Zia. You don't have to keep saying that." I laugh.

"But you do. I don't think you know how pretty you are."

I blush.

"And I'm so glad you're not wearing your glasses!"

"I brought them with me just in case I can't get used to seeing blurry."

"Don't you dare put them on! You hear me, Pia. You need to look stunning, not that you don't always look stunning. But a man wants to be able to stare into the eyes of the woman he loves with nothing blocking him."

I laugh. "Zia, this is just a first date. Gregory does not love me yet! He barely knows me."

"Don't you young people believe in love at first sight anymore?" Zia shakes her head disapprovingly.

"Zia, I don't think that concept ever existed. It's just something

Hollywood and romance novels created to hook audiences and readers."

"Have a little faith. If that boy doesn't fall in love with you, he's *stunad!*"

*Stunad* is how one would describe a fool or someone who's out of it.

I laugh and then return my attention to the cheap full-length mirror that Zia no doubt got at the More For Your Dollar store on Ditmars. Peering up close at my image since I'm nearsighted and can't see farther than a foot away, I have to agree with Zia. I do look very nice. When was the last time I got this dressed up? Suddenly, an image of me all decked out in black comes to mind—Erica's funeral. But that was a different sort of dressed up. Ever since I decided last night that I would go through with this date, I've been bouncing back and forth between guilt and convincing myself it's okay to experience joy again after my sister's death. Zia immediately notices the cloud that's come over my face.

"What's the matter? Don't you like this boy?"

"No, no. That's not it. I'm fine."

"You're lying to your aunt."

"I'm sorry, Zia. I really don't want to talk about it."

"Pia, I know you are not my daughter, and I know we haven't seen each other in years. But I do hope that in time you will feel more comfortable with coming to me if you ever need to talk about something that is troubling you."

"*Grazie,* Zia. That means a lot to me. It actually wasn't anything personal I was thinking about. I couldn't help but remember the last time I dressed up, and Erica's funeral came to mind."

"Ahh. I should have known. Whenever you are thinking about your sister, you get that faraway, sad look." Zia turns her back toward me, but I can see her image in the mirror. She's reaching for the handkerchief in her apron pocket. Great. Now I've made her cry. Doing what I do best when a situation gets awkward or too heavy, I change the subject.

"I wonder where Gregory is taking me."

My ploy does the trick. Zia whips around, looking like a little kid who's excited about going to the toy store.

"I'm sure it will be somewhere nice. You have to tell me all about it. That is, if you want to. I don't mean to intrude on your privacy."

I'm touched by Zia's happiness for me as well as by her desire to become more than just a relative to me. She wants to also be my friend.

"I'll tell you some of it. A girl has to keep a secret here and there!" I wink at Zia.

She laughs. "Beautiful and smart! But of course, you take after me."

The doorbell rings. My heart drops to my stomach. I can't help but look at Zia, panicked.

"Don't worry. You'll be fine." She squeezes my hand. "Now don't come down until a good five minutes have passed. You have to always keep the man waiting. Don't ever make it easy on him. Men love a challenge, and they go crazy for the women who play hard to get."

I nod my head. My mother used to impart the same wisdom to me, and I've always followed her advice. Unlike so many of my high school and college girlfriends who were so eager when it came to the guys they dated, I've always acted aloof in the beginning when I'm getting to know a guy. My friends always wondered why guys kept calling me for dates or developed crushes on me that wouldn't go away.

"I'm coming!" Zia shouts at the top of her lungs.

I stare at myself one last time in the mirror, making sure that I haven't forgotten anything. Zia is right. I'm wearing a black flounce skirt that falls slightly above my knees. And I've topped it off with one of my signature ultra-feminine peasant blouses. The scarlet-red blouse is sleeveless, and I'm happy to see my arms haven't yet fully lost my California tan. Instead of the usual ruffles that peasant blouses are known for, this one has the chiffon fabric gathered in an elaborate twist that ends in a rosette. The shirt's knot is strategically placed, allowing a view of my cleavage. It's just enough so that I'm not spilling out. But with my proportions, there's little chance of that happening. I don't have a large bosom, and it's never bothered me. Yet for some reason tonight, I decide to wear one of the padded bras Erica had bought me the last Christmas we spent together.

Erica took after my mother and was a full C cup. I'm an average B cup. Erica was always trying to convince me to wear padded bras, but unlike most girls, I've always been grateful to have smaller breasts that won't provoke men's stares. When I first put on my shirt tonight, it just looked okay on me. I then realized the elaborate knot of the blouse was flattening my chest a bit. But with the padded, lacey Victoria's Secret bra Erica gave me, the shirt was immediately transformed. Not only did the bra give me some cleavage, but it added some fullness to my chest and accentuated the lines of my small waist. I guess my little sister knew what she was talking about. Tears fill my eyes. I can't help but feel that she's looking out for me from above and placed the idea in my head to put on the padded bra. Having this thought makes me feel comforted, at least for the moment, that maybe going out with Gregory is a good thing, and maybe even Erica is encouraging me to go for it.

I suddenly hear footsteps coming up the stairs in the hallway. Glancing at the alarm clock on my night table, I realize with horror that I've kept Gregory waiting for almost fifteen minutes.

I grab my black alligator-skin clutch purse and run out into the corridor just as Zia is coming up the stairs.

First, she whispers to me, "You're even smarter than I thought, making him wait for so long! I finally started feeling bad for him and came up to get you. He's more nervous than you are. Remember that. So you have nothing to worry about. Just show him how calm you are." Then in a really loud voice, Zia says, "Oh, Pia. I see you're ready."

Feeling like I have to match her tone, I say just as loudly, "Yes, I'm ready."

I descend the stairs, expecting to find Gregory waiting for me. But he's nowhere to be seen. I strain my neck to see if he's still in the living room. He is. As I walk toward the living room, I call out to him nonchalantly, "Hey, Gregory. Are you ready to go? Or would you like to use the bathroom before we leave?"

He begins talking as he slowly gets up. I can't help but feel that he's putting on his own act, appearing just as calm as me.

"No, I'm good. Thanks for—"

His voice trails off once he turns around and sees me. His eyes immediately zone in on my cleavage. Instead of feeling self-conscious as I usually do when a guy is checking me out, I am pleased that he notices. Strange. I've never felt this way before.

Gregory swallows hard, then says, "Wow! You look gorgeous."

"Thank you."

I want to tell him he looks pretty hot himself, but that's another rule of mine: *Never compliment a guy on his appearance until you're in a committed relationship.*

Instead of his usual paint-splattered jeans, Gregory is wearing black khakis and a short-sleeved plaid button-down shirt. Of course, the shirt isn't tucked in, which is more the style now. I'm glad to see he hasn't completely gone conservative on me. And he's still sporting his motorcycle boots. I'm actually surprised Gregory doesn't own a motorcycle. It fits him more than the beat-up Honda he drives. Then again, he is a struggling artist.

Gregory walks over to Zia, extending his hand. "It was nice to meet you. I won't bring her back too late."

"Nice to meet you, too. Have a good time." Zia is beaming. I guess she likes Gregory.

As we step outside, Gregory says, "I parked the car at the corner."

I nod my head. For some reason, I'm feeling shy. Must be my nerves. I look down at the sidewalk as we walk. From my peripheral vision, I can tell Gregory keeps glancing at me. His eyes keep trailing down the length of my body. I can't help but smile. Luckily for me, my hair is hiding my profile. I've decided not to pull it up into its usual French twist.

"So, are you still feeling bad about what happened with Francesca?"

Good icebreaker.

"Ahhh." I shrug my shoulders. "I haven't thought about it too much. Getting ready for our date kept me preoccupied." I suddenly freeze. Oh God! I didn't just call this a date. I glance at Gregory, who's now keeping his gaze fixed to the cracks in the sidewalk. He doesn't seem to flinch at what I've just said. What's the matter with me? This *is* a date. So what if I've just called it that.

"Cool. I don't think you should worry. I'm confident Francesca will grant you the interview. It might just take a little bit of time." He looks up at me and smiles.

My heart drops. He is so sexy. All I want to do is run my lips over his. I don't think I've mentioned how he has the most incredibly delicious-looking lips I've ever seen on a guy. His upper lip has an extra fullness that gives him this irresistible pouty look. I force myself to break my gaze from his lips and smile back. Our eyes lock on each other's for a moment.

"Hey, Gregory!" A woman's voice brings us back to reality.

"Oh, hey, Connie! What's up?" Gregory wraps his arms around the petite frame of a gorgeous woman who looks to be around my age.

They kiss each other on the cheek. Jealousy quickly courses through my blood even though my brain is trying to reason with me, futilely reassuring me they're probably just friends. This Connie totally looks more like Gregory's type than me. She has short chestnut brown hair that's cut into sexy, spiky layers. Not many women can pull off such a dramatic hairstyle. But Connie's olive complexion and large hazel-colored eyes, which are outlined with smoky gray liner, make her totally rock the look. She's wearing dark-wash skinny Capri jeans and a retro-looking red and white gingham halter top that shows off her super-toned abs. Chunky, glittery bangle bracelets run down the length of her left arm, and a pair of super-long chandelier earrings dangle from her earlobes. Though she's wearing nude peep-toe Louboutin stilettos, which I can tell from their trademark red soles, she still has to stand on tiptoe in order to reach Gregory's cheek.

"You look great as always!" Gregory laughs, taking Connie's appearance in.

I know my face must be contorted into a tight scowl as I'm breathing flames in Connie's direction, warning her to back off from my guy. Whoa! My guy? We haven't even begun our first date. *Okay, Pia. Relax. Relax.*

"Thanks, Greg." Connie's looking at me expectantly, no doubt waiting for Gregory to make introductions. I don't detect any malice on her face, but I refuse to drop my guard just yet.

"Connie, this is Pia." Gregory holds his hands out toward me as if I'm a show prize. It's a harmless gesture, but it still irritates the hell out of me.

"Oh, you must be Antoniella's niece? My mom's told me about you." Connie steps over and shakes my hand. "I'm Connie DeLuca."

It takes me a moment to place the name. "You're Olivia's daughter?"

"Yes, well, one of her daughters. I also have two sisters."

Except for mother and daughter both being petite, I don't see any other resemblance.

I force myself to smile. Olivia has been nothing but kind to me, and I wouldn't want to offend her or her daughter by my standoffish behavior.

"So, where are you two off to?" Connie asks as she pulls a compact out of her oversized tote and begins feverishly powdering her face even though I don't detect a bead of shine on it.

"I'm taking her over to my hood. That's all I can say. It's a surprise." Gregory smiles sheepishly.

Suddenly recognition dawns on Connie's face that we're on a date as she exclaims, "Ohhh! I shouldn't keep you two. I'll catch up with you another time, Greg."

"Yeah, we should all hang out with Lou. It's been ages."

"He's been working a lot and so have I. Don't know how much longer I can keep up with the demands of all those nightmare Bridezillas we get." Connie rolls her eyes.

"That must be pretty stressful." I finally say something though it sounds lame.

"You have *no* idea! The stories I could tell you. Hey, you and me should have coffee some time. Let me get your number." She pulls out her cell. Now I can see a trait she shares with her mother—their super-friendly nature.

I spit out the numbers of my cell and to be courteous, I ask for her number, too.

"Great! I'll call you later in the week. Maybe Rita, my sister, can also join us."

"I'd like that."

Connie glances at her watch. "Shoot! I'm late for yoga. Good seeing you, Greg. Nice meeting you, Pia!" She turns around and begins jogging up the street. Her yoga mat is peeking through her tote bag as it bounces against her back. I'm amazed she can even manage a jog in her Louboutins.

Gregory laughs. "She's such a character. But she's one of the nicest people you'll ever meet."

"Really?" I suddenly realize how that must sound. "I mean how so?"

"She's very generous. They all are—her mom and sisters, too. Her oldest sister, Valentina, lives in Venice now."

"Olivia mentioned that to me. I can't even imagine meeting your Prince Charming and then moving to Venice. It sounds like something from the movies."

"Yeah, well, Valentina went through a lot. She deserves all the happiness she has."

I nod my head. I want to ask Gregory what Valentina went through, but it's none of my business. Maybe if Connie and I become friends, she'll tell me someday. I can't believe I let myself get so jealous of her without knowing anything about her. On the other hand, Connie immediately was kind and even invited me to have coffee with her.

We reach Gregory's car. He unlocks the passenger door and holds it open.

"After you." He bows deeply.

I giggle. "Oh, stop!"

When he gets into the car, I realize I should've thanked him for being a gentleman and holding the door for me. I'm being a total social klutz today.

"Thank you, Gregory."

"For what?"

"For holding my door, of course."

He smiles as he reaches over toward me. My pulse quickens. Is he going to kiss me already? Isn't the kiss supposed to happen toward the end of the date? But just as I'm having this thought, he places his hand on the side of my seat and reaches toward the back.

"Whew! They're still alive." Gregory hands me a small bouquet of pink tulips.

My face blushes. "Thank you. They're beautiful."

"I should've probably given them to you at your aunt's house, but I got shy to do so in front of her."

"That's okay. I love them." I inhale deeply and breathe in their scent. Tulips! Another sign from Erica? Tulips were her favorite flowers. I keep the flowers pressed to my face so Gregory doesn't notice the tears in my eyes. He starts the car and pulls away from the curb.

I force myself to make some small talk before I totally lose it.

"So, you're taking me to your hood?" I manage a small laugh.

"Yeah. We're going to Long Island City. No more questions. As I told Connie, I want to surprise you."

"Fine by me. I love surprises."

"You do?"

"Ever since I was a little girl, I was never one to peek at the gifts under the Christmas tree like most other kids. I just love the thrill of being surprised."

Gregory's staring at me while we're at a red light. He places his hand over mine.

"Great! That makes my job today that much easier." He grins before he returns his gaze toward the road once the light has changed. But he continues holding my hand as he expertly steers us through the traffic.

Soon we're in Long Island City. I'm amazed by how different the landscape looks from Astoria since Long Island City, or LIC as the residents often call it, isn't that far. Long Island City has a much more industrial feel to it. Warehouses upon warehouses line the streets. But many of the warehouses have now been converted into lofts or luxury apartments. As Gregory turns onto Jackson Avenue, the Empire State Building looms larger than life in the distance.

"Wow! It seems so close from here!" I strain my neck to keep looking at it as we drive farther away.

"Yeah, LIC is just about ten minutes away from midtown Manhattan on the subway. After we eat, we'll walk down toward the East River so you can see more of the skyline. They've really built the area up. There's a beautiful promenade now."

"So you live near here?"

"Yeah, over on Forty-Sixth Road, just off of Vernon Boulevard, which is where we're headed."

"We are?" The panic sounds off in my voice.

"Vernon is where all the restaurants are." Gregory looks at me, confused.

"Oh, right, right." I mentally slap my forehead.

He was referring to Vernon Boulevard and not his place when he said that's where we were headed. Fortunately for me, he doesn't seem to have realized why I sounded panicked. But I'm still not out of the woods. He might still suggest going to his place at the end of our date since he lives so close by.

We approach the Vernon Boulevard intersection, and as soon as the light changes, Gregory turns onto it. Immediately, I see the row of restaurants he was referring to. Trendy-looking clothing boutiques and other shops catering to yuppies and hipsters also dot the boulevard. There are a doggie daycare, a few coffeehouses, and several stylish hair salons. There's a cozy, intimate vibe to the street. It's reminiscent of what I've seen on TV of Manhattan's Soho, but not as big. When Erica and I visited Zia Antoniella as kids, we'd gone a few times into Manhattan. But, except for the horse carriages strolling through Central Park and the crowded, busy streets, I don't remember much else. Now that I'm interning at *Profile,* I've only had a chance to see midtown Manhattan, but I can't wait to check out other areas such as Soho, Chelsea, and the Upper East and West Sides.

"What do you think?"

"I like it, a lot. I was just thinking how it reminds me of what I've seen of Soho on TV, but, of course, on a much smaller scale."

"Wow! You really haven't gotten out much in the few weeks you've been here?"

I feel my face flush. I know he doesn't mean it as a criticism, but I can't help feeling slightly embarrassed.

Managing a little smile, I say, "I've been pretty busy with my internship, but I do plan on exploring more of Manhattan as well as other parts of New York."

"Great! That'll keep me busy." Gregory winks at me.

I'm about to ask him what he means, but it suddenly dawns on me. He's planning on being my personal tour guide around New York City. I'm tempted to say he doesn't have to do that, but I refrain as I feel my lips slightly turn upward into a grin. The truth is I'd love to have Gregory show me his city. What better way to see it than with someone who's lived here most of his life?

Gregory finally finds parking. I cringe as I watch him parallel park into a super-tight space. He maneuvers the car expertly without bumping either of the cars that are parked in front of and behind him.

"You're a pro!" I laugh.

"After doing this for so many years, you get used to it." Gregory shrugs his shoulders, but I can see he's glowing from the compliment I've paid him. Unlike my earlier rule of never complimenting a guy's appearance until you're in a committed relationship, it's okay to tell him he has great driving skills on the first date. Guys love being told they can drive and park well. It makes them feel very macho. And you have to give them some hint you're interested.

I begin to open my door, but he yells out, "Wait! Stay right here. I have to check something out."

Maybe I spoke too soon about his parking prowess, and he needs to make sure the car is parked correctly. But suddenly, Gregory whips open the passenger-side door and holds out his hand. Blushing again, I let him help me out.

"Thank you."

"My pleasure."

Believe it or not, no guy has ever held a door open for me. Again, I really thought chivalry had died and was something from my grandparents' time.

"The restaurant is a couple of blocks away. Sorry, but you have to get your parking wherever you can."

"Of course. I'm still getting used to all the . . ." I search my mind for a word that won't offend Gregory's New Yorker sensibilities. "Challenges. I'm still getting used to all the challenges that New Yorkers have to put up with."

"Ha! 'Challenges' is a nice way of putting it. Yeah, we have a lot to put up with. Then outsiders wonder why we can be abrupt and rude. Try living in the largest city in the U.S. with eight million people bumping into you, blasting their car horns at you, and waiting in line for virtually everything!" Gregory shakes his head.

"I think the crowds are the hardest part for me to deal with, especially on the subway."

"Your traffic in California is even worse than ours. You must still miss home though, right?"

I wrinkle up my face.

"No?" Gregory gives me a surprised look.

"No. Not yet at least. Besides, I needed a change." I hope he leaves it at that and doesn't pry me for details.

He nods his head. "I guess I can understand with your sister's death and all."

I avoid his gaze.

"So here we are. Tournesol. I hope you like French. If not, we can go to one of the other restaurants. It's totally your call." Gregory places his hand on my back and rubs it consolingly, but I get the feeling he's comforting me more over the mention of my sister as opposed to cuisine choice.

"I love French. This is nice." I flash him my most alluring smile, hoping to show him I'm fine and he can stop rubbing my back as if I'm going to break any second.

He stops and stares at my lips. My pulse quickens. He steps closer. His face leans toward mine until I can feel his warm breath.

"Something told me you'd appreciate French food," he whispers to me.

This time, I'm the one who's transfixed as I look into his eyes. His eyes crinkle lightly as he meets my gaze. Then, he takes my hand and leads me toward the restaurant's entrance. He doesn't let go as he opens the door, letting me enter first, of course. I'm about to disentangle my hand from his, but he grips it more firmly. As we walk into the dimly lit restaurant, I can feel him right up against me. I suddenly fantasize about turning around and kissing him wildly. Oh God! I need some air.

*"Bonjour, mademoiselle et monsieur!"* The hostess's voice seems to sing as she greets us in French.

*"Bonjour! Deux, s'il vous plaît."*

Gregory's French accent sounds impeccable. I only took a year of French in college, not enough time to learn it well or master the accent. He's turning out to be one surprise after another.

The hostess takes us to a table way in the back of the restaurant. The lunch crowd seems to be thinning out, so although the tables are quite close to each other, no one is seated at the moment near ours.

Gregory holds out my chair as I take my seat.

I decide to order a glass of white wine. Secretly, I really want a stiffer drink. My nerves could use it, but I'm trying to be demure and ladylike. And ordering a cocktail on a first date is far from demure.

"A scotch straight up." Gregory has no qualms about going for the hard liquor.

As if reading my thoughts, he says, "Sorry. Now and then I like to have something a little stronger."

"Oh, no. That's fine." I peruse the menu.

"Have you ever had duck?" Gregory asks me.

"I have, but I'm not crazy about it. A little too dry for me."

"Have you had it at a French restaurant with the orange sauce?"

"No, actually, I haven't."

"Well, the sauce definitely compensates for any dryness the duck might have. I think I'm going to order it. You can try mine if you don't want to commit yourself to it, just in case you still don't like it."

"Thanks. That's thoughtful of you." I smile at Gregory, which leads him to place his hand over mine as he nonchalantly looks back at the menu.

He strokes the back of my hand with his index finger. This guy is good, too good. My senses are going crazy. I try to focus on the entrees, but it's near impossible with what Gregory is doing.

"I'm going to order an appetizer. Care to share?"

I glance up at him. He seems to be asking with his gaze if I care to share more than just an appetizer. I swallow hard and quickly look back down at my menu.

"Sure. Whatever you want is fine with me."

"Even the escargots?"

"Yes, that's fine."

The waiter saves me. Gregory removes his hand from mine so he can point on the menu to what he's ordering, even though he really doesn't need to since his French is very good.

I decide to order the Chicken à l'Orange, which is chicken prepared the same way Gregory's duck is being prepared.

"Would you care for another glass of wine, *mademoiselle?*"

"*Oui, merci.*"

Gregory looks amused as he stares at my almost-empty wineglass.

I hold up my hands apologetically. "Thirsty. I don't normally drink this fast."

Gregory laughs. "No need to explain. We're here to have a good time and relax."

He raises his glass to me. "Oh, I should wait till he brings you another one."

The waiter returns with my Chardonnay.

"To Pia. May all your dreams be realized in New York."

"Thank you. And may you paint a masterpiece of Francesca Donata."

We clink our glasses and laugh before we take a sip.

"I guess neither of us believes in either of the toasts we made," I say.

"I do. You're hoping you get your start in journalism in New York. That is a dream of yours, isn't it?"

"Yes, but that's about it. You mentioned all of my dreams being fulfilled."

"Well, that's possible, too. Who knows what's in store for you here." Gregory's eyes twinkle once again.

I've just decided his eyes and his sly little smiles are his best features. Deciding to turn the tables on him, I ask, "So why did you laugh after our toasts? You don't think your painting of Francesca will be a masterpiece?"

Gregory wags his index finger at me, but first takes another swig of his Scotch.

"You're good, Miss Santore. You're a natural-born journalist."

I giggle. Only halfway through my second glass of Chardonnay, I'm beginning to feel buzzed. I better hold off on drinking any more until I've had something to eat.

Gregory continues, "There's only so much creative license an artist can have when painting a portrait."

"Oh, come on! You don't really believe that! Look at Picasso. He didn't paint literal portraits of his subjects." It's my turn to wag my finger playfully at him.

Gregory grabs my finger, laughing, and gives it a playful tug. "You are a lightweight!" He gestures with his head toward my wineglass.

"Would you rather I be a lush?" I toss my head so that my hair falls seductively over my left eye, and forgetting my earlier promise, I take another sip of Chardonnay. I'm thoroughly enjoying flirting with him.

"No! You're perfect the way you are." Gregory's eyes travel down to my cleavage and rest there.

I take a subtle, quick peek and am horrified to see that the top button of my blouse is undone, giving Gregory an eyeful of the deep cleavage my padded bra is giving me. But there's nothing I can do about it now. I'll have to wait until our food is brought out and then excuse myself to use the restroom.

The escargots arrive, and I'm horrified to suddenly remember what exactly they are—snails! I'd been so unnerved before by the feelings going off in me when Gregory was stroking my hand that my mind didn't fully register when he asked me about them. I can feel my intestines twisting at the thought of eating the slimy creatures. They seem to be covered in a bread-crumb coating, so at least they don't look like snails. Should I own up to my mistake or do I suffer in silence and force myself to eat them? I've never had escargots, so how do I know I won't like them? I just have to not think of their gooey membrane-like texture.

"Wow! These look great! Dig in. Ladies, first." Gregory hands over the tongs to me.

I take two, hoping he doesn't notice, but nothing seems to get past this guy. I thought men were the less observant of the sexes?

"Come on! Don't be shy. Take more."

I take two more. Gregory fills his plate and wastes no time popping the escargots into his mouth.

"Hmmm! Heaven!" He washes down the escargots with water, which makes sense. I can't see how downing Scotch with them would work.

I decide to just make this quick. I'll swallow the escargot in one shot. No chewing. That could prove disastrous, and I'll end up getting sick all over Gregory. Placing the escargot in my mouth, I press my lips together as I swallow quickly. That wasn't so bad. All I could taste were the seasoned bread crumbs the escargots were coated in. I don't notice any strong, lingering bad flavor on my tongue. Maybe I should try savoring them to see if perhaps I'd like them after all?

"Good, right?" Gregory is looking at me.

I hold up my thumb and nod my head. "Delicious."

I place another one in my mouth, but this time, I softly begin to chew it. Big mistake. While the bread-crumb batter is tasty, the gelatinous texture of the escargot is not. I feel like I'm going to gag. Fortunately, Gregory is too enamored with his snails to notice I'm about to projectile my half-chewed escargot right at him. I grab my napkin and discreetly spit it out. Trying to wash the flavor off my tongue, I take several gulps of Chardonnay. This would be a good time to take my restroom break.

"Can you excuse me, Gregory? I need to use the restroom." I smile sweetly at him, hoping he doesn't detect anything is wrong.

"Of course." Gregory immediately stands up and doesn't sit down until after I've passed him. Such a gentleman.

Once inside the restroom, I rinse out my mouth with cold water. Checking my complexion, I see that most of my makeup is still intact. I reapply a little lipstick even though I'm not done eating. I then notice my cleavage is still hanging out. The escargot fiasco almost made me forget my initial reason for wanting to come to the restroom. I button my blouse.

Returning to the table, I'm relieved to see the waiter has brought out our entrees. Gregory is sipping on a Coke.

"No more Scotch? You're such a lightweight." I place my hand playfully on Gregory's shoulder, tossing back his earlier retort.

He stares at my hand for a moment and then cocks his eyebrow up at me. "Trust me, I'm no lightweight." His devilish grin is back, and, as usual, it has a disarming effect on me.

Gregory waits until I've taken my first bite out of my Chicken à l'Orange before he cuts his duck.

"Oh! This is so good!" And it is. I don't have to pretend with this dish. Somehow the waiter knew I was done with the escargots I had left behind, and he took the plate away while I was in the restroom. There was no way I was going to eat any more.

"Better than those escargots, huh?" Gregory bellows in laughter.

"You knew I hated them?" Of course he knew. As I said earlier, he notices everything.

Gregory can't stop laughing. "I'm sorry. It's just when you ate that first one, I could tell by the way your lips were pressed so tightly together that you were forcing it down your throat."

I shake my head. "Fine. Have your fun at my expense."

"Oh, come on, Pia! You have to admit, it's really funny."

I hate being teased. Always have. Erica had known this about me and had reveled in teasing me from time to time. I'd become accustomed to it from her. I especially hate being teased by men. Refusing to look at Gregory, I continue cutting my chicken and eating it. Out of my peripheral vision, I can see he's staring at me. I've got his attention. Now, he's serious.

I'm about to pick up my wineglass when Gregory reaches over and takes my hand in his.

"You're so beautiful. I don't think you fully know that, do you?"

Finally, I return his gaze. But I haven't forgotten my wrath at being laughed at.

"I'm sure I was beautiful when I was forcing myself to eat those snails."

"Pia! I was just having a little fun with you. I'm sorry. I should've acknowledged sooner that I could tell you didn't like the escargots. But why didn't you tell me that you didn't like them when I asked if we should order them?"

I sigh. "You're right. I'm being silly. I actually forgot what escargots were until the waiter brought them out, and at that point, I felt bad about letting you eat all of them. I've never actually tried them so I thought maybe if I got past the idea of their being snails, I would enjoy them. I should've told you that I might not like them. I guess I just wanted to impress you."

Now I've really done it. I've totally let my guard down and let him know that I not only care about what he thinks, but that I was trying to please him. I'm afraid to meet Gregory's stare, but I do, and the tenderest expression greets me.

"Thank you."

"For what?" I laugh.

"For being so candid. There's nothing sexier in a woman than her not being afraid to show who she really is."

My cheeks are absolutely warming up. I know I should thank

him now, but I can't, especially when he brings my hand to his lips and kisses it lightly.

An hour later, we leave the restaurant and walk to the promenade overlooking the East River and Manhattan. Gregory and I are holding hands. It's muggy outside, and our sweaty palms stick together, but I don't mind.

I'm having a great time even with the embarrassing escargot episode. It's been nice getting out and doing something other than thinking about how I'm going to score an interview with Francesca Donata.

As if reading my thoughts, Gregory asks, "So have you prepared your questions yet for Francesca?"

"Of course not. I don't even know if I'm going to get the interview."

"I told you she will do it. It might take a little arm twisting, but she's not the only one who can be quite persuasive."

"Thanks again for asking her. I owe you."

Gregory waves his hand dismissively at me. "I'm not like that. I do things for my friends because I like to help."

"So I guess we're friends." I smile seductively at Gregory.

"Yes, but I'm hoping we can be more. I know this is our first date, and forgive me if I'm being presumptuous."

"You are being presumptuous." It's my turn now to have a little fun with Gregory as he had with me earlier over the escargots.

"I call it confidence."

He's so irresistible.

"I love it down here."

"Me too. It's really grown a lot in the past ten years though it's still quite small."

"Can I ask you a personal question?"

"Fire away." Gregory opens up his arms as if to say, "Hit me."

"How can you afford to live here? I've heard the rents can be quite pricey in this part of Long Island City and you're a—"

"Starving artist?"

"No offense. But yeah."

"First of all, I'm not a starving artist—maybe struggling is a more accurate way of putting it. Secondly, the house I live in is my parents'. Since they're now retired and living in Florida, I have the place to myself. It's a two-family house, and we rent the apartment above me. So it's good that I'm still living here when tenant concerns come up. Anyway, my parents don't expect me to pay rent so I'm saving a lot there. I take care of whatever maintenance issues come up with the house and the tenant's apartment, so they figure we're squared away."

"That's good."

"And while I have quite a ways to go until I'm a more established artist, I do sell a few of my paintings here and there. Plus, I teach art at an after-school program at the junior high in my neighborhood."

"That's great! I can't believe you haven't mentioned that."

"Well, this is—what? The third time I've seen you? I can't reveal all there is to know about me in one shot or else you'll lose interest." Gregory smirks.

"Who says I'm interested?" I give him my most haughty, disinterested look.

"Oh, you're interested."

"My, my, Mr. Hewson. You're quite conceited." I can't help but laugh.

"I'm just being honest. Why play games?"

I nod my head. He has a point. I've always hated the game playing that seems necessary to dating. But as a woman, I also know that it's best to protect oneself and play the game a bit, especially in the beginning. Another rule of mine which is in agreement with what Gregory said: *"Don't tell a guy everything about you in the first few dates."* But I'm finding it's easy to confide in Gregory. And I've already broken my rules by admitting to him earlier that I wanted to impress him by eating the escargots.

I glance up and find Gregory peering at me intensely yet again. Shifting my gaze to the skyscrapers across the East River, I pretend I'm taking in the scene. I can still feel Gregory's eyes on me.

A warm breeze comes up off the East River.

"Are you cold?" Gregory asks and then moves in closer to me, wrapping his arm around my shoulders.

I want to answer with a sarcastic response like, *"It's a muggy June afternoon, and you're asking me if I'm cold?"* but I remain silent since he's already decided I am cold.

I'm beginning to feel tired and lean into him. He immediately takes the action as a cue to start swirling his fingers up and down my arm. If he's this good at stroking with his fingers, his hands must be amazing at giving massages. A soft sigh escapes my lips involuntarily at the thought. Again, Gregory takes it as a sign, and before I know what's happening, he's kissing me.

I don't know why I'm surprised. We're standing at a promenade, overlooking the water and the beautiful Manhattan skyline. It's a romantic setting. I should've seen this coming, but I didn't. I'm not complaining though. Gregory's lips feel as lush as they look, and his tongue is expertly gliding along mine. Within seconds of his kissing me, I'm kissing him back, and it has to be the longest kiss of my life. And I don't want it to end.

As we kiss, Gregory's hands cup the sides of my face. I snake my arms around his waist. Finally, after what must be three minutes, he breaks the kiss and plants little kisses on my cheeks and along my jawline. I've never been kissed this way. There's a gentle, yet insistent, yearning in his kisses and embrace. I can tell he's holding himself back and trying to be gentle with me. Tears come to my eyes. I try to force them back, but it's too late. They're sliding down my cheeks.

"Pia? What's the matter? Oh God! I'm sorry. This is all too much, too soon for you."

"No, no. It's nothing. I'm okay." I shake my head.

"I've upset you. Please, tell me."

I see the anguished pleading in his face. Though I'm embarrassed, I don't want him beating himself up when he hasn't done anything wrong.

"I'm just moved. Sorry! I know that sounds so cheesy." I give an exasperated laugh.

"No, please go on. Remember what I said before. I appreciate honesty above all else."

Emboldened by his comment, I take a deep breath and let it all out.

"I'm moved by the way you kissed me. It was so tender. I can tell you were being considerate." I shake my head. "This is going to sound pathetic, but no one's ever kissed me like that." I cross my arms protectively over my chest and look off to the left of the promenade. A couple of teenage boys are attempting to climb the old train cars that stand as a landmark with the words "Long Island" painted on them.

"Hey." Gregory speaks softly, tilting my chin so that I'm forced to look right at him. "There's nothing pathetic about that. I'm extremely flattered to be the first man to kiss you the way you deserve to be kissed."

"Why is it you often have a way of saying the right thing to make me feel better? That's a gift, you know?" I smile.

He hugs me, rocking my body lightly from side to side. I could stand here forever like this. He feels so good. I want to make him feel as good as he's made me feel. I lean in and kiss him. Seemingly of its own accord, my body presses up firmly against his, eliciting a groan from him. He can't help himself this time, and his kisses are fierce as his tongue explores every inch of my mouth. I reach my hands behind his head and run my fingernails along his scalp. It's too much for him. He breaks away, gasping for air.

"Pia! You're killing me."

I laugh, and he laughs with me.

"Sorry. I couldn't help myself."

Gregory glances at his watch.

"I have another surprise for you before I take you back home. Oh! And there it is."

A motorcycle is making its way toward us. The rider stops about fifty feet away and gets off the bike. Removing his helmet, he yells out to Gregory, "Hey, man!"

Gregory walks over to him and gives him the same fist bump I'd witnessed him giving Paul the other day at the bakery.

"Pia, this is a good friend of mine, Lou Rabe. You met his girlfriend Connie earlier today."

So this is the Lou that Gregory and Connie had been talking about. He is handsome in a bad boy sort of way. Gregory has a hint of bad boy, but Lou seems to exude it from every pore. His hair is jet black and cut in longish, spiky pieces. A five o'clock shadow of stubble outlines his face. His eyes are the same intense black as his hair. His biceps are clearly defined in his snug, long-sleeved black tee. He is tall, at least six feet or six feet one. No wonder Connie wore those extremely high stilettos.

Lou walks over and shakes my hand. "How you doin'?"

His strong New Yorker accent further seems to add to his bad-boy persona.

"Fine. Thanks. How are you?"

"Can't complain. Took my baby out for a long ride to the Catskills and back. She's all yours now."

He was referring to his Harley Davidson motorcycle and not Connie.

"She's looking good, Lou. You did something different since the last time I rode her a month ago?"

"Just touched up the paint a little. That's all. She's perfect as she is."

I mentally roll my eyes. I don't know how much of this macho talk about a bike I can take.

"Are you ready, Pia?" Gregory asks me as he takes Lou's helmet from him and places it on his own head.

"What? We're going on the bike? What about your car?"

Gregory laughs. "We're just going for a short ride. We'll meet Lou on Vernon in about twenty minutes."

"Pia, I take it from your hesitation you've never been on a motorcycle?" Lou asks me.

"No, I haven't."

"Don't worry. It'll be smoother than riding in a luxury car. I promise. Connie can't get enough of her, but we have to ride outside of town. If her mother sees her riding the bike with me, she'll blow my head off." Lou snickers.

Gregory slaps Lou on the back as they laugh even harder together. I can see Olivia DeLuca going after Lou with a shotgun.

"Won't I need a helmet, too?"

"Oh, almost forgot." Lou takes his backpack off and pulls out a smaller helmet that matches his.

"It's Connie's. She keeps it at my place since she can't let her mother know she goes riding with me. She won't mind if I lend it to you."

"Thanks."

I put on the helmet, and Lou helps me strap it securely.

"Now remember, Pia, just hold onto Gregory for dear life."
My eyes open wide in fear, and Lou laughs.
"Just kiddin', sweetheart. Just kiddin'!"
"Don't listen to him, Pia. You'll be fine. Trust me."
Gregory nods his head reassuringly. I nod back. He slides down the protective visor over my eyes and then adjusts his. I get on the Harley and snuggle as close to him as possible, wrapping my arms around his waist. The action sends off a flutter of butterflies deep in my belly. I can't help wondering if Gregory is also turned on by having me so close. But my thoughts are soon forgotten as he starts the motorcycle's engine, and I feel a deep rumble beneath me.

"Ready?" Gregory shouts.

"Yes!" I shout back.

He takes off slowly, which gives me a chance to get used to being on a moving vehicle that has no protective exterior. But then when he gets to a deserted road, he accelerates rapidly. My heart is racing, and I want to shut my eyes, but I know that will just make me feel nauseous. After about a minute, I relax and actually start to enjoy the feel of the rushing wind blowing against me. It's as if we're one with the wind and the speed. No wonder Lou and Connie love riding so much.

We stop in a part of Long Island City that looks desolate compared to the Vernon Boulevard area. Gregory parks the Harley and helps me get off.

"So, how was it? Think you'll live?"

"I can't wait to get back on! I loved it after I was able to relax."

"I knew you'd love it!" Gregory gives me a quick hug.

"Do you borrow Lou's bike on a regular basis?"

"From time to time. I've been busy lately with my painting. But maybe one weekend, we can take it and go to the Catskills. It's beautiful up there, and it makes for a great, long ride."

"I'd like that."

"This is one of the surprises I have for you." Gregory takes my hand and leads me into what looks to be a park. As we enter, I see numerous sculptures.

"This is Socrates Sculpture Park."

Many of the sculptures are life-size. A view of the East River and the Manhattan skyline serves as the backdrop.

"This place has come a long way since it was first started by local sculptors and people in the community back in 1986. It used to be a landfill."

I could see the large open space serving as a landfill once. Now, grass covers the ground as well as gardens with blooming flowers. A lot of young people are milling about, either taking strolls or lying on blankets on the grass. I see a white screen off in the distance.

"I guess they're waiting for a movie to start?"

"In the summer, they show free movies. They host a lot of free events here, including theatrical performances, workshops, and fitness classes."

"That's great. Have you ever sculpted anything?"

"I took a class in art school, but I don't really have a knack for it. Painting and drawing are more my thing. But I do appreciate sculpting, and I'm always so fascinated at how some of these pieces are created."

"I like it here. There's so much character in the little I've seen of Long Island City."

"There is. And it keeps growing. Some of the change is good, but when a place gets too big or popular, things often seem to inevitably change for the worse. But we'll see. I don't want to be such a pessimist. Anyway, Socrates Park is one of my favorite hangouts."

"We should come back one night to catch a flick."

"Sure. That would be cool. We'd better head back before Lou thinks I've made off with his Harley."

We walk out of the park and toward the bike. Unlike earlier, I'm looking forward to the ride now. Gregory takes it a little slower this time. I can't help but feel that he's trying to prolong our date as the night comes to a close. Before I know it, we're back on Vernon Boulevard. I'm a little disappointed the ride is already over. As I get off the bike, I see Lou approaching us with Connie by his side.

"Hey! We have a virgin here. How was it, Pia?" Lou screams out for the whole world to hear.

"Great. I liked it a lot."

"See, I told you!" Lou gives my arm a playful punch.

I laugh and can't help feeling like I'm one of the in crowd.

"We just ate, but we're going for drinks. Want to join us?" Connie asks.

"Thanks, but maybe next time. I brought some work home that I need to go over."

"I never let work stop me." Connie winks.

"We'll see you guys around soon." Gregory waves to them and leads me away with his hand.

"Let's double-date next weekend!" Lou yells out.

"You're not my type, Lou. Can't you see I'm into blondes?"

"Badass!" Lou yells out.

"He's funny," I say to Gregory as I watch Lou and Connie walk into a bar.

"Yeah, Lou is a character just like Connie. You couldn't find a pair more suited to each other."

We walk over to Gregory's beat-up Honda. On the way back to Zia's, Gregory drives with one hand on the steering wheel and the other on my lap. Sadness is beginning to creep in. I don't want to go home. We pull up in front of Zia's house.

"Thanks for lunch. I had a really good time."

"Me too. What time do you get home from work?"

"It depends if I stay late. I'll probably be home by six-thirty tomorrow night."

"I'll call you around eight. If you're not too tired, maybe we can get an espresso at your aunt's bakery."

"Okay. Let's play it by ear."

We look at each other for a moment. Gregory leans in and kisses me softly. I pull away, nervous that Zia will come out any second. I notice the disappointment in Gregory's eyes that I've broken the kiss. Another rule of mine: *"Leave them wanting more."*

And that's exactly what I intend to do.

"I'm telling you, Mr. Cohen, I can do this."

"Pia, please call me 'Col.' Everyone else does."

Though Colin Cohen insists I call him "Col," I still have a difficult time doing so. I can see it's beginning to bother him. I'll compromise.

"Colin, I know I'm just an intern—"

"Who's only been on her internship for a few weeks."

"Yes, I realize that, too. But I'm telling you, I can interview Francesca Donata." *And write the article,* I add in my thoughts. I can't believe I've worked up the nerve to approach Colin about interviewing Francesca. My blouse is sticking to my back from all the sweat I've poured since I left Zia's this morning.

"So you say your aunt knows her?" Colin's looking at me with skepticism in his eyes, but I also detect a hint of something else—curiosity. I've got him.

"My aunt knows Francesca's sister—the one whose house Francesca is staying in."

"That's not the same as knowing Francesca Donata."

"Colin, Signora Tesca—Francesca's sister—is a bit of a recluse. She hardly lets anyone into her home, and now that her famous sibling is residing with her, I'm sure her guard will be up even more. My aunt can arrange for me to meet Francesca. She's really good friends with Signora Tesca." I'm stretching the truth of course, but no one has gotten ahead in life without a few white lies.

Colin is tapping his favorite Mont Blanc pen against his chin, a gesture he makes whenever he's contemplating one of his "exceptional ideas," as he likes to call them. He swings his office chair away from me and stares out his window. I wait for what seems like an eternity before he swivels his chair back toward me and says, "If you can arrange a meeting with her, I'll send Madeline with you to conduct the interview. You can assist her with everything involved with the piece."

My stomach burns from the acid that's churning violently inside. I swallow hard, trying to contain my anger. "Signora Tesca won't let Madeline in."

"Not even with you? What makes you so sure Signora Tesca will even let you into her home? Okay, your aunt is good friends with her, but you're a stranger as well. If she's as much of a hermit as you say she is, you're also pretty much an outsider."

I shake my head. "She'd let me in over Madeline because I'm a *paesana.*"

"A pie what?"

"*Paesana.* It's Italian for someone from your village. You know, kind of like a homeboy. I'm Signora Tesca's homegirl."

Colin erupts into laughter. "Pia, I was beginning to think you had zero sense of humor. You barely laugh at my jokes."

*That's because none of them are funny,* I think to myself.

I smile. This isn't the time to act my usual ultra-serious self. Slowly, but surely, I'm warming Colin to the idea of letting me interview Francesca. I refuse to walk out of here until he gives me carte blanche to do the interview.

"Anyway, I have the 'in' of not only being Italian American, but also my father's family is from the same town that Signora Tesca is from. Even though we've never met, the fact that I'm a *paesana* will help me to win her over."

Colin squints as he stares at me. His Mont Blanc taps his chin again.

Letting out a deep sigh, he finally acquiesces. "Okay, homegirl. You have my permission to interview Francesca—that is, if you get the interview. I still have my doubts, no matter your connections to her sister or that you're a piezon or whatever you call it. We're dealing with The Crazy Bride after all. She's notorious for being a bitch. You have your work cut out for you. If you do manage to get the interview, you will have earned my highest respect. I'll let you do the legwork on the interview—the research, notes—but I'm going to come up with the questions."

"But Colin—"

Colin holds up his hand. "Let me finish. As I was saying, I'm going to come up with the questions, but I'll also let you come up with a few of your own questions. We'll go over them together. I'll also have to prep you on the right way to interview her."

"I have done interviews before, Colin."

"The student council president and homecoming queen don't count." Colin gives me the most exasperated face.

"I interviewed local politicians back home and various artists who performed at my university."

"That's still peanuts compared to interviewing a world-famous movie star and one as legendary as Francesca Donata. She'll eat you up alive if I don't prepare you. Trust me on this, Pia."

He's right, as was evidenced by my meeting with her in Castello Jewelry the other day. And he is being fair by letting me come up with a few of my own questions. Dare I mention that I want to write the article or at least some of it? Why not? What do I have to lose at this point? He'll just say "no."

"Thank you for working with me on this. I really appreciate it."

"You have a lot of ambition, Pia. And you work hard. You're going to be a great journalist someday. But you have to pay your dues first. There's a reason people don't become journalists overnight."

Except for Madeline Drabinski, I want to say, but I remain silent. Now I'm not sure if I should bring up wanting to write the piece. Deciding not to push my luck, especially since he's compromised with me, I resolve to bring up the matter of writing the article at a later date. As Colin said, I have my work cut out for me just in interviewing Francesca.

"Thank you, Colin. I promise you won't be disappointed."

"Pia, I'm afraid *you'll* be disappointed. Just do me a favor. If you do score the interview with that nut, keep your expectations low. She's very unpredictable, and I wouldn't want your first major interview to scar you, especially if it doesn't turn out how you imagined."

"I'll keep that in mind."

And with that I exit Colin's office, trying hard not to feel intimidated by the extremely high bar I've just set for myself.

# ✒ 12 ✒

# Francesca

"**I** am too old for this. *Faccio schifo*. Poo!"

My back pain disgusts me. What is becoming of me that I cannot even sit erectly on the settee in my bedroom without having an ache? As an actress, I had to always maintain the most perfect posture. I should be accustomed to it, but instead every vertebra in my spine is screaming.

"You're doing great, Francesca. How about we take a break?" Gregory places his paintbrush down on his palette and begins wiping his hands with a towel.

Though I am in my mid-fifties, I can still appreciate a fine specimen of man, especially one as young and charming as Gregory. I know if I wanted to, I could have him, but I am from a different generation where good sense almost always prevails. *Si, si,* all the older actresses are now dating younger men, but it screams of desperation. And I, Francesca Donata, have never been desperate and never will be. Sighing, I take one last look at the young artist and pull my eyes away as I bend my neck toward each shoulder, giving my taut muscles a good stretch.

"How is my portrait coming along?"

"So far, I'm happy with the way it's progressing." Gregory smiles at me, causing his eyes to crinkle in the corners, much the way his mother's did when I last saw her.

Though Gregory is his father's child in every way where his talents as a painter and incorrigible personality are concerned, he's a dead ringer for his gorgeous mother.

"Will your parents be coming to visit you anytime soon? Scotch?" I hold up the bottle, and Gregory nods his head.

"Whoa! *Una goccia, una goccia!*" Gregory laughs, waving his hand for me to stop.

"You're a man. A drop will not do."

I wink at Gregory, causing his cheeks to turn slightly crimson. I am happy to see I can still have an effect on men as young as him.

Gregory drinks some of his Scotch before replying. "No, I probably won't see my parents until the fall. I did speak to my father last night, and he was pleased to hear that I'll be painting your portrait. He asked me to give you his best."

"And please give him mine."

Gregory clears his throat as if he is about to speak. I wait, looking at him expectantly, but he remains silent. Something is troubling him. I am the most patient woman in the world, which always surprises people when they come to know me. Everyone assumes that because I am a star I have little to zero tolerance and must get my way immediately. I can wait. For I always do get what I am seeking. I have also learned that when you want a person to confide in you, the best course of action is to act disinterested.

*"Sono stanca!"* I yawn, stretching my arms over my head, arching my back just the way Mewsette does as I thrust my ample bosom out. I close my eyes, but manage to keep them slightly open, just a slit, so that I catch Gregory stealing a glance at my breasts.

*Sì, Francesca. You have not lost your sex appeal,* my thoughts assure me.

I stand up and join Gregory, who is now standing at the window, no doubt forcing himself to look away from my cleavage that is on full display in the low-cut silk Armani dress I am wearing. I am surprised he was able to stare at my breasts while painting my portrait without blushing every time, but I suppose his having me look off to the side kept him at ease. My dress is a deep pomegranate red— one of my favorite colors—that accentuates my brunette hair. Red, for me, symbolizes youth and vitality, and that is what I am striving for Gregory to capture in my painting. He does not know this, but this will be the last portrait I will have commissioned. And I want to be certain that I look just as stunning as I did in the paintings his father did of me when I was younger. I feel confident that after I die, this will be the portrait that will be flashed across TV screens and magazine covers. The media loves contradictions, and what better contradiction than a former movie star looking her best in the prime of her life?

"Your sister has a beautiful home."

Ahh! The small talk. Small talk always precedes a confession or a request. My guess is that it is the latter. As a rich, famous woman, I have become accustomed to people always wanting something from me—except Giuliana. She never seems to want anything from me, which saddens me because I took so much from her.

"What's the matter, Signorina Donata?"

Perceptive as well as handsome.

"Would you be hurt if I lied to you and said 'nothing'?"

Gregory's face registers surprise at my honesty and something else I cannot pin yet.

"I prefer the truth, but I know sometimes people lie to protect themselves, and I can understand that." He returns his gaze back out the window.

He is a special young man, and someday, he is going to make a woman very happy.

"I was just thinking about my sister and how I have not always been the best sister to her."

Once again, Gregory looks surprised by my admission. But he quickly conceals his feelings and nods his head.

"Don't be too hard on yourself. You are only human after all, no matter what the media has made everyone believe." Gregory winks at me.

"You do value honesty, Gregory!" I laugh, playfully batting my eyelashes at him.

"Francesca, I wanted to ask you a question." Gregory's face turns somber.

Here it comes—whatever he wants from me. The warmth I felt a moment ago is quickly vanishing.

*"Si?"* I can hear the change in my tone, and this clever young man detects it, too. His expression immediately becomes angst-ridden.

Regretting my haughty tone, I place my arm around his shoulders in a motherly embrace and say, "Please, join me on the settee where you will be more comfortable."

He lets me lead him to the settee. I reach for the bottle of Scotch and pour more into both of our glasses.

"No arguing. I can tell you need this shot." I point my finger at him in warning.

We both raise our cups in a silent toast and toss back the Scotch. Gregory laughs.

"What's so funny? Huh?" I dab at the corners of my lips with a napkin.

"You shouldn't keep serving liquor if you want me to paint a flattering portrait of you."

*"Vero!"* I laugh.

The Scotch seems to have emboldened Gregory as he clears his throat and says, "I have a favor to ask you, and please, don't hesitate to tell me if you can't do it. You've already done so much for my family. I'm still so honored that you chose me to paint your portrait."

"Enough with the flattery, Gregory. Tell me what I can do for you."

"I have a friend." He pauses as he clears his throat once more.

Hmmm. A friend. No doubt, a woman.

"She's been through a lot the past few years, and she's working hard to make something of herself."

Gregory is trying to make me pity her. He is good, I must say. He looks imploringly at me. I nod my head, encouraging him to continue.

"Anyway, she's interning at *Profile* magazine, and I was wondering if you would grant her an interview? This is the break that could make her career. But again, if you feel strongly against doing it, I will respect your wishes."

*"Profile?"*

"Yes, I'm sure you've heard of them."

"Of course."

Gregory continues pleading the young woman's case and telling me how talented she is, but I have already turned a deaf ear toward him. *Profile.* Why does this sound familiar?

I interrupt Gregory. "What is her name?"

"Pia Santore."

Wait! It is that girl! The one who approached me at the jewelry store the other day. Well, well. At least Gregory has good taste in women. She was very pretty, and I was impressed by her bravado in approaching me. Suddenly, I also remember how harsh I was with her. For a moment, shame fills my heart, but I quickly shrug it off. As I told Edgardo, the girl needs to toughen up if she hopes to succeed. I decide not to tell Gregory of our encounter.

"So, will you let her interview you?" Gregory resembles the newborn puppy I rescued outside of my villa in Sicily. His eyes are extra wide, and worry lines are slashed deeply across his forehead. But even his charm and good looks are not enough to sway me.

"I am sorry, Gregory, but I am afraid I cannot grant her the interview."

Immediately, his expression becomes crestfallen. I do hate seeing him unhappy. Such a handsome young man should always be smiling. But I must remain firm.

"May I ask why?"

"You said she is an intern at the magazine, correct?"

"Yes."

"Gregory, how can I let an inexperienced journalist interview me? What would that say to the world? That would seal my career."

"Career?"

I shoot Gregory a dirty look, knowing what he is thinking.

"I'm sorry, Francesca. No disrespect, but I thought you retired from acting over a decade ago."

"I did, but I have my reputation to uphold."

"So, you still care what the public thinks about you even after all these years?"

Remaining silent, I take a long sip of my Scotch.

"Is that the only reason? Her inexperience?"

"Well, of course. What other reason would there be?"

"You tell me." Gregory stares at me. His unease from earlier is gone. He is challenging me. I am touched at what he will do to impress this girl. He must really like her.

"You've never been in *Profile* magazine." He breaks the stony silence.

"That is because they came out shortly before I retired. All the other major magazines have done interviews with me."

"This would be your chance to be in *Profile*. You said you still care what the public thinks about you."

"I never said that."

"Francesca, you've been very candid with me today. Why stop now? Anyway, if you agreed to this interview, this would show the media you're still significant."

"I *am* still significant!" My voice rises.

"I'm sorry. I didn't mean it that way. This was a bad idea. I shouldn't have asked you. As I said before, I will respect your wishes since you obviously do not want to do the interview."

Gregory gets up and begins packing his art supplies. "If you don't mind, I'd like to end our session now. I need to get some fresh air and run a few errands."

"You are upset, Gregory."

"No, no."

"Who is not being candid, now?" I smirk as I say this.

"You got me. But I'm not upset with you, Signorina Donata. You have every right to deny an interview. I just feel bad for Pia. She's had to delay by a few years getting her career started, and this would've really gotten her on the right track."

"What happened to her? You said earlier she has been through a lot."

"I wouldn't feel right breaking her confidence."

"I see." For some reason, this angers me. Or is it that I am jealous of his fierce protection of and admiration for this special woman? When was the last time someone felt that way toward me?

"It's okay, Francesca. Let's just forget I ever brought this up." He finishes packing his art supplies and begins to walk away.

"Wait, Gregory. I will grant her the interview."

He freezes and turns around.

"You will?" His voice comes out in a hushed whisper.

"Under certain conditions."

"Sure. Sure. That won't be a problem."

"Wait until you explain the conditions to Pia and she agrees to them before you say they won't be a problem for her."

"Fair enough. What are the conditions?"

"You had better write them all down or else you will forget."

Gregory looks at me a little uncertainly, but just nods his head as he fishes a pen out of his messenger bag.

*We will see what this girl is made of after her first interview with me,* I think to myself as I begin reciting to Gregory my long list of rules.

# ~ 13 ~

# Pia

1. *I must approve and vet ALL interview questions.*

2. *I must see the first draft of the interview before it is published.*

3. *No questions about my previous engagements or fiancés may be asked.*

4. *No questions about my movies that did not do well may be asked.*

5. *No questions about my family may be asked.*

6. *In the article, I must not be referred to in any way that implies I am old or that my career is over.*

7. *I must approve all photos that are to be used in the article.*

8. *Miss Santore MUST show the utmost respect toward me at all times.*

9. *Miss Santore MUST address me ONLY as "Signorina Donata." She is NEVER to use my Christian name.*

10. *Miss Santore MUST arrive ten minutes before the actual start time of our interview.*

11. *Miss Santore should not make any attempt to become my friend. This is a business transaction and nothing more.*

12. *Miss Santore MUST refrain from asking me for autographs or photographs. Every photo taken will be of me alone.*

13. *I reserve the right to end the interview when I believe it should be over.*

14. *The interview will be at seven a.m. sharp on Saturday here at my sister's home. That is the only day and time I can meet for this interview so no requests to reschedule may be made.*

15. *If any of these conditions are not met, the interview is off.*

"**S**he's a witch!" I fling Francesca's list of conditions in the air, letting the paper fall on the floor of Zia's bakery. Gregory is sitting across from me staring into his huge mug of cappuccino. He bends over and retrieves the paper, but dares not place it in front of me.

"Pia—"

"Don't defend her to me again! Don't!" I hold up my hand. A few of the bakery's patrons at the other tables look over toward me.

Gregory places his hand on my knee.

"I wasn't going to defend her. I agree the list is a bit much, but she's testing you."

"A bit much? It's so over the top! She's going to make this interview totally unbearable for me. I just know it." Crossing my arms over my chest, I heave out a long sigh.

"Pia, you can do this. Show her you're as tough as she is. That's what she wants to see. She values strength in character. Earn her respect, and you'll win her over."

"Why should I be bending over backwards to kiss her ass? Oh, wait, don't answer that. It's because she's silver-screen royalty. That allows her to treat the rest of us peons like dirt."

"I bet if you were to interview any other huge celebrity, his or her conditions wouldn't be that much different. Francesca isn't the only star guilty of acting like a diva."

I glance at the list of conditions. The one rule that irks me the most is her choosing when to end the interview. I'm the journalist, *not* her. And her assuming that I'd want to befriend her is ludicrous. You'd have to be certifiable to want to be friends with the likes of her.

"She isn't even giving me much time to prep for the interview. Saturday is only two days away. I only have one day to go over the questions with Colin and fax them to Francesca before we meet."

"You can do it. I have faith in you."

The tender expression in Gregory's eyes comforts me, making me regret my outburst. What's the matter with me? He's gone out of his way to get me this interview, and after seeing Francesca's list, I'm sure now she didn't make it easy for him either.

"I'm sorry. I'm acting as badly as Francesca with my temper tantrum." I place my hand on Gregory's arm, squeezing it lightly.

"No need to apologize. I knew you would lose it a little after seeing her conditions." Gregory laughs.

"I'm sure this meeting will be interesting. Maybe I can use it someday to write a fictionalized tell-all novel à la *The Devil Wears Prada*!" Now I'm also laughing.

"That's the spirit! Exploit every possible angle with this interview." Gregory holds up his thumb in approval.

"She'd probably get into a catfight with me just like in that hysterical scene of hers from *Dolci Labbra* in which she beats up the woman she's caught kissing her lover. They actually had her throwing fists at the woman. It looked so fake!"

"I've never seen that movie of hers, but I can imagine how outrageously funny that must've been!" Gregory wipes tears from his eyes. He can't stop laughing.

"I guess I can't ask her about that Oscar-winning scene since *Dolci Labbra* did horribly at the box office, and according to rule number four, I'm not allowed to ask about her flops."

"Let's treat ourselves to Antoniella's almond hazelnut biscotti. I can't believe we're just having cappuccino."

Gregory begins to wave to one of the waiters, but I quickly get up.

"I'll get them. We shouldn't be treated any differently because I'm Antoniella's niece. Unlike Francesca, I don't treat others like my slaves."

"No, you don't." Gregory raises his mug to me in salute. He thinks I've already looked away, but I see his gaze shift to my butt.

Since our first date, we've talked every night on the phone. He's taking me out on Saturday night and Sunday afternoon. Again, he's planning a surprise. Gregory wanted to take me out on Friday night, but once I found out that Francesca would be granting the interview, I needed that evening to prepare. My blood starts to boil again when I think about her requirements. But Gregory's right. I have to do whatever it takes.

I place four of Zia's almond hazelnut biscotti on my plate. Two are dipped in chocolate. They're the perfect accompaniment to coffee, espresso, or cappuccino, especially when you dunk the biscotti! My mom used to also make these. But I have to secretly admit, Zia's are better, which I guess is no surprise since she owns a bakery and has had more practice at baking than my mom has. My mouth waters as I anticipate biting into the sweet, crunchy biscotti.

"Only four? I can eat four all by myself!" Gregory pouts.

"You'll ruin your six-pack if you do."

"You've noticed?" Gregory is beaming from ear to ear.

I can't believe I've already broken my rule of withholding compliments from a guy on his appearance until you're in a commitment. Gregory is making me break every one of my dating rules!

Shrugging my shoulders in answer to his question, I take a bite out of a chocolate-dipped biscotti and simply say, "Maybe."

"Hey. If you want to run any of your interview questions by me tomorrow night, feel free to call. I'll just be home painting."

"Thanks, but Francesca's not the only control freak. Remember Colin said he's going to come up with most of the questions? He's letting me come up with a few of my own. I can't wait to see his reaction when I show him Francesca's conditions and how she's limiting what we can ask her."

"I'm sure you'll both be able to come up with some great questions."

A thought suddenly occurs to me.

"You know, for someone as clever as Francesca, I can't believe she forgot to list that I can't ask her about all of her notorious nicknames!"

"You wouldn't!" Gregory smirks.

"Why not? Is she the only one who gets to have a little fun?"

"You're bad, Pia! But please! Don't do it. Remember what she said? She can end the interview anytime she wants. And she expressly stated that you need to treat her with the utmost respect. Don't blow this opportunity, Pia."

Gregory's smirk has completely faded, and his eyes are pleading with me.

"Relax. I have class, more than Francesca, and I would never be cruel just for its own sake, as she's known to be. I'll find a way to ask about the nicknames so that she doesn't sense I'm giving her a taste of her own medicine." I giggle. "*That's* exactly what she needs."

My heart is pounding loudly as I walk up the block toward the Mussolini Mansion. I need to get my nerves under control before I come face-to-face with Francesca. I refuse to let her see me rattled.

I took great care last night in choosing my clothes. I'm wearing black trousers with a white button-down mandarin-collar shirt à la Diane Sawyer. By dressing in the fashion of my journalism idol, who normally wears neutral colors and mandarin-collar blouses and jackets, I'm hoping some of her talent will rub off on me during my interview. Though I hate wearing super-high heels since they just make me look like a giraffe, I decided to purchase a pair of four-inch Via Spiga peep-toe sling-back pumps in black patent leather. Maybe my now towering frame will intimidate Francesca. Of course, I don't seriously believe that for one second.

Zia Antoniella insisted I borrow her vintage Gucci black patent Kelly handbag since it matches my pumps. She also thought it would help to show Francesca that I, too, have good fashion taste. The purse is in mint condition even though it's from the late sixties, and it sports a beautiful bamboo handle. I love it. Zia bought it before she departed for America.

The paparazzi and the usual crowd of spectators are camped out in front of the Mussolini Mansion. Getting past them without being mobbed is going to be a challenge. The paparazzi have their backs turned toward the house as they sip on their morning coffee and smoke their cigarettes. The neighbors are gossiping among themselves as usual. I unlatch the front gate, hoping by some miracle I can make it up to the front door without being noticed, but of course, there's no such luck. I've barely pushed open the gate when Olivia DeLuca gives me away.

"Pia! Where are you going?"

Everyone, including the paparazzi, turns in my direction.

Deciding that lying is my best recourse at the moment, I say, "I'm here to see Signora Tesca."

"Signora Tesca?" Olivia frowns.

"Yes, if you'll please excuse me, I'm going to be late."

"You're here to see Francesca, aren't you?" a short, bald paparazzo asks me as he quickly walks over and then snaps my photo.

"Please, don't take any more photos of me."

Ignoring my request, he takes another as do the other paparazzi.

"What's your relation to the sisters?" a female paparazzo asks me. She's the only woman among them.

Instead of answering her question, I quickly run up the stairs. Out of my peripheral vision, I see Olivia is staring at me intently, still trying to guess why I'm seeing Signora Tesca. Ciggy waddles over to her with his huge beer belly and puffs smoke in her face as he whispers something to her. Olivia nods her head, and then they both look in my direction.

Thankfully, one of Signora Tesca's staff answers the door after just one ring of the bell.

"Miss Santore, I presume?"

"Yes, I have an appointment with Francesca Donata," I whisper, hoping my voice is low enough so that the paparazzi and the neighbors don't hear me.

"Right this way, Miss Santore. We've been expecting you."

The butler—I feel ridiculous saying that in this day and age, but don't know what else to call him—sounds just like you'd imagine one would sound like. He's an older man, probably in his late sixties, but is groomed impeccably from the perfectly combed-back gray hair to the just-pressed navy suit he's wearing. At least he isn't decked out in one of those ridiculous butler uniforms.

He leads me up a long, spiral staircase. Taking in Signora Tesca's home, I can't help noting that it definitely looks like a rich person lives here. But the décor seems dated as I glimpse the plastic-covered Queen Anne furniture in the library we've just passed. Monte di

Capo vases line the foyer and the base of the staircase. Oil portraits hang on the walls. The floors are all hardwood and are buffed to a high shine. We walk down a long corridor toward a room with a slightly open door. Sunlight is streaming through.

The butler lets me enter first. My heart begins racing again as I anticipate seeing Francesca in the room, but she's nowhere to be seen.

"Signorina Donata will be with you shortly. Please take a seat. I'll bring up espresso shortly."

"Thank you. I'm sorry, but I didn't get your name."

"Carlo." He bows slightly before he leaves. I can't help but feel like royalty.

I pace around the large sitting room and notice it adjoins another room. Beautiful French doors are at one end of the space. Surprisingly, the furniture here isn't covered in plastic, which is odd since it's an eggshell color. I would think Signora Tesca would be more concerned about soiling this furniture with its light shade. Unlike the hallways and what I could make out of the library downstairs, this room emits a lot of light with the paler shades of furniture, the lemon-colored walls, and the natural sunlight streaming in from the French doors.

A black-and-white photograph catches my attention. The photo is the only one present and rests on one of the end tables near the settee. I walk over and pick up the frame. Two teenage girls are sitting on a boulder. Their backs are turned toward the beach in the background. It's a stunning photo, since the photographer captured the image just as a huge wave was crashing against the shore. The girls have their arms around each other's waists and are laughing. They're both wearing halter dresses with full skirts that are billowing out against the ocean's breezes. One of the girls is unmistakably Francesca. Though she was quite young in the photo—no more than fourteen—her trademark beauty was already evident. Her face still possessed the innocence of youth. The haughtiness that I've often seen in her photos as well as the day I met her in the jewelry store is missing from her expression. But her eyes hold a hint of allure. She knew even then that she was beautiful.

The girl next to her is pretty. Unlike Francesca, her eyes hold no suggestive glance. She's just smiling from ear to ear. Tears fill my eyes as I think of numerous similarly posed photos of Erica and me. But I haven't been able to bring myself to look at them since Erica died. My father had compiled a few photos of Erica for her wake. As they flashed on the flat-screen TV at the funeral home, I had to look away. Seeing Erica when she was in the prime of her youth in those photos was too much.

"Good morning."

I'm startled by a woman's voice and look up. Francesca! My stomach immediately coils into knots. Placing the photo frame back on the end table, I walk over to Francesca and extend my hand.

"Good morning, Signor—ina Donata." Whew! I almost blew that again.

Francesca barely grazes my hand with hers in what has to be the weakest handshake I've ever experienced.

"Please sit down. Make yourself comfortable, although I see you already have in a sense." She glances toward the photo that I had been inspecting.

"I'm sorry. I couldn't help noticing the photo. Is that you and Signora Tesca?"

Francesca pauses as if she's wondering if she should answer my question. Then I remember her rule of my not asking about her family. I'm about to apologize again, but then she answers, "Yes."

Another awkward moment of silence elapses, but then I'm saved by Carlo, who wheels in a cart with a huge, silver tray that is covered. Just like the movies, I can't help thinking. Now I'm wishing that Carlo was attired in the stereotypical butler's uniform. It would complete this bizarre scene.

Carlo quickly sets up our espresso cups and then places a large platter of assorted *biscotti* and *sfogliatelle* on the coffee table in front of us. Does Francesca eat *biscotti* and the flaky pastry that's filled with ricotta cheese every morning for breakfast? If so, how does she manage to keep that figure of hers in her fifties? I can't imagine her being a slave to working out. She probably can't tolerate even a bead of perspiration.

"Is this fine? Or would you rather sit at the table?" Francesca tilts her head in the direction of a small, round table in the corner of the room.

"No, this is fine. Thank you." I'm actually surprised she's consulted me.

"I thought we would be more comfortable here."

I nod my head. Trying to act nonchalant, I take a sip of my espresso, which is strong. Even with the milk I've added to it, I can taste the pungent bitterness. If I don't want my nerves to be completely shot, I'll have to avoid drinking it. My stomach growls loudly.

"I'm sorry." Mortified is an understatement. Here I am, sitting across from silver-screen goddess Francesca Donata, who looks as good as she does on the magazine covers she's graced over the years, and my stomach has to grumble.

Francesca actually looks a bit embarrassed for me, but I know my eyes must be failing. She picks up a *sfogliatella* and softly bites into it. Even the way she eats is done with the utmost grace and flair. I'm too terrified to eat even though my stomach lets out another wail.

"Please, help yourself. Or do you not like *biscotti* and *sfogliatelle?*"

I can't help but laugh. "My aunt would murder me if I hated Italian desserts or anything Italian for that matter."

I pick up one of the Regina *biscotti* that are also on the platter and try to nibble on it delicately as Francesca had, but the sesame seeds that are sprinkled generously all over the cookie fall onto my lap along with an avalanche of crumbs. A few land on the cream-colored settee. Of course, Francesca is watching me and doesn't so much as blink when she notices that I'm made uncomfortable by her staring. I pick up the crumbs as best I can.

"Leave them. Carlo or Angelica will clean them up."

"I'm sorry."

"While I appreciate your manners, Miss Santore, you apologize too much. It is quite unbecoming of you." Francesca takes a sip of her espresso, never lifting her intense gaze off me.

I'm stunned by her brutal candor, but I don't know what to say, so I remain silent.

"Why would your aunt murder you if you did not like Italian sweets?"

"She owns a bakery on Ditmars—Antoniella's Bakery. Ever

since I arrived here, she's been feeding me nothing but *biscotti* and pastries."

"Is this the aunt you mentioned the other day when we met in the jewelry store, the aunt who knows my sister?"

"Yes." I'm silently praying she doesn't mention anything else about that disastrous meeting.

Her face grows somber for a moment.

"Maybe your aunt can come over for a visit the next time we meet. I have not met any of Giuliana's friends, and she could . . ." Her voice trails off. She shrugs her shoulder and continues, "Anyway, we will see how this first interview goes."

Strange. She's just pulled a Jekyll-and-Hyde on me. Still reeling from shock over her inviting my aunt, even if she reneged on her invitation a moment later, I nod my head and say, "I want you to be happy with this interview."

She starcs at me and says, "Naturally, I must be happy with it or else the interview will never make it to press."

The knot in my stomach twists even more.

"Gregory thinks highly of you." She's on her second *sfogliatella* now.

"I think highly of him, too."

"Do you?" Francesca asks in a somewhat incredulous tone.

"Yes. I have him to thank after all for getting me this interview. That was very kind of him, especially since he and I haven't known each other long."

"So, is that the only reason you think highly of Gregory? Because he was able to help you?"

"Oh no! Of course not. I can tell he's a good person."

Francesca's lips slightly curl upward so that she has an amused smile.

"I assume he gave you my list of conditions?" She gets up and walks over to a small escritoire desk. Pulling open one of the drawers, she takes out a legal pad and returns to the settee.

"Just in case you forget any of the conditions." She holds up the pad.

I can't believe she's keeping them handy. My blood, which has already been simmering, is rapidly approaching its boiling point. I take another sip of espresso so she doesn't see my scowl.

"Why don't we begin?" Francesca glances at her diamond-studded wristwatch.

She's actually going to time the interview! But why am I surprised? So far, her behavior is *precisely* what I expected. I'm trying to keep an open mind and not judge her like Gregory asked. But it's becoming increasingly difficult.

Opening Zia's Gucci purse, I take out my little notebook and pen. Francesca is staring at the purse with much interest.

"A knockoff, I see."

"Excuse me?" I'm not sure what she's referring to.

"Your purse. That is quite a good knockoff." The amused smile reappears. I want to slap it right off her smug face.

"This isn't a knockoff."

"I guess it is my turn to apologize now. It is just that Gregory mentioned to me you are an intern at *Profile,* and I cannot imagine how you would be able to afford a Gucci, no less a vintage one like that. I have not seen that style of purse since shortly after I started making movies. But I should not presume. Your family has money?"

"No, they do not. But you are right. The purse is vintage. It's actually my aunt's."

"The one who owns the bakery?"

"Yes."

I'm feeling embarrassed and angry as hell that I'm letting this prima donna bitch make me feel ashamed. I suddenly realize this is what she wants—to show me she's in control. Remembering my earlier resolve to stand toe-to-toe with her, I clear my throat and begin the interview.

"Please tell me which city and country you were born in?"

"Messina, Sicilia." She pronounces "Sicily" in Italian.

"At what age did you become interested in wanting to be an actress?"

The first ten questions sound like I'm taking a census survey. Though I'm following her conditions so far, I intend on sneaking in a few provocative questions. She's not the only cunning manipulator. By asking her the questions she's vetted in the beginning of our interview, I'm lowering her guard. After half an hour, I'm ready to test the waters.

"How did it make you feel to be a sex symbol?"

"I was flattered, of course, but I was more than a sex symbol. My awards attest to that."

"Yes, but you must admit, 'sex symbol' has always been attached to your name whenever the media talks about you. Did it ever bother you that more attention was placed on your physical attributes than your talents?"

Francesca's nostrils flare slightly. Obviously, I've hit a nerve. But she manages to quell any eruption that's threatening to surface.

"No, it never bothered me because my acting was also appreciated."

"Surely, it must have bothered you. After all, you detested the nickname you were dubbed with—*'Dolci Labbra'*—which was also the title of your fourth film release."

"I never said I hated that name. Where are you getting your information from?" Francesca's voice rises slightly.

"There's an interview you gave to Italian *Vogue* in which you admitted not only hating the nickname the media had christened you with, but also the movie's title because it sounded like a pornographic film. I'm surprised you don't remember this article since it created quite a stir in the media."

Francesca looks absolutely livid now. Her face is ashen.

"I stand corrected. Your research is quite thorough. I am just surprised that you would have gone that far back. That interview was done in the seventies. I almost forgot about it, and I never forget anything."

"So the name 'Sweet Lips' or *'Dolci Labbra'* was a thorn in your side?"

"A little. But can you blame me? I am a serious actress, not a porn star."

"So you still consider yourself an actress even though you retired from acting a decade ago?"

"I will *always* be an actress."

"Do you think you will ever act again?"

"I do not like to say never, but I doubt it. That part of my life is over."

"So how can you say you 'will always be an actress'?"

"It is part of my fiber. I cannot think of myself as anything else."

"So you have no other interests is what you're saying?"

"That is not what I am saying. Do not twist my words, Miss Santore."

Deciding I'm getting into dangerous waters, I shift gears.

"Clearly, you still have a passion for acting. A few critics have said that you still had a few good movies left in you when you retired."

"Really? They said that?"

"Yes, at least here in the U.S."

"Ahhh! America has always been good to me. Italy just wants to remember the Francesca Donata from decades ago."

"What does that mean?"

Francesca waves her hand in the air. "It is not important."

Just when I feel she's starting to open up, she clams back up.

"Were you not being offered the right roles?"

Recognition reaches her eyes. That's it. She was probably being offered more matronly roles, and her ego couldn't stand it even though she also didn't like all the attention that was placed on her sex-symbol status. Francesca is a contradiction.

"I was merely ready to retire. After acting for so many years, it was time I took a rest."

"You've rested for ten years. And now your visit to the U.S. has placed you in the spotlight again. Do you think there's even a slight chance you'll consider another role? That is, if you were offered one?"

Francesca's brows knit together as she stares at me through squinted eyes.

"I am always offered roles."

"Really? Even in this past decade that you've been out of the limelight?"

"Yes. Why do you sound so surprised?"

I mentally chuckle to myself. Who's in control now?

"It's just that I thought if you were offered roles at the start of your retirement and you kept refusing them, the knocks on your door would've inevitably stopped."

"Trust me, Miss Santore, they are still knocking."

"Which was your favorite film?"

"I think we're done for today." Francesca looks at her watch.

"Does this mean you'll continue with another appointment? We haven't even covered a quarter of the questions."

Francesca waits a few seconds before replying, "I am not sure. To be quite frank, Miss Santore, I do not appreciate some of the questions you asked me today. And more important, they were *not* on the list of questions that I approved."

"I apologize."

Francesca holds up her hand, imploring me to stop. For someone who can be such a bitch, she really hates it when people apologize to her.

"Why do you hate it so much when I apologize? Do you forbid your staff to apologize to you?"

"Of course I do not *forbid* my staff to apologize to me. If their actions warrant an apology, they should apologize. I just cannot stand to see a young woman like you so insecure. Trust me, you will get nowhere in your career or life if you play the good-girl part and apologize for everything."

She's managed to stun me once again. So this is how she sees me—lacking confidence and playing the good-girl role. I'm probably about to ruin my chances of receiving an invitation for a second interview, but I don't care.

"Miss Donata, as you stated earlier, you should not assume. You know nothing about me. You asked that I treat you with the utmost respect, but you have been condescending toward me since I first met you in Castello Jewelry. If you will excuse me, I will show myself out."

And with that I storm out of there.

## ～ 14 ～

# Francesca

"How did your interview go?" Giuliana is propped up with four pillows in her bed. This is the first chance she has had to ask me about my meeting with Pia Santore. She did not feel well yesterday and slept for most of the day.

"Eh." I shrug my shoulders. "Fine."

"You said the girl is Antoniella's niece?" Giuliana barely gets the words out before she starts coughing.

"Here, drink this." I offer her our favorite childhood drink, *orzata,* which is a combination of seltzer water and almond syrup.

"I can't believe you still drink these. *Grazie.*"

Giuliana is smiling, a sight I have not seen much since I have come here. Actually, she has not smiled much since her husband died all those years ago.

"And I cannot believe you ever stopped! You were even crazier about *orzata* than I was when we were growing up. Do you remember what you asked our father?"

"Of course. 'Baba, why can't you grow almond trees so we can make our own *orzata?*' " Giuliana starts laughing silently to herself.

"*Si, si.* I remember how expensive it used to be—well, at least for us." I shake my head at the memory.

"I remember when you first made it as an actress and you sent me five cases of *orzata*. Mama and I were astonished when we figured out how much the cases cost you."

"You remember that?"

"I remember everything, Francesca." Giuliana laughs, but then she notices my staid expression. Our eyes meet, and she quickly averts her gaze.

"So where were we? Oh, yes, Antoniella's niece, the girl who interviewed you. What is she like?"

"She is like any other young woman in her twenties—insecure, naïve, a dreamer."

"Like any other young woman in her twenties or like you?" Giuliana sips her *orzata,* but continues scrutinizing me.

"I see your candidness is still intact, Giuliana."

"It runs in our family. You can be just as blunt."

"I guess she does remind me a little of myself but more before I was discovered."

"Naturally."

Giuliana is done with her *orzata*. I see her staring longingly at the almond syrup bottle. I get up and make her another drink.

"She does have courage. I gave her a list of conditions that were to be met for the interview, one of which was that I had to vet all of the questions. But she still decided toward the end of our appointment to ask her own questions. And I am almost convinced she was intentionally trying to upset me."

"You've always been overly sensitive and paranoid, Francesca. Why would she sabotage herself that way? You mentioned she is still trying to make her mark as a journalist."

"Well, like me, I think she has a bit of a temper beneath that seemingly sweet exterior, and I think she got frustrated that I was making it hard on her."

"Of course, you were making it hard on her. That has always been something I never understood about you, Francesca. Why are you so intent on only showing this prima donna side of yourself? It has often cast you in a poor light."

"I make no apologies for who I am."

I get up and pace the room, not happy with where this conversation is going.

"There is more to you. We both know that."

I am surprised and touched by Giuliana's words. Has she perhaps finally stopped punishing me?

"How can you be so sure that the girl you once knew has not vanished completely? You of all people have witnessed the worst of me."

*"Vero, vero."*

Giuliana nods her head and looks down at her clasped hands in her lap. She finishes the second glass of *orzata* just as fast as the first one. From now on, I am going to make *orzatas* for her every day. It is a small pleasure, and Lord knows she has so few of those these days. I begin searching my mind, thinking of other ways I can make her happy.

"Giuliana, I was thinking we should go out. Get some fresh air. It would do you good."

"Ha! With that herd out there following us? That's not wise."

"I can ask Edgardo to make arrangements so that he and my other bodyguards can sneak us out of here. No one followed us the day I visited the jewelry shops on Ditmars."

"How did that go? You never did tell me. I also have not seen more gifts arrive. Perhaps word did get out that you were investigating and you scared off your secret admirer."

Giuliana looks amused.

"Perhaps."

Giuliana is right. No other gifts have arrived since the last one. It is for the better. I do not need a deranged stalker. *Stupida!* I silently scold myself. To think I thought there was a man who might be infatuated with me. I am in my mid-fifties, past the prime of my life. I must accept I am no longer the young woman whom every man desires.

"Francesca, if you would please excuse me, I need to take a nap. My medication makes me so drowsy."

"Certainly. Let me lower your pillows."

Giuliana has given up on resisting my help. Part of me hopes that her stubbornness is finally dissipating, but I also suspect she is getting weaker and welcomes the assistance.

"I will ask Edgardo to make plans for us to get away."

Giuliana opens her mouth to protest, but I quickly cut her off.

"Ah! I insist, so don't argue with me. *Basta!*"

"I see you still forget, Francesca, that I am the older sister. You are calling the shots as usual."

I have become accustomed to Giuliana's sarcastic comments. Though they still hurt, I am beginning to realize that sometimes she is merely trying to be humorous. With each day, I feel her slowly warming up to me again. And I pray fervently that she will forgive me if she has not already. That is all I have ever wanted—her forgiveness. But I dare not enter that discussion just yet. The time is not right.

Before walking out of Giuliana's bedroom, I shut the blinds. As I close her door, I hear the doorbell ringing. I make my way downstairs to the foyer and soon hear voices by the front door.

"I will make sure Signorina Donata receives these, but I am sorry. You cannot come in."

Angelica's voice sounds alarmed as usual. I am surprised that girl has not had a nervous breakdown yet in her life. She is so timid and anxious.

"Please. Let her know that Rocco Vecchio is waiting for her. I am the owner of Castello Jewelry."

My ears prick up. Perhaps he is here to tell me he knows who has been sending me the gifts.

I begin walking over, but stop as soon as I see what Angelica is cradling in her left arm—three bouquets of a dozen long-stemmed tea roses, my favorite flowers. The roses obscure Rocco's face. I notice in Angelica's right hand she holds three small gifts. The boxes look like jewelry boxes. They are stacked one on top of the other and are tied together with a beautiful pink ribbon. I take another look at the boxes and notice they are royal-blue velvet boxes—just like all the others I've received. My brain begins adding it all up. Could Rocco be my secret admirer?

"Angelica, it is all right. I will see Mr. Vecchio."

Angelica looks like she's seen a ghost when she turns around.

"Signorina Donata. I am so sorry. I tried telling Mr. Vecchio that you were not available."

"Don't worry, Angelica. I will see him." Rocco Vecchio looks pleased. "It is nice to see you again, Mr. Vecchio."

I extend my hand, and Rocco draws it to his lips, placing a light kiss on the back of my hand. Taking in Rocco's appearance, I realize he looks different than he did on the day I was in his shop. I must have been too enamored of the exquisite jewelry to have noticed he is a very handsome man. He looks to be in his fifties and is in tremendous physical shape, as the long-sleeved, form-fitted polo shirt he wears demonstrates. The three buttons in his shirt are unbuttoned, revealing tanned skin. His hair is mostly gray with a few traces of black peeking through. He is dressed all in black.

"Signorina Donata, I am sorry to drop in on you unexpectedly. But I did not have a phone number to call ahead."

I nod my head, waiting for him to continue. Angelica is staring at us.

"You may go now, Angelica."

"These are for you."

Rocco steps forward and takes from Angelica the roses and wrapped boxes.

"I'm sorry, Signorina Donata. I meant to give these to you." Angelica's earlier flustered state has returned.

"Angelica, please bring us a few refreshments. Espresso, Mr. Vecchio, or perhaps you would like something stronger—sambuca, whiskey?"

"Espresso is fine, thank you."

Angelica nods her head and quickly scampers away.

"Please come in, Mr. Vecchio."

I turn my back on Rocco as I lead him toward the library. Placing one foot carefully in front of the other, I do my catwalk, sashaying my hips so that they swing violently from east to west. Naturally, I feel Rocco's eyes on me as they follow the length of my body from my head down to my derrière and on to my legs. A sharp twinge of pain shoots up my spine. My aging body is no longer accustomed to walking so provocatively, but I continue the strut. I cannot help but feel like a newly crowned beauty queen with my bouquets and gifts.

Placing the roses on the grand piano, I reach for the Waterford vase that sits on one of Giuliana's bookshelves.

"Please, make yourself comfortable, Mr. Vecchio, while I fill this vase with water for your gorgeous roses. Tea roses are my favorite. But you knew that already, of course."

I flash my most seductive smile at Mr. Vecchio. He smiles slightly, but does not meet my gaze.

"I make it my job to know *everything* about a woman I admire."

I remain silent. Usually, I am a master at repartee, but he has managed to leave me speechless.

As I walk back toward the foyer, I feel his eyes on me once again. Suddenly, I realize I am no longer sashaying, but it is too late to transform my gait. Keeping my posture as erect as possible, I do my best to act nonchalantly while I exit the library.

Angelica almost crashes into me with the tray of espresso.

"*Mi scusi,* Signorina Donata!"

"Angelica! How many times do I need to remind you to calm down? Stop hurrying all over the place. You almost spilled all of that espresso onto my ivory dress," I whisper sternly to Angelica.

"I'm sorry. I did not want to keep you and Mr. Vecchio waiting long."

Angelica's eyes fill with tears. I am surprised this is the first time I have seen her come close to crying. Usually, she bears the brunt of my reprimands staunchly. Well, other than her extreme agitation.

"*Grazie,* Angelica. I will take the tray. Just please fill this vase with water. I forgot to take the roses to trim them. They are on the piano. Take them with you to the kitchen and trim them for me. And please do not return to the library until *after* Mr. Vecchio leaves. I need to talk privately with him."

Angelica's brows rise at this last bit of information, but she knows better than to inquire. I can tell she is like most other household staff—nosy. But she is too smart, or rather afraid, to overstep her boundaries by asking personal questions.

"Thank you, Signorina Donata. I will make the roses look beautiful."

I smile. "I am sure you will."

My reassuring words do the trick, as Angelica appears relieved that she has averted one of my full-blown tirades. She walks hurriedly away until I call out to her.

"Angelica! Slow down! Remember what I said."

"*Si, si, signora.*"

Angelica slows her pace, but I can tell it takes much effort to keep from running. She nods toward Rocco as she enters the library to retrieve the roses and then scrambles away. She cannot help herself. Everything she does is fast. It goes with her anxious nature. I decide to ignore her error in calling me "*signora*." I have more important matters to attend to.

"*Ecco!* Here is the espresso. Do you speak Italian, Mr. Vecchio?"

"Please, call me Rocco."

"I am sorry, but I cannot do that. I hardly know you."

Pouring espresso into our cups, I notice that Mr. Vecchio looks disappointed by my refusal to call him by his Christian name.

"That is true. I hope you do not mind if I call you 'Francesca'?"

I wait before answering. A confident woman *never* immediately gives a man what he is asking for, even when it is a mere answer to a question. He taps his foot lightly on the floor.

"Well, I suppose *you* may call me 'Francesca' since it seems you already know me quite well?" I shoot a mischievous grin in his direction.

"Only what I have read about, and of course, I cannot trust what has been written about you to be the entire truth." He meets my stare dead-on.

"You are a wise man, Mr. Vecchio."

"I take it my gifts have been to your satisfaction, Francesca."

I am a bit surprised he has decided to acknowledge so soon that he is my secret admirer. But I can tell Rocco is no fool, and he has chosen not to waste any more time by playing games. I like that. Of course, I will not reveal this to him.

"They were beautiful. Thank you. My love for jewelry is not a secret to the world."

"A woman who does not appreciate fine jewelry is not a real woman—at least in my eyes."

Hmmm. He is a traditional man. I remain silent, sipping my espresso, and keeping my expression unreadable.

"So tell me, Francesca, which was your favorite piece?"

Rocco leans forward so that he is sitting at the edge of the settee. I chose to sit in the chair opposite the settee, but I've stretched out my legs, which are crossed, as far toward him as possible. Naturally, Rocco cannot resist staring at them.

"What makes you so certain any of them were my favorite?" I cock my eyebrow.

"Ha! You are just as I imagined you would be." Rocco laughs, which irritates me along with his comment.

"And how is that, Mr. Vecchio?" Placing my cup down on the coffee table, I cross my arms across my chest. Rocco picks up on my defensive stance and suddenly looks worried.

"Strong. Confident. Dazzling."

He leans back on the settee, and now he crosses his arms across his chest. He is smiling in the most devilish way, which only makes him more appealing. *Disgraziato!* I mentally curse him. He is not only handsome and charming, but also very cunning. Rocco is ready for the fight if I give him one. I have never met a man who could match me. Then again, I am only beginning. As I am about to tell him I must go, he stands up and suddenly excuses himself, beating me at my own game.

"Please forgive me, but I have another appointment."

I have angered him.

"But I have not even opened your gifts."

"I am sure you will love them. Of course, if you don't like them, or even the earlier pieces you received, Castello Jewelry has a return policy—now that you know where they came from, *signorina.*"

Rocco's emphasis on *"signorina"* is unmistakable. He is smirking and does not even attempt to hide it. My pulse is absolutely racing with fury. He is taking pleasure out of this all. I will not let him win.

"Thank you, Mr. Vecchio. That is most kind of you. Yes, there were a couple of pieces that really did not suit my tastes. I would not want them to sit in my drawer when another woman could be enjoying them."

Rocco looks crestfallen. But he immediately recovers.

"Your satisfaction is what I aim for. Please do not hesitate to come into my store and exchange any of the jewelry."

I walk toward the foyer. This time I do not feel Rocco's gaze lingering on me. I can feel the tension in the air now.

"Thank you for agreeing to see me unexpectedly. I do hope you like the gifts you have received today, at least. *Arrivederci, signorina.*"

Rocco picks up my hand and kisses it. He is now smiling and seems to have forgotten his disappointment over my claim that I did not find his jewelry to my liking. But he is still choosing to refrain from calling me "Francesca." I should feel victorious that I am in control once again, but I do not. What is wrong with me? Surely, old age is dulling my senses.

"*Buongiorno,* Mr. Vecchio."

I stand behind the open door to conceal myself from the paparazzi and onlookers outside. Edgardo is standing guard outside the door and quickly grabs the door handle and pulls it shut, even though Rocco was attempting to wave good-bye to me. I walk over to the library window, which faces the street. Edgardo is looking at Rocco as he descends the steps. He is scowling. Edgardo must have seen him arrive with the gifts and knows now that Rocco is my secret admirer.

Will I see Rocco again after the way I treated him? Or have my games pushed him away? I am a stupid, proud woman who never learns from her past mistakes.

Sighing, I walk over to the piano and pick up the three jewelry boxes Rocco gave me. I open the first one. Once again, Rocco has managed to make me gasp, but this time, it is not because the piece is so breathtaking, but because it is the gold-filigree bracelet I was admiring as I was leaving Castello Jewelry the other day. Rocco must have noticed me staring longingly at it and decided this would be my next gift. I inspect its engravings and see it is eighteen karats and says "Italy," which does not surprise me. Rocco seems a man of good taste, and the jewelry I saw in his shop did seem like the best quality. Also, this bracelet reminds me of a necklace I own that was purchased in Firenze. I can wear the two as a complement to each other.

Removing the bow from the second box, I cannot help but feel giddy. I will never tire of receiving jewelry, especially when it is as gorgeous as what Rocco has given me. With a bit of shame, I remember my lie of telling him a couple of pieces were not to my satisfaction. I suppose I must carry through with the game now and return two of the gifts. But I simply cannot! I love them all too much and cannot bear the thought of parting with them.

Lifting the lid slowly to prolong the surprise, I want to cry when

I see the pair of gold teardrop earrings. Like the bracelet, they are yellow gold. The last gift must also be yellow gold. Wasting no more time, I quickly open the third box.

"*Incredibile!*" I all but shout.

How does Rocco Vecchio manage to astound me with every gift he has given me? In a departure from the other presents, this is not jewelry but rather a jeweled hair comb. The stones are diamonds without a doubt, and the comb's prongs are eighteen-karat platinum gold, which one can tell just from seeing the metal's high gleam. But I still inspect the engraving to be certain it is eighteen karats.

Walking over to the mirror that hangs in the foyer, I sweep up and to the side my hair and fasten the comb. Exquisite! Shutting my eyes, I remember again how I treated Rocco before he left.

"*Sei pazza!*" I whisper to myself.

This man thinks the world of me and has showered me with numerous expensive pieces of jewelry. And how do I thank him? By cutting him down and telling him that a few of the gifts did not meet my standards. I shake my head in disgust. I must make this right. But it is hard for me to apologize to a man—or to anyone for that matter. Well, there was one man whom I had no trouble apologizing to; I showed him the real person I am or rather was. But that woman died a long time ago.

I will stop by Castello Jewelry and thank Rocco again for the new gifts and tell him I do like all of the pieces. He will think I am crazy. I cannot do that. Perhaps I should just phone him? I will not make mention of the jewelry I had told him was unsatisfactory. He will know in time I did like the pieces when he sees that I have not gone to exchange them. Yes! That is best. I walk over to the phone on the table in the foyer. But my hand freezes once it rests upon the receiver. Francesca Donata has *never* called a man first and especially not so soon after becoming acquainted. But I need to give him a sign of encouragement. Ah! I will merely send him a thank-you note. *Sì, sì.* That is what I will do!

The doorbell rings, startling me. Could it be Rocco again? No, he is not the desperate type. He has too much class to come groveling back to me after the way I dismissed him earlier. I glance at the grandfather clock in the corner. Ten-thirty a.m. My interview! How could I have forgotten? I had called Miss Santore and asked her to come back for a second interview, but I made it for later in the morning since Giuliana's doctor was coming at eight o'clock. I wanted to talk to him to see if Giuliana's condition is improving. Unfortunately, he said she is the same. She has not gotten better or worse, which I suppose is some consolation. The doorbell rings a second time. What is the matter with these maids? If they were under my employ, they would be better trained.

"Angelica! Carlo! *C'è qualcuno alla porta!*"

Carlo comes rushing into the foyer, but stops short upon seeing me with the most exasperated look, as if to say, "Why are you not answering the door if you are so close to it?"

Hmmm! I suppose when Giuliana was feeling better, she answered her own door.

I walk up the stairs. The *Profile* girl can wait. She deserves it after breaking the rules and asking me a few of her own questions the last time we met. She is lucky I even invited her back.

As I reach the top of the stairs, I hear Pia greet Carlo. She is asking him how he is. Carlo responds, but I cannot hear him. I hear Pia laugh. They continue chatting as he leads her into the library. Mentally, I roll my eyes. I cannot even imagine what she finds to talk about with the household staff.

Deciding to get some fresh air, I quickly change my clothes. Edgardo had pointed out an Italian restaurant to me the day we were driving to the jewelry stores on Ditmars. He told me it was one of the best restaurants in Astoria, and they had received nothing but the best reviews. Trattoria L'incontro. I remember the name because I thought it was the perfect name for a restaurant. I will take the *Profile* girl with me. We can conduct our interview at the restaurant. Maybe eating will keep her preoccupied so that she will have no choice but to ask me the questions from the list I approved. This will also give me the chance to go out. I cannot stay indoors another day.

I pick up the phone and dial down to the kitchen. I wait several rings until Angelica finally answers.

"Angelica, please make lunch reservations for me right away at Trattoria L'incontro. I will need the reservation for eleven a.m. Make them for five people, and tell them I will need the VIP room.

Please ask them to be discreet. Make the reservations under your name, but you can tell them they are really for me. Explain to them that I will have my bodyguards with me, and they will need to inspect the restaurant and room before I enter."

"I don't think they have a VIP room, Signorina Donata. There is a party room to the back of the restaurant, which also has a separate entrance. Also, they open up for lunch at noon."

"Tell them I must arrive earlier. I am sure they can accommodate me. As for the party room, that is fine. I just cannot be in the same dining room as the rest of the patrons. I must not be disturbed. I am having my interview there today. Please explain to them it is a business lunch, and no one is to disturb me. None of the other diners or the restaurant employees must bother me for autographs."

"As you wish, Signorina Donata."

"*Grazie,* Angelica."

Now I must tell Edgardo that I am planning another last-minute trip outdoors. He will be furious, as usual.

An hour later, we are seated at Trattoria L'incontro. I did not bother this time disguising myself though Edgardo wanted me to. Everyone knows I am in town, and what is the point of having bodyguards if they do not perform their jobs? They can keep fans away from me if the fans approach me. I chose to wear a midnight-blue Chanel suit dress, deciding to keep my wardrobe simple so that the diamond jeweled hair comb Rocco gave me stands out even more. The comb is so stunning that I do not need any other jewelry. But I always wear a ring, and I decided to wear a five-carat diamond ring I purchased for myself after my first movie became a hit.

Pia cannot stop staring at my jeweled hair comb. Though the only jewelry she wears is a pair of chandelier silver earrings, I can tell she appreciates fine jewels by the longing look in her eyes. For I had that same look before I became famous, and I would stare at the jewels on the movie stars who were in the magazines I loved to read.

Pia no doubt is still mad that I made her wait so long this morning before I descended from my bedroom. And when I told her we would have the interview at Trattoria L'incontro, she looked like she wanted to slap me. Maybe I can unleash some of her repressed anger? Her calm demeanor bores me, and I would much rather see what she is capable of when her buttons are pressed.

Overly eager as always, Pia attempted to start the interview in the limousine. But I insisted we wait until we were seated. I was sandwiched between Pia and Edgardo in the limo, and the air could not have been more fraught with tension. Edgardo had yelled at me when I had informed him I wanted to dine at Trattoria L'incontro. I had warned him if he did not accompany me, I would just leave the house by the front door and risk getting mobbed. He has tested me in the past with disastrous results, so he knows better than to ever try me again.

The waiter comes to take our drink orders and recites a lengthy list of specials. While I am impressed that they have so many specials, I am also getting impatient for it is taking too long. Of course, the Americans always must have so much of everything. Though the waiter is talking to all of us, his eyes remain fixated on me. He is hoping I will make eye contact or give him an encouraging sign like a smile, but I talk to him without once lifting my gaze.

"A glass of Pinot Grigio, please. And I already know what I want for my appetizer. I will have the stuffed mushrooms."

"Excellent choice, Francesca."

I narrow my eyes toward the waiter, showing him I do not approve of his addressing me casually.

"I am sorry. I mean, Signora Donata."

"Signorina Donata." Edgardo speaks up, smirking at me.

"Anything else I can get for you, Signorina Donata?" The waiter now cannot make eye contact with me.

"Not at the moment. *Grazie.*"

After the waiter takes Pia's and Edgardo's drink orders, he walks away. I cannot help but notice he is a very handsome young gentleman. Pia catches me staring at him. I quickly return my gaze to my menu. I still cannot decide if I will have *insalata di polpo*—octopus salad—or *spiedini di vitello*—skewers of veal.

"I'm going to check on the guys out front." Edgardo rises out of his chair.

"Relax, Edgardo! We are fine. Let the poor men come in and eat. Angelica made the reservations for five guests."

"That's thoughtful of you, Francesca, but we're here to do a job, not to eat at our leisure."

And with that Edgardo charges off.

"Is he always that serious?" Pia asks me.

I wave my hand, indicating my annoyance. "He hates it when I spontaneously change plans without giving him adequate notice."

"So you do this a lot then? Act on a whim?"

Pia still looks angry with me for changing the plans on her as well.

"What does that mean, 'whim'?"

"Impulse. Do you always behave in such an impulsive manner, changing your plans according to whatever mood you're in?"

"Of course not. But why must everything be planned to the tiniest detail? Life cannot be lived that way. Do not tell me, Miss Santore, you organize your daily routines with so much precision!" I cannot help but say this in a snide tone.

"I try to think ahead as much as possible. It makes things go much smoother—at least for me. You can do whatever you want, Signorina Donata, but doesn't it bother you that you inconvenienced Edgardo? And I guess it didn't trouble you that I waited for half an hour until you came down for our meeting this morning."

"It was no more than fifteen or twenty minutes at the most."

"So you were well aware that you were making me wait."

"Miss Santore, may I remind you that our appointment is underway, so you had better begin asking your real interview questions instead of wasting time with nonsense."

That silences the girl. The nerve! Who does she think she is talking to me the way she just did? I guess Giuliana was right. The girl does remind me a little of myself and is most certainly not afraid to speak up for herself when she is upset.

"How long has it been since you last saw your sister?"

The waiter has returned with our drinks and my appetizer. He takes our order and bows to me before he leaves. I take a sip of my Pinot Grigio before answering Pia's question.

"A few years."

"What's a few years? Three? Five?"

"I do not remember. I am getting old."

Pia coughs up her iced tea.

"Am I hearing correctly? Francesca Donata is actually admitting she's getting old?" Pia laughs.

"We are all getting old, my dear, even you. There is nothing wrong with that."

"So you don't mind that you're not the young actress you once were?"

I cannot help but be pleased with myself. My intentional diversion is working. She has forgotten now about how long it has been since Giuliana and I last saw each other.

"No, I do not mind. Growing old is a part of life. You think that I am just like all these other vain actresses who cannot face the fact that their youth is over. I am *nothing* like them. I am me."

Pia nods her head as she quickly scribbles away in her little notebook.

"So you have not had any cosmetic procedures?"

"Most certainly not! Does it look like I have?" I lean closely toward Pia's face, challenging her to take a good look. To my surprise, she does not back away, but rather begins scrutinizing my face closely.

"You've had Botox."

"I most certainly have not! If you put that in your article, I will sue you and *Profile* for slander!"

"I'm sure you will."

"Miss Santore, you have once again managed to deviate from the list of approved questions I gave you. I must warn you if this continues I will have to cancel this interview and forbid you from even writing an article based on the two interviews we have had."

"I apologize, Signorina Donata. You're right. I did agree to your conditions."

She takes a sip of her iced tea. I must admit I am disappointed she gave in so quickly and apologized. I was beginning to enjoy our match of words.

"May I be frank, Signorina Donata?"

She is up to something. I can feel it. Pia Santore is more calculating than I originally gave her credit for.

"Yes. Please, be honest."

"Thank you. I just don't see how this interview will be any good with the limited list of questions you approved. And it won't be that much different from past interviews you've given. The public needs to hear something new about you. They want to know more about what you've been up to the last ten years."

"Well, then I am afraid I will bore them. Everyone knows I have been a hermit since I dropped out of the spotlight. There is no story there, Miss Santore."

"Do you have any hobbies that were keeping you busy? I never read in any of your previous interviews interests of yours besides your love of acting and jewelry. Is that how you want the world to remember you when you're gone? I know there is more behind your carefully constructed public persona. The media has always acknowledged you are a bit of an enigma. And your suddenly coming out of hibernation to travel to Astoria and visit a sister no one knew you had is fascinating. Getting back to my earlier question, when exactly was the last time you saw Signora Tesca?"

"I cannot remember the exact number of years. I told you."

"Was it more than five years, a decade? You must have some idea!"

"Probably about a decade."

"Why so long?"

"We live on different continents."

"But you have money. You could easily travel here whenever you want. So could Signora Tesca. I've heard she's not hurting financially either."

"Leave my sister out of this interview. I am warning you, Miss Santore."

Pia pauses before asking, "What's the big secret regarding your sister? Why so much secrecy?"

"The interview is about me, *not* her."

"But since she is your sister, the subject is related to you."

"Miss Santore, you are breaching the conditions. I explicitly stated that no questions about my family were to be asked. That includes my sister. I see that I will have to have a copy of those conditions with me present during our appointments so I can remind you of them."

"So, this is what you really want? A flat interview?"

"You are the journalist. Whether the article is flat or not rests solely with you and your talent as a writer."

"You are not going to lay the blame on me!"

"Miss Santore, I know you are still *quite* inexperienced as a journalist. Maybe you are not ready for this interview after all. If you have the talent as a journalist and writer, you will be able to construct a compelling article with what I give you."

"You won't even allow me to call you by your first name. How am I supposed to write an intimate article about someone who insists I call her 'Signorina Donata'?"

She's mocking me. I am about to lash out at her when the busboy saves her by arriving with our food.

We eat in silence. Edgardo must have decided to stay with the other bodyguards outside or he is keeping watch out back. Now I must suffer through this awkward lunch alone with this disrespectful girl. I decide to have a little fun to make the remaining time pass quicker.

"How is Gregory?"

"Fine. But you must know that already since he's painting your portrait."

"What I meant to say is, how are things between the two of you?"

"That's really none of your concern, Signorina Donata."

I stare at Pia as she eats her Penne Puttanesca. Her cheeks are turning pink, but she refuses to glance in my direction. I wait another minute before I resume eating my octopus salad. The food is quite good here.

"How about I compromise with you, Pia? May I call you Pia?"

She does not even attempt to hide her surprise at my calling her by her Christian name. Waiting a moment before replying, she finally answers, "Yes, you may call me Pia."

Smart girl. She was not exaggerating earlier when she said she plans as much as she can. She even chooses her responses carefully. She knows that allowing me to use her first name might make me more willing to let her call me Francesca.

"You may ask me a question that is not on my approved list if you answer a question for me."

Pia frowns. Again, I can see her carefully weighing her answer before replying.

"Okay."

"Gregory mentioned to me that you had been through a lot the past few years."

Pia whips her head up quickly from her plate. This is the angriest I have seen her yet.

"He told you?"

I debate whether I should let her think he told me, but then I realize he will tell her the truth. Will she believe him?

"No, he did not. So my question is, what happened to you?"

"I'm sorry, but I don't want to talk about it."

"Are you sure? You may ask me any question you want."

"Oh, so now you're ready to break your sacred list of conditions just because you're dying to know about me? This is all a game for you, isn't it? You're wasting my time."

Pia reaches for her purse, taking her wallet out.

"Put your wallet away, Miss Santore."

"So it's back to calling me '*Miss* Santore' just because I won't tell you something personal about me? You really are a piece of work."

She throws a few twenty-dollar bills onto the table.

A waiter walking by our table hears Pia's angry tone and glances over.

Placing my hand on her arm, I whisper, "Pia, take your money. I wanted to treat you to a nice lunch. I know I can be . . . difficult at times. But remember what I told you the first day we met in Castello Jewelry. You need to develop a thick skin to make it in your line of work as well as mine. I am doing you a favor. I know you do not see that now, but you will someday. Now, please, stay. I will answer one of your own questions."

I do not give her time to think about it. This girl, like me, does not bluff and is ready to walk out.

"I have not seen Giuliana in over thirty years."

"Thirty years?" Pia gasps.

"Now you see why I was embarrassed to admit to you the exact number of years."

"But why?"

"We were not on speaking terms."

"Oh."

I wait for Pia to ask me why, but she does not. Placing her purse back down, she sips her iced tea.

The busboy clears our plates. Once we are alone again, Pia asks, "Were you ever close?"

"Yes, when we were girls."

"So I guess you have made up since you are here and staying with her?"

"Not exactly. But she needs me, and we will always be family no matter what."

Pia nods her head. She looks over to a mural of Capri that is on the wall to her right. But her attention seems to be elsewhere. I can tell she is tempted to ask me more about my strained relationship with my sister, but she does not want to pressure me, especially now that I have finally given her something more personal about me.

"My sister died."

It is now my turn to look surprised.

"I am so sorry."

"That was what Gregory was referring to when he told you that I'd been through a lot the past few years."

"May I ask how she passed away?"

Pia shuts her eyes. I regret my question and fear that she is going to start crying.

"She drowned."

I want to place my hand on her shoulder, but I refrain from doing so.

"It's still a shock to my family and me. She was a strong swimmer and had even been on her school's diving team. But I guess she went out too far and got tired. Or maybe she wasn't feeling well suddenly. I don't know."

"Were you close?"

"Very. We were supposed to come to New York City together. She was going to attend art school. She loved to paint like Gregory."

No wonder she is attracted to Gregory. He reminds her of her sister. I remain silent, waiting for her to continue.

"I always wanted to come here and intern or work for a magazine. Our ultimate goal was to return to California and start our own magazine someday. She was into photography, too, and was going to take the photos and do the layouts for the magazine. But after she died, I dropped out of college and took a break. I'm finally getting back to my life and putting the pieces back together."

"Of course."

Pia looks spent. My sixth sense is telling me there is more to her sister's story, just as there is more to my story with my sister. But I do not plan on becoming Pia's best friend and telling her all of my secrets.

"Would you like coffee?" I signal to the waiter before she answers, giving her no choice.

"By the way, Pia, you can call me Francesca from now on. But I have not changed my mind about my conditions. I really do not want to argue with you every time I see you."

"Fair enough, Francesca."

Pia gives me a sly smile, which I return. We both know she has no intention of following my rules.

## ❧ 15 ❧

# Pia

Gregory and I are strolling around the streets of Manhattan's Chelsea district, exploring the art galleries. In the past few weeks, he's shown me around New York City. East to west, uptown to downtown, I love it all! But I think my favorite neighborhoods are Soho and Chelsea.

"See yourself living here some day?" I ask Gregory.

"Maybe. Why do you ask?"

"The obvious reason. So many artists live in Chelsea now."

"So I have to conform and live here, too?" Gregory tucks a wisp of my hair that's fallen out of my ponytail behind my ear. I can't help but blush. Even though we've been dating now for almost a month, his tender gestures still move me.

"That's right. You're a nonconformist. How could I insult you the way I have?" I giggle and pull Gregory closer to me as I wrap my arms around his neck and kiss him lightly on the lips. Gregory deepens the kiss. After a few seconds, we pull apart and notice several pedestrians staring at us. We literally just stopped in the middle of the sidewalk and kissed. Reading each other's thoughts, we laugh and continue walking. Gregory's swinging my hand, much like kids who are skipping and singing as they make their way to school. Sometimes he surprises me with his boyish manners, especially since he's got a bit of a wild streak to him, as is evidenced whenever we borrow Lou's motorcycle and he charges down the roads. I'm drawn to this dual nature of his, so when Gregory told me he's a Gemini, I could totally see it.

I'm in love. There. I've admitted it to myself. Though I've been resisting falling so hard for him, I can't deny the feelings Gregory sets off in me whenever we're together. But I can't tell him. It's too soon. And besides, I don't even know if he feels the same.

"So, Pia, I was thinking of cooking for you tonight. But if you'd rather go out to eat, that's fine."

Gregory's voice sounds a little nervous. I haven't been to his place yet. And we both know what this could mean.

"I'd love for you to cook for me."

"Whew! That's a relief because I went shopping yesterday and bought a ton of groceries so I'd be prepared if you did come over."

"Why didn't you just ask me yesterday before you went to the supermarket?"

Gregory sticks his tongue in the side of his cheek as he realizes I've just busted him.

"Ah . . . I just like to wing it as much as possible."

Deciding to let him off the hook, I change the subject.

"So my third interview with Queen Francesca is tomorrow when the rooster crows." I roll my eyes.

"You're not a morning person at all." Gregory squeezes my hand playfully.

"No, that's not it. Making me show up so early is just another one of her manipulative ways to exert control over the situation. There's no reason why she can't meet later in the day. Our last interview was late morning because she had another sucker meet her at the crack of dawn. Get real! What does she have to do? She's been cooped up in the Mussolini Mansion since she arrived—oh, except for the time I ran into her at Castello Jewelry and our last impromptu lunch meeting."

"Just be patient, Pia. At least she did call you to return."

"True. After I angered Francesca by asking about her numerous nicknames during the first interview and then asking at our second meeting how long it had been since she and Signora Tesca had last seen each other, I thought I had blown it for good."

"I wouldn't test her again. You're right. She does need to feel like she's in control but not because she's trying to be a bitch."

I nod my head and think about how Francesca surprised me by saying she hadn't seen her sister in thirty years. I haven't told Gregory about how she opened up.

"Have you ever noticed, Gregory, that Francesca rarely uses contractions when she's talking? It just makes her sound snootier." I roll my eyes.

"I never really noticed, but yeah, you're right now that I think about it." Gregory laughs. "It must be because English isn't her first language. I know when I was learning Italian, and I would practice it on native Italians, they always told me I spoke so formally. Of course that was because in school we were taught the proper way of speaking a language rather than slang. They should cover both."

I'm secretly annoyed that Gregory had to find such a plausible reason for Francesca's hardly ever talking in contractions when she speaks English. I'd much rather believe she's omitting the contractions to sound far superior to everyone else.

"Pia, I know it's still early, but what do you say we head back to my place? I'm going to need all the energy I can muster for the feast I'm preparing."

Gregory's eyes are filled with hope and a hint of something else—lust.

My own eyes feel heavy as I anticipate what might happen.

"Okay." My voice comes out huskier than I intended.

He kisses me again but with a sense of urgency this time.

"So, you completely place your trust in my culinary skills. You're one brave woman."

"Who says I trust you?" I cock my eyebrow.

The 7 train stalls on our way to Long Island City. Gregory can't stop tapping his foot as we wait for the train to resume service.

"The next stop is Vernon Boulevard." The automated voice announcing the next station is a balm to both our ears.

"Finally!"

"You know we can just eat out, Gregory, if you're too tired. You can cook for me another time."

"Nah! Cooking is therapeutic. I need it after the stress of sitting on that train for so long."

We turn off Vernon Boulevard onto 46th Road. Gregory's house is all the way down the block, the second to last house on the corner. It's one of the older two-family row houses that are commonly seen in Long Island City, although quite a few have now been demolished to make way for modern apartment complexes. Gregory's house doesn't look as dilapidated as many of the other houses in the neighborhood. I can tell that he and his parents have maintained it over the years.

We climb up the stairs. Gregory pulls out his keys and inserts one into the lock. I feel nervous, but it's a good kind of nervous.

"*Voilà!* Welcome to Maison Hewson." Gregory bows deeply, extending his arm out for me to enter first.

"I had no idea you lived in such palatial quarters, Monsieur Hewson!" I giggle.

"Are you saying my estate does not meet your very fine standards?" Gregory speaks in an ultra-nasal tone as he attempts a French accent.

"*Fa schifo!* This will not do for Signorina Donata!" I do my best imitation of an Italian accent. Thrusting my chest out and standing as erect as Francesca does with her perfect posture, I place my hands on my hips and strut into his living room.

"That's pretty good!" Gregory laughs as he walks over to me and takes my hands in his. "I especially like your posture." His eyes immediately dart to my chest, which is still thrust out, making my average B-cup breasts appear larger.

My anxiety gets the better of me and I pull away, pretending to examine his living room. I stop in my tracks when I see the large canvas hanging over the couch. The portrait features the exposed back of a woman who is sitting on a chair. A drape is wrapped around her waist, but threatens to collapse, giving a peek of her derrière. The subject's dark curly hair is piled up onto her head, but as a few of the cascading curls show, it's also about to come undone. The woman's figure has beautiful curves. I take a few steps closer to better examine the stunning painting.

"Francesca?"

Gregory stands behind me. He wraps his arms around my waist and places a light kiss on my earlobe. I place my hands around his.

"Yup. In all her glory. That's one of my father's paintings of her."

"Why does he have it?"

"It was a gift from Francesca."

"Does your father have any other paintings of her?"

"No."

"I wonder why she gave him this one."

"My father said she wanted him to have at least one of her portraits. She used to always tell him it was a shame that he had to part with his creations or his 'children' as he liked to call them."

"That was kind of her, especially since she's such a narcissist. I would've imagined her to want every single portrait painted of her along with every magazine whose cover she graced."

"I think a lot of people would assume that, but as I keep reminding you, there's more to her than meets the eye."

"I have to admit, Gregory, I did get a glimpse of a different side during our last interview."

"Holding out on me, I see." Gregory leans his face over my shoulder so that I'm forced to look at him. He's smiling.

"She told me something personal, and I was just respecting her privacy." I shrug my shoulders.

"That was very thoughtful of you, but of course, I'm not surprised."

Gregory kisses my neck. I'm about to completely melt when he stops and walks away.

"Must prepare my culinary masterpiece."

*He's actually going to cook?* I can't help thinking.

"Let me help you," I yell out. But before I even make it to the kitchen, Gregory is back with a bottle of Cabernet Sauvignon and two wineglasses.

"You're my guest. I just want you to relax."

He pours the wine into a glass and hands it to me.

"I'll have mine when I'm done cooking. Wouldn't want to screw up the food." He winks.

"You're absolutely spoiling me!"

"You deserve it." Gregory strokes my cheek before returning to the kitchen. I kick off my mules and lie on his couch.

He's so good to me. I want to reciprocate. I start mulling over ideas of how I can surprise Gregory, but nothing solid comes to mind. Francesca's portrait is distracting me as I repeatedly glance over. Even when she's not looking at you, as in this painting, she still manages to captivate. The way her head is tilted slightly down so that her full, sensuous lips and her long thick eyelashes are all one can see of her profile. And the way Francesca holds her body shows she's very aware of her power and beauty. Yet there is a certain vulnerability, too, which is illustrated by the hair that is escaping its pins and the fabric that is slowly, but surely, falling from her waist. The way she looks down it seems almost as if she knows she's losing control and rather than fight, she surrenders.

Perhaps that is why she gave this painting to Gregory's father? She did not want to be reminded of her vulnerability.

My eyelids are getting heavy. I knew I shouldn't have had any wine to drink before eating. Relaxing fully, I give in to sleep. Dinner probably won't be ready for a while anyway. As I begin dreaming, I find myself to be the woman in the painting. But unlike Francesca, all of my inhibitions are dropped as I blatantly stare back at the painter.

I awake to the aroma of peppers and garlic. My stomach rumbles as I realize I'm absolutely famished. Glancing at my watch, I see that I was out for almost an hour.

"Did you have a good nap?" Gregory walks in wearing a plain white apron. He looks incredibly sexy.

"Yes. Sorry." I grin sheepishly.

"Stop it! I said I wanted you to relax."

He pours Cabernet for himself and refills my glass.

"To your burgeoning career interviewing celebrities." He holds his glass up in a toast.

"To your burgeoning career painting pain-in-the-ass stars!"

Gregory laughs as I clink my glass with his. We take a few sips.

"Ready?"

"For what?"

"I've been toiling away for nothing! You've already forgotten that I'm preparing a culinary experience like none you've ever had." Gregory shakes his head incredulously.

"Sorry! I'm quite out of it when I first wake up from a deep slumber. Of course I haven't forgotten. The aromas coming from the kitchen are what woke me up. It smells heavenly!"

"Let's go eat then."

Gregory takes my glass and places it on the coffee table. He then takes my hand and leads me to the dining room, which is small but still holds a formal table and six chairs comfortably. Lit candles flank either side of a beautiful centerpiece of orchids. He really has gone out of his way to make this dinner special. I lean over and inhale the orchids' sweet fragrance.

"Those are yours to take at the end of the night, by the way."

"Orchids are one of my favorite flowers. You really didn't have to go to all this trouble, Gregory."

"I know, but I wanted to."

I turn around and place my arms around his waist. Leaning my face up, I kiss him. Immediately, the kiss becomes heated. I suddenly realize this is what I'm hungering for, not his cooking. We keep kissing. I know I should pull away, but I don't want to. Gregory is the one to finally break the kiss. He looks into my eyes as he holds the sides of my face.

"I promise we'll pick this up later."

A jolt shoots straight to the pit of my belly. Swallowing hard, I nod my head and whisper, "I'll hold you to that."

Gregory can't resist the impulse to kiss me again. I don't hold back. I kiss him as aggressively as I did a moment ago. If it were up to me, I'd skip straight to the dessert. But I know he's slaved over this dinner. He wants to impress me. So with much effort, I pull away.

"Let me help you serve the food."

"Princess Pia, this is your night. When you cook for me, you can do all the work and I'll sit back."

"What makes you so sure I can even cook?"

"I can feel it."

We stare at each other for a moment before Gregory heads back into the kitchen.

He returns with our salads.

My first bite of the salad surprises me. It's warm, and, upon closer inspection, I see pieces of scrambled egg and salami in the salad.

"Wow! This is really good. I rarely have warm salads. And I would've never thought to add eggs and salami to a salad."

"It's actually not salami. It's *soppressata*."

"Supper-what?"

"You don't know what *soppressata* is?" Gregory asks me in disbelief.

"No, is that a crime?"

"Yes, for someone of Italian heritage. How can you not know?"

"I've never had it. You also forget that I live in California. Italian imported food products aren't as readily available as they are in New York."

"Let me instruct you then in *soppressata*. You can buy it either sweet or hot. They're both good, but I usually buy the sweet one, especially when my recipes call for it. *Soppressata* is in the same family as salami, but as I'm sure you noticed, it's saltier."

"It's really good."

"You can get it at most delis in New York City. You should try it sometime in a hero with provolone and tomatoes."

"So who taught you to cook?"

"My parents. Both of them have always loved cooking, and I helped them as a kid."

"Does it ever bother you that you're an only child?"

"A little when I was growing up. I wondered what having a sibling would have been like."

"I can't imagine not having siblings."

"I know you were close to Erica, but how about your brother?"

"We're not as close, but that's mainly because there's more of a gap in years than there was between my sister and me. He's a good guy though. He's helping my parents out a lot while I'm here."

And for the first time since I've left California, I begin to miss my family. The guilt returns. I should be there to help Kyle with my parents. Gregory must notice the change in my mood. He reaches over and places his hand over mine.

"Pia, I don't want to tell you what to do, but it's still very apparent you haven't fully come to terms with Erica's loss. I don't mean to pry, but did you ever talk to anyone about her death?"

"Not really. I talked to my doctor a little bit when I began having . . ." I let my voice trail off as I realize I'm about to confess to my panic attacks. That's all I need—for Gregory to think I'm some basket case.

"Having what?"

"Gregory, thank you for your concern, but I really need to deal with this my way. Okay?" I stroke his hand, signaling to him that I'm not mad.

Gregory sighs, but adds, "Of course. But please know that I want to be here for you. And I am. You can talk to me whenever you're ready."

"I appreciate that. Now what awaits me next?" I rub my hands together and say, "Yummy!"

"My cooking's not that great. You don't need to overact."

I can tell Gregory is just being modest and is fishing for more compliments.

"What's this I hear? You go from calling your cooking a 'culinary masterpiece' to 'it's not that great'! You *so* know you're good."

"I humbly thank you." Gregory bows before taking our salad plates to the kitchen.

"Ratatouille for dinner."

I remember the fragrance of sweet peppers that awakened me from my nap.

"I haven't had ratatouille in ages!"

"I'm relieved you've heard of it!"

"Ha! Ha! You're so funny!" I stick my tongue out at him.

"You can eat the ratatouille straight with some plain Italian bread or you can place it in these rolls that have a pesto spread on the inside."

"Hmmm! *Pesto!* I love *pesto!* Gregory, you truly have gone above and beyond! Thank you!"

Gregory grabs a roll and stuffs it full with the shimmering caramelized peppers, onions, eggplant, and tomatoes that make up the ratatouille. He hands me the plate.

If I hadn't already admitted to myself that I'm in love with this man, his extraordinary cooking is all it would have taken to make the admission.

After we eat the ratatouille along with a side of spinach and sautéed mushrooms, my stomach is ready to burst.

"Please, don't tell me you also made dessert. While I'd love to see what you came up with for dessert, I don't think I can get any more food down my throat."

"You're in luck. There's no dessert. I didn't want to keep you waiting for more than an hour."

"So, in addition to cooking you also know how to bake?"

"Guilty as charged. Next time I'll just make something light so that I can wow you with my baking."

"Next time, I'm going to do the cooking! But now, I insist you let me help you clean up or else I'm going to fall asleep again and you might not get me up."

"That wouldn't be such a bad thing." Gregory's eyes travel lazily down the length of my body.

"For my aunt, it would be. She'd have your head on a platter, and my ass would be shipped back to California."

I help Gregory clean up; it is good he's accepted my help since like most men he doesn't wash his prep dishes and pots while he's cooking. After we're done, we both collapse onto the couch.

"That dinner was really amazing, Gregory. Thank you so much!"

"My pleasure. Come here." Gregory turns me away from him and begins kneading my shoulders.

"Hey! I should be giving you a massage after all the hard work you did!"

"I'll gladly take the massage when you cook for me."

"Okay," I sigh, giving up instantly.

Gregory's expert hands are performing their magic on my usually tight shoulders. The stirring I felt earlier in my abdomen is back, gradually increasing until I can't stand it any longer. Opening my eyes, I catch Gregory staring at me before he lowers his head and kisses me softly.

"I should get you back home," he says, pulling away. "It's getting late."

Turning around to face him, I say, "I wouldn't say ten p.m. on a Saturday night is late, Gregory." I strain my neck forward to kiss him again, but he holds his hand up, stopping me.

"I don't want you to think this is why I had you over tonight."

"I know it's not. And you've been nothing but the utmost gentleman with me in the past month that we've been dating. I want you, Gregory."

Gregory's eyes squint hard as if he's just felt a jolt of pain. He begins stroking my hair.

"You have no idea how much I want you, Pia."

"Show me."

"I really care about you a lot."

I stroke his cheek and say, "I care about you a lot, too."

"I just want our first time to be special."

"You've already made this night so special with your hard work in preparing a romantic dinner. No one has ever done that for me."

"Pia, I have another confession to make. I don't just care about you. I'm falling in love with you. I understand if it's too soon for you. And I'm not expecting you to say—"

"I'm in love with you."

"You are?"

"Crazy in love." I laugh.

And it's true. I've never felt this way about a guy before. Sure, I had my teen crushes and what I thought was first love in high school, but I see now those were just infatuations. I was more in love with the idea of having a boyfriend rather than being in love with the person I was with. No wonder my relationships didn't last long. I really wasn't into the guys I dated. And I could tell they mainly liked me because of my looks. It didn't go deeper.

With Gregory, it's completely different. I care about his welfare. I want him to reach his dreams as an artist just as much as I want to succeed as a journalist. His tenderness makes me love him all the more. And I can tell he genuinely cares about me—everything about me, not just what he sees on the outside.

Reaching over, I kiss him tenderly. Gregory returns the kiss just as softly. I begin unbuttoning my blouse. Leaning back from the kiss, I arch my back, giving Gregory an ample view of me in my bra. The thought enters my mind that once it comes off he's going to see I'm not as big as this push-up bra makes me out to be. But I don't care. I feel so safe with Gregory. I know what we have is more than just our physical attraction.

Gregory stretches out so that he's now lying over me. He kisses the nape of my neck and I moan softly, encouraging him to keep going.

I begin fumbling with the buttons on his shirt until one flies off and hits the hardwood floor, rolling away. Unable to wait until the shirt is completely unbuttoned, I slide my hands across his chest, feeling the smooth contours of his skin and the firmness of his muscles.

Gregory sits back and in one quick motion pulls his shirt over his head. He begins undoing his belt, but I push his hands out of the way and unfasten it. He kicks his jeans off and then stretches over me as he plants kisses from my cleavage down to my navel. I'm so completely lost in the sensations he's setting off that I don't even notice he's unbuttoned my jeans until I feel him sliding them down my hips. Then, with one swoop, he lifts me up in his arms, carrying me to his bedroom upstairs. As we make love, Gregory repeatedly stares into my eyes and whispers, "I love you, Pia. I'll always love you."

After we make love we lie on the bed and stare at the ceiling, taking in the enormity of what transpired moments before. My head rests on Gregory's chest and my left arm is draped over his abdomen. Gregory strokes my hair and every so often he bends down to kiss my head.

"I'd better get going." Sighing deeply, I sit up and reach for my bra, which somehow made its way around the bed's foot post.

"Wait. Don't go yet." Gregory reaches for my arm, pulling me back toward him.

"My aunt is going to get worried if I don't get home soon."

"If it makes you feel better, call her and let her know you'll be late."

The thought of calling Zia isn't appealing. But I also don't want her to worry. I feel like Cinderella, who must race to her coach by the stroke of midnight. Instead of my coach turning into a pumpkin, Zia might lock me out. I know it's crazy, but I can't help feeling that once she hears my voice on the phone, she'll know I just had sex with Gregory. I care a lot about what Zia thinks, and I don't want to disrespect her. She's been nothing but kind and loving toward me, and she's allowing me to stay with her for the summer—rent free. Although I am in my twenties, and I'm sure my mother must suspect I'm no longer a virgin, we don't discuss the matter. My mother and Zia are from another generation, and I'm sure they'd like to believe I will remain a virgin until I get married.

"Okay, I'll call her."

"Great! You do that, and I'll be right back."

Gregory jumps out of bed. I watch him as he runs out of the room. He's so incredibly sexy. Part of me just wants to make love to him again, but I know if that happens I'll definitely get home late.

Zia doesn't seem to care that I'll be home later. She thanks me for being considerate by calling and tells me she's going to bed. Relieved, I hang up just as Gregory returns with a few paintbrushes, a palette, and a small wire basket that contains a few small cans of paint.

"What are you doing?"

"I'm going to paint you."

"Oh no, you're not—and especially not naked!" I start getting dressed, but Gregory rushes over to me, grabbing my hands just as I'm trying to fasten my bra. I look up at him, and his eyes twinkle as he slowly pushes the bra off my shoulders. My heart starts to throb. I want him again so badly, but instead of kissing me, Gregory leads me back to the bed, holding my hand.

"You're so beautiful. I want to capture you exactly as you are right now. Don't be self-conscious about your body. It's perfect."

"Thank you, but this just feels so . . . so revealing." I can feel the color rising in my cheeks. Part of me is tempted to let Gregory paint me in the nude. There's something alluring about it, and I'm flattered that he even wants to.

"No one has to see the portrait. It could just be for you and me."

"Okay. I guess it's all right. But promise me that no one else will ever see it."

"I promise." Gregory seals the oath with a kiss, which I try to prolong, but he's more intent on painting me.

"Let me get my canvas. Don't move!" He points his index finger sternly at me before he runs out again.

When he returns, he gives me instructions to lean fully back on the bed so that I'm turned on my left side as I was earlier, with just part of the sheet covering my torso so that my breasts are completely exposed. My head is resting on the pillow. Gregory adjusts my body a little so I'm closer to the edge of the bed. He pulls out my right calf so that the sheet lightly drapes over it. My toes peek out. He then takes my hair and lets it fall over my right shoulder. My right arm is bent at the elbow and my hand rests on my hip.

"There! That's exactly how you were. Don't move. Just relax and forget that I'm even here."

"Maybe if you threw a shirt on that would be easier." I give Gregory my most sultry look, still hoping he'll change his mind and make love to me a second time. He blows a kiss my way, but starts working. He's focused on painting my body first since he doesn't notice I'm staring at his face. His eyes are off somewhere far away as he feverishly brushes strokes onto his canvas. I'm fascinated watching him. Painting is his passion. It's obvious. I'm glad I gave in. My earlier anxiety has vanished along with my modesty.

I awake an hour later to Gregory softly calling my name.

"Pia, it's time to go home." Gregory picks up my clothes from the floor and hands them to me. I notice the canvas is gone.

"Weren't you painting me or was that just a dream?"

"No, it was real all right." Gregory laughs. "I put everything back in my studio."

"Did you finish it?"

"Half of it."

"I want to see."

"Not until it's finished."

"So will I have to pose for you again?"

"No, I've got it all up here." Gregory points to his head.

"What's the big deal if I see it unfinished?"

"Trust me. You looked like a goddess. But I have a rule that no one, not even tempting sirens like you, sees my paintings until they're completed. Don't take it personally, Pia. It's just the way I work."

"Oh. Okay. But you are going to show it to me once you're done?"

"Of course!" Gregory walks over and kisses me. "Has anyone ever told you, you worry too much?"

"Erica used to tell me that all the time. But she was the only one."

"Sounds like she knew you the best."

"She did." My voice sounds very sad.

Gregory lifts my chin. "You don't have to feel alone anymore. You've got me, and in time, I'm going to know you just as well as your sister did. I know I can't replace her, and I would never try, but again, I want to be here for you. Remember that."

I nod my head. We hug, and I whisper in Gregory's ear, "So far, you're the best thing that's happened to me here in New York."

"You mean I beat scoring an interview with Francesca Donata?"

I punch Gregory's back lightly and laugh. "I'm not even dignifying that with an answer."

"We'd better go before Antoniella shows up and shoots me."

As we leave Gregory's house, I think about how happy I am. But I also can't help thinking, *What's going to happen at the end of the summer when it's time for me to go back home to California?*

# ✒ 16 ✒

# Francesca

There is that tapping again. *Disgraziati!* Doesn't anyone sleep in this godforsaken city! If it is not one noise, it is another. Though I have now been in Astoria for over a month, I am still not accustomed to all of the sounds.

"Ping! Ping! Ping!"

There it is again. At first, I thought it was rain or perhaps hail. But the taps are too light to be hail. Finally forcing myself to wake up from a deep slumber, I sit up in my bed, lifting my eye mask.

"Ping! Ping!"

Pulling the covers off me, I get out of bed and walk over to my window. There is a man standing outside, looking up at my window. I back away suddenly as he throws another pebble.

I am about to go call Edgardo, thinking it is either a deranged stalker or one of the paparazzi. But I take another look before I leave. My eyes widen.

"Rocco?" I whisper aloud to myself.

Drawing the blinds up, I lift the window.

"What are you doing?" I ask him sternly.

"I am sorry, Signorina Donata. I hope I did not wake you."

"Of course you woke me. It is midnight."

"I'm sorry, but I have a surprise for you."

Immediately, jewelry comes to mind, but I do not see him holding any of his trademark gift boxes.

"Well, it will have to wait until a decent hour. I am going back to sleep, Mr. Vecchio."

I begin lowering my window when Rocco calls out in a much louder voice, "Please, please, *signorina!* Just hear what my surprise is."

Pursing my lips together, I cannot deny I am tempted. So far all of this man's surprises have been absolutely delightful—but of course, they were all jewels. After our last visit, I sent him a card thanking him for his most recent gifts. I almost apologized for being abrupt with him, but in the end, I could not bring myself to do it even though I knew I had ruined my chances of seeing him again. As I have said before, it is very difficult for me to apologize even when I know I am in the wrong. The man is persistent, I must say. Many men would have let their egos prevent them from ever contacting me a second time after being treated so callously.

Leaning forward so that my head is outside the window, I whisper to Rocco, "Hurry up! And keep your voice down. I do not want to alert the paparazzi out front."

Rocco nods his head. Cupping his hands around the sides of his mouth, he says in a low voice, "I want to take you out on a date right now."

"Right now?" My voice rings out loudly.

"Sshhh!"

"You are absolutely out of your mind, Mr. Vecchio!" I laugh, but I cannot help but be delighted at his impetuousness.

"I am sorry I did not give you a warning, but I like to surprise you."

"*Si, si.* I have noticed that." I am smiling.

"I can sneak you out so that the paparazzi won't see us."

"And how do you intend to carry out this grand plan?" I cross my arms in front of my chest and suddenly realize that I forgot to put on my robe. Rocco must be reading my thoughts because his gaze drops to my cleavage, which is on full display in the low-cut satin slip I am wearing. I still like to wear slips, which I have owned since they were more in vogue in the seventies. But I only wear them to bed now as nightgowns instead of undergarments. I cannot help but feel slightly titillated that Rocco is staring at my cleavage. Removing my arms from my chest, I lean forward out the window, but this time, I thrust my chest well out, letting my breasts spill dangerously. Rocco swallows hard, but does not stop staring. After a good long minute, his eyes finally travel to my face. A slight smile curls at the corners of his lips. I return the smile. Rocco's smile deepens, and in that moment, I know he realizes what I am doing.

"I am still waiting for your answer, Mr. Vecchio."

"Of course. Of course." With much effort, Rocco relays his plans for sneaking me out of Giuliana's house. He keeps stammering and cannot help stealing glances at my décolletage. I have not changed my position, loving the torture I am causing Rocco.

"I brought a rope ladder, which you can climb down from your bedroom window. It is one of those rope ladders that hikers use so you don't have to worry. It is very secure. My car is parked in the neighbor's driveway. We will climb over the fence that separates your sister's yard from her neighbor's. My Lexus has tinted windows so none of the paparazzi will see you as we drive by. Besides, they probably won't think to look twice since the car will be coming out of the neighbor's driveway."

Rocco looks quite pleased with himself, and I have to admit, I am also impressed by his careful planning.

"And where will we go? Or is that a surprise as well?"

"Naturally. Trust me. That is all I am asking of you, Francesca— I mean, Signorina Donata."

He has me. I am completely intrigued. The thought of escaping for a night is just too tempting. I cannot take being cooped up any longer in this house. Refraining from showing Rocco my eagerness, I wait a few seconds before responding.

"I guess I can come out. But I must be back by three a.m."

"Can we say four a.m.? I am afraid it will be hard for me to get you back by three a.m. where we are going, and if we want to relax and enjoy ourselves a little before we return."

Hmmm. It has been well over a decade, maybe longer, since I was out until four in the morning. I like this man's style more and more.

"Okay. But no later than four a.m. Let me change."

"Make sure to wear flats. I don't want you slipping on the rope ladder. I don't suppose a star like you owns a pair of tennis shoes? That would be safest. You can change into your dress shoes once we're in my car."

"Of course I own tennis shoes. I am not always dressed like a Barbie doll." I roll my eyes. Rocco's face flushes. "Give me fifteen minutes, and I will be ready."

Rocco nods his head. "Take your time." Somehow I do not think he really means that. I can see the anxiety written all over his face. He is not completely confident he can pull this off. I still respect him for trying. If the paparazzi catch us, then so be it. I am more worried about Edgardo finding out. He will have my head on a platter if he learns I sneaked out of the house with no security. Too bad! I am not getting any younger, and I want to have some much needed fun.

I pull out of my armoire a slinky pair of black pants that hug my figure. You might think I am too old to wear tight pants, but these make me look alluring and not cheap. Deciding to wear all black lest any of the paparazzi or the neighbors decide to try and peer into the driveway, I slip over my head a sleeveless cotton knit top. Not bothering with socks, I throw on a pair of running shoes, which I bought five years ago and have never worn. I do not know what I was thinking. Just the thought of running and sweating so much turns me off. I throw into an oversized Gucci handbag a pair of Chanel patent-leather flats. This is the most casual you will ever see Francesca Donata. I rarely wear jeans and even when I do, they are always paired off with a fancy blouse and shoes.

I only put on a little bit of makeup—the essentials: concealer, powder, eyeliner, mascara, and lipstick. There is no time to elaborately make up my eyes the way I normally do with eye shadow. Hmmm. I think I look younger without the eye shadow I usually wear. Maybe I should start going without it? Running a brush through my hair, I say a quick prayer to God, thanking Him for letting my tendrils behave. I hurry over to the window when I remember I have forgotten my perfume. Returning to my dresser, I spray two pumps of Prada L'Eau Ambrée. I am about to flick off the switch to the bedroom when I think better of it. No one will dare disturb me or check up on me if they notice the light on beneath my door.

I walk over to the window and see Rocco is waiting with the rope ladder in his hands.

"I was beginning to think you changed your mind and weren't going to tell me." Rocco smiles.

"You are getting to know me well quite quickly," I say.

"I'm going to throw the ladder up to you. You'll see two hooks. Secure them to the window ledge."

I nod my head and wave my hands, indicating for him to hurry up. He throws the ladder but not high enough the first time. It skims past my fingers as I try to catch it.

"You throw like a schoolgirl!"

"You never saw me play football when I was younger. I always made the pass."

To prove his point, he grabs the rope with one hand and thrusts it with what looks like all of his strength. This time, the rope reaches the desired height, and I have no trouble catching it. I shake out the rope, uncoiling it as Rocco grabs the ends that are dangling. Fastening the hooks onto the window ledge, I feel better seeing that they sink into the wood quite securely. And the rope looks thick and durable.

"Here, catch!" I throw out the window my Gucci handbag. Rocco just barely catches it. Placing my bag down on the ground beside him, he implores me with his hands to begin my descent. Mentally shaking my head, I turn around so that I can begin descending. This feels like a scene from a movie.

"Careful, Francesca!"

My precarious position stops me from correcting him. Suddenly, I realize my derrière is on full display as I carefully begin climbing down the ladder. Cursing myself for wearing the slinky pants, I focus on not killing myself.

"*Brava! Brava! Vai piano! Piano!*"

I do not know why Rocco has resorted to talking in Italian. I did not even know he could speak the language.

Once I reach the third step from the bottom, Rocco comes over and swoops me into his arms and then lowers me to the ground. He is quite the gentleman!

"Thank you, but I could have managed the last few steps."

"I know, but I love chivalry." He winks.

I shake my head. Rocco takes my hand and tiptoes toward the neighbor's fence.

"What about the ladder?" I ask.

"There's no way for me to unhook it from the ground. We'll just have to leave it. Besides, we'll need it for you to get back up."

For some reason, the thought of climbing the ladder terrifies me. I had no fear of descending it. I will have to deal with that later.

"Are you strong enough to get over the fence? I can help lift you."

"I should be fine. I am not that old!"

I scowl, but I see Rocco is quietly laughing. He loves teasing me. At least he has a thick skin and can take my barbs.

I begin climbing the fence and immediately realize what Rocco meant. My abdomen is killing me as I climb higher. Seeing me struggle, Rocco pushes my derrière up without warning so that I can easily drape my leg over the top of the fence. He does not even wait for me to jump down before he begins climbing up himself. Swinging my other leg over the fence, I take a look below before I jump. It is only about a five-foot jump.

"Wait for me before you jump," Rocco whispers.

Ignoring him, I jump down and lose my balance as I fall onto my knees.

"Ai!"

"Francesca!" Rocco is now at the top of the fence as he looks down at me with concern written all over his face.

"I am fine! I am fine!" Holding up my hands to calm him down and then motioning for him to keep his voice down, I slowly get up.

Rocco jumps expertly down onto the ground.

"Why didn't you wait for me? I would've helped you down."

"I am fine, Rocco." I bend over and beat out the dust from the knees of my pants.

"Finally!" Rocco looks victorious.

"Finally, what?"

"Finally, you are calling me 'Rocco'!"

Shrugging my shoulders, I say, "It is quicker to say than Mr. Vecchio. Fewer syllables. We have to hurry. There is no time for formalities."

Rocco nods his head, but he appears unconvinced by my pathetic excuse.

We walk over to his car, which is in the driveway as he said it would be. I am surprised that the neighbor who lives here has not noticed it. Then again, it is past midnight. Rocco opens the passenger door and quietly shuts the door once I am in. The car is a beautiful luxury sedan. The exterior is black, which definitely came in handy tonight since the color only further concealed it in the dark. And the interior has cream-colored leather seats and thick, plush carpeting on the floor.

"Ready for the night of your life?" Rocco smiles like a mischievous boy who knows he is getting away with murder.

"Ha! You are quite confident of yourself! You are well aware that as a movie star, I have had plenty of 'nights of my life,' as you put it."

"Of course. But you have never had any like the night you are about to have."

Rocco places his key in the ignition and starts the car. Slowly, he backs the car out of the narrow driveway. Shutting my eyes, I cannot bear to look, certain he will hit the walls on either side.

I can feel the glare of the streetlamp on my face and open my eyes. We drive slowly, not wanting to make it seem like we are escaping. I see the crowd in front of Giuliana's house turn their heads in our direction, but then they look away.

"Thank God you have tinted windows!"

"They're also not expecting to see you in a Lexus. They know you always arrive and depart in the Maserati."

"You sound like you have been stalking me, too."

I stare at Rocco intensely, but he does not flinch under the weight of my gaze.

"So where are we going, Mr. Vecchio?"

"Oh, so now it's back to the formalities, I see."

"As I told you earlier, it was quicker to say your first name when we were making our grand escape."

"Yes, quicker, Francesca."

I begin opening my mouth to correct him, but suddenly feel foolish—and uptight. He is right. How can I insist we continue calling each other by our surnames when we are about to share an intimate night? Well, not intimate in *that* regard.

"You still have not answered my question."

"All I'll tell you is that we're going to Manhattan."

I am so thrilled that I want to cry, but I do not let him see my excitement. It has been over a month now since I arrived in Astoria, and I cannot believe I still have not ventured to one of my favorite cities in the world.

Rocco leans over and presses one of the buttons on his CD player. Classical music comes on. Again, I am pleasantly surprised by his good taste. Sinking back into my luxurious seat, I sigh deeply, letting myself fully relax as I take in the sights outside. I am horrified to see we are in what looks to be a very bad neighborhood with its dilapidated buildings, shops that have gone out of business, and groups of teenagers hanging out at street corners.

"Are we safe driving through here? Could you not have taken another route?"

"You're fine, darling. You're with me. There's one other route to get to the Fifty-Ninth Street Bridge, or rather, the Ed Koch Queensboro Bridge, as it's now called, and that only looks marginally better than this neighborhood. Trust me, it's not as bad as it looks."

Now he is calling me "darling." I do not like that, but again, I dare not protest. I do not want him thinking I am so rigid.

We drive up the ramp leading us to the upper level of the Ed Koch Queensboro Bridge. I gasp at the gorgeous Manhattan skyline, all lit up with its multitude of twinkling lights.

"She's beautiful, isn't she? I never tire of this view when I drive into Manhattan at night."

"I have never seen the view from one of Manhattan's bridges at night. It is truly astounding."

We continue in silence over the bridge. I am so enthralled by the glittering city landscape that I have not even noticed Rocco has draped his arm behind my seat's headrest until we are exiting the bridge. He keeps his arm draped behind my seat as we drive through Manhattan's streets.

"Even this late, there is traffic."

"Well, it is Saturday night."

I blush, realizing my error. Each day has blurred into the other during my stay here so that I cannot distinguish the weekend from the rest of the week. I have been cooped up too long in that house.

We arrive at Little West 12th Street. I have never ventured lower than midtown when I have come to Manhattan. Rocco finds parking at the corner. I take out of my purse my sunglasses and scarf. I begin wrapping my hair turban style in the scarf.

"What are you doing?"

"Disguising myself."

"You'll be fine."

"Rocco, I do not want people bombarding us."

"I have already thought of everything. A friend of mine owns this restaurant. He's expecting us. We'll enter through the kitchen in the back of the restaurant. They have a private room reserved for us. He's also made other arrangements to ensure your privacy."

I am taken aback by Rocco's thoughtfulness.

"I should still wear the scarf and sunglasses while I am outside. You did not find parking after all near the restaurant."

"Francesca, you'll only draw more attention to yourself in that getup, especially with the sunglasses. Only celebrities wear sunglasses at night."

He is absolutely right. But my nature refuses to surrender so easily.

"I will just wear the scarf—at least until I am indoors."

"I give up." Rocco holds his hands up in resignation.

I quickly wrap my hair and step out of the car. We walk briskly, keeping our gazes to the ground so as not to attract attention. However, no one takes a second look, and many of the other pedestrians are walking just as quickly and looking down at the sidewalk as well. It has been years since I have been in Manhattan. I had forgotten that New Yorkers are not as starstruck as residents from other cities, and even when they see someone famous, they tend to leave the person alone.

We approach a restaurant called Revel. We pass the restaurant and go around to the side street that takes us to the back of the restaurants that line Little West 12th Street. A door is propped open behind the building that belongs to Revel. Rocco takes out his cell phone and dials.

"Yup, we're here. I know. I know. We had a bit of a delay. Okay."

Rocco ends the call and shoves his cell back into the pocket of the sports jacket he is wearing. He looks debonair as usual. He is decked out in black once again, but this time, he wears a midnight-blue button-down silk shirt. There is no one in this alleyway, and I suddenly feel self-conscious wearing the turban. I pull it off and shake my hair out. Rocco is staring at me.

"Gorgeous as always." He strokes my cheek with his thumb.

I feel my cheeks begin to warm. I quicken my step so that I am ahead of him, not wanting my brief flustered moment to show. A man dressed in a black suit greets us at the door.

"Rocco! It's been ages." He steps out and hugs Rocco, patting him on the back.

"Franco. Thank you for accommodating us on such short notice."

"Anything for a friend, and anything for Miss Donata." He bows deeply toward me and then takes my hand in his and plants a light kiss.

"Thank you. Please, call me Francesca."

Rocco's eyes shoot daggers at me, but he quickly conceals his anger as Franco turns toward him.

"She is even more beautiful than the photos or the images on screen. It truly is an honor to meet you, Miss Donata."

"Francesca!"

"I'm sorry. As you wish, Francesca."

I can feel Rocco's scorching gaze on me. This is the first time I have felt like I have really angered him. He has always taken my sarcastic comments and harsh words with such grace.

"Follow me. You can rest assured, Francesca, no one will bother you here."

"Thank you. I hope we are not inconveniencing you. I would imagine that you would be getting ready to close the restaurant this late."

"Yes, Francesca, the restaurant does close at midnight on Saturdays, but I am making an exception for my good friend Rocco. You and he have the entire restaurant to yourselves tonight. We knew if he had brought you earlier in the night, you would not have much privacy with the restaurant's patrons dining. He was also worried about making your great escape if you had left home much earlier. Now if you would please follow me." Franco leads us through the kitchen, where all of the workers freeze the moment they see me enter. I nod my head in greeting toward them. They nod back and continue to gawk until Franco barks, "Back to work!" Like robots, they immediately return to their tasks and do not risk another glance in my direction.

We exit the kitchen, and Franco descends a narrow spiral staircase. I cannot help but wonder if we are being relegated to a shabby basement, and this is Rocco's idea of a "private room." But once downstairs, I see that Rocco's good taste does not disappoint yet again. The basement is completely finished and is almost as lavish as the main dining room. The space is cavernous, and as we follow Franco, we pass barrels upon barrels. Soon, I see bottles of wine on shelves from floor to ceiling—a wine cellar! How charming! Finally, we arrive at a spacious room that is decorated beautifully. Vines snake their way around marble columns and along the beams running across the ceiling. Huge vats of rhododendrons and geraniums are placed around the room. The walls feature exposed brick.

"We reserve this room for large parties or for guests who want privacy such as you and Rocco want tonight." Franco makes eye contact with Rocco, then pats him on the shoulder as he passes him.

"Francesca, please."

Franco holds a chair out and gestures for me to take my seat. With the flash of one hand he unfolds my napkin and drapes it over my lap. He then opens the menu and hands it to me.

Rocco takes his seat. When Franco attempts to unfold his napkin, Rocco grabs it and says curtly, "I can manage, Franco. Thanks!"

Franco looks at him, a bit surprised, and then shrugs his shoulders.

Rocco seems upset still that I let Franco call me "Francesca" immediately. He is being silly. Yet a part of me is pleased by his jealousy.

Franco takes our drink orders and says he will return shortly to take our appetizer order.

"If it's too late for you to eat a full meal, we can just stick to the appetizers."

"No, no. I would love to sample their cuisine. I am accustomed to these late suppers from Italy."

"That's true. I forget that Europe has an active nightlife and eats late just like we do in New York City. Would you mind if I took the liberty of ordering for us?"

I am immediately pleased by his assertiveness.

"I would like that very much. *Grazie,* Rocco."

I flash him my most seductive smile. It does the trick. The tense muscles in his jaw visibly relax, and the lines in his forehead have eased, too. His eyes crinkle slightly as he returns my smile. It does not take much to please this man or to erase his anger. The waiter arrives with our cocktails. I have ordered a Campari. Rocco ordered a martini.

He raises his glass in salute to me. "To the beginning of a long friendship and to the best night of your life."

I laugh as our glasses clink.

"To the best night of *our* lives. You are after all in the company of Francesca Donata."

# ～ 17 ～

# Pia

Making my way through the crowd in front of the Mussolini Mansion, I'm still amazed by their tenacity. It's seven a.m., and though it's obvious many of them spent the night here, they don't give up in their quest to spot the star again.

"Good morning, Miss Santore." Angelica can barely be heard above the cries of the paparazzi and neighbors behind me as they shout to her, "Any chance of Francesca's coming out today? Please, tell Francesca we just want to say hello."

One of Francesca's bodyguards quickly pushes me through the door as another bodyguard warns the crowd to stay back. I don't see Edgardo, who is usually guarding the front of the house.

"What kind of a mood is she in today, Angelica?"

"I haven't seen her yet, Miss Santore."

"Please, Angelica, call me 'Pia.' "

Angelica nods her head and gives me a shy smile as she leads me into the library.

"Can I get you coffee? Something to eat?"

"Just a glass of water. Thank you, Angelica."

Angelica hurries off. I can't help but wonder what kind of a life she has as a servant. It's a shame. She must not be more than in her mid-twenties. If she wore a little bit of makeup and let her hair down, she would be a very pretty girl. Ugghhh! I sound like my aunt, who's still getting on my case to stop wearing my glasses. She offered to take me to the optical store the other day and buy me contacts. I made the mistake of telling Zia that Gregory thinks my glasses are sexy, and she went ballistic.

"Sexy? Is that how he sees you? Maybe you should stop seeing that boy!"

Zia loves Gregory, but of course, the thought that we might be having sex is too much for her to bear. Thankfully, she didn't ask me if we were.

Angelica brings my glass of water in record time.

"I'll go check on Signorina Donata. It's odd that she isn't down yet. She wakes up quite early and is often down here in the library reading her newspaper when I start working."

Angelica turns to go, but a thought comes to my mind.

"Wait! Angelica, please come back."

"Can I get you something, Miss Santore?"

"Please, Pia."

"Oh, I'm sorry. It's just that Signorina Donata is quite adamant about me not calling her by her first name."

"I know. She took my head off the first time I met her and made the mistake of calling her '*signora*' instead of '*signorina.*' "

"That happened to you, too?"

"I think it happens to everyone." I roll my eyes, at which Angelica laughs. Finally, she relaxes. It must be stressful anticipating Francesca's mercurial moods.

"I wanted to ask you a question if you don't mind, Angelica."

Angelica shrugs her shoulders. "Okay. If I can answer it, that is."

"Where is Signora Tesca? This is my third visit to the house, and I still have not seen her."

Angelica's face reddens.

"Ahhh. She's around."

"Be honest with me, Angelica. Why does there seem to be all this secrecy regarding Signora Tesca?"

"I don't know what you mean, Pia. I'm sorry."

Angelica looks away. She cannot lie to save herself. I see I'm making her very uncomfortable. Unlike Francesca, I don't take pleasure in seeing others suffer.

"Thank you, Angelica. That was all I wanted."

Angelica nods her head and practically runs off.

Ten minutes later, Francesca has still not come down. It's deathly still in the house with the exception of Carlo's passing through the outer corridor on his way back and forth to the kitchen. I can smell eggs and coffee. My stomach growls even though I had a couple of biscotti for breakfast. I really need to cut the sweets out. My pants are getting tighter.

Standing up, I peer outside the library. No one is in sight. I decide to take a walk. The safest bet is the staircase. I won't run into Carlo or any of the other staff who are in the kitchen. I might run into Angelica, but I can just say I was looking for her. As I near the top of the staircase, I hear coughing coming from the second door on my right-hand side. I remember from my first visit that this is the bathroom since I had used it before I left.

Leaning my head closer to the door, I listen. The coughing continues, followed by a voice.

"I am calling the doctor."

A choked voice screeches, "No!"

More coughing follows.

"Giuliana, you are coughing up blood. That is not normal!"

My heart pounds as I realize Francesca and Giuliana are in the bathroom. Obviously, Giuliana is quite sick. Perhaps that is why I never see her and why Francesca has been so protective of her.

"Just leave me alone. It'll pass. It always does."

"There has been bleeding before?"

"Just a little."

"I am calling your doctor."

I hear Francesca's heels tapping on the marble tiles.

Running down the stairs, I almost crash into Carlo, who's carrying a large covered platter to the library.

"I'm sorry," I whisper as I scramble around him and into the library.

Carlo frowns, but doesn't say anything as he places the platter on the coffee table in front of the couch in the library.

"Signorina Donata said you can help yourself to breakfast. She apologizes, but she will be down as soon as she can."

"Thank you, Carlo."

Carlo nods and leaves.

My mind is racing. Trying to calm my nerves, I remove the cover from the platter and scoop out a crepe and scrambled eggs.

The food tastes like something you'd get at a five-star restaurant. I can't believe I've deprived myself of it the other times I've been here.

While the food is helping the gnawing in my stomach, it's not doing much to ease my flurry of thoughts. Signora Tesca is ill. Could that have been Francesca's motivation for coming to see her after their long estrangement? The more I think about it, the more I'm convinced. This is why Francesca bristles whenever a question about her sister comes up. She's trying to keep her illness private. I'm surprised that none of the household staff has leaked it to the press. Their loyalty to Signora Tesca is impressive.

"Good morning, Pia. I am very sorry about the delay. I had a . . . an urgent matter I needed to attend to." Francesca looks pale, and her hands tremble as she helps herself to some breakfast.

"No need to apologize. I'm beginning to get used to it."

Francesca shoots me a dirty look, and I quickly apologize. "I didn't mean any sarcasm by my response. I'm sorry if it sounded that way."

Pursing her lips tightly, Francesca remains silent and takes a long sip of her espresso.

"I hope everything is okay?"

"*Si, si.* Well, I might have to end our appointment early. I am sorry. I am expecting someone and will need to talk to him as soon as he arrives."

"Of course. I understand. I can wait if you want?"

"No, I could not ask you to be any more patient than you already have been today."

Deciding to take a chance, I go for it.

"Is it your sister?"

Francesca's eyes widen in shock, but she quickly recovers.

"Giuliana is fine."

She then narrows her gaze as she continues to stare at me while sipping from her cup.

She knows that I overheard and now she thinks even less of me. I'm such an idiot!

"Let's get started since you will have to leave early," I say, attempting to act nonchalant.

Pretending nothing has happened is my best recourse in this awkward moment.

"You were engaged four times, correct?"

"Five."

"Five? I thought I had all of the names of your ex-fiancés."

Flipping through my research notebook, I find the page on Francesca's past paramours.

"Mario Scarpone, Sal Giametta, Luca Barone, Stello Cascio. Whom am I missing?"

"Vladimir Novikov."

"A Russian?"

"Yes, Vladimir was Russian. What? Just because I am Italian, I must date only Italian men?"

"No, no! Of course not! So, do you care to share what went wrong with these relationships?"

Francesca gets up and walks over to the escritoire in the corner of the library. She pulls open a drawer and takes out a sheet. Walking over to me, she points to an item on a list.

"Remember this, Pia?"

She's holding her list of conditions and pointing to item number three: *No questions about my previous engagements or fiancés may be asked.*

"I shall give you this copy since it appears you have lost your own."

Francesca places the sheet next to me on the couch and returns to her seat.

"Francesca. I may still call you by your first name as you stated I could during our last interview?"

"*Si, si.* I do not go back on my word."

"Francesca, let's be honest."

She looks up at me with the most feigned innocence as if to say, "Me? Not be honest?"

"You really do want to talk about your ex-fiancés or else you would have cut me off as soon as I first mentioned them. What's the harm in sharing with your adoring fans why you have not succeeded in love and gotten married?"

My words sting her. The ashen complexion she had when she first walked into the room has returned.

"It is private."

I remain silent. This is not working. Colin threatened to pull the plug on this interview if I don't get Francesca to open up soon. To buy myself more time, I told him how she admitted to me that she hadn't seen her sister in thirty years and how they've been estranged. Part of me felt guilty that I sold her out this way, especially since I've been able to tell she wants to keep her sister out of the media. But she never did tell me I was forbidden from revealing that they had not been talking to each other for so long. Colin gobbled the tidbit up and agreed to wait so that I could get more out of her.

Suddenly, I remember Francesca's tactic from our last interview when she offered to tell me something personal in exchange for my answering her question. Standing up, I walk over to the windows and look outside.

"I'm sorry, Francesca. I haven't been completely straightforward with you, and here I am expecting you to be honest with me."

"Oh?"

Keeping my back turned toward her, I can tell from her tone that I've piqued her interest.

"The reason I wanted to know more about your past relationships is that I wanted to compare them to mine with Gregory. That's crazy, I admit, but I just wanted to see if what we're going through is similar to what others have experienced in their relationships."

Holding my breath, I pray she doesn't see through my ploy.

"You and Gregory are having problems?"

"Not necessarily. But I have never felt this way for anyone else before, and I'm getting scared."

Okay, now I've come quite close to the truth with her. I've never had such strong feelings for anyone I've dated, nothing quite like I do for Gregory. And I am starting to grow anxious. I don't want to get hurt. I haven't had anyone to confide in about him. I always confided in Erica. Though I've become friendlier with Megan and even Connie, I still don't feel close enough to them to spill all the beans.

"That's normal. Everyone is afraid when they first fall in love. I assume you are falling in love with Gregory?"

I hesitate. Part of me wants to keep that between Gregory and myself. It's special. But I know I need to make a sacrifice in order to get Francesca to open up to me.

"Yes, I'm not just falling. I am already in love."

I turn around and lock my gaze onto hers. I see sadness I've never seen before fill her eyes. She quickly averts her gaze.

"You must always use your assets as a woman to aid you in keeping your man hooked. Remember, men's first instincts are physical. You are a very pretty girl, Pia, but you're hiding a lot of your beauty behind those glasses and in the way you always keep your hair pulled back in a ponytail or up in that messy chignon."

"I let my hair down and take off my glasses sometimes when I go out on dates."

"Good! But start wearing it down all the time. And invest in a pair of contacts."

"You sound like Zia. She can't stand my glasses."

"And rightly so! Your aunt and I might be older, but we know what we are talking about, especially when it comes to men."

"Well, Zia never married so I don't know about that."

I suddenly realize my faux pas since Francesca never married either.

"I didn't mean any offense by that. You're different than Zia. You exude a lot of sensuality. Men still find you very attractive. I love Zia, but she has never seemed to have an awareness of her essence as a woman."

"Thank you for your compliments, Pia. But just because your aunt seems to be a certain way now does not mean she was always this way. You must remember we were all once young. Take my sister for instance. She was breathtaking as a teenager and into her early twenties. I looked up to her and thought she was the true beauty in our family."

"Really?"

Francesca gets up and walks over to one of the bookshelves. She pulls out what looks to be a photo album. Flipping it open, she hands the album to me.

"*This* was Signora Tesca?"

The photo looks like it was taken when Signora Tesca was in her twenties. Though I could tell in the photo I had seen in the library a few weeks ago that Signora Tesca had been pretty as a teenager, it paled in comparison to this image. As a young woman, her beauty truly stood out. If only the neighbors could see this photo, they would never dare call Signora Tesca "plain as vanilla" again.

"Gorgeous, right? She could have been a model. But, correct me if I am wrong, Pia, you have never met my sister. Why are you surprised then if you do not even know what she looks like now?"

I try to think of the most delicate way to say it, but there simply isn't one.

"I heard that she is quite plain."

"Who said such a thing?"

Francesca sounds angry and rightfully so. This is her sister, whom it's obvious she loves very much.

"A few of the neighbors just expressed surprise when they learned that you were sisters. They said she was plainer than you."

"I should have never come here. Because of me, she is a prisoner in her own home, and now she has people gossiping about her behind her back. She does not deserve that! She is an angel! I am the one they should be talking badly about! Not her!"

Francesca is very agitated and is waving her index finger in the air. She reminds me of footage I've seen of the former Italian dictator Mussolini when he was giving his speeches.

"I'm sorry, Francesca. I did not mean to upset you."

"Stop apologizing! How many times do I need to tell you that?"

She shakes her head in disgust, but I'm not sure if she's disgusted with me or herself for losing control.

"I apologize. You were simply being honest with me. Thank you for that. So many people tiptoe around me because of my celebrity. I am protective of my sister, as you have seen. She has had a very hard life, and I am to blame for much of that."

I remain silent. I can't believe how much she is revealing, but I know I can't push her. She has to feel like she's in control.

"But enough about me. I will help you with your problem."

She motions with her hand for me to follow her. We go upstairs. I hear voices behind one of the closed doors and the coughing I heard earlier. Francesca pauses for a moment, knitting her brows together, but then resumes walking down the hallway.

We enter the sitting room where our first interview was conducted and pass through an adjoining door, which leads us to a bedroom. She opens her armoire and begins rifling through the outfits. I'm amazed that someone can own that many clothes, especially since she is just visiting and this isn't her permanent home.

"Try these on. I know they will not fit you exactly, but we will make whatever adjustments are necessary."

"Oh, I can't. That's really okay, Francesca."

"Pia, do you want my help with Gregory or not? You said it yourself. Men are still attracted to me. That is true. I have even seen your Gregory notice my curves."

Fury pulses wildly through me, and in that moment, I want to rip her eyes out. I'm not usually prone to fits of anger or violence, but I guess this just proves how much in love I am with Gregory. The thought of him checking Francesca out makes me absolutely insane.

Francesca laughs. "Calm down, Pia. He is a man after all. He never tried to seduce me or anything like that." She pats my arm. "*Dai!* Come on! Try on the dresses. If you will please excuse me, I think the visitor I was expecting is here. But I will be back. And feel free to try on any of my shoes that you like." She waves to an assortment of heels that are lined up neatly in shelves above the racks where her clothes hang.

"Thank you, Francesca."

Smiling before she walks out, Francesca actually looks pleased that she will be helping me. She really is one bizarre woman. As soon as she leaves, I tiptoe over to the door and open it a crack. I hear her talking to a man outside the door we passed earlier. That must be Signora Tesca's room.

Carefully, I lean closer so that I can get a view of the man. He's carrying what looks like a doctor's bag and a stethoscope is wrapped around his hand. His face is gravely serious. Francesca dabs at her eyelashes and nods her head at whatever the doctor is saying. He places his hand on her shoulder.

I feel bad that I'm spying on her private moment, especially since she is so upset. What exactly is the matter with Signora Tesca? Whatever it is, it does not seem good. Francesca escorts the doctor downstairs. She'll be back up soon. Quickly, I run over to one of the two dresses Francesca laid out on her bed for me.

I choose first the stunning royal-blue sheath dress, which has a beautiful sheen and slightly retro look. I can tell before trying it on that it will be too big in the chest. Frowning, I'm tempted to not bother. There's no way I can compete with how Francesca must look when she wears this dress. But it's gorgeous, and the thought of wearing a dress that belongs to the star, if even for a few minutes, convinces me. Taking my clothes off, I shimmy into the dress and am struggling with the zipper when there's a knock on the door.

"Are you dressed, Pia?" Francesca opens the door slightly, peeking in.

"I just need help with the zipper."

After Francesca zips the dress up all the way, I'm surprised that it's only gapping a little bit around my chest. I then remember I'm wearing one of the padded bras from Victoria's Secret. I had decided to treat myself to new bras. After seeing the effect I had on Gregory with the padded bra I'd received from Erica as a gift, I felt more comfortable with the idea of wearing them. No doubt the bra's padding is helping to fill the space in the dress.

"Beautiful! I knew this royal blue would make your blond hair come alive, and it only needs to be taken in a little."

Francesca pulls the dress in at the sides a bit and motions for me to look in the mirror.

She's right. The color is perfect with my hair, and now that she's holding the fabric in, the dress looks like it was custom-made for my body.

"May I remove your clip?"

She doesn't wait for my response as she removes the banana clip that's holding my tresses up in a loose chignon. I liked the way my hair looked up. It gave me a certain chic with this dress. But once my hair spills over my shoulders, and Francesca shakes it out with her hands, the effect is amazing!

"Now for the shoes." Francesca walks over to her closet and takes out a pair of four-inch navy and white pumps. I'm not so sure about the white, but I don't say anything.

"I forgot to ask you what size you are? Seven? Eight?"

"Seven and a half."

"Oh! So these should fit you. I am an eight. If they are a little loose, we will just put a few cotton balls in the toe of the shoe."

I step into the pumps. My legs are instantly transformed. My calves look shapely and longer. And the white in the pumps that I was hesitant about adds a certain sexy effect to the shoes.

"Wow!"

"Wow, indeed. You look just as good as I do in this outfit."

Of course Francesca wastes no time in turning the attention back on herself. Mentally, I roll my eyes.

Francesca continues. "I remember the first time I wore this dress."

"The first time? Was it a special occasion?" I ask her.

"I wore it in my twenties at one of my movie premieres. And the shoes . . . well, I definitely remember the first time I wore those shoes, but I was wearing a white Valentino tailored suit with them."

"You wore this dress in your twenties and it still fits you?" Francesca frowns.

"I'm sorry. I just mean that we all . . . change as we get . . ." I let my voice trail off as I realize I keep sticking my foot in my mouth.

"Well, I did have my tailor let it out a bit. But just a bit."

"Of course." I avert my gaze from Francesca's. I'm actually surprised that she still wears clothes from her youth since the styles change. Though the dress does have a retro feel, its classic sheath silhouette does not make it seem too dated. But what shocks me more is that I would have figured with all her money, she'd prefer buying new clothes every chance she got. But as soon as I have this thought, I notice Francesca's eyes are far away—no doubt returning to the memory of when she last wore this dress and these shoes. Suddenly, it all makes sense to me. She still wears clothes from her youth because she is sentimental.

"So, what was the event for the shoes?" I ask.

Francesca sighs. "It was the first time I became engaged."

"Really?" I can't help revealing my surprise.

"Yes. I had a feeling Mario would propose so I made sure I was dressed to the tens."

"You mean 'to the nines.' "

"Nines? I always thought the expression was 'dressed to the tens'? Ten is perfection. Why would it be nine?"

"I don't know. But trust me, it's the nines."

Francesca shrugs her shoulders.

"Mario Scarpone. He was your leading man in your first film, *La Sposa Pazza*?"

"*Si.* And at the time, all of Italy was in love with him. He was the equivalent of Brad Pitt. I still think he was one of the most handsome men I ever dated. We made quite a dashing couple."

"And who was the most handsome man you were ever with?"

Francesca's eyes immediately darken. But she gives a light laugh. "I do not know. There were several handsome men. It is difficult to say."

"Difficult or rather you refuse to say?"

Francesca's eyes meet mine. She seems startled that I'm challenging her. I'm waiting for my scolding, but now it's my turn to be surprised.

"You are quite perceptive. Yes, you are correct. I refuse to say."

"I guess I can respect your protecting the other man, especially since he's no doubt famous."

"He was not famous. But you are right. I am protecting his privacy."

Hmmm. In my research of Francesca's relationships, I never came across anyone she dated who was not either in the movie industry or known for his immense wealth. Knowing I can't press her any further on this, I change tactics since I'm getting quite a bit out of her.

"And what did you wear when you became engaged the second time?"

Francesca walks to her armoire and pulls out a candy-red halter dress with a few scattered rhinestones. The rhinestones are just enough so that the dress has sparkle without overdoing it.

"That's gorgeous!"

"You can try it on if you want."

"Oh, no. I can't take another dress. And I insist on just borrowing them. I can't keep these dresses now that I know they hold such sentimental value for you."

"Me? Sentimental?" Francesca laughs. "I simply could not part with these dresses because I love them so much and they still look gorgeous on me."

I don't believe her, but I keep my mouth shut.

"Anyway, I was planning on giving you two dresses. The other dress I laid out on the bed I thought you would like because it is black, and what young girl does not like a little black dress? But I will let you choose. And I do not want to hear any more talk about borrowing. These are a gift, and I will be highly insulted if you return them." Francesca gives me a reproachful look.

"Thank you, Francesca."

"My pleasure. Now decide if it will be the black or the red dress."

I'm unable to resist the red dress. I begin unzipping the royal-blue sheath dress when Francesca comes over and helps me. For a second, I see her give me the once-over when she sees me in my underwear. Does she wish she were still as thin as I am? I would kill for a few of her sultry curves.

Sliding into the red dress, I catch a glimpse of myself in the armoire's mirrors. I've never looked this sexy before. Though I usually like to dress in a more understated way to prevent lots of stares, I am utterly mesmerized by this dress. I want Gregory to see me in it.

"Slip these on." Francesca hands me red patent-leather sling-back, peep-toe sandals.

They seem a bit too conservative for this dress, which I envision matched with a vampy stiletto pump. But when I slide my feet into them, I see the effect Francesca was going for. The outfit still looks very sexy but in a classier way than it would've looked if I had worn stilettos.

"This dress will only need a few alterations."

I admire myself in the mirror. Francesca comes up behind me and brushes my hair to the side and over my right shoulder. She then inserts two hair combs, giving me a forties starlet appearance.

"Glamorous. I should have become a fashion consultant." Francesca's hands are clasped together, and she's beaming like a proud mother who's sending her daughter off to the prom.

"So, Sal Giametta was your second fiancé—the one who proposed to you when you were wearing this dress?"

"Yes. Unlike with my first engagement, I had no idea he was going to propose to me. We were having dinner at a restaurant in Rome and were planning on going to a nightclub. He was the director of my second film, *Donna Fortunata.* The chemistry between us was intense. I did not even care that he was quite significantly older than me."

"Sal Giametta was in his early forties when you were seeing him, and you were in your twenties, correct?"

"*Si, si.* You have done your research well. He was also married, but I am sure you know that already."

"Actually, I didn't." I can't believe such a scandalous fact hadn't surfaced in my research.

"I guess you are not that thorough." Francesca winks at me and smiles, indicating she's only teasing. But the remark manages to annoy me.

"You didn't have any problems dating a married man? And then becoming engaged to him?"

"His marriage was already over when we began seeing each other. They were separated, but not in the legal sense. It was very difficult in those days to get a divorce in Italy. It still is not easy. After I accepted his proposal, he convinced his wife to file for the divorce. We had a long battle ahead of us with the courts and the Church, but our engagement only lasted two months. I could not take the headache involved with his trying to get divorced. So I ended it."

*Quite loyal and patient,* I can't help thinking to myself.

"You didn't say why you ended your first engagement to Mario Scarpone. That is, if you were the one who broke it off."

"Of course I was the one. I ended all of my five engagements."

"Yes, I did read in my research that the rumors were that you had the change of heart. But a few people were skeptical. They thought you were just trying to save face because of your sex-symbol status, and to admit you'd been rejected would've been the worst insult to you."

"So, is that what they thought?" Francesca's hands are on her hips, and she's staring me down as if she wants to punch me.

Holding up my hands, I say, "Hey, this is what I read. I'm not the one saying it."

"I would love to see this research you came across."

"Why, Francesca? I thought you have always prided yourself on not caring what the media thinks."

"Ha! Do you really believe that, Pia? I am an actress. We all care what the media thinks. Plus, I am Italian. We always care about making a good impression and what others say or think about us."

She's right. My mother is the same way and so is Zia. *Fare la bella figura* or making a good impression. I'd heard that from both of them throughout my life.

"So, why did you end your engagement to Mario Scarpone?"

"I was young. I was not ready to get married, especially since my career had only just taken off. I knew I needed to establish myself with more movies before I could think about settling down and having children."

"And what happened with your third fiancé, Luca Barone, the heir to the Barone Leather House?"

"Ahh, Luca. I was engaged to him the longest—a year. We were just one month shy of our wedding. What can I say? I realized I was not in love with him. I did acquire so many beautiful leather coats and shoes while I was with him though." Francesca smirks.

I'm disgusted by her remark, but I don't dare say so. It's typical anyway. She's a narcissistic celebrity with a taste for the finer things in life.

"Why weren't you in love with him?"

Francesca laughs. "What kind of question is that? You either feel it or you do not. Why are you in love with Gregory?"

Refusing to let her turn the tables on me, I ignore her as I pull off the strap of the sling-back sandals and begin unzipping my dress.

"Wait! What are you doing? Keep the dress and sandals on."

"Why? I have nowhere to go this dressed up."

"Of course you do. After you leave here, you are going straight to Gregory's. He must see you dressed this way. I promise he will love the outfit and will be completely enchanted with you!"

"I don't know. I feel weird walking around this way. I'm not a movie star like you, and it isn't even nighttime. Besides, the dress needs to be altered."

"We can easily fix that with a few discreetly placed safety pins."

Francesca walks over to her dresser and takes a few safety pins out of a porcelain box. Returning to my side, she begins taking the dress in and carefully places the pins so that they're concealed within the folds of the fabric. When she's done, she places her hands on my shoulders and tilts my body so that I'm facing the armoire's mirrors. "Take a good look at yourself. You are a very beautiful young woman. Start believing it."

I'm feeling self-conscious, but I can't resist staring at myself one last time. A part of me does want Gregory to see me in this alluring, glamorous outfit. But I'm not accustomed to looking this way. As if reading my thoughts, Francesca whispers, "Trust me."

"Okay." I begin packing up my things. Fortunately, I have my large tote bag with me today so I can throw my clothes in there. I still want to hear about Francesca's last two fiancés. Glancing at my watch, I see that I've been here for two hours. Of course, it didn't help that I was kept waiting yet again. I'm supposed to meet Gregory at Zia's bakery. Suddenly, with horror, I realize I can't let Zia see me like this. I can just hear what she'll say: "That *puttana* dressed you like a Hollywood whore!" I'll have to call him and ask him if we can meet somewhere else.

"So, why did you call off your last two engagements?"

"I have shared enough for one day, Pia."

"Does that mean we'll pick up where we left off at our next meeting?"

"I think I would like to focus on my acting method and why I won two Oscars."

Great! She's clamming up once again. But I'm not worried. I can tell now that Francesca does want to open up more to me. She just has to feel that it's on her terms.

"That's a great idea. I really want to get into the nitty-gritty of your acting style and dissect the movies you won Oscars for scene by scene."

"Oh! Yes, that sounds wonderful." Francesca plasters on a phony smile, but there's a hint of disappointment in her voice.

I pick up the hanger holding the royal-blue sheath, but Francesca stops me.

"I will ask Angelica to take it in for you. She's quite an expert seamstress. I will tell her what needs to be done."

"Really?" I can't help but wonder again why Angelica chose to be a maid when she could've used her seamstress skills working for a designer or even opened up her own business.

"Yes, she told me she makes most of her clothes. When she comes to work, before she changes into her uniform, she is dressed impeccably. I am thinking of asking her to make a dress for me. It has been ages since I have had a custom-made dress."

"You shop off the rack?" My voice comes out in a high shrill.

"No, of course not. I am Francesca Donata. I have a personal shopper who brings clothes from only the finest boutiques in Milan and Paris to my villa in Italy."

"I would think with your money, all of your wardrobe would be custom-made."

"I do not have the patience to wait for the clothes to be made, and I never liked someone fawning over me with a tape measure."

I suspect the latter reason is her real motive for shying away from custom-made outfits. Though she has a to-die-for figure for a woman her age, she is fuller than she was in her youth. Fortunately for her, most of the weight seems to have gone to her breasts, hips, and derrière and has further enhanced her already sensual physique. If only every woman could age as gracefully.

"Thank you for the dresses and for asking Angelica to make the necessary alterations."

"It is my pleasure. The dress will be ready tomorrow."

"There's no need for Angelica to rush. I can wait."

"Nonsense! Besides, I want to hear all about Gregory's reaction when he sees you in the red dress. Be sure to bring it with you so that Angelica can alter that one as well."

"Okay."

"Actually, Pia, I cannot wait until our next interview to hear how it went with Gregory. How about you come by tomorrow afternoon? The dress will be ready by then, and we will have tea. Well, you can have tea if you wish. I never drink tea. I will have espresso—or something stronger." Francesca gives me a conspiratorial smile.

Returning the smile, I say, "Okay. I'll see you then. You don't need to come down with me. I'll let myself out."

"Yes, you know your way around here well now." Francesca

narrows her gaze. Again, she's giving me a hint that she knows I eavesdropped on her earlier when she was in the bathroom with Signora Tesca.

Walking down the spiral staircase, I can't help but feel elated. This interview went very well. Finally, I feel like Francesca is warming up to me and revealing more. Though I still think she can be haughty and self-centered, I do feel that she is longing for companionship. Her acting like my girlfriend and giving me two of her dresses attests to that.

"Miss Santore?"

I'm about to walk out the front door when I hear Francesca's bodyguard, Edgardo, calling me.

"Hello, Edgardo."

"Good morning, Miss Santore. How are you?"

"I'm well, thank you."

Edgardo is staring at my legs. Suddenly, I remember the sexy outfit I'm in. How could I forget?

"We'd like you to start using the back entrance when you arrive and leave here. It would just make the bodyguards' job easier, so that they don't have to constantly fend off the mob outside whenever someone comes and goes. Plus, I've noticed how the paparazzi have been hounding you lately."

Edgardo is referring to the fact that the paparazzi found out I'm interning at *Profile*. Not only were they harassing me with questions about Francesca, but they even took to insulting me out of jealousy for my having full access to her. I'm so grateful I could kiss him, but I merely voice my appreciation.

"Thank you very much, Edgardo. That makes my life easier, too."

Edgardo nods. "Just follow me, and I'll show you where the back door is."

He leads me through the immense kitchen. The staff doesn't even look up. That's how engrossed they are in their work. We go down about five steps, to where there's a door that looks like it leads to the backyard.

"Hold on." He motions for me to stay back as he glances out the door's window. Confident the coast is clear, he waves me forward. "This leads out to the backyard. The neighbor generously allowed us to cut some of the fencing that separates her yard from Signora

Tesca's, so that we can go through her property and avoid detection by the mob outside."

"How much did you pay her?"

Edgardo smiles. "Money does talk. She was reluctant at first, but we definitely made it worth her while."

"Thanks again."

Edgardo holds the door open for me. I'm also secretly relieved I didn't have to leave the house through the front, looking the way I do. The paparazzi would have no doubt noticed and eaten me alive.

As I step out into the yard, my heels quickly sink into the lawn. Sighing, I take out a tissue from my bag and bend over to wipe the mud from my heels. When I stand back up, I almost scream. A man towers over me, staring intensely.

"Oh my God!"

"I'm—I'm sorry. I did not mean to alarm you," the man stammers. He appears flustered. "I was lost in my thoughts before I looked up and almost slammed into you."

"It's okay. If you'll please excuse me, I'll be on my way."

"Were you here to see my aunt?"

"Aunt? You mean Signora Tesca?"

"No, she's my mother."

"Oh!" I remember the neighbors had mentioned Signora Tesca has a son who visits infrequently.

"My Aunt Francesca." He comes closer to me and with a devilish grin whispers, "The Crazy Bride."

I can't help but laugh. "Yes, I was here to see her. How did you know?"

"My mother mentioned to me that a young woman has been coming by to do a series of interviews with Francesca. I'm sorry. Where are my manners today? First, I give you the fright of your life, and then I forget to introduce myself. Lorenzo Tesca."

Shaking his hand, I say, "Pia Santore. Nice to meet you."

As I get closer, I see his hair is much darker than Signora Tesca's red hair. Since I have yet to see Signora Tesca in person, I cannot tell whether they share any resemblance. From the photos I've seen of her when she was younger, I don't see any. He takes off his sunglasses, revealing a captivating pair of hazel eyes that complement his bronzed skin perfectly. He's slightly taller than average height for a man, but he looks to be in incredible shape. I can tell he works out religiously.

"I hope my aunt has not been very difficult to work with."

Smiling, I say, "So even her family knows she can be difficult."

"Of course! But I have never met her and am only going by the little my mother has told me about her and what I've heard from the media."

I must not have heard him right. Did he actually say he's never met his aunt?

"I'm sorry. You said you've never met your aunt?"

"Yes. I will meet her for the first time in person today."

"How can that be?"

"She and my mother haven't seen each other in a long time."

Then I remember Francesca and Signora Tesca's estrangement, so it does make sense that he's never met his aunt since the two sisters haven't even seen each other in thirty years.

"We have talked on the phone a handful of times and corresponded by letters, but this will be the first time I am meeting her in person."

"You must be excited to meet your famous aunt at last."

"Not as excited as a starstruck fan." Lorenzo laughs. "But I'd be lying if I said I wasn't a bit eager. I am curious to see what she really is like. Any warnings you can throw my way would be greatly appreciated."

Lorenzo is easy to talk to, and he seems very down-to-earth. He's dressed casually. His chocolate-brown khakis look like they've been pressed. Who irons their khakis? A cream-colored button-down shirt is tucked in his pants but not tightly. It appears as if he intentionally tucked it haphazardly to go for a slightly messy look, but it totally works. And the sleeves are rolled up to about three quarters, showing off more of his tan. A thick leather belt wraps around his trim waist. His leather sandals are the only part of his wardrobe I'm not crazy about.

"Miss Santore? I know you're probably afraid to divulge anything about Francesca that might get back to her, but I'm pleading with you. I'm a desperate man. I need to know what awaits me behind those walls."

Realizing with horror that I never answered his question and that I've been checking him out, I apologize.

"I'm sorry. I was in a daze. It's been a long day."

"I'm sure." Lorenzo smiles, looking amused. His eyes wander from my hair down to my toes and back up to meet my gaze. My knees feel weak.

"Ahhh, a warning, right? Whatever you do, don't refer to her as Signora Donata. Then again, that should be easy for you since I'm sure you'll just be calling her Aunt Francesca or Zia Francesca."

"Ahhh, yes, I have heard about her testiness when it comes to her marital status and title. But when the world knows her as 'The Crazy Bride' and for breaking off five engagements in addition to her film characters' running out repeatedly on their grooms, can one blame her?"

He's right. I'd never thought of it that way. For the first time, I feel some compassion toward Francesca.

"Well, it was nice to meet you, Lorenzo. I need to get going. Good luck!" I start to walk away.

"You still owe me a warning. The one you gave me doesn't count since I would never call my aunt *signora* or *signorina*."

Turning around, I shrug my shoulders and say, "Just make her feel like she's in control at all times. Don't question her, and I'm sure excessive flattery will get you far, too. Then again, I might be wrong. Francesca Donata is one of the most mercurial people I have ever met. But you have an advantage as her nephew whom she's never seen face-to-face. Something tells me once she takes a look at you she'll be nothing but sweet toward you."

"Really?" Lorenzo smirks, and my words come echoing back to me. Oh God! What did I just say? I implied to him that he's handsome and that when Francesca sees him, that alone will sway her.

"Again, it was nice to meet you, Lorenzo. I'm sorry, but I'm going to be late for my appointment."

I hurry toward the opening that Edgardo showed me will lead to the neighbor's driveway.

"Just one more question, Miss Santore, and then I promise I'll let you go."

I continue walking and call out, "What is it?"

"Are you done with your interviews?"

"No, I have at least two more, maybe even three."

"Good. So I'll be seeing you again. I look forward to it."

Glancing over my shoulder, I see Lorenzo just standing there staring at my legs. When he notices I've caught him, he winks at me and waves before he heads for the entrance to the house. A movement from one of the second-story windows catches my eye. But as soon as I look up, whoever was standing there steps back, letting the curtain fall back into place. I'm almost certain that window corresponds to Francesca's bedroom. Did she witness my whole encounter with Lorenzo?

Pushing Francesca out of my mind, I try to forget about Lorenzo, but it's useless. I feel slightly unsettled. It's nothing, I tell myself. He's an attractive, charming man. What woman wouldn't be fazed by him?

My phone beeps, alerting me to a text message. Pulling it out of my purse, I see the message is from Gregory:

ARE YOU STILL AT FRANCESCA'S? I'M AT THE BAKERY. BEEN HERE FOR ALMOST FIFTEEN MINUTES.

Shoot! I should've texted him before I left the Mussolini Mansion to tell him to meet me at 718 Lounge instead. It's too late now. I'll just have to deal with Zia's reaction to my makeover.

I text Gregory back:

LEAVING NOW. WILL BE THERE IN FIVE MINUTES.

Remembering my heels, I change it to ten minutes instead. Then I make my way through the fence and walk down the neighbor's driveway. Once I'm out front, I walk as fast as I can in my heels to Zia's bakery. A few cars honk their horns as they pass by, and the men walking down the street stare at me.

The walk from Signora Tesca's house to the bakery usually takes me five minutes, but in these monstrous heels, it feels like a half hour. Pushing open the door to the bakery, I take a quick glance behind the sales counter and am relieved to see that Zia isn't in sight. Gregory is sitting at a table to the back. He's with Connie and another woman with long, dark curly hair. My heart skips a beat. I can't deny that I'm feeling a bit self-conscious since I'm so dressed up. Can't do anything about it now. Taking a deep breath, I try to walk as gracefully as possible to Gregory's table. Gregory glances in my direction, but returns his gaze to Connie, who seems to be talking a mile a minute and gesturing with her hands animatedly. I can't believe it. He doesn't recognize me. Stepping up to the table, I say in my most cheerful voice, "Hey, guys!"

Gregory looks up at me and for a second has a frown on his face as if to say, "Who are you?" But then his eyes open wide as recognition finally dawns on him.

"Pia!"

"Hey, Pia! Wow! You look stunning! Doesn't she, Rita?"

The woman next to Connie nods and says, "Yes, you do."

"Pia, this is my sister, Rita."

"Nice to meet you." I lean over and shake her hand. I can't help feeling like a towering giraffe.

"We saved a seat for you." Connie pulls out the empty chair between her and Gregory.

"Thanks!"

Gregory is just gaping at me. He still hasn't complimented me.

"Do you have a wedding to go to?" Rita asks me.

"No. It's a bit of a long story." I can feel my cheeks begin to blush. I should've changed into my own clothes before coming here. But the thought of having Gregory see me like this was too enticing. Now he doesn't even seem to care.

"Well, we're not in a rush, and we love good stories!" Connie elbows Rita, and they both nod their heads. I guess Connie can't take a hint.

"Yes, I'd love to hear the story of why you're so dressed up," Gregory says in a deadpan tone.

"You hate it."

"No, you look very nice. I'm just surprised. It's the middle of the morning, and we don't have plans to go out to brunch to a fancy restaurant. It's just so—so different from your style. Not bad, just different." Gregory shrugs his shoulders.

Connie and Rita exchange nervous glances and look down as if they're embarrassed for me.

"Francesca gave me this dress and insisted I wear it. And you know how it is, Gregory; you can't say no to Queen Francesca."

Gregory presses his lips tightly together. I can tell I've angered him.

"*That* is Francesca Donata's dress?" Rita asks me. Her eyes are practically bulging out of her head.

"Oh my God, Pia! Can you imagine how much that dress is worth or will be worth some day? Don't tell me it's a dress she's had for a while and one with some historic significance?" Connie holds her hand to her heart.

"Actually, yes, she told me she was wearing this dress when her second fiancé proposed to her."

"Millions! That dress is worth millions!" Connie is gesturing with her hands again.

"Yeah, you've totally stepped in shit, girl!" Rita is shaking her head, incredulous at my good luck.

"She also gave me another dress, which she wore to one of her movie premieres when she was just in her twenties."

"She gave you *two* dresses?" Connie's eyes are bulging out of her head.

I nod.

"Did she say which movie premiere she wore the dress to?" Connie is leaning closely now, staring at the dress as if she's inspecting a rare gem beneath a magnifying glass.

"No. I forgot to ask her."

"You have to find out and tell us," Rita says. "Oh, wait!" She slaps her forehead. "I can do a search online on my phone right now for her movie premieres. Maybe a photo of her wearing that dress will show up."

"That could take forever, Rita," Gregory says in the most exasperated tone.

Rita ignores him as she pulls out her phone and begins her search.

"The shoes look vintage, too." Connie is now bending over to stare at my shoes.

Rita forgets about her online search and also looks at my shoes. My earlier awkwardness is gone now in light of Connie and Rita's awe over my outfit.

"Wow! I guess you've finally fallen into her good graces," Gregory says with obvious sarcasm in his voice.

Our eyes meet, and mine betray the hurt I'm feeling. Of course, perceptive as ever, Gregory notices and nervously glances away.

"So, what is she like?" Connie asks me.

"Yeah, tell us *everything!* Is she really as much of a diva as she appears to be?"

I hesitate, not wanting to compromise Francesca's privacy. But I also don't want to disappoint the DeLuca sisters. They're like a couple of schoolgirls who have just seen their celebrity crush.

"She does have the diva qualities, but I get the feeling what she shows the public is very different from who she is."

"So it's all just an act?" Rita asks.

"No. I guess what I'm saying is that there's more to her than what we see. She also is very guarded about her personal life. It's been tough interviewing her and getting more out of her."

"You're so lucky to have this opportunity to interview her. This will help your career *tremendously!*" Connie nods her head, looking to Rita for approval. Rita nods her head.

"Yes, I have Gregory to thank for getting me the interview with Francesca." I glance toward him. He's staring at me and manages a small smile.

"You didn't tell me that, Greg! You're holding out on me as usual!" Connie playfully swats his arm.

Rita gets up. "We need to go. Ma is going to send the search party for us soon."

"Sorry, Pia. We'd love to hear more about Francesca, but we have all these bridal gown alterations we need to complete today. I'll call you. Maybe the three of us can go for drinks later this week and you can tell us more about your interviews with Francesca? Oh my God! Aldo has to come! He'd never forgive us. He's been camped out in front of the Mussolini Mansion ever since he heard the neighbors saw her twice."

"Who's Aldo?" I ask.

"He's a good friend of ours and our older sister Valentina's best friend. He was visiting her in Venice when Francesca was first spotted. He's been cursing his bad luck at not being here to see one of his movie idols," Rita offers.

"Please say it's okay for Aldo to join us, too? You'll love him, I swear." Connie holds her hands in a prayer position over her heart and gives me an irresistible smile. I can see why Lou fell in love with her.

"That's fine, but I don't want to get your hopes up. As I said, I haven't been able to get a lot out of her." I know I'm telling a small white lie, but I don't feel comfortable revealing anything about Francesca's past to them yet. They'll just have to wait to read about it in my article when it's published.

"We'll talk to you later in the week. Again, you really look gorgeous, doesn't she, Gregory?" Connie throws a stern glance in his direction.

"Yes, yes, you look very pretty," Gregory says sheepishly, as if he's been scolded by his mother.

Connie kisses me good-bye as if we've been the best of friends forever, and Rita follows suit.

After they leave, Gregory asks, "Where are my manners? I forgot to ask you if you wanted anything to drink or eat?"

"No, thanks. I'm fine."

Gregory nods his head. A few moments of silence follow. Finally, he says, "I'm sorry. You do look beautiful. It's just I was surprised. You have your own style, which I love, and I guess I just didn't want you falling prey to letting Francesca or anyone else try to make you over."

"You're right. I do have my style, but I'm also a woman who's prone to wanting to look pretty for her boyfriend. I'll go change. I do feel overdressed and a bit silly after clonking all the way over here in these heels." I smile shyly.

Gregory places his hand over mine. "You don't need to change. I just wanted to make sure that you weren't conforming to pressure and becoming someone you're not. I love you exactly the way you are."

I lean over and kiss Gregory.

"Hmm . . . Hmm!"

"Oh, hi, Zia. I didn't see you."

"I know!" Zia is frowning. I immediately blush.

"*Sei bella!* Do you two have something special planned?" Zia then inspects Gregory's usual ultra-casual clothes and frowns once again.

"No. I just came back from one of my interviews with Francesca, and she insisted I take one of her dresses. She seemed so pleased that I didn't want to disappoint or insult her by refusing the gift."

"Listen to me, Pia. You do not need that *puttana*'s charity! You hear me?" Zia's voice borders on yelling. A few of the bakery's patrons glance in our direction.

"That's not how it was, Zia. She was just doing something nice for me."

"You don't need the likes of her doing something nice for you! She's trying to turn you into her. Not everyone needs to be a Barbie doll. All that *puttana* cares about are her looks." Zia scrambles away, muttering under her breath.

Great! Now Gregory must feel even more vindicated in his own disapproval of my outfit.

"Ignore her. It's obvious she's not a fan of Francesca's."

"Oh no! From day one, she couldn't get what all the fuss was about with the neighbors camped out in front of the Mussolini Mansion."

Gregory laughs, and I join him.

"Let's get out of here."

"Do you mind if I stop home really quick to change into something more comfortable?"

"Sure."

I stand up, and Gregory's eyes drop to my legs.

"On second thought, forget about changing. Your outfit is growing on me more and more." He winks.

"Men!" I shake my head. "Then they accuse women of not knowing what they want."

We walk out of the bakery hand in hand.

# ❧ 18 ❧

# Francesca

There is no mistaking who the young man is talking to Pia in Giuliana's backyard, although I have never met him in person, and the last photograph Giuliana sent me of him was from when he graduated college a dozen years ago. He was a bit of a party boy from what his mother told me and took an additional two years to complete his bachelor's degree. But he more than made it up for it by becoming a doctoral student in comparative literature at Columbia University. This year, he finally received his doctorate.

I was expecting him today. Making my way downstairs, I see him enter the library. Before I step into the room, I take a moment to study him further. He helps himself to a cup of espresso and then stares at the vase of daisies perched on the coffee table. His eyes fill with sadness. No doubt he is thinking about his mother and her love of daisies.

"At last we meet in person, Lorenzo." I stride over, smiling warmly.

"Zia Francesca! You never age—well, at least from the photos I've seen of you." Lorenzo smiles as he walks over and gives me a hug. After a second, I begin to back away, but he holds onto me for a moment longer. Then, he kisses both of my cheeks.

"It really is you, isn't it? I guess my mother wasn't lying all those years, telling me the great Francesca Donata was my aunt."

"I am surprised she even owned up to it."

"Isn't it time you two bury the hatchet?" Lorenzo rolls his eyes.

"I would love nothing more, but your mother is stubborn. Although I am amazed she has not thrown me out yet, and it has been a few weeks now since I first arrived in Astoria."

"Give it time. I'm sure she'll throw you out soon." Lorenzo belts out a boisterous laugh. I cannot help noticing how different his temperament is from my sister's. He is more like his father, who was often joking and enjoying life.

"I saw you were talking to Pia Santore."

"Yes, she's a lovely young woman. I understand she's interviewing you for *Profile?*"

"She is."

Lorenzo nods his head thoughtfully.

"So, how is my mother doing? How does she look? I need to brace myself before I see her, especially since I haven't seen her since Christmas."

"She has lost some weight and looks pale, but I think it was more of a shock for me to see her since we had not seen each other in over thirty years."

"What could have happened between you to avoid each other for so long? Italians are supposed to be close-knit and never abandon family."

"I never abandoned her, Lorenzo."

"I'm not saying that. You know what I mean. I hear of stuff like this happening to American families. You can't even begin to imagine how lonely it was for me growing up with only Mama in my life. Nonno and Nonna were in Sicily, and I don't even remember the one time I met them as a boy when we visited."

"*Mi dispiaccio,* Lorenzo. I truly am sorry we could not have known each other when you were younger. I suppose it all seems very senseless now that Giuliana is not well."

Lorenzo sighs. "I'm sorry, too. I should not be making you feel guilty. Life is complicated. Family is complicated."

"Even Italian families?" I laugh.

"Yes, we're proof of that!" Lorenzo laughs with me.

"We should be grateful that we are all together now. Honestly, I never thought I would see her again."

"My mother thought she'd never see you again either."

"Shall we go find her? She has been excited all morning."

"Yes, let's go, Zia Francesca. And, Zia, you made the right decision in coming."

Lorenzo places his arm around my shoulder as we make our way up to my sister's bedroom. And for the first time in my life, I feel a sense of belonging.

# ❦ 19 ❦

# Pia

Here I am once again, sitting in Signora Tesca's library waiting for Her Royal Highness. I've become accustomed to Francesca's tardiness, and I actually expect it now when I arrive. Since we had decided I would drop by to pick up the royal-blue sheath dress Francesca was giving me and that Angelica was altering, I called her and asked if we could move up our next interview to this afternoon as well. Colin is getting impatient and wants to see a first draft of my proposed article in a week. He told me it doesn't have to be the entire article, but he wants to see something. I haven't even begun writing it. He's letting me take a few days off this week so I can have more time to meet with Francesca. Now that I'm finally getting Francesca to feel comfortable around me and open up more, I want to wait until all of our interviews are done before I begin writing. We have one more scheduled after today. Then I can review my notes and get a better sense of how to shape the piece.

I remembered to bring the red dress Francesca gave me so that Angelica can also alter it. Placing the garment bag holding the dress beside me on the couch, I'm still almost tempted to return it and not even take the first dress she gave me. But I know that would be the ultimate insult to Francesca. After working so hard to gain her favor—and I'm still not sure I've completely won it—I can't risk incurring her wrath now. Besides, I can always wear the dresses to a wedding or some other fancy event.

"Hello. You must be—heh . . . heh . . . hehhhhh!"

I'm shaken out of my reverie by the sound of an older woman's voice followed by a fit of coughing. Looking over my shoulder, I'm stunned. Signora Tesca! Though I've only seen the photos of her from when she was younger, there's no mistaking Giuliana. The penny-red hair is still evident amidst the graying strands that are overtaking it. Sadly, most of her beauty from her youth has faded. Her complexion is very pale with a yellowish tinge—obviously, it's not the complexion of a healthy person.

As Olivia had told me, Signora Tesca's hair is cut in a pixie style, and her narrow, weasel-like eyes squint intensely in my direction. Vanity must prevent her from investing in a pair of eyeglasses. I guess that's one trait she shares with her famous sister. With both hands, she holds onto a cane, which I'm afraid is about to buckle from her violent coughing. I stand up and walk over to her. By the time I reach Signora Tesca, her coughing has subsided.

"Hello. You must be Signora Tesca. I'm Pia Santore." I extend my hand.

"Please excuse me, but I doubt you really want to shake my hand after I just hacked a lung into it." Signora Tesca smiles feebly.

Returning her smile, I lower my hand. I feel embarrassed for her, but she seems unperturbed by the awkward moment.

"I see my sister is keeping you waiting. Late should be her middle name. Even when we were children, she took forever getting ready. If you don't mind, I can keep you company until she arrives."

"I'd like that."

We head over to the couch. Signora Tesca shuffles her feet very slowly. I try not to notice and act as if I'm staring at the arrangement of daisies on the coffee table. Finally, she sits down in the chaise chair opposite the couch.

"How is Antoniella?"

"She's fine. Working hard as always. Thank you. I'll tell her you asked about her. Zia always wants to know if I've seen you when I come over."

Signora Tesca nods her head. "Please give her my best. I haven't gotten out much these past few months. I'm sure you have gathered I am not well."

"Only recently."

"Francesca has not said anything?"

"No, she hasn't."

"Of course not. I'm sure she is focused on regaling you with tales from her glorious acting career." Signora Tesca looks over toward the French doors. Her voice is dripping with sarcasm and hostility.

"Actually, when I have tried to ask about you, Francesca has been fiercely protective of your privacy. I think that is the reason why she hasn't mentioned your not feeling well."

"Perhaps." She nods her head.

"I'm sure this all has not been very easy on you."

"What do you mean?" Signora Tesca looks at me, startled.

"The crowd outside."

"Oh yes, yes. Well, at least my walls are pretty thick, and I haven't heard them too much."

I'm sure she must have thought I was referring to her being reunited with her estranged sister. An awkward silence ensues. I'm tempted to ask about her estrangement from Francesca, but fear prevents me from doing so. Signora Tesca appears to have a bit of the same mercurial temper Francesca has, and I don't want to offend her. Searching my brain for small talk, I say, "You must be happy your son is here."

Her eyes light up.

"Yes. He's been away from home since Christmas, but now that he has received his degree, I hope to see him more."

"What has he received his degree in?"

"He has his doctorate in comparative literature."

"Impressive."

"Yes, I am very proud of him. He's traveled a lot in the past two years, doing research, so I haven't seen him as much as I would have liked."

I now remember the cruel words the neighbors had said about Lorenzo's not visiting often, as if he couldn't stand his mother.

The front door opens, and I can hear the crowd that's parked outside yelling, "Francesca!" After a second, the door closes with a loud bang. Signora Tesca and I look toward the door.

"Animals!" Lorenzo cries out as he steps into the library. He freezes when he sees me and immediately scans me from head to toe. My face flushes.

"I'm sorry, Mama. I didn't realize you had company. Miss Santore, it's a pleasure to see you again." Lorenzo walks over and shakes my hand.

"Hello." I avert my eyes.

"Lorenzo, is the crowd as large as it was when your aunt first arrived?" Signora Tesca asks.

"I wasn't here when Zia Francesca first arrived. Remember, Mama?"

"Oh, that's right. I'm sorry, son." Signora Tesca looks momentarily embarrassed by her lapse in memory.

"No worries." Lorenzo walks over to his mother and kisses her on the cheek.

"I'm sorry to have interrupted. Do you mind if I join you?" Lorenzo searches my face, and I have no choice but to meet his gaze. His lips curl up slightly in a smirk as if he knows he's making me uncomfortable.

"Of course not, Lorenzo." Signora Tesca motions with her cane for Lorenzo to sit next to me on the couch.

"I'm waiting for your aunt," I say lamely, not knowing what else to say.

"I gathered as much."

Suddenly, we hear conversation coming from the staircase that leads to the second-story bedrooms. The talking becomes louder as Francesca and whomever she's talking to descend the stairs. There's something familiar about the other woman's voice as it reaches my ears.

"The artwork is absolutely breathtaking. Your sister has quite a collection!"

Madeline Drabinski! What is *she* doing here? Paranoia quickly enters my mind. Is Madeline trying to snag her own interview with Francesca? She's been giving me the evil eye whenever I run into her at *Profile*'s offices. Did Madeline contact Francesca behind

Colin's back? Granted, she is *Profile*'s art critic, but she's also been known to conduct interviews of people other than artists or the rich and famous with extensive art collections.

"Oh, she has another appointment," Lorenzo says. "Mama, are you planning on selling your artwork? I thought you were leaving it all to me when you pass on."

Signora Tesca and I shoot daggers in Lorenzo's direction. I can't believe how insensitive he's being given that his mother is apparently very ill.

"I see your trademark bluntness is intact as always, Lorenzo. You share that with your famous aunt," Signora Tesca says in a deadpan voice. I find myself liking her more and more.

"Forgive me, Mama, I didn't mean any offense. You know me— always joking." He gets up and kisses his mother. Her tight scowl lines from a moment ago quickly vanish. He does know how to charm her. I give him that. But his use of "mama" is quite annoying. Who still calls their mother "mama" unless you're in England? It sounds very affected.

"I'm not selling the artwork, Lorenzo. That woman is a friend of Francesca's."

"Really?" I can't hide my surprise.

"She's with that magazine where you are interning. She used to work at *Architectural Digest* a long time ago. While there, she interviewed Francesca for an article she was writing on her artwork in her villa in Taormina, Sicily."

Madeline is turning out to be one surprise after another. I guess the rumors about Madeline's going from her modeling career to her current position at *Profile* are unfounded, as is the gossip I heard recently that she slept with someone to get her job. Still, there's something about her I don't like or trust.

We hear the two women exchange good-byes. Francesca enters the library.

"My apologies, Pia. That appointment lasted a little longer than I had planned."

I want to say, "You never plan," but I bite my tongue.

"I see Giuliana and Lorenzo have kept you company. *Grazie!*"

Lorenzo greets her, but Giuliana doesn't even so much as glance in her direction. Whatever happened between these sisters must've been a doozy for Signora Tesca to have so much resentment still toward Francesca.

"We'll leave you so you can conduct your meeting in private. I have some matters to discuss with Mama." Lorenzo gets up and shakes my hand. Is he going to shake my hand every time he says hello and good-bye to me? I can't help wondering. Again, he holds my hand for a moment too long, and again, butterflies flutter in my belly. He then kisses his aunt on the cheek. Francesca gets the same sparkle in her eyes that Signora Tesca had when I asked her about Lorenzo. No doubt they love him very much.

Signora Tesca leans on Lorenzo's arm as they leave the library.

"So? I am dying to hear all about Gregory's reaction to your makeover!" Francesca takes a pastry I don't recognize from the covered platter that's on the coffee table. It's amazing she hasn't turned into an elephant yet, since every time I come over she's helping herself to whatever sweets Carlo or Angelica have put out.

"Have you ever had fried ravioli?" she asks.

"Those are ravioli? They look nothing like pasta."

"They are not pasta but pastry ravioli. You *must* try one! You'll love it, I promise!"

The raviolis remind me of funnel cake in their appearance— fried dough with a sprinkling of powdered sugar. I bite into one. The filling has a sweet, creamy texture. I can also taste cinnamon. They're absolutely heavenly!

"Wow! They're delicious. What's in them?"

"Ricotta with sugar and cinnamon. They are an old recipe my mother used to make when Giuliana and I were children. The recipe was passed down from my grandmother."

"You made these?" I ask incredulously. Though I try hard, I just can't envision Francesca toiling away in a kitchen.

"*Si!* You sound surprised. I can do more than just act, Pia." Francesca's annoyance flashes through her face.

"I thought you would have cooks like most other celebrities."

"And I do, but I enjoy cooking and baking. It relieves my stress."

I nod my head and continue eating my ravioli.

"Have another one." Francesca holds the platter toward me. They're too good. I can't resist having a second one even though I can feel how tight my jeans have gotten in the past few weeks since

I've arrived in Astoria. Having an aunt who owns a bakery is dangerous.

"Out with it. Gregory could not resist you in my dress, could he?"

"Actually, not only could he resist me in my dress, but he wasn't thrilled with my new look."

"Ah! He is a man! They are moody!" Francesca chuckles and waves her hand dismissively.

"Moodiness usually applies to women and their monthly cycles, not men." I'm not amused by Francesca's take on why Gregory hated my makeover.

"Oh, Pia! You really have no idea what Gregory was doing? He was afraid you would attract other men with your sultry new look. I must admit, Pia, I am a little disappointed in you."

"In me? Why?" My voice rises.

"Calm down. Here you are this confident, budding young journalist who can stand foot-to-foot with me."

"The expression is toe-to-toe," I say and can't help laughing.

"You know what I mean. Do not correct me!" Francesca stares me down. I stare back. The more I get to know her, the less she intimidates me. We continue staring at each other for what feels like a full minute. She finally looks away. I win!

"As I was saying, you are this self-assured woman, and you quickly revert to your . . . your . . . more ordinary fashion sensibilities because your boyfriend did not approve. That is why I am disappointed in you. I expect so much more from you."

"Do you?" I'm totally not buying her speech.

"Yes." Francesca pours herself a cup of espresso and takes a long sip.

Deciding it's time I change the subject before my own temper unleashes, I flip through my notebook to my questions for today. But first, I need to get to the bottom of why Madeline Drabinski met with Francesca—the *real* reason.

"Why was Madeline Drabinski here?"

"Were you eavesdropping . . . *again*?" Francesca's gaze meets mine, no doubt to try to ascertain whether I will lie to her.

"I wouldn't call it eavesdropping. We all overheard your conversation. You were both talking so loudly."

"I am surprised your editor has not shared with you that Madeline is interested in writing a piece about Giuliana's vast art collection," Francesca says in a snide tone.

Willing the muscles in my face to remain relaxed, I say as sweetly as possible, "That's none of my concern, so of course my editor wouldn't share that with me. He doesn't tell me whom the writers are planning on interviewing."

"But he knows you are interviewing me, and I would think having another writer at *Profile* also interview me might be a conflict of interest. Do you agree?"

For some reason, it's as if Francesca is trying to goad me. Just when I think we might be on the verge of becoming BFFs by sharing clothes and doing girly things like making me over, she switches to Mr. Hyde mode and becomes her usual bitchy self.

"It's not a conflict of interest. I am interviewing you about your life and your acting career. Madeline is interviewing you about your sister's art collection. Two very different topics."

"I guess." Francesca seems to be at a loss.

"Shouldn't Madeline be interviewing Giuliana since it is her art collection?"

"Giuliana has no interest in being in the spotlight, and she has never wanted the world to know that we are sisters."

"But the world now knows."

"She does not wish to be bothered, especially since she is . . ."

"Ill?"

Francesca's cheeks turn slightly pink. I've never seen her blush before.

"It's okay, Francesca. I figured out the last time I was here that Giuliana is sick, and she just admitted it to me when I met her. It's quite obvious once you see her."

Francesca's eyes fill with tears. She tries to conceal her face behind her espresso cup as she takes a sip, but the ridiculously small demitasse cup barely hides her nostrils.

I pull out a tissue from the dispenser that's on the end table and hand it to her.

"Thank you." Francesca lightly dabs at the corners of her eyes. "I suppose it has been silly of me to try and hide from you the fact that my sister is very sick. I needed to know I could trust you and that you would not put it in the article. She has never wanted my life. I must honor her wishes and privacy."

"You have my word I will not mention her in the piece."

"*Grazie molto.*"

"May I ask, Francesca, what exactly is the matter with her?"

"She has leukemia. Lorenzo wrote to me, asking me to come. The doctors have given her a few months. When Giuliana was diagnosed, she refused treatment other than some pain medication to keep her comfortable. Lorenzo tried to convince her to fight, but it was no use. I even tried persuading her after I arrived, but as I told you we were estranged for so long that I do not hold much influence over her."

"She does care about what you think, Francesca."

"Why do you say that?"

"I could tell from the brief conversation we had earlier. Look, Francesca . . ." I hesitate, but I know I must tell her what I'm thinking. "You need to try and make amends with her before it's too late. Trust me. I know."

"You are talking about your own sister, correct?"

"Yes."

"But I thought you were very close."

"We were. But we had an argument the last time we saw each other before her accident."

Now my eyes fill with tears, but unlike Francesca, I can't keep them at bay.

"Please excuse me." I get up and rush to the bathroom. The panic attacks are back. I haven't had an attack in two weeks. I thought perhaps they were gone for good. Sitting on the toilet, I place my head between my knees, trying to breathe. It's not working. If anything, the attack is lasting longer than it normally does.

"Pia!" Francesca knocks at the door. "Pia! Are you all right? You have been in there for almost fifteen minutes. I am worried about you."

Not now, I think. I don't want her to see me like this, but I don't want her to think I'm passed out on the floor either. I get up and open the door. My chest is heaving. I motion with my hands that

I'm having difficulty breathing, not that I need to. Francesca can hear my raspy breaths.

"Wait here!" She leaves the guest bathroom. She's only gone for a minute at most.

"Take this." Francesca hands me a pill and a glass of water, but I shake my head.

"It is a Xanax. I sometimes get anxiety attacks, too. Take it."

I don't have to think about it for another second. The constriction in my chest feels like it's becoming more unbearable. I wash the pill down with lots of water. Then hold the cool glass to my forehead.

Francesca puts her arm around my shoulders and leads me back to the library.

"Lie down. The medication should start to take effect soon."

I let Francesca ease my body down onto the couch as she props my head with a few throw pillows. She then walks over to the thermostat and adjusts the temperature. Soon, I feel a cool draft blowing down on me from the vents that are directly above my head in the ceiling. That alone is already making me feel better.

Francesca leaves and returns with a wet washcloth. She presses it to my forehead.

"Thank you. I'm sorry I scared you." I smile feebly.

"Stop apologizing! How many times have I told you that?" But she winks at me so I know she's only teasing.

"I should be apologizing," she says.

"For what?"

"For asking about your sister."

"You had no idea."

I sit up.

"I'm feeling better."

"Take the rest of these." Francesca gives me the bottle of Xanax.

"That's okay."

"You need these. I am amazed your doctor has not prescribed them for you."

"He has, but I didn't want to take them. I've been able to manage the attacks. But I haven't had one that lasted as long as today's."

"I will feel better knowing you have these. Just take one if it gets as bad as the one you had today, okay?"

This woman sure does have a way of making it hard to say no to her. I take the bottle.

"Can we just forget this happened and resume our interview?"

"You still want to continue? You should go home and rest."

"Francesca, I'm feeling fine now. It's just during the attack that I feel lousy."

"You are stubborn! Okay. We can continue, but if you change your mind, please let me know."

"Fair enough."

Silently, I curse my panic attacks for making an appearance since I felt like I was possibly on the brink of finding out what was the cause of the estrangement between Francesca and Giuliana. But the thought of my argument with Erica was too much to bear. Thankfully, Francesca realizes I'm not ready to talk about the last time I saw Erica alive, and she doesn't ask me to finish where I left off.

"We were talking about your fiancés the last time. We're up to fiancé number four—Stello Cascio."

"Do we have to talk about the rest of my fiancés?"

"No, but your fans would understand you better if they knew why you broke off your engagements with them. You didn't seem to have a problem discussing fiancés numbers one through three the last time."

Sighing, Francesca relents. "Stello. I still think about him sometimes."

"Why is that?"

"We never acted together in a film, and I always wondered what the chemistry would have been like if we had."

"Stello was quite a famous movie star in Italy when you and he dated."

"He is still very popular. I cannot tell you how many people have come up to me in Italy and told me he was their favorite of all my fiancés."

"Does he still act?"

"*Sì,* but he does not get the quality films he used to get. He even does television commercials now."

"You've never done commercials, correct?"

"Actually, I did commercials for Nivea in Italy in my late twenties."

"You didn't feel commercials were beneath you?"

"Not for a huge product like Nivea! And the money they paid me." Francesca fans her hand in front of her face.

"That much, huh?"

"Yes."

"How long were you with Stello?"

"We became engaged after only dating for a month, but the engagement lasted for nine months."

"From my research, I read your relationship with him was quite volatile, probably the most volatile of any of your relationships."

"They were all volatile, my dear. But the paparazzi were better at catching us arguing than they were with my other fiancés."

"And why did you break this engagement off?"

"He was full of himself! I was getting tired of his conceited ways. He used to rub in my face his fame and make me feel like I was nowhere near the star or actor he was. Ha! I showed him. I became more of a legend than he."

Naturally, there couldn't be two legends in a marriage, I think to myself.

"He tried to win me back for almost a year, but it was hopeless. Besides, I met Vladimir Novikov not long after Stello and I broke up. I was too enamored of Vladimir to even entertain the idea of going back to that narcissist."

"After our meeting yesterday in which you mentioned Vladimir, I did some research on him. He was a very wealthy Russian businessman."

"Very wealthy is an understatement. He was filthy rich." Francesca laughs.

"And he lavished you with expensive jewelry."

"He was very good to me." Francesca's eyes get this dreamy look. I'm not sure, though, if it's over fond memories of Vladimir or the gorgeous jewels he gave her.

"Unlike with Stello, you went back to Vladimir after you broke off the engagement."

"We were engaged for seven months. I got back together with

him a month afterward. Or was it two months? It is so hard to remember. Oh, wait. *Si, si.* We got back together after a month, but broke up again two months later. That was it."

"You broke off the engagement both times with him?"

"Of course. As I have already told you, I ended all of the engagements."

"Just making sure."

Francesca frowns.

"Excuse me, Signorina Donata. You have a guest waiting in the foyer." Carlo interrupts us. Francesca glances at her watch.

"*Dio mio!* I almost forgot. What a crazy day! Appointment after appointment. I am sorry, Pia, but we need to finish up."

"You know, we have only one interview left, Francesca?"

"I am aware of that. I think by then you will have enough material to write an article, do you not agree?"

I want to say, "I'm not sure," but I don't. After our next meeting, I will have no choice but to show Colin my cards, so to speak. I will produce a first draft and pray that he thinks there's enough to publish the article and that it will appeal to *Profile*'s readership. "Yes, I think you have given me quite a bit to work with." I stand up.

"Excellent! Oh, I almost forgot. Your dress." She screams, "Angelica! Angelica!"

In two seconds flat, Angelica races into the library.

"*Si,* Signorina Donata?"

"Bring Pia the dress you altered for her and then kindly show her out. Oh, and she will need to have this other dress altered as well. I assume that is what you have in the garment bag, Pia?"

"Yes. But again, if Angelica is too busy, I can take it to the local tailor shop." I feel bad that Angelica will have more work on my account.

"Nonsense! Angelica would be more than happy to alter this dress as well." Francesca takes the garment bag and hands it to Angelica.

"It's no trouble, Miss Santore," Angelica says meekly before she hurries away to get my other dress.

"Now, if you will excuse me, Pia, I need to tend to my other guest. I will see you next week. And make sure Gregory sees you in the blue dress before our next meeting. He is absolutely *pazzo* if he doesn't love you in this one." Francesca leaves.

Walking out into the foyer to wait for Angelica to bring my dress, I hear Francesca talking in whispers to a man. They are both giggling. My curiosity gets the better of me. I tiptoe quickly toward the sound of the voices, which are coming from the living room. The door is slightly ajar, allowing me a peek. Francesca is standing at the bar next to a man who looks to be in his late forties or maybe early fifties. He's dressed impeccably with fine tailored trousers and a pale gray silk shirt. I bring my eyes closer to the door's crack. It's none other than Rocco Vecchio, the jeweler from Castello Jewelry! I remember now, Francesca was exiting his store the day I first met her on Ditmars. Rocco is a regular customer at Zia's bakery.

There's no mistaking the tone of their conversation. They're flirting with each other. Hmmm. How long has this been going on? I'm surprised the paparazzi haven't leaked rumors to the media.

"Miss Santore?" Angelica is standing two feet away from me.

"Oh, Angelica, you scared me!" I whisper to her. Fortunately, Angelica picks up my cue and whispers back, "We should get away from here." Her nervous eyes dart toward the living room. This poor girl is absolutely terrified of Francesca.

Nodding my head, I follow her back out to the foyer. Fortunately for me, she doesn't ask why I was spying on Francesca and Rocco. She hands over the dress she altered for me.

"I hope the alterations are fine. If for some reason they're not, please let me know. I'll adjust them. I should have the second dress ready for you by the end of the week unless you need it sooner?"

"No, the end of the week is fine. Thank you, Angelica. I appreciate it. I hate to ask you for another favor, but please don't tell Francesca I was eavesdropping."

"Don't worry! I won't tell her. I have to admit, I've been pretty curious myself about her and Rocco Vecchio. I'm convinced he's her secret admirer."

"Secret admirer?"

"Can you keep a secret?"

"Of course. Plus, you've got me now that you witnessed me spying on Francesca." With my index finger, I motion as if I'm zipping my lips and putting the key away.

"She was getting all these gifts of jewelry from an anonymous person. It *has* to be him."

"Really?"

"Yes."

"How many times has he visited her here?"

"Only one other time, and he came with a gift that time as well."

"Maybe she's buying jewelry from him, and he's just delivering it personally since she can't go out without the paparazzi hounding her?"

"I thought of that, too, but my vibe is telling me there's more going on."

"You and me both. Well, thanks for the info."

I wave good-bye to Angelica and make my way toward the kitchen to exit through the back of the house. Francesca and Rocco? Nah! She's accustomed to dating billionaires and famous movie stars and directors. Then again, the man owns a jewelry store. That's enough for Francesca with her obsession with gems.

"Pia?"

I literally jump and drop my dress.

"Lorenzo! You scared me!"

Bending over, Lorenzo picks up my dress, taking the opportunity to stare at my legs since he has a closeup view of them. Silently, I curse my choice of wearing shorts today.

"I'm sorry I startled you. How did your interview with Zia Francesca go?"

"Fine. Fine. Thank you."

"I was thinking, Pia, perhaps you might want to interview me?"

"You?" I can't help but reveal the surprise in my voice, and then I realize too late I probably insulted him. "I'm sorry. I just meant—"

"There's no need to apologize. I know what you meant." Lorenzo waves his hand. "I thought I might be able to offer some perspective into Francesca. I know she's the draw, and I'm just her nephew."

I think about it for a moment, but I'm not won over. "I'm sorry,

Lorenzo, but I can't see how you would be able to offer any helpful insight given that you only met your aunt in person a few days ago."

"True. But we did correspond by letter and talk by phone a few times over the years."

I'm still not convinced, but a good journalist covers all of her bases. You never know when a lead that appears inconsequential could prove to be valuable.

"Okay. I'll listen to what you have to offer."

"Fantastic! How about tomorrow?"

"Tomorrow is already all booked up for me. I'm sorry, but actually this whole week is bad. How about a week from today?"

"If I must wait, then I guess I must. What is it they say? All good things come to those who wait." Lorenzo smiles deeply. He's shamelessly flirting with me and has no reservations about concealing it. I pretend not to notice and keep my tone as nonchalant as possible.

"How about we meet at Antoniella's Bakery at six p.m.? I'm working that entire day so I'm afraid that's the only time I can squeeze in."

"That's perfect. Antoniella is your aunt?"

"You heard?"

"Yes, my aunt told me."

I want to ask him what else Francesca has told him about me, but I decide to continue acting aloof.

"I'll see you next week. I really need to get going or I'll be late meeting my friend."

"Have a nice day, Pia." Lorenzo takes my hand, and I'm expecting him to shake it as he's made a custom of doing upon saying hello and good-bye, but then he leans forward and kisses me on the cheek. I'm too stunned to kiss him back. I merely wave and walk out the kitchen door leading to the backyard.

I don't hear the door close until I'm walking through the partition that divides Signora Tesca's yard from her neighbor's. Obviously, Lorenzo was checking me out the entire time.

Why didn't I tell him I was meeting my boyfriend? Guilt immediately washes over me as I chastise myself for referring to Gregory as "my friend." And why do I feel like I've just made a romantic date with Lorenzo as opposed to a business date?

Sighing, I walk down Signora Tesca's neighbor's driveway. Before stepping out onto the sidewalk, I make sure none of the paparazzi is looking in my direction. As usual, they're too focused on the Mussolini Mansion or their inane conversations about when The Crazy Bride will make another surprise appearance.

I cross the street undetected and make my way down the block toward Zia's house. A motorcycle speeds down the street with two men. The driver slows down and lets the rider off. It's Gregory.

"Hey! What are you doing here? I just finished up my interview with Francesca and was going back to my aunt's to relax a little before I met you. I thought we were meeting at the coffeehouse in your neighborhood?"

Gregory doesn't say anything as he comes over to me. A mischievous smile dances along his lips.

"What's going on?"

Instead of answering me, Gregory picks me up and spins me around. I begin laughing.

"You're in a good mood! What happened?"

"I've been discovered, Pia! I've been freakin' discovered!"

Gregory keeps spinning me. I'm thrilled for him, but I'm also worried I'm going to throw up soon. Laughing, I beg him, "Stop spinning me! Stop! I'm really dizzy!"

He lowers me to the ground. We stare into each other's eyes. His are filled with the satisfaction of success. Mine are filled with tears. I hug him, and he kisses my neck. I whisper to him, "I'm so happy for you! I knew you'd make it!"

"I love you, Pia. That means the world to me. Even though you've only known me a short time, you had faith in me." He pulls back and, holding my face with both of his hands, he kisses me. The kiss is as mind-blowing, if not more, than our first kiss. Tears are streaming down my face.

He stops kissing me and wipes my tears with his fingers.

"Why are you crying? This is good!"

"Tears of happiness, you fool!"

"Ah! Yeah, I have to admit. I almost cried when I found out."

"You have to tell me all about it. Who discovered you?"

"Only Nathan Horowitz—one of the top art dealers in New York City!"

"Oh my God! I've even heard of him!"

"Of course you have!" Gregory laughs.

"How did he find you?"

"He called me last week and told me he was scouting artists in Long Island City. I guess he'd talked to people and a few of the other artists in my hood. He wanted to come over and see my work. So we set up an appointment for this morning. And the rest is history. He loved what he saw. He thinks he can use most of my pieces in the show he's giving me at his gallery in Chelsea. But he wants me to create new pieces, too. I'm going to be painting 24/7 until the show, which is only a month away."

"Gregory, that's awesome! Congratulations! I can't believe you didn't tell me that Nathan Horowitz called you, and you've known for an entire week!" I playfully hit his arm.

"I just didn't want to jinx it. I'm sorry. Please don't be mad. I was ready to explode and tell you a few times. I couldn't sleep last night. I picked up my cell probably every hour and almost called you, but then my insecurities got the better of me."

"I forgive you this time. But don't ever hold anything back from me—especially good news like this!" I wrap my arms around his neck and kiss him.

"Let's go celebrate! Lou is rounding up a bunch of people at 718 Lounge to buy us drinks."

"Us? You're the one who's got an occasion to celebrate, not me."

"You're my girl, so as an extension of me you get free drinks, too."

"Oh, really, is that how you see me? As an extension of you?"

"I don't mean it in a bad way, Pia!" Gregory groans. "I know you're your own independent woman. I just mean you're my other half."

"Gregory Hewson, you're too much." I'm about to start crying again, but don't want to fall apart. I'm so moved that Gregory already thinks of me as being his significant other. So I do the only thing I can before I totally lose it; I kiss him again. But it's no use, the tears still stream down my face.

"I love you so much, Gregory."

"Not as much as I love you, Pia."

We run back to Zia's so I can drop off my dress and messenger bag. We want to hurry to meet Lou and the gang at 718, but once we're alone in my bedroom, the temptation to make love is too great. It must be the adrenaline we're both feeling over Gregory's success in being discovered. Neither of us says a word as we frantically strip each other and fall onto my bed, not bothering to pull back the comforter or remove the throw pillows. I don't even care if Zia happens to come home early from the bakery and discovers us. All I care about in this moment is showing Gregory my love.

# ‿ 20 ‿

# Francesca

The breeze off the Hudson River's currents blows my hair. I wrap my Hermès silk scarf around my bare shoulders as I take in the twinkling lights from the Manhattan skyline.

"Here's your martini with an extra olive just for you." Rocco hands my cocktail to me.

"This is wonderful, Rocco. You truly are a wealth of surprises."

"I'm glad you're enjoying them." Rocco grins mischievously.

"*Si,* I admit it. I am like a schoolgirl who cannot get enough gifts. That has always been my greatest weakness." I take a sip of my martini. Rocco is even skilled at making the perfect drinks.

We are on a yacht that belongs to another good friend of his. Of course, it would have been better if Rocco had his own yacht, but he does have many friends with access to the finer luxuries. This is our second date. Although he had promised when he whisked me to his friend's restaurant that I would never forget that night, this outing is proving to be more memorable. But our last date was also special. I was impressed that he went to the trouble of asking his friend to keep the restaurant open so late just for the two of us. Though we were the only patrons in the restaurant, Rocco had insisted we dance, and he was the utmost gentleman—and a romantic!

Again, I climbed down the rope ladder from my bedroom window. Although it was quite difficult for me to climb back up the ladder after our previous date, the lure of escaping and having fun in Manhattan for another night was too enticing. No one had suspected that I was missing the last time.

Rocco had tried to kiss me while we danced at the restaurant, but I never kiss on a first date. That might seem silly given that I am a middle-aged woman who has been . . . How do the Americans say? Around the block a few times? But I am and always will be a lady above all else.

The yacht's captain took us for a short ride around a few of the popular New York City landmarks. Now the yacht is anchored a couple of hundred feet from the shore along with a few dinner cruises. Cheers from the crowds on the other boats reach our ears.

"To be young," I say, followed by a long sigh.

"Do you wish you were young again?" Rocco comes by my side and drapes his arm around my shoulders. I lean into him.

"Not really. I am sure the world thinks that an aging star like me wishes she were young again, but I made too many mistakes to want to go back to that stage of my life."

"Yup. That's part of being young. Making mistakes and hopefully learning from them. But it is great being that age and discovering so much for the first time. I sometimes wish I were young again. Let's be honest, growing old is tough," Rocco says sadly.

"You seem to be aging gracefully."

"You think so?" Rocco meets my gaze and smiles, pleased at my compliment.

I stroke his face with my index finger, letting it trace the strong lines of his jaw. Rocco grabs my wrist and guides my finger over to his lips as he lightly begins sucking my finger. My heart races at the intimate gesture. Though I am shocked, I do not stop him. I stand mesmerized, watching his eyes grow heavy. He then stops and takes my face in both of his hands and begins kissing me tenderly. I cannot take the teasing any longer. I throw my arms around his shoulders and kiss him aggressively.

We are interrupted by the yacht's captain.

"I'm sorry to disturb you, sir, but I just wanted to give you a heads-up that I'll be returning to the port now."

"Thank you. That's fine." Rocco looks slightly annoyed by the interruption.

I, on the other hand, welcome the distraction. Taking out my compact, I reapply my lipstick. Shame fills me. I have never thrown myself at a man. My stomach still feels unsettled from the lingering kiss as I try to calm my racing pulse.

"I can't believe the night is just about over. Time flies too quickly when I'm with you. All I want is for it to go by as slowly as possible." Rocco grins sheepishly.

"That is good, no? If time were crawling that would mean you were bored." I flash him a seductive smile as I put my lipstick and compact back in my purse.

"I don't think you possess a boring bone in your body." Rocco stares appreciatively at my figure. Goosebumps dot my bare legs and arms, but they are not just from the cool breeze off the river. Every nerve in my body is heightened, aching for Rocco to kiss me again.

We reach the port, and after Rocco hands a generous tip to the captain we walk toward his car. Once inside, Rocco leans over and kisses me hungrily. I do not resist. His hands waste no time in cupping my breasts, which elicits a groan from him. A tiny voice in my head whispers, "You are not behaving like a lady, Francesca." But I do not care. It has been so long since I have been with a man. Why should I deprive myself, especially since I have taken painstaking measures to keep my body looking as fit as it does. It is about time someone enjoys it.

I straddle Rocco, which is a bit uncomfortable with the steering wheel in our way. Immediately, I feel his hardness. I let out a cry when he abruptly pushes me off, sending me bouncing onto the passenger seat.

"I'm sorry, Francesca. I got carried away." He wipes his brow with the handkerchief he has pulled out of his trousers pocket.

"There is no need to apologize." I lean over and begin nibbling his ear, but he places his hand on my lap and lightly nudges me away from him.

"What is the matter?" I ask.

"Trust me, Francesca. I've wanted you ever since I first saw you in *La Sposa Pazza*. I keep pinching myself to know that I'm not dreaming and you're really here with me. But I respect you. I can't

make love to you for the first time in my car like a teenager who's
hoping that his parents won't catch him."

Now I feel embarrassed. What must he think of me?

"You might not believe me, Rocco. But you are the first man I
have thrown myself at. I do not usually act with such . . . such . . ."

"Abandon?" Rocco laughs.

"Yes, *grazie*. That is the word I was searching for."

"I wish you could go away with me, Francesca, but I know how
ill your sister is."

"Giuliana needs me. God forbid if something happened
overnight, and I were not there." With this thought, I glance at my
watch and am horrified to see it is almost five a.m. By the time we
drive over the bridge and get back to Astoria, it will be dawn and
more likely that someone will be able to spot me climbing up to my
bedroom window.

"I am sorry to rush you, Rocco, but I did not realize how late it
is. I have to get back."

"Don't worry. We'll be back in time."

Rocco starts the ignition and speeds away. We remain silent for
the rest of the car ride back to Astoria. I know we both cannot stop
thinking about the passion between us.

About an hour later, I am making my way up the rope ladder. It
took us longer than usual to drive back. Even at five in the morning, there was traffic on Manhattan's streets. Rocco kept cursing,
saying he had never seen so many cars that early in the city.

The climb up the ladder is more difficult this time, probably because I am so tired. My legs feel wobbly. Nervous, I decide to slow
my pace. As the sun reaches higher in the sky, more birds cry out,
announcing the new day. With each cry, I become more anxious, as
if they are pointing me out.

"Come on, Francesca. You can do it. Just five more steps."
Rocco encourages me from below as I stop to take a break.

"I am getting too old for this." I wipe my forehead with the
back of my arm. Taking a deep breath, I continue the climb up
when suddenly, I see a flash followed by, "It's her!"

Glancing down, I see a photographer snapping another photo.

"Get the hell outta here!" Rocco yells at them. He forgets about me as he walks over toward the photographer. The moment he lets go of the rope ladder, I feel it sway lightly. I freeze, gripping onto the next rung so tightly my knuckles turn white. Suddenly, my fear of heights kicks in full force. I am paralyzed. Though I have only three steps left, I cannot move. Knowing Rocco was holding the rope ladder for me gave me the psychological sense of security I needed to overcome my phobia of heights. Rocco had assured me that he really did not need to hold onto the ladder. The metal hooks that are fastened in my bedroom window's ledge are very secure. He had also reminded me that rock climbers use these types of ladders on mountains that regularly erode and crumble and at much greater heights. But I had still insisted on his holding the ladder.

The flashes increase. Looking down once more, I see Giuliana's yard is now full of paparazzi and neighbors, some of whom are in their pajamas.

One young man waves to me in an exaggerated manner and calls out, "Francesca! Francesca! My name is Aldo, and I am your number one fan! You are a goddess, tee ah-moh! Tee ah-mohhhh! Tee ah-mohhh!"

He sounds like the Native Americans from the old spaghetti Westerns. Suddenly, a wave of vertigo hits me, and I panic, screaming, "Somebody help me! I am terrified of heights!"

The crowd rushes forward. I no longer see Rocco trying to fight them off. What have I done? *Dio mio, aiuto!* My God! Help me! I want to make the sign of the cross, but dare not let go of the ladder.

"Francesca!"

Edgardo is leaning out my bedroom window, trying to reach me with his arms, but they fall short.

"I cannot move, Edgardo. My fear is paralyzing me."

"If you don't move, that crowd is going to knock you off this ladder, and then there will be no fear left since you'll be sprawled on the ground dead." Edgardo is fuming mad, no doubt at discovering my escape.

Taking another peek below, I see the young man who was screaming *"ti amo"* earlier is beginning to climb the ladder. He probably wants to help me, but then again, he might be some lunatic.

"Don't worry, Francesca. Aldo is coming to help you." He smiles up at me.

The ladder pitches violently to the left with the added weight of this buffoon.

"Francesca, quick! Climb! There are only three steps. No, wait; make that one step you have to climb on your own. I can reach you after that," Edgardo says, waving his hand hurriedly.

Shutting my eyes tightly for a few seconds, I summon every ounce of internal strength and then propel my legs forward. Somehow they obey and move. As Edgardo promised, he grabs me on either side of my waist and hoists me through the window. The young man with his cell phone in hand has reached the top rung of the ladder just in time for Edgardo to shut the window in his face. But Aldo still snaps my photo even though the image will probably come out grainy with the glass obstructing his view. Edgardo locks the window and checks the locks on the other windows.

I sit down on my bed, massaging my calves. Every muscle is taut with tension.

"What the hell were you thinking? You could've been killed!" Edgardo is in my face, screaming at the top of his lungs.

"Shhh! You will wake up Giuliana!"

"Oh, trust me, she is awake already. Listen to that crowd out there."

I can hear the crowd outside, yelling my name repeatedly, begging me to come back out.

"Who helped you get out, Francesca?"

"No one!"

"I'm not an idiot! Where did you get that rope ladder?"

"Online."

"You rarely go on the Internet. And you have personal shoppers!"

"I am a prisoner here! I have only been out when we went to the jewelry stores and when we had lunch at Trattoria L'incontro. I am going *pazza! Pazza!*" I point to my head, not caring if I wake up the entire household now.

"You should have thought of that before you came then," Edgardo says in a low voice.

"Yes, Francesca. We all know how hard it is for you to sacrifice and think of someone else besides yourself." Giuliana stands in the threshold of my bedroom. Her stony gaze meets mine. Even in her fragile state, her eyes still possess great strength. But instead of feeling ashamed over my actions and words, I become infuriated.

"How dare you! You more than anyone know how much I have sacrificed and what I have sacrificed!"

Giuliana hobbles over to me with her cane. She is a good two inches shorter, yet it feels as if she towers over me.

"That was not a sacrifice. After all, you admitted to me your first love was acting."

Giuliana turns to leave. I begin to rush after her, but Edgardo stops me with his hand, whispering, "No more." But it is Giuliana's coughing that convinces me to drop my battle.

Tears silently fall down my face. Only Giuliana has the power to completely devastate me.

# 21

# Pia

I'm sitting at a table in the back of Zia's bakery, waiting for Lorenzo to show up. He seems to have inherited his aunt's notorious tendency to be late. Glancing at my watch, I see he's already a good fifteen minutes late. He texted me five minutes ago to say he was on his way. I'm reading the rag mags that the previous customer left behind. Francesca is all over the front pages—or rather I should say her derrière is.

The headlines run the gamut from "Caught!" to "Crazy Forever!" and even "Jewel Thief!" The last headline is next to a photo of Rocco Vecchio holding the rope ladder Francesca was using to climb up to her bedroom.

Shaking my head, I whisper to myself, "What the hell were you thinking, Francesca?"

Now I really need to find out if she is involved with Rocco, but from the looks of it, she has to be. Putting the rag mags aside, I take out my cell and call Gregory, hoping to kill some time until Lorenzo shows up.

"Hey, sweet pea. What's up?"

"Sweet pea" is Gregory's endearment for me. "Hey! Painting?"

"What else? I love to paint, but I think the fumes from all the painting I've been doing are getting to me. I feel as if I'm literally eating, breathing, sleeping paint!" Gregory heaves a long sigh.

"Here you go, Gregory."

I hear a woman's voice cooing to my man.

"Who is that?" I snap, not caring that my voice is dripping with jealousy.

"Madeline Drabinski."

"What is *she* doing there?"

"She knows Nathan Horowitz and came over with him. She wants to interview me for *Profile* and write about the upcoming show."

"How long have you known about this?"

"I just found out about it today when she and Nate came over. What's the matter with you, Pia?"

Realizing how crazy I sound, I decide to tone it down.

"Sorry. I'm not crazy about Madeline."

"Why? Has she been nasty to you in the office?"

"Not necessarily, but I think she was very upset that Colin let me interview Francesca alone. She had wanted to conduct the interview and just bring me along for the ride since I had an in with my aunt's knowing Signora Tesca. I know this is going to sound ridiculous, but I can't help feeling she scored this interview with you to sort of rub it in my face."

"That is ridiculous, Pia. She doesn't even know we're dating, does she?"

"I'm not sure."

"See! How would she know we're dating if you haven't told her, and I definitely haven't gotten around to it since I only just met her an hour ago?"

He's probably right. I decide to drop it.

"So I was thinking of bringing dinner to you tonight. Give you a break since you've been a hermit for the past week."

"Thanks, Pia, but I've got cold cuts. I'll just make myself a quick sandwich. I really can't take more time than it takes to eat quickly and get back to work with the show just three weeks away."

"Oh, okay. I guess I'm not going to see you much until close to that show."

"Sorry, sweet pea. Please understand. It's just that when I'm in the zone, I can't afford any distractions. Luckily, the creative streak has been hitting full force and I haven't gotten stuck."

"You'd better get back to your painting, Gregory!"

Ughhhh! Madeline's voice again.

"We'll catch up with you next week. See how the work is coming along."

A man's voice, no doubt Nathan Horowitz.

"Hold on, Pia. Let me say good-bye to them."

"That's okay, Gregory. I should let you go anyway."

"All right. I'll call you tonight."

"Just as you did last night," I gently remind him.

"Shoot! I forgot. I'm sorry. Okay, I really gotta go. Later!"

Gregory hangs up. My spirits feel low. I'm just being selfish. If the tables were turned, and I got a huge writing assignment, I know I would be blowing Gregory off, too, and doing nothing but writing.

"Hey! Why the long face?"

Lorenzo is standing over my table, holding a cup of espresso in one hand and a cannoli in the other. I can't believe I didn't even notice him come into the bakery.

"It's nothing. How are you?"

"Fine. Sorry again I'm late."

"That's okay. I had a phone call to make that kept me occupied."

"Along with these?" Lorenzo holds up the rag mags with his aunt's photo plastered all over the covers. He smirks as he flips through the pages.

"Those aren't mine. I found them here."

"Uh-huh! And my name is George Clooney."

"Whatever. Believe what you want." I laugh.

"You wouldn't believe the fracas at the house yesterday morning over my aunt's nighttime escapades." Lorenzo whistles and shakes his head.

"Care to share?" I take out my notebook.

"You can't write about this or Zia Francesca will disown me as her nephew and have both of our heads on a platter."

"All right. All right. Off the record." I put my pen down.

"Edgardo, you know her beefy bodyguard, chewed her a new one again today."

"I take it he also let her have it right after she got caught?"

"Of course! I could hear them shouting from my bedroom. They were bickering like old lovers."

"Interesting you say that. I kind of picked up on a vibe from Edgardo the time we had lunch at Trattoria L'incontro. I think he has feelings for her."

"He'd be a fool to. No offense to my aunt, but we've all seen how her past paramours have been crumpled up and thrown in the wastebasket."

"Now why do you think that is?"

"Because she can. She's drop-dead gorgeous even in her middle age, and she's a legendary movie star. No complexity there."

"I'm not so sure about that, Lorenzo."

"Ahhh! So you're playing detective now as well as journalist."

"In the time I've spent with her these past few weeks, I've come to see there is much more to Francesca than what she lets the public see."

"True. But do me a favor. Don't waste your time digging too much or trying to get her to open up about herself. That would be like breaking down a wall of iron. Now, what do you say we go for a drive?"

"What about our interview?"

"You can ask me questions in the car. Come on! It's a beautiful day. I've got the top down on my car." Lorenzo gestures toward his car, which I see is parked right out front. It's a gleaming candy-red Alfa Romeo.

"Okay. But we're sticking to the topic of Francesca, and it'll all be on the record."

"Scout's honor." Lorenzo holds up his hand as if taking an oath.

"Zia, I'll be home a little later," I call out to my aunt and look over my shoulder. She's stopped her usual frenetic sweeping and is staring at me with her mouth open. For the life of me, I have no idea why she looks almost shocked. She probably is surprised to see me with a guy other than Gregory. I guess in her day you were only seen with the man who was courting you. And I'm sure women didn't have friends of the opposite sex.

"*Ciao,* Pia! Take your time. It's okay if you get home late. Have fun!"

That's odd. Since when has Zia not cared about my getting

home late? Whenever I go out with Gregory, she's always telling me to be home by a reasonable hour. Pushing her strange behavior out of my mind for the moment, I step into Lorenzo's convertible. Once Lorenzo is buckled in, he says, "Get ready for some serious driving." And with that, he peels away from the curb, screeching his tires. A few pedestrians look at us. I'm a little embarrassed, but soon, I love the way his car takes command of the road. Lorenzo is driving past the old Con Edison plant, where the streets are deserted, allowing him to go much faster than he would've been able to on the more crowded Ditmars Boulevard.

He talks to me about himself, and soon, I forget that we're supposed to be talking about his aunt. Right now, he's talking to me about his studies in comparative literature.

"Are you familiar with Greek mythology?"

"I just know some of the more popular stories, but I never actually read the Greek myths or studied them in school."

"You don't know what you're missing out on. That's actually my specialty."

"You can specialize in Greek mythology?"

"Well, classical literature, which covers the texts of ancient Greece."

"I did read *The Odyssey* in high school and enjoyed it."

"Yeah, *The Odyssey* is pretty much standard high school or even undergraduate reading. I've read it five times."

"Wow!"

"I find something new to learn from *The Odyssey* every time I read it. It's brilliant!"

"So which is your favorite Greek myth?"

"Ahh! I love the story of how Hades, the god of the underworld or hell, kidnaps Persephone, whose mother is Demeter, goddess of the harvest. Overcome with grief, Demeter no longer allows the fields to thrive, but instead they grow barren and cold. The flowers lose their blossoms and wilt, and the trees lose their leaves. All of nature is grieving with Demeter. She threatens to never make the earth green again unless Hades returns her daughter. Zeus commands Hades to do so. Persephone is reunited with her mother. But there's a catch. Since she's eaten a few pomegranate seeds in the underworld, she must return, because no one who's eaten the food of the dead can stay on earth. But Zeus decides to let Persephone stay in the underworld for only one month for every pomegranate seed she'd eaten. So when Persephone is with Hades, her mother grieves and it is winter on earth. But when mother and daughter are reunited, it is spring and they are together until winter sets in."

"What a beautiful myth and way to rationalize why we have seasons."

"Yes. That's probably what I love so much about Greek mythology—their attempt to offer a reason or a lesson for why life is the way it is."

I like this part of Lorenzo better than the guy who can be so blunt. There's more to him beneath the surface.

"Why do you think that myth is your favorite?"

Lorenzo shrugs his shoulders. He's driving much slower now than he was earlier. No doubt he was trying to show off for me.

"I guess because it moves me the most. Nothing can compare to the love between a mother and child. That myth shows how powerful that bond is."

Lorenzo's eyes fill with sadness. He must be thinking about his mother and how he'll lose her soon.

The next three weeks fly by, and the day of Gregory's show has arrived. I've only seen him three times in the past few weeks, and each time it was brief. Gregory finally relented to my visiting as long as I stayed no longer than half an hour, but I could tell his mind was on his work. Though I kept reassuring him that his show would be fabulous and the new paintings would be just as extraordinary as the older ones, he wouldn't relax. I asked him to stop promising to call me since he kept forgetting to do so. And I went from calling him every other day to twice a week. I couldn't help wondering if he would be like this every time he'd have a show coming up. He's definitely been acting like the stereotypical crazy artist who has no life other than his art while he works. All I know is that I'm happy I'll have him again until his next show.

"Pia, are you still here?" Zia knocks softly on my door.

"Yes, Zia. Come in. I'm waiting for Connie, Rita, and Aldo to pick me up. Connie's going to drive into the city."

Zia walks in. She often doesn't go in to work on Sundays. She trusts her employees to take care of the bakery while she's gone. She's wearing one of her favorite housecoats that she likes to relax in when she's home. Today's coat is an aqua green with a pattern of small, bright yellow sunflowers. I know it sounds hideous, but it actually looks really cute on her, and the green is a perfect complement to her caramel-colored hair, which today is coiled around foam rollers. A pink scarf holds her roller set in place. Gregory invited Zia to his show, but the thought of traipsing into Manhattan was too much for her. Instead, she's going to Olivia's house for dinner.

"Shouldn't you be more dressed up?" Zia frowns as she appraises me from head to toe. I'm wearing a new pair of Lucky designer jeans, which are a dark-wash denim, making them appropriate for evening. I also treated myself to a new halter top that dips quite low in the back. Instead of my trademark boots, I'm wearing a pair of nude stiletto heels I bought a month ago when I spotted them in the window of a Zara's boutique near *Profile*'s offices. I knew they'd be perfect to wear to Gregory's show. I'm going for urban chic as opposed to over-the-top glam. Besides, after the Francesca makeover debacle, I know Gregory will appreciate that I'm staying true to my style.

"It's an art show. I'm sure a few people will also be dressed casually."

"Ahh! *Va bene.* What do I know? I'm just an old lady who hates going into Manhattan unless I must. Tell Gregory I said congratulations and thank him again for inviting me."

"I will, Zia. Are you sure you won't change your mind? Even Olivia can come."

"I'm sure. This is more for young people. Have a good time. You need it. You have been working too much lately between your internship and interviewing that loon!" Zia shakes her head.

"She's not that bad once you get to know her."

"Hmph. She is just acting as always. She's afraid if she continues to behave like a crazy woman in front of you, it will end up in your article."

"You're probably right, Zia." I laugh.

"Pia, I have been meaning to ask you a question, but I don't want to interfere. Is everything okay between you and Gregory?"

"Of course it is. Why do you ask?"

"I know he has been busy preparing for his show, but I cannot believe he hasn't made any time to take you out in these past few weeks. And then I see you with Lorenzo not once, but three times over the course of the past month. I see the way he looks at you. Is something happening between you two?"

Zia's face looks hopeful, and then I suddenly remember her shocked expression when she first saw me with Lorenzo that day we were leaving her bakery. Could it be she wants me to dump Gregory and date Lorenzo instead? But she's always spoken glowingly of Gregory.

"Lorenzo and I are just friends. He's given me some insight into his aunt." I'm lying right now to save myself. Although I have seen Lorenzo a few times as Zia pointed out, he has yet to give me his perspective on Francesca. I tried prodding him, but he has always managed to skirt the subject. I've given up since I realized he probably doesn't have much to offer on an aunt he's only met in person recently. And Zia's gotten it wrong. She's seen me in Lorenzo's presence three times, but I've actually seen him on five occasions. The other two were at the Mussolini Mansion. Naturally, my last interview with Francesca was cut short by her being late and then having an emergency to tend to. So I had to go back again to wrap up the interview. Lorenzo seemed to be waiting for me after both appointments and coaxed me into staying longer to have a drink with him. I did finally fess up about Gregory.

"I just want you to be happy, Pia. Forget that I asked you about all of this." Zia walks over to my dresser and begins taking out her hair rollers. I can tell she's embarrassed by having brought up an intimate topic and is now ready to drop the subject.

"Thank you for being such a good aunt by looking out for me." I kiss Zia on the cheek. Her eyes fill with tears.

"It's okay, Zia. I'm sorry. I didn't mean to make you cry." I wrap my arm around her shoulders.

"You don't need to be sorry. It's just that I have become very accustomed to having you here. I'm going to miss you when you go back home."

"I promise I won't stay away so long this time. And I'll call you regularly."

"You don't need to do that. You're a young woman with a life of her own. But thank you." Zia pats my hand.

Now it's my turn to ask Zia a delicate question that I've always wanted the answer to. I asked my mother once a few years ago, but all she said was, "It just didn't happen for her."

"Zia, may I ask why you never married?"

Surprise washes over Zia's features as she stops unwinding her curls. Her lips are pursed tightly together. I've angered her. I'm about to apologize when she says, "He was very sick."

I wait for her to continue. She sits down on my bed.

"His name was Domenico. We fell in love almost immediately. He was a bricklayer, and I met him when I was only twenty-one. Back in the 1960s in Italy, I was already considered old to have not wed yet. We became engaged after three months. Since I was the oldest child and daughter, my parents wanted to throw me a big wedding so we needed time to prepare. We set the wedding date for six months later. I know that might not seem long compared to how Americans plan their weddings for an entire year or even two in some cases, but again, those were different times. To me, it felt like six years. I could not wait to become Domenico's wife." Zia takes a deep breath. I join her on the bed.

"If this is too hard for you, Zia, please don't continue."

"No, no. You have been honest with me about your personal life, and now I would like to share mine with you. We're friends in addition to aunt and niece, after all." Zia gives me a shy smile, and guilt immediately pierces my heart over having lied to her about why I've been spending time with Lorenzo.

"About three months before the wedding, Domenico began acting strangely. He told me he was convinced the other workers at his job were conspiring behind his back to have him fired. At first, I believed him, even though I could not understand why they would do that. Domenico was one of the friendliest, nicest people I have ever met in my life. Everyone loved him. Then, he told me his brother, Luigi, was telling him to break off our engagement because I was not good enough for him. Again, I believed him until Domenico came to me one day and told me that the reason why Luigi wanted him to leave me is that he wanted me for himself. I knew that was crazy, and I told Domenico that. Luigi was married. He got married a year before my engagement, and you could see by the way he looked at his wife that no other woman existed for him. When I defended Luigi, Domenico got angry with me and told me I was in love with his brother. We got into a horrible fight, and for the first time, I became afraid of Domenico. He didn't hit me, but the look in his eyes . . . He looked capable of the worst violence. A week later, he told me he heard a voice, and he was convinced it was God telling him to kill Luigi. I knew then without a doubt that Domenico was very ill. I went to Luigi and told him everything. Luigi admitted to me that he and his parents had been very worried about Domenico for the past few months. He was saying strange things to them as well, and one night, Luigi woke up to find Domenico standing over him with rage in his face.

"The family tried to deny that Domenico was mentally ill until my meeting with Luigi. Also, the day after I talked to Luigi, Domenico's foreman at his job visited the family and told them that Domenico had almost killed one of the other bricklayers after they argued. The foreman said he had tried to look the other way the past month and had blamed Domenico's strange behavior on the stress of getting married. The foreman said he now had no choice but would have to let Domenico go after what had happened that morning. He wanted to tell the family first and have them break the news to Domenico. To make a long story short, Domenico's family had to commit him to an asylum for the insane. At first, the doctors were hopeful they could help him. They said he was in the early stages of paranoid schizophrenia and believed medication would allow him to return to a functional life. So I postponed the wedding and waited. But one month became two and two then became three. Domenico kept getting worse. After a year, I finally gave up."

Zia wipes her eyes with the back of her hands.

"Is he still alive?"

"Yes. And he is still in that place."

"I'm so sorry, Zia. You were so young."

"I know. And I know what you're going to say. I could have married someone else, but I didn't."

"Why?"

"No one measured up to him. I should have known he was too

good to be true. He was such a kind person, so generous. My family tried to arrange dates with a few other men from our village, but all I could think about was Domenico. Even after I canceled the wedding, deep down I never gave up hope he would get better. I was a fool." Zia hangs her head low and stares at her clasped hands.

I'm about to lose it and start sobbing, but I need to hold it together for her. All these years, I thought she loved work more than having a life. I thought she had no interest in marriage and children. Part of me looked up to her for being such a strong, independent woman who chose her career over a man during a time when women who did so were ridiculed and ostracized. But she was a victim of circumstance just as my sister was.

"You weren't a fool, Zia. You were smart. Can you imagine if you married one of those other men, how unhappy you would have been? You can't force someone to fall in love. It's either there or it isn't."

"But I had many friends whose parents arranged their marriages. True, they did not love their husbands at first, but later, the love came."

"I think some of those women lied to you. I'm not saying it's impossible to fall in love with someone after you marry, but the chances have to be far fewer. And look at your successful business. You have done so much on your own. You should be very proud of that. I look up to you as a businesswoman."

"You do?"

"Yes! Even my mother has always said, 'Antoniella is so strong and smart.' My mother has always envied you."

"And I have always envied her because of her children and husband. Sometimes I think my jealousy brought her bad luck, and that's why she lost Erica." Zia begins crying uncontrollably. "God, forgive me. I'm a terrible person. Pia, please forgive me."

I'm stunned by her admission, but more so because I now see other people have carried the guilt of Erica's death—not just me. I've blamed myself for her death, but it never occurred to me that perhaps other members of my family might be feeling the same way.

"Zia, stop it! You're human. We're all jealous of someone at some point in our lives. Your envy of my mother did not give her or

Erica bad luck. Erica died because it was her time. That's it. No one is guilty. Not even me."

My admission is what finally stops Zia's sobs.

"What do you mean?"

"I've been blaming myself for Erica's death, too. We got into a horrible fight the morning that she died. That was the last time I saw her." The last sentence comes out so low that I'm not sure I even uttered it aloud.

"Oh, Pia. Come here." Zia wraps her arms around me, and I collapse against her. I don't even try to fight back the tears. I'm tired. I'm tired of fighting my feelings where Erica's death is concerned. I'm tired of acting to everyone that I am okay. I'm tired of keeping the burden of this secret buried deep within me.

"Erica had met someone a few months before she died. His name was Bill. She was crazy about him. She had changed her mind about coming with me to New York. I was so mad at her because I felt like she was giving up on her dream—on our dream. I thought she was making a mistake choosing love over her career aspirations. But I think what angered me more was that she was choosing Bill over me. You remember how close we were?"

Zia nods her head as she begins stroking my hair, pulling the strands that have stuck to my wet face back.

"This was the first time anyone had come between us. Even with her friends. They always came second. She was upset that I wasn't supporting her decision to stay in California so she could build her relationship with Bill. We said such ugly things to each other. She told me I was jealous of her since my relationships never lasted long. She told me I was cold and that's why no one fell in love with me. I told her she was becoming selfish and letting nothing more than a teen crush blind her. I told her she was making the biggest mistake of her life and she wouldn't amount to much. Oh God! I can't believe I told her that."

My body shakes as a new round of tears erupts.

"Pia, listen to me. We all say hurtful things to one another when we're mad. You were both hurt. Erica was hurt because for the first time she didn't have your approval, and you were hurt because for the first time she was making her own decisions—decisions that left you out of the picture. Yes, it's sad that the last time you saw her had to be that way, but don't let that one moment ruin the beautiful relationship and love you had for each other. Your mother used to tell me that she hardly ever saw you fight. Is that true?"

I nod my head. "That's what makes this so hard to accept. Why did our one major argument have to be the last words we ever spoke to each other? Why couldn't God give me just one more chance to tell her I was sorry before she died? I just wish our last memory together could have been a good one."

"I know, Pia. I know. But I want you to start remembering all of the happy times you shared with Erica. I want you to remember the special bond you and your sister had. Whenever you start to think about that fight, just replace that thought with one of the many happy memories instead. And like you just told me, no one is to blame for her death. She wouldn't want anyone to feel that."

"Thank you, Zia. You're the only person I've confided in about this."

"Don't worry. Your secret is safe with me. And thank you for making me feel better."

Zia and I hug. I realize that this is the first time I haven't gotten a panic attack when I've thought about the argument Erica and I had.

The doorbell rings.

"That must be your friends. I'll go answer the door. Fix your makeup, and I'll tell them you'll be down soon."

I nod my head. Walking over to the dresser, I grab a Q-tip from a crystal jewelry box, which was no doubt a wedding favor, and dab at the mascara that's run beneath my eyes. Applying a few drops of concealer, I examine myself to make sure all signs of my tears are gone before I head downstairs.

I can hear a man's voice. It must be Aldo. I have yet to meet him, but feel like I know him already since Connie and Rita have regaled me with many tales about him. I spotted in the rag mags the photo of him climbing up the rope ladder that led to Francesca's room. Connie and Rita weren't joking when they told me how crazy he is about Francesca. The guy has guts; I give him that.

Megan will be meeting up with us at the gallery later. Since it's

Zia's day off, Megan is closing up the bakery tonight, so she'll miss the first hour of Gregory's show. Lou is going to meet up with us later, too.

The gang is seated on Zia's couch, and just like much of Signora Tesca's furniture, it's also covered in plastic. Many older Italian women cover their furniture in plastic to prevent stains and don't seem to care that most people stopped this custom decades ago.

"Hey, guys."

"Hey, Pia!" Connie gets up and kisses me on the cheek. "This is the famous Aldo. Now more famous since he's made it to the pages of *Inquisitor*."

"I can die now that I've landed in the gossip mag to the stars!" Aldo stands up and kisses me on both cheeks. "Ahhh! I can smell California all over you."

I don't know whether to take that as a compliment or not. But then Aldo smiles warmly at me, so I'll assume he wasn't being sarcastic.

"I'm in awe of your tenacity and your ability to get within mere inches of your idol." I bow deeply before him.

"Thank you. Thank you. I must say I didn't even recognize myself. My mind just kept repeating the same phrase: 'Eyes on the prize. Eyes on the prize.' That's what kept propelling me forward. It's so true what they say about envisioning your goals and repeating self-affirmations. I'm living proof that they work."

Aldo looks quite proud of himself.

"We'd better get going. I'm sure Pia doesn't want to be late for her boyfriend's big night," Rita says. Her eyes meet mine, and she rolls them with a slight nod of her head toward Aldo. I guess she's sick of hearing about nothing else but his close brush with Francesca and his making it in *Inquisitor*.

"Zia, we're leaving."

Zia comes from the kitchen. "Have a good time!" She kisses me on the cheek and smiles at everyone else.

"Ma told me to tell you she's cooked a new dish that she knows you'll love," Rita tells Zia.

"Thank you, Rita. I'll be heading over soon." Zia opens the door for us. Before I walk out, she whispers in my ear, "It's okay if you want to come home much later tonight. Don't even worry about calling me. Just enjoy yourself. *Va bene?*"

I nod my head and squeeze Zia's hand to show my appreciation. I feel so much closer to her after having confided about Erica.

We climb into Connie's lime green Volkswagen buggy. The car fits her and her funky style perfectly.

"I'm *so* glad we're not schlepping into the city on the subway. Riding the subway on weekends totally blows with all the track repairs they've been doing." Aldo is sitting in the front passenger seat, regularly murmuring warnings to Connie as we drive. "Car coming on your right . . . Slow down, yellow light . . . Watch this moron in the opposite lane who's getting too close to you." I don't know how Connie manages to ignore him. She's definitely a role model for serenity.

My jaw feels like it's locking up. I don't know why, but I'm feeling anxious. I guess I'm nervous for Gregory and want this night to go off well for him. I know how much is riding on the show's being a success. This can really make or break his career.

"You must be so proud of Gregory," Rita says to me.

"I am. This is all just so amazing."

"He's lucky to have you. We think you're so good for him." Connie looks over at me while at a stoplight. She sounds more like Gregory's gushing mother than a friend.

"Behind every great man is a greater woman—if I got that saying right," Aldo says extra loudly as his voice competes with the traffic on the bridge.

"Thank you, Aldo. You're good for a woman's ego."

"Anytime you need a little boost, Pia, just call me." With lightning speed, Aldo produces from his sports jacket a business card. I can't help but laugh out loud.

"I'm serious! What's so funny?"

"Aldo, you're just too much, but in a good way. Trust me." I pat Aldo's shoulder.

"Aldo has what I like to call the 'I'm-clueless-that-I'm-funny complex,' " Rita says in a very deadpan tone.

"Oh, shush, Rita! You have the 'I'll-only-find-something-funny-if-an-asteroid-knocks-me-in-the-head complex.'" Aldo rolls his eyes.

Connie and I are laughing so hard now. Rita's arms are crossed defensively over her chest, and Aldo is staring out his window, doing his best to act like he isn't still stung over Rita's comment. The two have more in common than they'd like to admit.

Changing the subject, Aldo says, "I can't believe they renamed this bridge the Ed Koch Queensboro Bridge. *Yuck!* Why do they feel the need to rename everything lately?"

"I know. I still refuse to call Shea Stadium by its new name Citi Field. And who the hell calls the Triborough Bridge the RFK Bridge unless you're a 1010 WINS radio news broadcaster!" Rita exclaims.

"You got that right, sistuh!" Aldo turns around and high-fives Rita. Their earlier spat is forgotten as they unite over their hatred of New York City landmarks' being renamed.

"Make the sign of the cross, guys. Quick before we pass the Devil's Building," Connie yells out as she steers the car with one hand while making the sign of the cross with her other. I'm about to ask her which is the Devil's Building and why it's called that when the numbers "666" loom before me in red neon lights at the top of an office building.

"I love that building," Aldo gushes like a schoolgirl.

"Don't say that, Aldo!" Connie swats his arm as she slows down at an approaching red light.

We're going down Fifth Avenue, making our way to Chelsea. Though we're making good time, it's not fast enough for me. Again, my jaw tightens as I feel my anxiety returning. I can't lie to myself any longer. I'm nervous about more than just this night turning out well for Gregory. I can't put a finger on it, but my nerves won't allow me to relax.

Finally, Connie turns onto 26th Street, and we make our way west toward 11th Avenue. The show is being held at First Street Gallery. Ironically, Gregory and I had walked into First Street Gallery when we were gallery-hopping on one of our early dates. I can't believe his work will now be featured in Chelsea—the heart of New York's art world.

Connie finds parking on 11th Avenue. Fortunately, we find a spot after searching for only five minutes. As I step out of the car, a warm breeze that's coming in from the nearby Hudson River greets me.

"Come on, girls!" Aldo links his arms through mine and Rita's and ushers us forward.

"Wait up for me, guys!" Connie teeters over in her zebra-striped stiletto sandals. She's wearing a white shirtdress, with a black patent-leather belt that's cinched really tight to emphasize what must be a size zero waist. Rita is wearing a plum silk empire-waisted sundress. It suddenly dawns on me that I look the least dressed up of the group. Even Aldo is dressed to the nines in a short-sleeved, cream-colored button-down shirt with a gray pin-stripe vest and a periwinkle bow tie. Whatever. This is New York City. It's rare you'll see everyone dressed in similar fashion whether you're at a party or a lounge.

Walking arm in arm, we take up the width of the sidewalk, ignoring pedestrians who are behind us talking loudly, hinting to us to get out of their way. Normally, I hate it when people hog the sidewalk, oblivious to those behind them, but tonight I don't care as I adopt a typical New Yorker attitude. This is my baby's night to shine, and I can't wait to share it with him.

As we approach the gallery, I see numerous people entering. A group of older women are all wearing couture. They look like wealthy socialites. A Hummer limo pulls up in front of the gallery. Two couples get out. They look like the models who grace the bill-board ads in Times Square.

"I wonder if we'll spot any A-list celebrities. These B-list types aren't doing it for me." Aldo snickers.

"Those people getting out of the limo are B-list celebrities?" I ask him.

"They're models. I keep forgetting their names, but I've been seeing them everywhere lately from billboards to magazine covers. If they were really huge, I'd remember their names, of course."

"Of course," I echo back. Although it's apparent that Aldo is a bit of a snob, I can't help but feel that a lot of it is done for show. There's an inauthentic vibe to his snobbery. I think part of him wishes he belonged to this elite world, but there's also a side of him that knows he's not quite cut out for it.

Connie gives our names to the woman at the door. After she checks them off her clipboard, she motions with a quick flick of her fingers for us to step through the gallery's entrance. Two bouncers, both sporting bald heads and sunglasses à la Kojak, scan the crowd, looking for troublemakers. Silently, I laugh to myself, unable to picture this haughty, wealthy crowd containing even one instigator.

Already there's a decent-sized crowd milling about the interior of First Street Gallery. A six-foot-one auburn-haired woman is handing out flutes of champagne to the guests. Her strapless black gown has a thigh-high slit that provocatively shows off the full length of her leg. No doubt the woman is a model. I suspect the gallery has hired several models and actors to stage the show so to speak. My eyes are scanning the room, searching for Gregory, but he's nowhere to be seen.

"Drink up, Pia." Aldo hands me a flute of champagne.

"Thanks." I take a few gulps, and when I'm done, I see Aldo, Connie, and Rita staring at me.

"Want another one?" Rita asks, nodding toward my glass.

I notice with horror that I've almost downed the entire flute of champagne.

Smiling shyly, I say, "Ahh, no, that's fine. Thanks. I guess I was thirsty."

"I'll say." Aldo smirks. Connie subtly elbows him.

"I wonder where Gregory is. This is, after all, his show," Rita spits out. I've noticed how direct she can be.

"I'm sure he's somewhere. There's more to this gallery than this room. Come on, let's head to the back." Connie puts her arm protectively around me and guides me to the back. The girl must have ESP in addition to her ultra-serene state of mind. Somehow, she's sensed my nervousness.

"You look really sexy, Pia. You're going to look great in the photos they take of you and Gregory."

"Photos?" I ask.

"I'm sure there are a couple of reporters here to cover the show. Relax. You will be the perfect accompaniment next to the up-and-coming hottest artist." Connie winks at me.

Now I'm really questioning my more casual wardrobe. The only guests I've spotted in jeans are the male models and a few other guys. But most of them are wearing sports jackets or collared shirts with lightweight V-neck sweaters, which I don't get since it's the middle of summer on a muggy New York City night. The air conditioner isn't even set to full blast, and I'm already feeling warm with the crowd in this enclosed space.

"There he is!" Connie points Gregory out. I stop dead in my tracks. Madeline Drabinski is holding on to his elbow, leading him to the corner of the room. She whispers in his ear, and Gregory belts out laughter so loud that a few people look in his direction.

"That bitch" escapes my lips. Connie stares at me in horror.

"Did you say what I think I just heard you say?"

"Sorry, Connie. I know that snake who's draped around Gregory."

"Oo! Drama! Do tell!" Aldo comes up behind me. Great. He overheard me, too.

"It's nothing. Forget I ever said anything."

"Oh no! Spill it, Pia."

Even Rita is looking at me, waiting to hear the juicy story.

"Her name is Madeline Drabinski. She's—"

"*Profile*'s art critic! I know who she is. Remember, I work in the art world." Aldo sounds really proud of himself as he states this fact. I had almost forgotten that Connie had told me Aldo used to work for Christie's and now works for an art gallery not too far from here.

"Yes. She's doing a story on the show and interviewing Gregory. I guess you can say I'm not a fan of hers."

"You think she has the hots for your man?" Rita blurts out.

"No, no, of course not. She's a lot older than him."

"That's how they like them, Pia. Haven't you ever heard of cougars, and boy, does she have cougar written all over her." Aldo is practically drooling as he stares in awe at Madeline. I guess he holds cougars in high esteem.

"It's nothing like that. Madeline wanted to interview Francesca with me. She got mad because my intern supervisor gave me the green light to interview Francesca alone. She's given me the dirtiest looks around the office ever since. I'm not the only one who doesn't like her at *Profile*. There are certain rumors swirling about her and how she got her job at the magazine."

"Really? Like what?"

"Sorry, Aldo, I don't believe in spreading gossip. Besides, I recently discovered some info about Madeline that throws some doubt on a few of these rumors."

"Well, then, it's okay for you to tell us since they're probably not true." Aldo opens his eyes widely, giving me his best innocent face.

"Drop it. I'm not saying anything." I give Aldo my sternest voice.

"You're spoiling my fun, Pia!" Aldo pouts before he finishes off the last of his champagne, in time to plop the flute onto the tray that's being passed around by another Amazonian model.

"Well, let's go say hello." Connie nudges me forward.

"I'd rather wait until Madeline leaves." I remain rooted in place.

"Come on, Pia. Show that cougar who's boss." Aldo grabs my hand and pulls me in Gregory's direction. Wresting my hand from his grip, I plaster on my best smile and repeat to myself, *Look cool and confident. Look cool and confident,* hoping desperately that Aldo's advice to live by self-affirmations works for me as well.

"Sorry to interrupt, Gregory. But we wanted to say hello." My voice comes out extra boisterous, and I pray it's not obvious that I'm overdoing it.

"Pia! You guys made it. I was beginning to wonder where you were." Gregory gives me a half hug, nothing like what I'd imagined would happen when we first saw each other tonight. I was expecting a prolonged embrace, followed by a kiss on the lips—even if it were just a quick peck since we're in public. Instead, the hug he's given me feels like one you'd give to an acquaintance. He shakes Aldo's hand and gives Connie and Rita the same weak hug he gave me.

"Madeline, I'd like to introduce you to my friends and my girlfriend." Gregory recites our names. I note how he introduced me last instead of first. I know I'm nitpicking, but I'm still seething mad over his less-than-exuberant greeting.

Madeline shakes everyone's hands. When she directs her gaze toward me, she merely nods her head and says, "Pia and I already know each other, of course. How are you, darling?"

I want to puke all over her Christian Louboutin pumps. Her tone is dripping with condescension.

"Fabulous, Maddie. Are you here alone?"

Madeline's nostrils flare slightly at my use of "Maddie." Colin confided in me that she hates the nickname. I can't believe I've not only dared to call her that, but also asked her if she's here alone. I'm sure the answer will be "yes." But instead of answering my question, Madeline chooses to ignore me.

"I'll let you chat with your friends, Gregory. There's someone in the corner I'd like to say hello to." Madeline squeezes Gregory's arm before she slithers away. As she passes by, she gives me her trademark dirty look that I've grown accustomed to whenever I see her at *Profile*. I shoot back my own evil stare.

"Thanks so much for coming, guys. This means a lot to me." Gregory finally places his arm around my waist, but I don't feel reassured. I'm sensing he's holding back. Or am I just being paranoid?

"We wouldn't miss it for the world, Greg. Congratulations!" Connie walks over and gives Gregory a kiss on the cheek.

"Yeah, congrats, Gregory." Rita gives Gregory a quick hug.

Aldo raises his glass of champagne, which has to already be his third drink, and says, "Oh, Gregory, I've talked to the owner of the gallery where I work about giving you a show. He was very open to it. In fact, he was going to try and make it tonight."

"Wow! That's great, Aldo. Thanks so much for your support. So have you all had a chance to look at my paintings?"

"Actually, no, we wanted to find you first and give you our congratulations. Let's go check out the masterpieces." Connie ushers Rita and Aldo away, making it quite obvious she's trying to give us some time alone.

"This is great, Gregory. I can't tell you how thrilled I am for you." I lean forward and kiss Gregory on the lips. He pulls back and looks around, almost as if embarrassed by my PDA. Since when has he been shy about public displays of affection?

"Thanks, Pia. And thanks for coming."

"You don't need to thank me! As if I would miss the most important night of my boyfriend's life." I laugh, but instead of joining me, Gregory just nods his head.

"I thought you would've worn that dress Francesca gave you. Didn't she also give you a second one?"

My heart sinks. I knew it. Zia was right. I am underdressed for the occasion.

"I figured a casual, trendy look would be more appropriate. I see a few other people who aren't that dressed up. Connie thinks I look sexy." God, I sound so desperate, trying to gain his approval. *What are you doing, Pia?* I silently scream to myself.

"You do. You always look sexy, sweet pea. Don't get me wrong. It's just I thought this would've been an occasion where you could've taken advantage of wearing that dress Francesca gave you. That's all."

The note of disappointment rings loud and clear. Without thinking, I snap, "Don't be a hypocrite, Gregory. First, you tell me Francesca's makeover isn't me. Now, you're telling me I should've worn that dress? Make up your mind."

"Whoa! Whoa! Relax! All I meant when I first saw you that day is that you were overdressed for our date. But for these art shows, you can get dressed up more."

"That's not what you said. What's the matter? I'm not dolled up enough for your snooty art crowd? Maybe Madeline Drabinski should be your date tonight."

"Pia, what's the matter with you? This isn't like you."

Suddenly, a wave of shame washes over me. I'm about to apologize when Madeline shows up.

"So, Pia, doesn't Gregory look smashing tonight?"

I've been so caught up in my jealous rage about Madeline and anger about Gregory's lukewarm reaction to me that I hadn't even noticed he's dressed very stylishly. Instead of his usual paint-splattered, torn jeans, he's wearing black dress pants. His shirt, which doesn't sport so much as a crease in it, is a beautiful shade of gray and is buttoned all the way to the collar. It's fitted and shows off his lean physique. Expensive-looking black leather boots complete the ensemble. Though his hair is still slightly on the longer side, the way he likes it, I can tell it was just trimmed. And his signature five o'clock shadow that I love so much is absent. A hint of cologne reaches my nose.

"Yes, you look great," I say softly. Gregory looks into my eyes, not missing the sad note in my voice. For a second, his eyes look guilty, as if he regrets knocking my wardrobe choice. But the moment is interrupted once again by Madeline's annoying voice.

"I told him these clothes were made for him when we bought them."

"You went shopping with him?" I can't even hide my surprise.

"Nate was with us, too," Gregory quickly adds. "He took one look in my closet and told me I needed new duds for the show." Gregory laughs nervously, not meeting my gaze.

I can't believe Gregory. He has the nerve to get mad that I let Francesca make me over, and now he's allowed Madeline to transform him. I never thought Gregory would fall prey to the curse that comes with celebrity. But I see he's quickly becoming fame's slave. Now, it's the clothes. Tomorrow, it'll be a hot model to replace his girlfriend.

"By the way, Pia. How's that article coming along? The Francesca Donata interviews should have been wrapped up weeks ago. Colin thought he would've seen at least a first draft by now." Madeline links her arm through Gregory's and is tilting her head slightly to the side. Gregory looks slightly uncomfortable, but makes no effort to disengage himself. To one of the other guests, it would appear that they're the happy couple celebrating his success.

"The article is going better than I expected, and wait until you see the secrets I was able to get Francesca to reveal. I *know* Colin will not be disappointed." I flash Madeline my most saccharine smile. Though my heart is breaking into a million little pieces on the inside, I'll be damned before I let this woman rattle my exterior so easily.

"That's wonderful, Pia. I cannot wait to read it. I am sorry but if you'll excuse Gregory and me, there's someone whom I promised I would introduce him to." Without waiting for my acknowledgment, Madeline leads Gregory away. Gregory glances over his shoulder and mouths, "I'm sorry." I give him a little wave, letting him know it's okay even though it really isn't.

I need a drink and something much stiffer than champagne. Making my way over to the bar that's been set up in the gallery, I order a martini. While the bartender's back is turned, I sneak a few of the olives from the bar and pop them in my mouth. The bartender returns with my drink. I glance around the gallery, trying in vain to locate Connie and the rest of the gang among the crowd, which keeps growing. Someone behind me taps my arm.

"Megan! You made it."

"Yeah. I'm pretty exhausted, but I couldn't let Gregory down." Megan gives me an air kiss on the cheek and asks the bartender to make her a martini as well.

"Where's everyone else?" She takes one of the maraschino cherries sitting in a cup on the bar and twirls it in her mouth as if she's sucking a lollipop. Unlike me, she doesn't care if the bartender catches her stealing the condiments.

"They're somewhere. I'm sure they'll find us sooner or later."

"What's the matter, Pia? You sound glum."

"Just tired." I shrug my shoulders. Megan gives me a worried look, but doesn't ask further.

"I saw Gregory when I walked in, but he was surrounded by so many people. I'll catch up with him later when this crowd thins a bit."

"Yup, he's quite preoccupied tonight."

Out of my peripheral vision, I catch Megan staring at me.

Suddenly, the crowd rushes to the front of the gallery. Everyone seems excited.

"What's going on?" I ask Megan.

"Let's find out." Megan takes my hand and, like a pro, squeezes through the throngs of people.

"Oh my God! *She's* here!"

I follow where Megan's index finger is pointing. But I can't immediately make out who it is with everyone's cell phone cameras flashing. Then I hear, "It's Francesca Donata! It's Francesca Donata!"

I'm shocked, though when I think about it for a moment, I don't see why. It makes sense that Gregory would've invited Francesca considering their long friendship and that he's now painting her portrait, although he's had to take a hiatus from it since he's been busy preparing for the show. While it's no surprise that Gregory extended an invite to her, I never would have thought she'd risk the mob scene her presence elicits. Then again, as I've come to learn, Francesca is a glutton for attention.

Finally, she comes into view. Am I seeing right? She's wearing a coral-red jumpsuit. Normally, I'd say a woman her age shouldn't be wearing a jumpsuit, but Francesca totally rocks it. Then again, is there any look she doesn't rock?

She's flanked on either side by Rocco and Lorenzo. My heart quickens at the sight of Lorenzo. He looks more handsome than usual. I didn't just admit he's handsome. *Okay, Pia, no big deal.* I can notice other good-looking men. It doesn't mean I'm cheating on Gregory.

"Thank you! Thank you!" Francesca repeats to the swarms of surrounding people who keep professing their love for her. You'd think the art show was for her and not Gregory. I'm starting to get annoyed and plan on giving Francesca a piece of my mind. But just when I'm thinking the worst about her, she announces, "I would like to make a toast to the young man whose art we are celebrating."

"Sshhh!" travels through the crowd.

Nathan Horowitz rushes to Francesca's side with a microphone.

"Everyone, please allow me to introduce the legendary Francesca Donata, who has been so kind to grace us with her presence this evening."

The audience applauds. Nathan gives them a moment and then motions with his hands for silence. "I'll now pass it over to you, Francesca." Nathan smiles as Francesca leans over and air kisses him on both cheeks.

"Where is the man of the hour?" Francesca cups her hand over her eyes, scoping out the crowd. I see an arm shoot up in the air.

"There you are, Gregory. Do not be shy. Please come join me."

I strain my neck to see Gregory. He kisses Francesca and then bows slightly to the crowd. Everyone laughs. I try to make eye contact with him, but it's no use.

"I have had the pleasure of knowing this man since he was a young boy; he used to accompany his father, who painted several portraits of me. He was even shyer then than he is tonight." The crowd laughs again, and Francesca smiles at Gregory. She places her arm around his shoulders.

"When his father retired from painting, I never imagined I would find another talented artist to paint my portrait. So you can imagine my extreme pleasure when I learned that Gregory had followed in his father's footsteps and was an artist in his own right. I had to—how do you Americans call it? Twist his arm?" People in the front row nod their heads, and Francesca continues. "*Si*, that is it. I had to twist his arm a little, but I was able to persuade Gregory to paint my portrait."

Gasps of surprise float through the air. A reporter yells out, "Is the portrait here?"

"No, Gregory is not finished painting it yet. He had to take some time off to prepare for this show. But this night is not about me. It is about Gregory Hewson and his brilliant paintings. I know this is the start of a wonderful career for you, Gregory, and it makes me so proud to toast you tonight. Please, everyone, raise your glasses to this extraordinary man." Francesca raises a flute of champagne, which I hadn't even noticed she was holding. Someone must've quickly passed it to her. Gregory kisses Francesca again, and after everyone has toasted him, he takes the microphone.

"Thank you, Francesca, for your warm toast. I cannot tell you how much it means to me to have your support and friendship. I would also like to take this opportunity to thank my friends who came out tonight. You've been patient with my neglect of you in the past few weeks. I hate long speeches, as I'm sure all of you do, too, so I'll end this now, but first I'd like to send out a special thanks to my girlfriend Pia." Gregory raises his glass toward me. I swallow hard as everyone looks my way.

"Please enjoy yourselves, and feel free to come up to me and say hello if you haven't done so already. Thank you." Gregory hands the microphone to Nathan as he escorts Francesca toward the back of the gallery. Francesca links her arm through his. Her bodyguards trail after them, making sure the crowd keeps their distance.

"How does it feel to be dating a star who's on the rise?"

I jump.

"Lorenzo! You scared me."

"Sorry. I didn't think that was possible among this horde."

"I didn't know you and Francesca were coming tonight."

"Gregory invited Francesca, and she asked him if I could come. I'm surprised you didn't extend an invitation to me."

I'm about to defend myself when Lorenzo winks. Of course, he's joking as usual. I'm so not in the mood for his barrage of jokes.

"Gregory's art is very impressive."

"Yes, he's talented. I'm really happy for him."

"Then why do you look like someone's rained on *your* parade?"

I want to wipe the smug grin off Lorenzo's face. For some reason, he seems to be taking pleasure out of making me squirm.

"Look, Lorenzo, tonight's not a good time for your sarcasm. So I'd appreciate it if you would back off."

"Ouch! Okay, you have my word, no more snarky comments. Sorry, Pia. I can't help myself sometimes. Forgive me?" Lorenzo pouts his lips and holds his hands together as if he's praying to me. I cave in and laugh.

"You're too much." I shake my head.

"That's what I've been waiting for. That perfect smile." Lorenzo pushes a strand of stray hair back behind my ear. The action freezes me. I look down into my empty glass.

"Let me get you another drink." Lorenzo takes my glass and heads over to the bar.

"Pia!"

I turn around and see Gregory making his way toward me.

"I swear. I keep losing you."

"You've been looking for me?" I can't hide the surprise in my tone.

"Of course I have. I'm sorry. I'm being pulled left and right tonight."

"That's okay. This is great. I can't believe Francesca came."

"Yeah, I owe her."

I glance around the gallery.

"Where is she?"

"She's in the VIP room. She and Rocco are having drinks and talking to Nate and Madeline. She'll probably cut out of here soon. She just wanted to make a quick appearance."

I nod my head.

"Pia, I need to talk to you. Let's go somewhere quiet."

Gregory takes me by the hand, leading me to the back and through a door that is marked "Employees Only." The room looks like a storage area. Various paintings fill the space. I notice the same artist's signature is on all of them. No doubt it's the work that was last on display at the gallery.

"Sorry for the stuffy quarters, but I wanted to talk to you alone and where we won't be interrupted."

I nod my head. An uneasy feeling spreads in the pit of my stomach. "So, what did you want to talk about? It sounds important." I try sounding casual, but instead my voice comes out shaky, betraying my nervousness.

Gregory runs a hand through his hair and then swallows deeply.

"Okay, this isn't easy, so I'm just going to blurt it out. That portrait I painted of you is here."

"The one of me naked?" Panic flashes through me.

"Ahh. Yeah, but your breasts were the only part of you that was exposed."

"Oh, great! Everyone will know now just how small my apples really are."

"Pia, stop it! They're perfect."

"I thought you weren't even finished painting it. You were going to show it to me once you were done."

"When Nate came over to see my work, I went to get him a beer and left him alone in my studio. Of course, he snooped around and lifted the tarp that was concealing your portrait. Even though it was only half done, he loved it. He said I captured so much emotion in your face and the way I positioned your body was brilliant. He wanted it to be part of this show and asked me to finish it."

"I didn't see it hanging on any of the gallery's walls. Where is it?"

"It's in a small room upstairs. Nate plans on revealing it halfway into the show. He thinks it's the jewel of the collection and knows he'll get many bids on it."

"Bids? You're going to sell it?"

"Pia, please try to understand. I can't say no to what Nate thinks is best for my career when it's only just launched."

"Gregory, you promised me that no one was going to see that portrait. It was just supposed to be for the two of us. Now some stranger is going to be staring at me every day of his life and doing God knows what else when he looks at that portrait."

"Pia, come on. It's art. You're acting like it's porn. I know you're upset, but I hope in time you'll realize you're overreacting."

"Overreacting? You broke your promise to me. *That's* what upsets me the most. If this is how you keep your promises, how am I supposed to trust you?" I should be yelling at him, but I'm too hurt to muster up the energy to raise my voice. Tears race down my face, and I don't even bother trying to fight them.

"Pia, I'm sorry."

"And you didn't even tell me before the show!"

Gregory tries to hug me, but I knock his arms away.

"I need to get out of here."

"Pia, please, don't go. You're going to be just as famous as I'm going to be once your portrait is revealed. This will be great publicity for you as a writer."

My hand is on the stockroom door. Before I leave, I turn around and say, "You really don't know me, Gregory. Yes, I want to be a successful writer, but I care more about my relationships than I do about fame. I thought you shared the same ideals as I do, but I guess I don't really know you either."

I slam the door shut behind me and walk quickly to the exit before Gregory has a chance to catch up. But I have nothing to worry about. He isn't even following me.

Once outside, I run up to a yellow cab that's just gone down the street and is at a red light at the corner.

"I'm going to Astoria."

The cabbie motions with his head for me to get in as he adjusts his meter.

"Hold on!"

"Oh my God!"

Lorenzo is banging on the passenger window.

"I'm sorry. He's with me."

The cabbie pulls over as the red light turns to green. Lorenzo gets in. I wanted to be alone of course, but I have a feeling if I hadn't let him in, he would've chased the cab, yelling until we stopped.

"I saw you leaving the gallery. I could tell you're upset and was worried about you."

Lorenzo's voice sounds sincere. Mentally, I thank him for not being his usual sarcastic self for once.

"Thanks, Lorenzo."

We ride in silence until we're going over the bridge back into Queens.

"You got into a fight with Gregory, didn't you?"

"Yup." I smile sheepishly at Lorenzo.

"Okay, I get it. You don't want to talk."

"Sorry. I'm just spent."

"He's taking you for granted, Pia."

"Gregory has been very busy preparing for the show. I don't blame him. I can be a workaholic myself."

"Stop defending him. He should always make some time for you."

"Thanks. That's sweet of you."

"I mean it, Pia. You're a wonderful person."

I laugh. "You don't even know me, Lorenzo, but thank you for the sentiment."

Lorenzo looks out his window. His brows are knitted furiously together. I've upset him. Instead of apologizing or even changing the heavy subject we're on, I just remain quiet. I already fought one battle tonight.

The taxi stops in front of Zia's. I open my purse, but Lorenzo has already handed the cabbie a fistful of cash. He steps out and holds my door.

"Thanks for the cab fare, but that wasn't necessary."

"I know, but I wanted to. I like doing things for you even if they're minor like paying for your cab fare."

"Well, thank you again. And thanks for making sure I was okay. Have a good night."

I turn to leave, but Lorenzo grabs my wrist, pulling me toward him, and before I can protest, he's kissing me. I know I should make him stop, but I don't. Strangely, kissing him is making me feel comforted.

Suddenly, I realize with horror that we're standing on the street and anyone could see us. What if Gregory came by looking for me? Guilt propels me to push away from Lorenzo.

"That shouldn't have happened. I really need to go."

"I'm sorry, Pia. It's just—"

I hold up my hand. "It's okay. I just really have to go now. Okay?"

Lorenzo nods his head and looks at me sadly. I run up the stairs to Zia's, quickly fumbling with my keys. Lorenzo waits until I've opened the door and then waves as he walks away toward his mother's house.

Shutting the door behind me, I turn my back and lean against it, exhaling what must be the longest breath of my life. Listening for any sounds that would indicate Zia might be awake, I kick off my heels and say a silent prayer thanking God for not letting my aunt witness her niece acting like a hussy.

What a mess! The whole night was just one disaster after another. And I can't believe I kissed Lorenzo back. I came to New York seeking some clarity in my life in addition to experience at a magazine. But it seems like I'm only adding to the confusion.

Pulling my cell phone out from my purse, I check to see if Gregory called or texted me. There are a few missed calls from Connie and Megan. I call my voice mail and listen to the two messages they left me, asking me to let them know if I'm okay.

I send them both texts, telling them not to worry and that I made it home safely. Connie immediately texts me back:

ARE YOU OKAY???? GREGORY TOLD US YOU GOT INTO A FIGHT.

Great! He had to blab that to everyone.

I text Connie back:

I'M FINE. JUST TIRED. WE'LL TALK TOMORROW.

My stomach grumbles even though it's close to midnight. Heading into the kitchen to get a snack, I can't help thinking about Gregory and what's he's doing right now. The show is probably wrapping up. We were supposed to be together to celebrate his big night. Guilt stabs at me—both for getting upset with him and for kissing Lorenzo.

I don't need to eat right now. I need something to help me fall asleep and forget this terrible night. I search Zia's cupboards to see if she has any brandy. After much searching, I locate a few liquor bottles behind her baking pans in one of the cupboards above the stove. I pour milk into a large mug. I then stir in a teaspoon of vanilla and a few teaspoons of sugar. I heat the milk in the microwave for a minute and a half. Once the timer goes off, I take the mug out and stir in an ounce of brandy and a quarter of a teaspoon of nutmeg. Taking a sip, I let out a sigh of pleasure. Zia made this for me one night last week when I couldn't sleep.

Carrying my warm milk with brandy up to my bedroom, I tiptoe past Zia's room. But once I hear her cacophonous snoring, I relax, knowing nothing will wake her out of that deep slumber. Too lazy to remove my makeup, I step out of my clothes and ease into bed. I don't even bother with my pajamas tonight. Drinking slowly so I can savor my drink, I replay my argument with Gregory. But as the warm milk with brandy works its magic and makes me drowsier with every sip, my mind keeps replaying Lorenzo's kiss.

## 22

# Francesca

Giuliana is sleeping. I am sitting in the upholstered chair that is usually in the corner of the bedroom, right next to her bookshelf. But I have brought it closer to Giuliana's bedside. Even in this room, Giuliana is surrounded by her treasured books. As I take closer notice, many of her beloved possessions are in this room.

Jewelry boxes of all shapes and sizes cover the surface of her dresser. She has adored them since she was a little girl. I am happy to see she even kept a few that I had sent her over the years for Christmas. At least her contempt for me did not transfer to the boxes.

A light scent of flowers always fills her room, much like a funeral home. Daisies, Giuliana's favorite flower, are in vases throughout the room. Though daisies have a shelf life of seven to fourteen days, Giuliana has instructed Angelica to check them regularly and replace any that are beginning to wilt. The daisies are taken from the garden out front. But in the winter, Angelica buys them at the local florist. Luckily for Giuliana, daisies are available year-round.

Giuliana fell in love with the flower after Dante, her deceased husband, showered her with them during his courtship. When my mother was alive, she told me that Dante used to call Giuliana his "delicate daisy." Even when we were children, Giuliana loved the wild daisies that grew on the hillside of my parents' farm in a tiny mountain village outside of Taormina, Sicily.

I close my eyes and am instantly transported to when we were young girls.

Giuliana was thirteen and I was ten. Our arms were linked as we skipped and sang, playing a silly game in which one of us would suddenly drop to the ground, pulling the other along with her. Every time we fell, we pulled more daisies and placed them in the little wicker baskets we each held.

"I am going to beat you, Francesca! You hardly have any daisies in your basket!" Giuliana laughed.

I shrugged my shoulders. "So what? You always share yours with me anyway."

"*Davvero?* I think I am going to stop being so generous and will keep all of my flowers to myself this time!"

"You will not!" I laughed, knowing Giuliana was incapable of acting so selfishly.

"Wait and see!" Giuliana broke her hold from me and ran down the hill. I chased her. We were both giggling. Finally, out of breath, Giuliana stopped halfway down the hill and collapsed on the grass. I joined her. We both shielded our eyes from the sun as we looked up into the sky.

"I can never get sick of living here," Giuliana said. I glanced over at her. She was smiling and seemed so content.

"Not me. I want to see what the rest of the world outside of Sicily looks like." Though I was just ten years old, my wanderlust had already set in, and I spent much of my time daydreaming about traveling to other countries. I did not know yet I wanted to be an actress. I merely knew that I was not going to spend the rest of my life in the city where I grew up. How much we change when we grow old. Now I only long to be in my native country, in my home, where my memories of my unspoiled childhood bring me comfort.

"You would not dare leave me!" Giuliana reproached me. Her voice betrayed a hint of fear.

"Then, you will have to join me, Giuli." I nudged my elbow lightly into her side. When I was first learning how to speak as a toddler, I could not say "Giuliana," so I called her "Giuli" instead.

I continued calling her this until we had our falling out, and we stopped being the best of friends.

"I cannot imagine traveling so much. I think I would miss home too much." Giuliana's voice sounded wistful.

"Trust me, you would forget about home almost immediately. I know I would."

"I would not be so sure of that if I were you." Giuliana propped herself up onto her forearms and watched me with a smirk on her face. She then took the daisies she had collected earlier and placed a bunch in my basket. Pulling two out, she intertwined their stems and leaned over me as she inserted both into my hair, right above my ear.

"*Perfetta! Sei molta bella!*"

"*Grazie,* Giuli. Your turn." I took six daisies out of my basket and pulled off the stems. I then tucked each flower into the crown of Giuliana's head, forming a headband of daisies. Her thick, wavy hair held the daisies securely in place, and the white petals stood out against her fiery red hair.

We then made our way down the hill, back to our home. I do not remember what we talked about, for we were always chatting and laughing. What I do remember is our close bond and how I thought, in those days, nothing would ever come between us.

Tears flow freely down my face as I watch Giuliana lying in bed. How different this sick woman looks compared to the vibrant girl I knew from my youth.

On Giuliana's night table, her wedding photo rests. She was so beautiful. If only I could have seen her in person that day. Her light breathing reaches my ears.

"Giuli," I softly whisper to her. "Please come back one last time before you go."

The day after Gregory's art show, Giuliana's health took a dramatic turn for the worse. Lorenzo rushed her to the hospital, where she stayed for a day. Her cancer has spread throughout her body. The doctor told us she could last a month or less. They recommended transferring her to a hospice, but Lorenzo and I want her to die at home. Lorenzo said he knew his mother's wishes would have been the same. A few days have passed since we brought her home. She was barely conscious the first forty-eight hours, but yesterday she slipped into a coma and has not woken up. It is just a matter of time now before she leaves us forever.

My tears fall onto my clasped hands that are clutching a rosary. I have been praying for my sister to wake up since yesterday.

*Please God, just for five minutes. That is all I am asking of you. I have wasted these past few weeks thinking about how bored I was cooped up here, thinking about my secret admirer, thinking about myself as always when I should have forced Giuliana to talk to me. I want to tell her how sorry I am for hurting her so much. Please God, do not let her die before I tell her.*

A soft knock at the door interrupts my prayers.

"Zia, why don't you go lie down? You haven't left her side since yesterday." Lorenzo comes in and hands a glass of water to me.

"I must stay in case she wakes up. There is something I need to tell her. I will never forgive myself if I leave and she wakes up." With the back of my hand, I wipe my tears.

"Just talk to her anyway. They say when someone is in a coma he or she can still hear his or her loved ones." Lorenzo strokes his mother's cheek with a light touch of his fingers. His eyes well up. I stand up and join him, placing my arm around his shoulders. He breaks down sobbing and leans into me. We hug each other as we both cry inconsolably.

A raspy breath comes from Giuliana, startling Lorenzo and me. Her eyes flutter open for a second and then close again.

"Mama!" Lorenzo calls out to her.

A few seconds go by, and then Giuliana's eyes open once more. She blinks a few times.

"Loren . . . sho." Her voice is barely above a whisper.

"Mama, yes, it's me. Zia Francesca is here, too." Lorenzo squeezes his mother's hand.

I walk over to the other side of the bed and take her free hand.

"Giuliana, I have prayed for you to wake up. It is so good to hear your voice. We are here with you. There is nothing to fear. You are not alone."

"I have . . . I have . . ."

"Take your time, Mama," Lorenzo pleads.

*"Poco . . . poco tem . . . po."* Giuliana has reverted to speaking in her native Italian as she tells us she has little time left.

"Don't waste your energy, Mama." Lorenzo is crying once more, but he is fighting to keep the emotions from being evident in his voice lest Giuliana hear.

"*Ti vo . . . glio . . . bene.*" Giuliana looks at Lorenzo.

"I love you too, Mama." Lorenzo bends over and kisses his mother on the forehead.

Giuliana then looks at me. My heart stills.

"I for . . . for . . . give . . . you, my . . . my little . . . sis . . . ter. I did . . . a . . . long time . . . ago."

"*Carissima.*" I call my sister by the endearment my fans have used for me all these years. But she is truly the dearest one, not me. She should be adored and honored. She is the one who possesses a good heart. "I am sorry I hurt you so much, Giuli. Every day for the past thirty years, I have regretted the pain I caused you." I bend my head and kiss Giuliana's hand.

"You . . . made mis . . . takes. You were . . . just . . . just a child . . . who grew up . . . fast. We all loved . . . you . . . *sor . . . sorella mia.* Promise me. Promise to tell the truth." Giuliana's eyes begin to close, but then they open once more. She is struggling to stay with us. Lorenzo and I wait patiently, hoping her time has not come, though we know our bargaining with God is almost over.

"Lo-Lo-renzo. Please. I . . . must . . . talk . . . to her . . . alone."

Lorenzo nods, but I can tell he is reluctant to leave, afraid this really will be the last moment he has with his mother. He leans over and whispers into her ear. He kisses her hand before he lets it go and steps out of the room.

"Promise . . . me . . ." Giuliana stares intently at me.

"I promise, *carissima.* But are you sure?"

Giuliana squeezes my hand so tightly that I am shocked her weakened body still has such amazing strength. She stares intently at me and repeats, "Promise . . . tell . . . truth."

"I promise. I promise, Giuli."

Little by little, Giuliana's grip relaxes until she is no longer holding my hand, and her breathing has stopped.

Placing my head on her chest, I hug my sister as I weep uncontrollably and whisper, "Do not leave me. Do not leave me, *carissima.*"

## ❧ 23 ❧

# Pia

A week has passed since Gregory's art show. And it's been one of the worst weeks of my life. The day after the show, I waited for him to call, but he never did. Connie had come over and admitted that Gregory had asked her to check in on me. He wanted to make sure I had arrived home safely the night of the show, and I couldn't help feeling he wanted to know how mad I still was before he contacted me. All that did was infuriate me more. I told Connie I didn't appreciate her acting as his spy. I wasn't mad at her though. Connie pleaded with me to call Gregory, but my stubbornness wouldn't allow for it.

Gregory finally called me a few days ago, leaving voice mails each time. Of course, he apologized in each message. Deciding I've made him suffer enough, I'm in a cab right now heading to his house.

While I know I have every right to be mad at him for not telling me he was including my nude portrait in the exhibit, I can't help feeling guilty for ruining what was to be his biggest night. Then again, from the photos that Connie showed me, which were taken after I bolted out of the show, he appeared to be enjoying himself. A few other celebrities, besides Francesca, had arrived after I left, and they all posed with Gregory. For someone who often made snide remarks about stars and hating pop culture, he's embracing it all too readily now.

Then again, how well do I know Gregory? We haven't been dating long. With that reminder, my spirits suddenly plummet. I can't believe we're already heading into the second week in August. I'm supposed to be returning to California the first week in September. Zia has been asking me to change my airline ticket and stay in New York for another month. I have to admit I am tempted. I don't know why I can't make up my mind. It's just postponing my return by a few more weeks. Sighing deeply, I squeeze my eyes shut. Whom am I kidding? Of course I know why I can't decide. If it were Gregory instead of Zia asking me to delay going back home, I would change my ticket in a heartbeat. But he hasn't brought up the subject. How can he tell me he loves me and then not ask what my plans are at the end of the summer?

The cabbie pulls up in front of Gregory's house and my pulse starts racing. I pay my taxi fare and get out. I quickly make my way up the steps leading to Gregory's door before I can change my mind and hightail it out of there. I ring the bell several times, but there's no answer. Turning around to leave, I suddenly remember that when Gregory is painting he plays his music really loud and often doesn't hear his bell. I try his cell. He picks up on the first ring.

"Hey!" Gregory sounds genuinely pleased to hear from me.

"Hey."

"I'm so glad you called."

"Actually, I'm downstairs. You didn't hear the bell ring."

I hear music, followed by a voice in the background. Gregory calls out to the person, "Hold on a sec!"

"Is this a bad time? Sorry. I should've called before coming over."

"No, no. I have company, but she was about to leave."

"She?" I can't help myself, and I know Gregory can hear the jealousy in my tone.

"Ahhh. It's just Madeline. She's finishing up my interview for the *Profile* piece. But you can come up."

All I want to do now is leave, but I can't. Partly because I'm try-

ing to act like I'm cool with a former Eastern European super-
model spending time alone with my boyfriend, and partly because
I want to see for myself that everything is fine. Crazy! I know Gregory would never cheat on me, but still. I can't ignore this recent
insecurity I've been feeling either.

"Okay, if you're sure I'm not interrupting."

"Nah! I'll be right down to let you in."

We hang up. It feels like an eternity until Gregory finally makes
his way to the door. I can see through the glass, he's pulling on his
T-shirt. Granted, he rarely wears a shirt when he's home and painting, but how can he be shirtless in front of Madeline? I mentally tell
myself to calm down and not explode.

"Hi!" Gregory is smiling from ear to ear, much like a schoolboy
who's in love with his teacher. He leans over and kisses me on—the
cheek? But then he holds me close to him once I step inside.

"I'm so happy you're here. I've been going crazy this week. I'm
so sorry about everything."

"I'm sorry, too. I ruined your big night." I hug Gregory back.

"You didn't ruin it! Stop!" Gregory is doing a good job of acting like his night was still perfect, but his voice sounds a bit forced.

"I was just hurt that you broke your promise to me about not
showing my painting to anyone. I guess I overreacted."

Gregory tilts my chin upward so that my gaze meets his.

"Pia, I'm really sorry I broke my promise to you. I don't know
what came over me. Well, I guess I do. I let all this craziness with
getting discovered go to my head."

"I would've probably acted the same way."

"No, I don't think you would've. You're just saying that to make
me feel better. And I love you for it." Gregory pulls me close to him
once again.

"You had pretty much no choice, Gregory. Nathan Horowitz
wouldn't have given you the show without my portrait."

"He said that, but in retrospect, I think he was bluffing because
he wanted that painting in the exhibit. I didn't try hard enough to
protest about your painting being unavailable."

"So what did everyone think of it?"

"They loved it! Are you kidding me? It got the most buzz of all the paintings in the exhibit. I wish you had been there to see how excited everyone was."

"I don't know about that. They would've recognized me as the subject, and I would've felt naked." I laugh.

"Gregory!"

Madeline's shrill voice rings out. Soon, her rail-thin body is coming down the stairs with precise, calculated movements. It's as if she's doing a fashion show and the staircase is the catwalk. Does she ever walk as if she's not strutting down a runway?

"Sorry, Madeline, Pia and I needed to talk."

"Hello, Pia."

"Madeline." I nod my head.

"You left the show early last week. Did you have somewhere else to be?" Madeline's lips turn up slightly. She's absolutely sneering at me.

"I wasn't feeling well."

"Hmmm. Well, I need to be going, Gregory. I'll come back with Anton for the photo shoot."

"Photo shoot?" I ask.

"For the *Profile* interview Madeline's doing," Gregory explains.

"I'm sure Anton can handle that by himself. I mean, it's not like you have photography expertise as well, do you, Madeline?" Now I'm the one who's sneering.

"I need to direct Anton to ensure the photos go with the theme of the article. When *I* write a piece, I oversee every aspect of it. Nothing gets overlooked. But you are still learning. I wouldn't expect you to know that." Barely showing her teeth, Madeline smiles. She walks over to Gregory and kisses him on both cheeks even though his arms are still wrapped around my waist. She doesn't seem to care that she interrupted us.

"I'll call you as soon as Anton lets me know when his schedule will allow for him to come over."

"Thanks, Madeline." Gregory breaks our embrace and opens the door for Madeline. Before she steps out, he leans forward and kisses her on both cheeks. Madeline snakes her arm around his waist and hugs him briefly. She doesn't even say good-bye to me. I want to run over and give her bony butt a good kick that will send her careening down the stairs.

"Whoa, Pia! You need to cool it with Madeline. The tension between the two of you is so palpable," Gregory says after he shuts the door.

"Why do I need to cool it? She started by asking me why I left the show early and then giving me a little 'hmmm' when I told her I wasn't feeling well. She obviously didn't believe me."

"Well, you were lying."

"I wasn't lying. I really wasn't feeling well. My boyfriend admits that he broke a promise to me as well as my trust in him. How do you think I felt? Great? You want me to tell her our personal problems, Gregory? Or maybe you have already and that's why she didn't believe me. She already knew the truth from you!"

Gregory remains silent, but he's staring at me. After a few more seconds elapse, he finally says, "I thought we just made up. But I can see this is still raw for you."

"Sorry. I do forgive you. I just don't like Madeline."

"Pia, you hardly even know her. It's natural that the two of you have some professional rivalry, but I think if you both put that aside and realized you're on the same team, you'd get along better."

"Why is it you're always defending these women to me? First, it was Francesca; now it's Madeline. Can't you see women like them take pleasure out of chewing people up and spitting them out? They act like they're super-confident women when they're really insecure. That's why they have to knock everyone else down around them—except for the people they want something out of, like you."

"Oh, so now you're saying I'm being used?" Gregory breathes an exasperated sigh.

"Sort of. Actually, yes, if I may be frank."

"Pia, stop!"

"Gregory, I know this is hard to hear, but Francesca used you by convincing you to paint her portrait because she wanted you for the job. You didn't even want to paint her initially, but we both agreed she played on your guilt and your family's long relationship with her. And now Madeline is using you to write her article."

"I said stop!" Gregory is shouting now. I've never seen him so mad. I turn around so he doesn't see my tears.

"I'm sorry I shouted. But Pia, you're not making sense. Madeline is just doing her job. She's an editor at *Profile*. Don't you think it would sound bizarre to you if I accused you of using Francesca so you could get your interview?"

"Okay, okay." I hold up my hands in resignation, but I'm not about to give up. "You've got a point there. But I know Madeline is up to something. I can feel it. She wants more from you than a great interview."

Gregory shakes his head, still not believing me. I'm saved by the ring of my cell phone. The screen flashes "Lorenzo." My heart drops to my belly.

"Sorry, Gregory. Let me just get this really quick."

I don't know why I don't let Lorenzo's call go to voice mail. Maybe because it'll buy me a couple of minutes to get myself out of this messy conversation I started with Gregory.

"Hello."

"Pia, I'm sorry to bother you, but I have some bad news."

"What's the matter? Is it your mother?"

"Yes. She passed away early this morning."

"Oh, Lorenzo! I'm so sorry!"

Gregory quickly glances up at me when he hears Lorenzo's name. My sadness over hearing the news of Signora Tesca's death made me forget not to say Lorenzo's name aloud. Then again, why do I feel I have to hide the fact that I'm talking to him? We're friends. Nothing more. Yeah, except for that kiss we shared the other night. I can feel my face warming up.

"Pia, Francesca wanted me to call you to ask you to let the neighbors who were my mother's friends know. We're going to have a wake for her, but I can't disclose yet where it will be for security reasons. We want to try and fend off the paparazzi. When I know more of the details, I'll call you. My mother left behind a letter, saying that she wants to be buried next to my father in Rome. So after the wake, we'll be transporting her body to Italy. The wake will be the only chance her friends will have to say good-bye to her."

Lorenzo utters the last sentence very quietly. I can tell he's struggling to keep it together.

"Of course, I'll let the neighbors know. I'll do it as discreetly as possible, and I will ask them not to say anything. But I can't promise the news won't leak. People have a way of talking."

"Yes, yes. Francesca and I are aware of this. As I said, we'll do our best to minimize the media frenzy, but if the paparazzi find out where the wake will be held and follow us, then so be it. We felt it was more important that her friends have the opportunity to see her one last time."

"I understand. I'm so sorry, Lorenzo. Please give Francesca my condolences. I'll see you both at the wake."

"Thank you, Pia. I will call you when the plans are finalized."

"Okay. Good-bye, Lorenzo."

I hang up the phone. Gregory is standing right behind me. His eyes look grave.

"Signora Tesca died." He's heard enough to know it's a certainty rather than a question.

"Earlier this morning. Her son and Francesca are going to bring her body back to Italy. Signora Tesca wanted to be buried in Rome, beside her husband's grave."

"I guess Lorenzo got your number from Francesca?"

I shrug my shoulders. "I guess. He said that Francesca wants me to let the neighbors know so they can attend her wake. They're going to have it here, but they need to iron out the security details first. They want to try and avoid having the media find out, to prevent a circus outside the funeral home. Once he knows more, he'll call me."

I can't believe I've just lied to Gregory about Lorenzo's getting my number from Francesca. There's no excuse, but I've never done well with awkward situations that arise spontaneously. Then again, don't most awkward situations occur spontaneously? I look at Gregory and force a small smile. He's staring intently at me.

"Please let me know where the wake will be. I'd like to attend and pay my respects."

"Okay."

"I'll pick up you and your aunt, and we can head over to the funeral together. That is, if you want."

"Sure. That would be fine."

"I'm sorry, Pia, but I need to get back to work."

"I thought you were going to have a bit of a break before your next show?"

"Yeah, I thought so, too, but since my first show was such a success, Nate has moved up the date of my second exhibit. Apparently, he already has a list of anxious buyers for my new paintings even though they haven't seen them yet."

"All right, I'll leave then." I can't hide my disappointment as I walk to the front door. I never even made it past the foyer, and now I'm going home.

"Pia, I promise I'll make it up to you."

"Don't make promises you might not be able to keep."

"Ouch! You're never going to let me forget about letting Nate show your portrait at my show, are you?"

"It . . . it just came out of my mouth. I wasn't thinking."

"No, you were thinking. Your subconscious made you choose *exactly* those words. Come here. Let's talk some more." Gregory pulls me by the hand and leads me to the staircase. We sit down on the bottom step.

"Lay it all on me—even your anger."

"It's no longer about the portrait. I have forgiven you over that."

"Then what's it about?"

"I just thought you were going to have more time for me after the first show. It's been hard not seeing you much."

"I know. I know. It's been hard on me, too, but this is the sacrifice I need to make, especially right now when I'm at the start of my career. You'll understand when you get your big break."

"I do understand. But I can't help wondering if this is going to be the norm for you from now on. I'm afraid that whenever you're busy, work is all you will do. It seems like you have a hard time balancing your personal life with your professional. I don't want to be with someone who's married to his work."

"So you're saying you see a future with me?"

Oh, geez! What did I just imply? I didn't want to be the first one to bring up the subject of our future. But I can't shy away from it now.

"Maybe."

"Don't worry. I've never been that much of a workaholic. I enjoy more in life than just painting. I will make the time for you. How about we have a special date next Saturday night? You're right. I have been neglecting you."

"I didn't say that, Gregory."

"You didn't have to actually say the words. It's crazy that I haven't even made time for you on the weekends since all this started."

"Gregory, I do want you to succeed."

"I'm so lucky to have you, Pia." Gregory picks up my hand and kisses the back of it and continues to hold it as he stares into my eyes.

"And I'm lucky to have you." I stroke his cheek with my thumb.

"Pia, I've been meaning to talk to you about Francesca."

"What about her?"

"Are you almost done with the article?"

"Yes, I just have one more interview left, but I've already written most of the first draft."

"Pia, I think you've been too focused on this project. Are you learning other valuable skills at least when you're in *Profile*'s offices?"

"What's going on, Gregory? You know I wasn't learning much there besides proofreading. This is Madeline talking, isn't it? What has she been saying to you?"

"Again with Madeline! Geez, drop it already, Pia!"

"Not until you tell me what this conversation is about!"

"I just don't want you to put all of your eggs into one basket. What if Colin doesn't like the article and decides not to publish it? I don't want you getting your hopes up and then being crushed. I think you should see if you can write or edit other articles. Maybe you can help Madeline edit the piece she's doing on me."

"Are you out of your mind? There's no way I'm working with her so she can lord it over me! Why did you even say yes to doing the interview with her?"

"You're being irrational, Pia. How was I supposed to know you didn't like her when Nate introduced us? How could I turn down media coverage of my show and a story on me when I've just been discovered? In fact, I'm surprised you didn't think of it, since you are interning at *Profile*."

"So that's what this is about. You're annoyed that I didn't suggest interviewing you myself, and you think it's because I've been too focused on Francesca."

"You have been too focused on her."

"And you've been too focused on yourself and your new rise to fame."

"That's not fair, Pia, and you know it."

"You've been different ever since Nate discovered you. You even let them dress you for your show! You're their puppet on a string. Don't you see that?"

"And you haven't been Francesca's puppet?"

Sighing deeply, I get up and walk to the front door.

"So you're going to storm off again?"

"Good-bye, Gregory. I think we both need to cool down before we say something we'll regret."

"I think it's too late for that. But fine. Whatever." Gregory runs his hands through his hair and storms upstairs.

And with that, I make my exit, making certain to slam the door.

Signora Tesca's wake is held two days after she died. Though I got into an argument with Gregory, he still insists on picking up Zia and me. Zia walks in between us as we make our way up the block to the Mussolini Mansion. It's the longest walk of my life. Neither Gregory nor I say anything, and Zia keeps looking from one to the other of us. But she also doesn't make any attempt at small talk to break the ice.

All of the neighbors are meeting inside Signora Tesca's house. Francesca's security team is too paranoid about giving out the name and location of the funeral home. They've rented a couple of SUVs to transport us. Lorenzo told me they were going to have decoy SUVs to throw the paparazzi off the trail. I pray it works. Signora Tesca deserves to have a peaceful wake, and I know it means a lot to Francesca. Lorenzo confided in me that she'd felt guilty about the crowds outside of the Mussolini Mansion ever since her arrival.

I can't help feeling extremely bad for Lorenzo. I called him before he contacted me with the wake arrangements. We talked for almost an hour as he told me stories from his childhood in Rome and about his mother. It sounded like he had a lonely childhood. What a shame that Francesca and Signora Tesca hadn't been talking all those years. He could have had his aunt at least. Neither of us brought up the kiss from the night of Gregory's show.

Finally, we arrive at the Mussolini Mansion, and Gregory rings the bell. Carlo lets us in and shows us to the library, where the rest of the neighbors are milling about. They're whispering as they sip espressos. I also spot Rocco in the corner.

"I can't believe I've never seen the inside of these digs before!" Paulie Parlatone's voice booms over the din of the crowd.

"Clah-see! Clah-SEE all the WAY!" Ciggy drawls. I'm relieved to see he isn't smoking his cigar, but I'm annoyed that both he and Paulie are being obnoxious. Where's their respect for the dead?

Suddenly, I feel Zia squeeze my arm so tightly I almost shriek in pain.

"Oh, Pia! I cannot believe I didn't make any time to see Giuliana before she died!"

I pat Zia on the shoulder. "You didn't know she was sick. It's okay."

"Still. I should have come, but I felt weird with her sister being here."

Now, I feel guilty that I didn't confide in Zia just how sick Signora Tesca was. If I had, maybe she would have had the chance to see her one last time before she passed away.

"It's normal to feel guilty after someone dies, Antoniella. We all find something to feel guilty about when we've lost someone close to us." Gregory puts his arm around Zia and gives her a slight hug. To my surprise, Zia leans into him as she pulls her handkerchief out of her pocketbook, another Gucci vintage purse from the sixties, and blows her nose. Gregory continues to hold on to Zia.

"Antoniella, Pia," Olivia DeLuca calls out softly and motions for us to join her. Connie and Rita are with her. Connie is wiping tears with a tissue. Rita isn't crying, but her lips are pursed tightly together as if she's trying to fight back tears.

"If only she had told us she was ill. I heard she knew for a year," Olivia says. Zia shakes her head and the two of them lower their voices as they continue talking. No doubt they're exchanging the gossip they've heard regarding Signora Tesca's illness and death.

"Were you guys close to her?" I ask Rita and Connie.

"We became closer to her after Valentina's shower," Rita says. Now she looks like she might start to cry any second.

"That's right. Your mother told me Signora Tesca threw your sister's bridal shower here. She also told me about the beautiful brooch she gave her as a wedding gift."

Connie nods her head. "I feel horrible. We used to be scared of her when we were kids. We even joked that she was the witch on the street because of the scary statues in her yard. But she was the furthest thing from a witch. She was so kind and generous. You'd never know she was related to Francesca. She was very quiet and unassuming."

"What's important is that you did get to know the real her, Connie," Gregory says. "Don't dwell on stuff you can't control, especially from when you were kids."

Boy, Gregory is a wealth of wisdom tonight. I can't help mentally rolling my eyes. I'm still seething mad about our argument. As if reading my mind, Gregory leans over and whispers in my ear, "Follow me. I want to talk to you."

"Again?" I whisper back, not attempting to hide the anger in my tone.

He takes my hand and is about to lead me away when Lorenzo suddenly is standing before us.

"Pia, Gregory. Thank you for coming."

I let go of Gregory's hand and hug Lorenzo as I give him my condolences. Gregory shakes his hand.

"I'm sorry for the delay. We're just waiting for Francesca."

*Naturally,* I can't help thinking. *She's even late for her sister's wake.*

The neighbors' whispers increase as Edgardo and another of Francesca's bodyguards enter the room. A moment later, Francesca enters the library, and the neighbors go silent immediately. Everyone is staring at her with shock on their faces as if they can't believe they're really here in her presence.

Francesca is wearing a black pants suit. Even her blouse is black. Her hair is up in a simple chignon, and she wears no makeup or jewelry. Her eyes are bloodshot. Though she looks less glamorous without any makeup, her beauty is still evident.

"Hello, everyone. I wanted to thank you for coming. I know this means a lot to Giuliana, and she is looking down on us right now, smiling." Francesca's voice cracks a little. She pauses for a moment to regain her composure before continuing.

"I also wanted to thank you for being her friends all of these years. As I'm sure you know, my sister was shy and kept to herself a lot. But I know she loved Astoria very much. She spoke fondly of it. Though she had come to think of America and Astoria as her home, she did express a wish to be buried in her villa in Rome, next to her husband."

A few whispers are heard among the neighbors.

"We will be leaving for the funeral home now. I wanted to thank you all again for being friends to my sister when she was alive and for coming tonight."

Francesca turns around and leaves with Edgardo and another bodyguard flanking her sides. As soon as she exits the room, the neighbors talk excitedly among themselves, but at least they're keeping their voices low out of respect.

"Pia, would you like to ride in the SUV that Francesca and I are taking?" Lorenzo asks me.

Gregory shoots a look between me and Lorenzo.

"Oh no, thank you, I couldn't. That should be for family."

"Of course, you may also come, Gregory."

"We came with Pia's aunt, and we're also with our friends. But thank you for the offer." Gregory puts his arm around my shoulders.

"Well, I guess I'll see you both then at the funeral home." Lorenzo nods his head and walks away.

We follow the crowd that's started to file out the back door leading to the yard. The security guards are checking each of our funeral invitations before letting us step into the SUVs. Yes, we actually received invitations for the wake to ensure that only those invited would be in attendance. Olivia, Connie, and Rita are with us and are doing a good job of chattering away so that I'm not forced to get into another awkward conversation with Gregory. He still has his arm around me. I keep stealing glances his way, but his mind appears to be somewhere else.

After about half an hour, we arrive in Roslyn Heights, a suburb on Long Island. As we step out of the SUV, which has parked in the yard behind the funeral home, I see huge white tents set up, much like the ones Hollywood celebrities have when they're getting married or having some other event they want to keep private. We walk under the tents and through a back door into the funeral home. I guess the tents are just to conceal Francesca.

We step into the viewing room where Signora Tesca's body is lying in repose. Flowers in abundance line the sides of the room and surround Signora Tesca's casket. As we get closer, I see all of the flowers are daisies. That does it. I start crying, remembering all of the daisies I've seen in the Mussolini Mansion. Obviously, they were Signora Tesca's favorite flower. I don't know why this moves me so much, but it does. Gregory grabs my hand and squeezes it tightly. Like Zia earlier, I collapse into him, not caring anymore about the stupid argument we had.

Instead of feeling comforted by Gregory, my anxiety grows, and suddenly, it's not Signora Tesca's wake I'm at but Erica's. As we approach the casket, I see Erica, wearing her violet prom dress that she loved so much. Her long brown hair, which hung all the way down to her waist, is wrapped over her shoulders and down her arms like bolts of ribbon. Her first communion rosary was interlaced around her clasped hands. I wish I could say she looked every bit as beautiful in death as she did in life, but except for her lustrous hair and her princess-like prom dress, her beauty had faded with her life. Her face was puffy and her lips, which had always been naturally pink, were now a dull beige hue. The sheer lip gloss the mortician had applied hardly added any color. At least the mortician hadn't gone overboard with applying her makeup.

There were many flowers at Erica's wake, too, but they were all different varieties. I look at the front row of seats and see my mother's haunted stare, my brother being so brave for all of us, and my father crying inconsolably. And then I see myself, dressed all in black with a skirt and top that Erica had given me for my birthday the previous year. Like Francesca, I also chose not to wear any makeup or jewelry.

"I can't breathe. I need to go out," I say to Gregory.

"Come on." Gregory quickly ushers me away.

"Pia, are you okay?" Zia asks.

"She'll be fine. She just needs some fresh air." Gregory waves his hand. "All the flowers in here."

Zia nods her head and seems to believe him. I thank God for Gregory in that moment. We approach the back entrance, which is where we came in. One of Francesca's bodyguards is blocking the door.

"We need to step out for a few minutes. She's not feeling well."

"We're not supposed to let anyone leave until the wake is over and Francesca has left first."

I start gasping loudly and my chest is heaving as I go into full-blown panic-attack mode. The bodyguard's eyes widen.

"Okay, but stand where I can see you."

I hear Gregory curse at the bodyguard under his breath. "Asshole! What does he think we're going to do? Sneak in a reporter?"

As soon as we're outside, I grasp onto one of the poles of the tents that have been set up and bend my head close to my knees. Gregory rubs my back.

"Just give me a couple of minutes. It should stop soon."

"Take your time, Pia. I'm in no rush to go back inside. All those daisies were starting to make me feel woozy."

"Can you go to the restroom and wet a paper towel with cold water for me?"

"Sure. I'll be back before you know it." Gregory smiles, but I can tell he's worried about me.

I focus on my breathing and try to keep my mind from wandering back to Erica's wake.

"Breathe into this."

I glance up and am startled to see Lorenzo looking at me with concern. He bends down so that his face is level with mine and hands me a paper bag.

"Thanks," is all I can manage. I want to ask him how he knew I was out here and not feeling well since he magically has a paper bag, but it'll have to wait until my attack subsides. Breathing into the paper bag is helping tremendously as my heart rate begins to slow down and my breaths come more naturally. I should carry a paper bag in my purse all the time. Then again, I keep hoping that I won't get any more panic attacks. Am I doomed to get them forever?

"Francesca asked Antoniella where you were when Antoniella came over to pay her respects. Francesca was worried and asked me to check on you. I'm sorry about all of the flowers. I tried telling my aunt she was overdoing it, but she wouldn't listen."

"It wasn't the flowers that made me feel sick."

"Then what was it?"

"I couldn't help flashing back to when my sister died a few years ago and I was at her wake."

"So you understand."

I nod my head as I begin to slowly stand up.

"Let me help you." Lorenzo gives me his hand and helps lift me.

"I've got it from here." Gregory's stern voice rings through the air.

I didn't even hear Gregory return. He's giving Lorenzo a dirty look. I'm embarrassed. Can't he see Lorenzo was just helping me stand? Where's his compassion? Lorenzo just lost his mother.

"Are you sure you're feeling better now, Pia?" Lorenzo seems hesitant to leave.

"Yes, thank you, Lorenzo. I'm fine. I'll return in a moment."

"If this is too much for you, my aunt and I would understand if you went home."

"Maybe that would be for the best, Pia. You still look really pale," Gregory says as he dabs at my forehead with the wet paper towel. I want to tell him to stop, but I don't. Instead, I just take the towel from him and dab my own forehead.

"No, I really want to pay my respects to Signora Tesca. I'm much better now."

"Okay. Let me know if you need anything." Lorenzo walks away. Even his gait is filled with sorrow.

"You gave me a scare, Pia. I didn't know you suffer from panic attacks."

"I've been getting them since Erica died. It didn't even occur to me that Signora Tesca's wake would trigger memories from Erica's funeral."

"It seems like you and Lorenzo are friendly."

"Of course we are. I've seen him at the house when I've interviewed Francesca."

"I think he likes you."

"That's crazy, Gregory. He could have his pick of women with his money and . . ." I let my voice trail off.

"And what?"

"Nothing."

"And his good looks?"

"Let's go back. I don't want my aunt to worry."

Without waiting for Gregory, I enter the funeral home. He catches up to me and grasps my hand. I can't help feeling he's doing it more to show Lorenzo his ownership of me. I'm turned off, but I don't let go of his hand. I don't have the energy after my anxiety attack to start what will surely be another ugly argument.

Taking a deep breath, I repeat in my head, "Signora Tesca, Signora Tesca" to keep my mind from straying back to Erica. As I kneel down on the pew in front of Signora Tesca's casket, I can see from my peripheral vision that Lorenzo is watching me. I close my eyes to pray, but all I can think about is what Gregory said. "I think he likes you."

Francesca called me the day after the wake. I was surprised given that she's in mourning. Part of me was afraid that I'd never hear from her again. After all, she would be under no obligation to return to New York after delivering her sister's body to Rome. She could finish our last interview over the phone, but I wouldn't blame her if she were too consumed by her grief and forgot that we still needed to finish up our interviews.

Francesca wanted to see how I was feeling, but she also had a request. I'm still reeling from the shock. Not only did Francesca remember we have one interview left, but she wants me to write her autobiography! She asked me to fly to Rome this coming weekend and stay with her for a month at her apartment. She and Lorenzo need to settle Signora Tesca's estate, which will take quite some time. Francesca even joked that she wouldn't have any list of conditions or approved questions this time around.

This autobiography, along with the *Profile* interview, would seal my career as a journalist. I'm excited, but I'm also nervous. I'm on my way to tell Gregory the good news, and I'm planning on asking him to join me in Rome—if not now, then as soon as he's done with his paintings. But what I'm really afraid of is his reaction when I tell him that I am seriously considering moving to New York permanently. I'm scared he's going to tell me that while he cares about me, he doesn't see us having a long-term relationship. But he did tell me he loves me. Ugghhh! I have to stop with this mental torture and just get this over with and deal with the consequences.

Again, I've decided to surprise Gregory rather than calling him before showing up. I was too excited to wait to see him. I already know the answer will be "yes." As soon as I hung up the phone with Francesca, I called a gypsy cab and left.

It takes longer than the usual fifteen minutes to get to Gregory's because it's four p.m. and rush-hour traffic is already underway. Finally, I'm at his house. I run up the steps and trip midway. I ring the bell, but again, Gregory doesn't answer. I'm about to call him on my cell when I notice the door is slightly ajar. Shutting my phone, I push open the door and let myself in. Radiohead is blasting from his computer as I make my way up the stairs.

Gregory's studio is at the end of the hall on the right-hand side. It used to be a guest room when his parents lived here, but Gregory has long since converted it into his studio. As I walk down the hall, I hear voices. The music is so loud that I can't hear what's being said. I approach the studio and peer into the room. The door is only half open, but I can make out part of Gregory's bare back as he's seated on a stool. As I stretch my neck all the way to the left, my blood turns cold. Madeline is standing next to Gregory with her arm around his shoulders. Her opposite hand holds a glass of wine. She's wearing a super-tight, hot-pink ruched dress that shows every curve in her body. Leaning provocatively so that her hair brushes against Gregory's bare back, Madeline whispers into Gregory's ear. He laughs and says, "You're *so* bad!" Then Madeline holds her wineglass to Gregory's lips as he takes a sip.

I knew it! They're sleeping together. How could he? How could he do this to me? Tears blind my eyes as I kick open the door, startling Madeline and Gregory so much that she spills wine all over his chest.

"Pia! What are you doing here? Did you ring the bell?"

"Apparently I needed to so you'd have enough warning just like the last time I showed up!"

"Pia, calm down."

"I know what I saw! Don't try to deny it! This is why you've been too busy for me to visit? But you let *her* hang out with you while you work?"

"There's no changing her mind, Gregory. Let her believe what she wants. You don't need this stress." Madeline looks triumphant, as if she's won the Oscar.

Gregory ignores her and walks over to me.

"Pia, I was just getting some feedback from Madeline on my latest painting. I was going to call you to come over tonight to give me your opinion."

"Stop!" I hold up my hand. "Stop with the lies." I turn around and run down the hall, but Gregory catches up to me before I can head down the stairs.

"Don't do this, Pia. Please." Gregory is whispering, but the urgency in his voice is still apparent. "Let's talk, okay?"

Madeline appears in the hallway.

"Gregory, it's best that I leave. I don't want to cause any more trouble than I already have." As she passes us, she flashes another malicious grin as her eyes lock onto mine. Gregory doesn't notice.

"I'm sorry, Madeline. I'll call you later."

Another dagger pierces my heart, but I don't say anything.

"Gregory, let me go. I don't want to talk." Gregory is holding onto my wrists with both of his hands.

"No! You keep running away every time we have a fight. I'm not letting you do that to me again!"

"Oh! You're the victim! You cheated on me with that trash! Again, you've broken my trust in you. It doesn't matter, Gregory. Nothing you say will change anything, especially now that I'm going away."

"Going away? Are you going back to California? It's not even the end of August."

"Francesca has asked me to go to Italy with her. She wants me to write her autobiography. I'll be staying with Francesca at her apartment in Rome for a month. That's why I came here unannounced. I wanted to surprise you. I was really excited that she wants me to write her autobiography, and I was going to ask you . . . Well, I guess it doesn't matter now. It's over between us."

"You were going to ask me what, Pia?"

"I was going to ask you to meet me in Rome when you're done with the paintings for your second show."

"Of course I'll come."

"No, Gregory. Don't. This is really for the best. You were right when you hinted at my being a user, too. Only, I didn't use Francesca. I used you. I knew you were my ticket to getting an interview with Francesca. I knew it from that first night when I saw you come out of Signora Tesca's house."

"You don't mean that, Pia. You're just saying that to get back at me because you're hurt."

"It's true, Gregory. Just like what you said about my having been too focused on Francesca. You were right. So please don't bother coming to Rome and trying to change my mind about us. I never really loved you. I was just using you."

"I don't believe you! I've never had a woman look at me when she told me she loved me the way you have. I've only felt this way with you. No one else. I was going to ask you to stay in New York and not go back to California. I was going to ask you to move in with me."

Hearing his admission brings a new round of tears to my eyes. That's all I was waiting to hear from him these past few weeks. Why couldn't he have told me sooner? What does it matter? He's a good actor. He wants me for his girlfriend, but Madeline as his lover. She'll assure him access to famous art dealers and all of her other valuable contacts. He calls that love?

I still have to torture myself, so I ask him, "Why didn't you ask me to move in with you sooner? We're already halfway into August. Or are you just bluffing now so that I won't walk?"

"I was going to ask you on Saturday. Remember I promised you a special date? I wanted to make the occasion memorable. It's not too late, Pia. When you're done with Francesca in Rome, come back here, and I'll help you make your arrangements to move permanently to New York."

"I don't trust you, Gregory. I know what I just saw."

"You act like we were having sex, for crying out loud!"

"I didn't have to catch you in the act to know you're sleeping with her!"

"You're pushing me away. You accuse *me* of being the liar?" Gregory has let go of my wrists and is now pointing with his index finger at his chest, which still has drops of red wine from when Madeline spilled her drink.

"Pia, you're afraid of commitment. You're seeing what you want to see with Madeline and me to make it convenient to walk away."

"Stop turning the tables on me! You're the one who cheated. Don't act like I'm the bad guy!"

"For the millionth time, I did not cheat on you with Madeline or anyone else. I have never cheated on anyone in my life. That's not who I am. Pia, don't you see what you're doing? You're afraid of getting too close to me. You're afraid you'll lose me like you lost Erica."

"Don't mention my sister! That is *not* what I'm doing."

"You run away whenever there's conflict, Pia. Whenever things get too difficult for you, you escape. You left California to avoid dealing with your unresolved emotions over Erica's death; you ran out on me the night of my show. You tried running out on me again when you were last here. You're running now. Fine. You want to run. Go to Rome. I won't stop you. Maybe the distance will give you better perspective, and you'll see in the next few weeks that you've been trying to sabotage this relationship."

So that's it. He's giving up. He's not going to keep trying to change my mind about breaking up with him. It's just further proof that he is sleeping with Madeline and doesn't really care about me.

We stare at each other for what feels like an eternity but is really probably no more than a minute. I know we're both thinking the same thing. This could be the last time we ever see each other.

"Good luck with your paintings and your next show." I begin going down the steps.

"Congratulations on Francesca's asking you to write her autobiography. I know you'll be a great success someday."

I freeze on the third step. His last words sound so final. We really are doing this. I don't turn around when I say, "Thanks."

I can feel his eyes all the way until I get downstairs and shut the door behind me.

# ❧ 24 ❧

# Francesca

Though Rome was my home for almost thirty years, La Città Eterna still manages to hypnotize me as if it is my first time visiting. Everywhere I look, her boundless vitality and regal beauty surround me as I take my *passeggiata* through Rome's jewel, Piazza Navona. The magnificent sculptures of giants at the Fontana dei Quattro Fiumi, or the Fountain of the Four Rivers, herald my return to the city. The four giants symbolize the four great rivers of the world: the Ganges, the Danube, the Nile, and the Plate. Here in what must surely be Rome's most elaborate *piazza,* Baroque architecture is on dramatic display. One of my favorite Baroque masterpieces is the church of Sant'Agnese in Agone. The church is believed to have been built on the site where in AD 304 the young St. Agnes was stripped naked in front of a crowd in order to force her to renounce Christianity. Her hair miraculously grew to cover her body. St. Agnes was martyred at this site.

I decide to enter the church and light a candle for Giuliana as well as my deceased parents. Edgardo and an additional bodyguard are present, but they stay a good five feet behind me. On occasion, Edgardo allows me to walk without him or the other guard flanked on either side of me. Today Edgardo is not worried that anyone will recognize me with my red wig and large oval sunglasses. Rome is so congested with people that I am easily swallowed among the throngs.

Two weeks have passed since Giuliana died, and Edgardo does not wish to give me further grief. I am tempted to sneak in among a group of tourists and run off so I can truly be alone. But I do not have the energy for the escape or for Edgardo's anger. Giuliana's death has been so draining. Sighing deeply, I step into Sant'Agnese in Agone. Removing my sunglasses, I replace them with my reading glasses to help conceal my face. I also pull out a silk scarf and tie it around my head to further disguise my identity.

After lighting my candles, I sit down in the last pew at the back of the church. Edgardo and the other bodyguard stand behind the pew. I can feel Edgardo's heavy breathing on the back of my neck. He has never done well with extreme humidity, and August in Rome is insufferably hot. I lower myself onto the kneel rest and close my eyes.

*Dio, dammi forza per dire la verita. Per favore, Dio, dammi forza.*

As I pray to God to give me strength to carry out Giuliana's last wish, I feel beads of perspiration forming along my temples and my heart races. Giuliana's last words replay over and over in my mind. I have not been able to stop them since she died. I know what I must do, but I am not ready to do so.

Lorenzo and I buried Giuliana in the private mausoleum where her husband rests in the yard of her villa. Lorenzo stayed behind to have the house cleaned, but I am staying in my old apartment in the Piazza Navona district. Pia arrived a week ago and is staying in the guest bedroom of my apartment. I have asked Lorenzo to take her out whenever she is not interviewing me for my autobiography.

Pia was quite surprised that I am having her write my autobiography, as I am sure the public will be when they get wind of it. I have always been a very private person. But throughout my career, there have been so many misconceptions about me in the media. I am now ready to set the record straight and let the world know who the real Francesca is. I have grown to trust Pia and admire her. She seemed a bit nervous to take on such an overwhelming task, but I have full confidence in her even though I have not read yet the article she is writing for *Profile*. In my life I have learned to trust my instincts, and they are telling me that Pia is the right person to tell the story of my life.

Pia confided in Lorenzo that she is no longer seeing Gregory.

She has not told me herself yet. You would never know the girl is in Rome. Even though this is her first visit here, she looks as if she is the one who has just lost a family member. Ahh! First love. It is always the first experience we have with love that crushes us the most. My first love devastated me. Closing my eyes, I let my mind wander to the first time I came to Rome, and I remember how in love I was. The memories come fast and furious. My heart feels like a balloon ready to pop. Flashing my eyes open, I notice Edgardo is staring at me. I avert my gaze as I make the sign of the cross and stand up to leave. I feel faint, and the scent of incense in the church is making me feel worse.

I head in the direction of the Piazza di Spagna district. My destination is Via Condotti, where upscale designer boutiques line the street as well as the adjacent ones. Shopping has always immediately lifted my spirits, and as I contemplate what clothing treasures await me, Edgardo intrudes upon my thoughts.

"Where are you going?" he whispers to me, which is silly with all the noise surrounding us.

"I thought I would do some shopping on Via Condotti."

"Francesca, you need to tell me what your plans are."

"I am doing so right now." I frown at Edgardo and shrug off his grip on my arm as I quicken my pace to increase the distance between us. But he quickly catches up.

"I thought we had an agreement, Edgardo. You and Tonio keep a few feet away from me so I can feel like I am a grown woman who does not need her babysitters."

"You're planning on going inside shops where the merchants and customers will be able to get a better look at you. So we need to be right at your side should anyone attack you."

I dramatically roll my eyes and say, "In the four decades that I have been an actress, no one has ever attacked me, and I do not think it is going to happen now that I am in my old age."

"You are not in your old age." Edgardo's eyes sweep across my body even though I am wearing a loose tunic over relaxed capris. I did not want form-fitting clothes that might give away my famous figure to the public.

"Fine, fine, Edgardo. You and Tonio may stay beside me. I do not want an argument for once."

I hear Edgardo release a long sigh of relief.

"Look, Francesca, I know things have been tense between us since I blew up at you the night I discovered you had escaped from your sister's home. I'm sorry. You have to understand you gave me the scare of my life."

Edgardo is looking at me with the tenderest expression. He truly does care about me. I pat his arm and say, "I, too, am sorry. Sometimes I do not think. I was having too much fun with Rocco."

At the mention of Rocco's name, Edgardo's eyes cloud over and his lips crease. I did not mean to hurt him. I am only speaking the truth. When I said good-bye to Rocco in Astoria, I told myself I would not miss him. But I do. We did not speak of whether or not I would return to Astoria, but I could tell it was weighing on Rocco's mind. Good man that he is, he did not bring it up out of respect for Giuliana's passing away. He has called me a few times since I arrived in Rome. But I have only taken two of his calls. I am certain he will tire of me soon. Besides, I have too much on my mind right now. I must honor Giuliana's last wish. And until I do so, I cannot think about anything—or anyone—else.

Finally, we arrive at Via Condotti. I step into the Giorgio Armani shop, and as my senses take in the fine clothes, euphoria replaces the anxiety I was feeling seconds ago. Ahhh, Roma! You have always been good to me.

# ❧ 25 ❧

# Pia

So I've traded in the crowds from New York City for the crowds in Rome. But in the Eternal City, the masses seem less menacing. Maybe that's because everyone looks excited to be here. From the numerous tourists, *romani,* priests, and nuns walking the *piazzas* to the students whizzing by on their *motorini, la dolce vita* is reality in Rome.

The Spanish Steps sprawl before me like an enormous hand fan. I'm sitting at the very top of the stairs with my laptop, hoping to glean some inspiration. For famous writers such as Byron, Honoré de Balzac, and Stendhal among others also sought their muse at the Piazza di Spagna. But all I've been able to accomplish is a rough outline for Francesca's autobiography. You might think I'm crazy trying to write in one of Rome's most busy and famous squares. I've always had a knack for shutting out the noise and focusing on my work, but today I'm failing miserably. Teenage couples making out are as numerous as the churches in Rome, and they're proving to be a huge distraction. I always thought that images of amorous Italians on every street corner were just part of a stereotype the movies created. But in the past week since I've arrived, they've bombarded me. If I'd known that there were so many happy couples in love, I would've stayed in New York. For these young lovers remind me of my own failed relationship with Gregory. And Rome's romantic landscape only makes me wish even more he were here with me.

I noticed he tried to call me last night, but he must've forgotten about the time difference. My phone was turned off and I was in bed already. I even opted to get the pricey international plan my cell phone carrier offers just so that I could talk to Gregory if I wanted to. But now I'm seeing what a bad idea that was—and not just for the sake of money. How am I supposed to move forward and forget about him if I keep talking to him? But am I ready to forget him? Is it really over between us? Or is this just a break to figure out what we both want, and we'll get together once I return from Italy? Ugghhh! I'm crazy! I can't believe I'm even entertaining the idea of getting back together with the man who cheated on me. That seals it. Tomorrow, I'm canceling my international cell phone plan. The sooner I forget Gregory, the better.

The bell tower of Trinità dei Monti clangs loudly above the din in the piazza, coinciding with the headache that is pounding against my temples. The church is behind me, at the top of the Spanish Steps. Deciding this is a good time to check out the Antico Caffè Greco, a two-hundred-year-old haunt for famous artists and writers, I pack up my laptop and stand up. Two boys around fifteen years old blow kisses at me, smacking their lips loudly. I ignore them and head over to Via Condotti, where the historic café is located.

Antico Caffè Greco is packed. Mostly locals, all dressed fashionably of course, stand at the bar sipping espressos. To the back, I see the typical tourists dressed in Bermuda shorts and white tennis shoes. Lorenzo mentioned that the café is a must for any aspiring writer, but he warned me to just get a quick espresso at the bar, which is much cheaper than if you were to get table service. What I'm really dying for is a cappuccino, but Zia Antoniella told me before I left that Italians only drink cappuccinos in the morning because they don't want to combine the dairy in it with the foods they eat throughout the day and possibly cause stomach upset. How clever! I order an espresso *macchiato*. I can't take my coffee black whether it's *Americano* style or Italian. After just two sips, I feel my headache starting to subside.

"I thought that was you!"

A redheaded woman with enormous sunglasses approaches me. Must be a tourist. Maybe German or Eastern European with her accent.

"I'm sorry. You must have mistaken me for someone else."

The woman leans in closer and whispers, "It is me, Pia. Francesca."

And then I notice Edgardo and another bodyguard nervously scanning the crowd taking their espresso breaks. I can't believe I didn't recognize her voice, though her sinfully curvaceous figure is hidden in the baggy trousers and tunic she's wearing.

"I see they let you out." I smirk toward Edgardo and the other bodyguard.

"*Madonna mia!* That one is getting worse with age—well, except for his looks. Unfortunately, Giuliana's death is working to my advantage by gaining Edgardo's sympathy."

"Would you like an espresso? I can order one for you."

"*Si, si. Nero, per favore. Grazie.*" Francesca begins to open her purse, but I wave her hand away. I know it's ridiculous of me to treat a rich, famous movie star to coffee, but it would also be obnoxious of me to expect her to pay for everything when I'm with her. She tries to insist, but I walk away.

After ten minutes of waiting in line, I finally get Francesca's espresso. I don't see Edgardo any longer.

"Where are your bodyguards?" I whisper to Francesca once I return.

"I do not know. I am sure they are close. I cannot worry about them. It is their job to worry about me. *Vero?*"

Naturally, I nod my assent. Though I feel more comfortable around Francesca after getting to know her better these past few months, I still realize I must never disagree with her.

"Are you enjoying Rome? I know Lorenzo has taken you to a few places this past week. He felt bad that he could not be with you today, but he had to meet with my sister's attorney about her estate."

"That's okay. I don't expect Lorenzo to be my personal tour guide. I can get around the city on my own. It's even fun to get lost on a few of these side streets and alleys. I almost always discover something unique when that happens."

"Ah, *si!* That is the beauty of Rome. I am glad to hear that you are getting some pleasure out of being here. I must admit, Pia, I have been worried about you."

"I suppose Lorenzo told you about me and Gregory." I say it as a statement rather than a question.

"Do not be upset with him. He was anxious for you, too. And even if he had not told me, I could see it with my own eyes. You have not looked the same since you have arrived."

I shrug my shoulders. I don't know what to say. She's right. I'm a mess both on the outside and inside.

"Pia, this pain will pass. Trust me. First love is complicated and rarely works out."

"How do you know this was my first love?"

"Because you are absolutely crushed."

"So when other loves break your heart, you're not as hurt is what you're saying?"

"In a sense, yes. I am not saying that it does not hurt when another person you fall in love with after your first boyfriend breaks your heart. It is just that with first love you experience the feelings much more strongly because it is the first time you have felt this way. You think the world is over and no one can replace that love."

"Is this the way it was with Mario Scarpone?"

Francesca purses her lips tightly before taking a sip of her espresso. She then turns her back toward me and scans the pedestrians walking by the café.

"Where is Edgardo? That is strange he has been gone for so long."

Apparently, Francesca doesn't wish to talk about Mario Scarpone or her past experience with first love. Whatever. I'm tired of her games. Just when she begins opening up to me and revealing more about herself, she then pulls back. This has happened repeatedly, first with the *Profile* interview and now in Rome with the questions I've asked her in order to write her autobiography. I'm here on her dime. If she wants to waste her money, that's fine by me.

Out of nowhere Edgardo suddenly looms over us with his towering frame. I'm relieved to see he isn't wearing a suit. Even in New York City, it was ludicrous that he was wearing one since the summers get just as hot and humid there as they do in Rome. In olive-green khakis and a tan button-down shirt that he doesn't wear tucked, he strikes a handsome and menacing presence. I can't help but wonder if he and Francesca ever had a fling. She certainly seems to appreciate a good-looking man.

"We need to get going," Edgardo says, but he does not look at Francesca. He dares not relax his guard for even a moment.

"Never free. This is the curse of being a legend, Pia. Be very grateful that you are not famous and have no desire to be." Francesca downs the last of her espresso, leans over, and kisses me on both cheeks.

"Am I hearing correctly that Francesca Donata regrets being a famous movie star?"

"I do not have any regrets. After all, being an actress was my destiny, but sometimes it can be a burden is all I am saying." Francesca turns to Edgardo, and just as he did moments ago, she talks to him, but looks off in the distance lest anyone notices. "Please give me a minute to talk to Pia in private."

"I'm timing you." Edgardo points to his expensive Rolex watch—no doubt a gift from Francesca. Then again, I'm sure she pays him a handsome salary and he could afford it on his own. He walks over to Antico Caffè Greco's entrance, resuming his scan of the crowd.

"Pia, I think you should take some time off from work."

"I'm fine, Francesca. Really."

"Do not lie to me. You most definitely are not fine. All you do is work. That is commendable, but even when I was busy acting in film upon film, I took my vacations. You will burn. Is that how the Americans call it?"

"Burn out."

"*Si.* You will burn out if you keep going this way. Just take a week off, even more if you need it."

"You must not want this autobiography to be written all that badly."

"There is time for that. I am not going anywhere."

"But I am, Francesca. I have a life back in the U.S."

"*Va bene.* Then take only a week. Lorenzo can show you more around Rome. He is an expert on her treasures. You will have your own personal tour guide for free. I can see that he has grown very fond of you and appreciates your friendship, especially during this difficult time he is going through."

I'm tempted. My mind has not been focused. Surely a week won't hurt. Besides, if I feel refreshed after a few days, I can return to work. Maybe I'll still interview Francesca in the evenings after I take in Rome's sights by day. I could leave the actual writing to the following week.

"I'll compromise. I won't write for a week, and I'll relax by exploring the city during the day. But I would still like to continue our interviews in the evening. It's not labor-intensive taking notes of our discussions. That would make me feel better. I don't want to fall behind schedule. And Lorenzo doesn't have to accompany me. I'm sure he has better things to do than babysit me."

"He loves teaching, and showing Rome to someone who has never been here will be an absolute delight for him."

I see there's no point in arguing with Francesca. I'll just let Lorenzo know he doesn't have to be my guide every day.

"*Grazie,* Francesca."

"For what?"

"Your hospitality and for caring about me."

"*È niente.* It is nothing. I will see you back at my apartment." She waves and walks by Edgardo, who soon follows along with the other bodyguard.

I finish my espresso and join the teeming crowds on Via Condotti. I still have not been to the Trevi Fountain and decide to begin my week-long respite now. Pulling out my map, I locate Via del Corso and head over.

As I approach Rome's largest and most famous fountain, the hordes of tourists flipping their coins into the pool make it difficult for me to get a good view. But once I'm up close, I see the Trevi Fountain is more glorious than the first time I saw it as a child in the 1954 flick *Three Coins in the Fountain*. The sculptures that comprise the fountain are of Neptune and two Tritons, or mythological Greek gods of the sea. The site that the Trevi Fountain was built on was once an aqueduct built in 19 BC. I feel a rush of adrenaline course through me as I take in the masterpiece before me.

Suddenly, the landmark's enormous size makes me feel very small—and alone. I look around, but I appear to be the only person who isn't with someone.

*Stop feeling sorry for yourself, Pia. You're in one of the greatest cities in the world, and you're too busy moping around.*

My internal pep talk gives me some courage. Ever since I saw *Three Coins in the Fountain*, I've always dreamed about standing here someday and flipping my own coins into the magical waters. I feel a bit foolish doing it with no one to cheer me on. Then again, it's not like any of the tourists are staring at me. They're all too busy taking photos and enjoying themselves. With all the drama my life has had recently, it's only sensible to throw a few coins into the Trevi Fountain, to not only ensure I return to Rome someday, but also to give me some much needed good luck.

Searching the bottom of my large handbag, I finally find three euros and turn my back toward the fountain. I remember reading that the proper ritual is to toss the coins with your right hand over your left shoulder or left hand over your right shoulder. Since I'm right-handed, I opt for that hand. Instead of just one, I decide to toss all three coins, hoping to increase my luck.

I'm about to toss my coins when I realize I haven't thought of a wish. Naturally, I want to return to Rome. That's a given. I need to make a wish that's more concrete than just hoping my life takes a turn for the better. Searching my mind, I finally decide what I want most. My own fountain of tears threatens to spill any moment. Closing my eyes, I make my wish and toss my coins into the Trevi Fountain.

## ~❧ 26 ❧~

# Francesca

Last night, Giuliana visited me in my dreams. But it was not the old Giuliana. Instead, she was the young girl who braided my hair and sang to me . . . my confidante who always made me laugh as we ran along the beaches in Sicily, collecting pebbles and sea-shells but pretending they were fine gems . . . the beautiful woman who always saw to my needs first before her own . . . the older sister who told me about the secret ways of love between a man and a woman . . . the only best friend I ever had.

*"Francesca, svegliati."* Giuliana implored me to wake up in my dreams. I did, but she kept repeating, *"Svegliati. Svegliati."*

"I am awake, Giuli."

"No, you are not. You have not told the truth yet."

*"Per favore, piu tempo.* I need more time, Giuli."

"Three decades. You have had three decades."

"No, I have not had all those years. We made a pact. We were never going to tell."

"The truth, Francesca. You promised me to tell the truth."

Suddenly, the young Giuliana I remember from my youth is re-placed by the old Giuliana who stared at me intently on her deathbed as I made my oath to honor her last wish. I reach out to stroke her cheek, but Giuliana disappears. I wake up. My heart is racing, and my pillow is wet. Getting out of bed, I walk over to the window and open it wider. The stifling humid heat Rome is known for in August greets me. At least the usually noisy streets are a bit quieter.

Italians have already left for Ferragosto, a holiday that has been celebrated since ancient Roman times. It is also a holy day in the Catholic Church and is known as the Feast of the Assumption of the Blessed Virgin Mary. Most of the country takes off for their summer vacation in August, and though the Ferragosto holiday falls on the fifteenth of the month, many Italians begin their vacations the first week in August and do not return to work until the first week in September.

I turn on the lamp that sits on my night table. The small wooden clock that has been passed down in my family for three generations tells me it is only midnight. I went to bed at eleven. Giuliana's passing has fatigued me incredibly. Normally, I do not go to sleep until midnight or even one a.m. Sighing deeply, I slip my silk robe over my lace camisole and matching shorts. It is too hot to wear even a short nightgown. Though the apartment has air conditioning, I prefer not to use it, like most other Italians. I am convinced the air conditioning from Giuliana's home in Astoria gave me aches in my bones I have never had.

My apartment is on the top floor of a historic building in Rome. When I bought it, the neighboring apartment was also available so I purchased that one as well and knocked down the walls to connect the two residences. This allowed me to expand the kitchen to the size of one that would be found in a large house.

Cooking and baking have always calmed my nerves. While it is late, I decide to make one of my favorite desserts, Riso Nero di Pasqua or Black Easter Rice. It is a chocolate rice pudding dessert from Messina, Sicily, where Giuliana and I grew up. Traditionally, the dessert is made for Easter in honor of the Black Madonna of Tindari. A cathedral in honor of this Black Madonna sits at the foot of a dramatic cliff in the town of Tindari. Once a year, I hike up the mountain to atone for my sins, much to the chagrin of Edgardo and the rest of my bodyguards, who grudgingly must keep up with me on the arduous ascent. I love making this dessert throughout the year and not just for Easter.

As I wait for the Arborio rice to cook, I pour a shot of sambuca. I almost drop my glass when I hear the phone ring. Who is calling at this hour?

I walk over to an old rotary-dial phone that hangs on the wall in my kitchen next to my refrigerator. My maid, Maria, always answers the phone lest it is a fan or a *paparazzo,* but she is a heavy sleeper and no doubt does not hear the phone ringing. What is the harm if I answer my own phone? No one will recognize my voice. But naturally, just as I say, *"Pronto,"* I hear Edgardo's voice on another of my phones.

*"Pronto. Chi parla?"*

"Hello, Edgardo. It's Gregory Hewson."

"Gregory, is everything okay?" I ask him.

"Francesca, get off the phone," Edgardo roars at me.

"Stop being so paranoid, Edgardo! This is my house and phone!"

"I need to make sure it really is Gregory."

"Trust me, it's me. I'm sorry for calling so late. But I've been having a hard time reaching Pia on her cell. I think she might've canceled her international plan since my calls aren't going through. May I please speak to her, Francesca?"

"She is probably sleeping, Gregory. But I will check."

"Can you please wake her up if she is sleeping? I really need to talk to her."

"I will do my best. Hold on."

I place the phone down on the counter and make my way toward the guest room where Pia is staying. Knocking on Pia's door, I push it slightly ajar when I do not hear her voice, expecting her to be sound asleep. But she is standing by her window looking out.

"Pia? I knocked, but you must not have heard me."

"Is everything all right, Francesca? I heard the phone ring."

"It is Gregory. He insists on talking to you."

"Tell him I'm sleeping."

"He asked me to wake you up and said he had to talk to you."

"I don't want to talk to him."

"He said he has tried to call you a few times, and now he thinks you canceled your international plan with your cell phone carrier."

"I did. How am I supposed to move forward with my life and forget about him if I continue talking to him?" Pia shakes her head and turns her back to me as she resumes gazing out the window.

"You can do what you want, Pia, but maybe you should talk to him and make it clear that it is truly over or else he will keep calling."

Pia turns around. Her arms are crossed defensively across her chest. I wait. Finally, she says, "Okay. I'll talk to him. I'm sorry. I shouldn't be placing you in the middle like this."

"You can use the phone on your nightstand. I will hang up once I go back into the kitchen. I am making chocolate rice pudding. It should be ready by the time you are off the phone. Join me afterward."

"You're making dessert this late? Aren't you worried about ruining your famous figure?" Pia smiles.

"Life is meant for living and enjoying all of its pleasures." I return her smile and walk out, closing the door behind me.

More than half an hour passes before Pia joins me in the kitchen. I have just finished stirring the chocolate and milk into the ceramic dish that holds the cooked rice. After sprinkling the top generously with cinnamon, I scoop a few heaping spoons of the rice pudding into crystal dessert glasses.

"Aren't you supposed to chill the rice pudding before serving it?" Pia asks, but I see she cannot wait as she samples the dessert.

"I like it both warm and cold, and since it is rather late, I am not going to wait for it to cool before I eat it."

"Hmmm! So good! I've never had rice pudding while it's still warm, and I've never had chocolate rice pudding. I didn't even know it existed. Wow, Francesca! Who would have known that a silver-screen star like you is also a diva in the kitchen?"

Closing my eyes, I savor the deep, bitter taste of the chocolate in the rice pudding before swallowing it. After just a couple of teaspoons, I feel relaxed. We continue enjoying our dessert in silence. I wait for Pia to bring up her discussion with Gregory. Maybe she needs a little prodding.

"How is Gregory?"

"Fine. Busy, of course, finishing the paintings for his second show."

I see this is going to be more difficult than I anticipated. I have never been one for subtlety, and why should I begin now?

"He is not ready to let you go, is he?"

"It's not his decision. He betrayed me. So there's nothing he can say to convince me to take him back." Pia shrugs her shoulders before continuing. "Even if he hadn't betrayed me, I don't think our relationship would have worked out. He's changed ever since he was discovered." Pia's face looks pained.

"I know it is hard not to take it personally, Pia, but he is human. Becoming rich and famous changes you, whether you want it to or not."

"Of course you're talking from personal experience?" Pia asks.

"*Sì.* Please, do not take this the wrong way, Pia, but to be quite frank with you, I never thought you and Gregory were right for each other."

"Really?"

I can hear a slight annoyance in Pia's tone. I have offended her.

"You have to remember I am on the outside and can see things differently than the people involved in the relationship."

Pia nods her head. "So, why didn't you think we were a good match?"

"I have known Gregory since he was a boy. He has always had an impulsive nature. He becomes bored quite easily except for his art. He has never strayed from his passion for painting. I cannot see Gregory ever settling down with one woman. He just is not the type to commit to anyone."

"If that's true, why did he just tell me then that he hasn't given up on me?"

"He does not know himself. *That* I can tell you with the utmost certainty. I hate to say this, Pia, and I pray to God I am wrong, but you will probably never hear from him again."

"I don't know. He keeps calling me even though I've told him repeatedly not to."

"He is a man above all else. He has his pride. Gregory is not going to keep chasing you at the risk of looking pathetic each time you scorn him. Besides, I thought you said you will not forgive him and you need to move forward with your life. What I am telling you should not be troubling you."

"No, no. You are right. I just don't see him as the womanizer type who moves on to the next one so soon. I don't know. Then again, I never thought he would . . ."

"He would what?"

"Betray me. Look, Francesca, I appreciate your advice, but I'd like to stop talking about this now if you don't mind."

"*Va bene.*"

"So I know what's been keeping me up. Why can't you sleep?"

"Ah. I had a dream about Giuliana."

"It will take time, Francesca. I lost Erica three years ago, and the pain still feels fresh."

"*Si.* But there is something else weighing on my mind." And with no warning, I break down crying.

"Francesca, what's wrong?"

"I cannot talk about it."

"Francesca, I like to think that we now have more than just a professional relationship. You have given me advice. Please, let me help you now."

"It is too terrible."

"I swear I will not tell anyone."

I stop crying and decide I need something stronger than sambuca. Walking over to the bar that sits below my kitchen counter, I take out a bottle of grappa.

"Would you like some?"

"No, thank you. My aunt made me try some, and I hated it."

"I suppose it is an acquired taste."

After drinking the grappa in one gulp, I pace the kitchen.

"Maybe if I tell you, it will be easier later. But you must not breathe a word of this to anyone, and it goes without saying that it cannot appear either in the article for *Profile* or in my autobiography. My reputation would be ruined forever."

"I swear again I will tell no one."

"Not even Gregory or your aunt."

"I did say no one."

I stare directly into Pia's eyes before I say, "If you do break my trust, you will pay dearly for it. Is that understood?"

Pia nods her head and looks down. She is still just a child, trying to figure out who she is and what she wants in the world. But that is the exact reason why I must put the fear of God into her. After all, we make some of our most foolish—and gravest—mistakes when we are young.

"I am going to make espresso. This is a very long story although I am certain it will keep you awake."

I pull out my stovetop moka espresso maker, which is also known as a moka pot. My hands shake as I measure the espresso grinds. Pia comes over and takes the espresso from me.

"Let me do it."

"Do not fill the espresso too high."

"I know. I've been making espresso since I was a little girl. That's all my mother drinks."

I nod my head and sit down once I am assured she is making it properly.

"Would you like more rice pudding?"

"No, thank you."

"So I will start my story while we wait for the espresso to be ready. *Va bene?*"

"Whenever you're ready."

"We were talking about first love when I saw you earlier today at the Antico Caffè Greco."

Pia nods her head, waiting patiently for me to continue.

I swallow hard before continuing and keep my eyes averted from Pia's.

"I have not been completely forthcoming with you."

"I suspected as much, Francesca."

I look up at Pia surprised, but I have known from the first day I met her that she is a very smart young woman.

"You asked me why I kept breaking off my engagements, and while the reasons I gave you were also true, they were not the primary motive for me."

"I figured that as well." Pia stares at the intricate crochet weave of my tablecloth as she traces the shapes with her index finger.

"Do not act like you have had the answers all along, *Miss* Santore." I glower at Pia. She meets my gaze, but this time she does not look away.

"I never assumed I had all the answers, *Signorina* Donata."

The espresso pot's whistle breaks the tension between us. I begin to get up, but Pia beats me to it.

"I've got it."

She takes two demitasse cups out of the cupboard and pours the espresso. As soon as she hands my cup to me, I take a long sip before continuing.

"The main reason I did not marry any of the men I was engaged to is that I still had feelings for my first love."

"Mario Scarpone? Wait. I'm confused. Then why didn't you marry him unless . . ." Pia's voice trails off as recognition dawns on her. "Unless Mario was not your first love."

"Correct. Mario was not my first love. My first love's name was Dante."

"That's a beautiful name."

"Yes, and the name suited him. He was a beautiful person." My eyes almost betray me as I remember the young Dante.

"Giuliana was seventeen and I was fourteen when we first met Dante, who was just a year older than my sister. Dante was the son of the local pharmacist, and he came to our house to deliver antibiotics that my mother needed after suffering a respiratory infection. From that day forward, Giuliana and I would walk by the pharmacy every day to get a glimpse of Dante.

"I had not begun developing yet. I was a late bloomer, if you can believe that." Pia's eyes drop to my figure, and I can see disbelief in her expression.

"Pia, do you remember the photo of Giuliana that I showed you, when she was young?"

"Of course I remember. She was stunning," Pia says in a hushed whisper.

"So it was no surprise that Dante would take a liking to Giuliana. Besides, she was closer in age to him than I was. He probably thought I was younger than my fourteen years since puberty had not paid my body a visit. My chest was as flat as the washboard we used to do our laundry. When Dante came to visit, the three of us would take walks together. But soon, Giuliana asked me to walk ahead of them so they could have a few minutes alone to talk. This angered me for I wanted to spend time with Dante. Though I knew he saw me as nothing more than a child, I did not care and still pined away for him. I honored Giuliana's wish and walked a few feet in front of them, but I also made sure to interrupt them every two minutes or so. Soon, Giuliana stopped taking me with her when she went to visit Dante at the pharmacy. She made certain to leave a good half hour before the usual time we went, knowing that I was still in school and would not be able to follow her. I was so angry and jealous. But now looking back, I see I was not just envious of Giuliana having Dante all to herself, but I was also jealous that this boy had replaced me as my sister's primary companion and confidante. I was hurt that she no longer asked me to join her when she went to the pharmacy. For once in her life, Giuliana was placing herself first before me, and I did not like it one bit. But in her defense, I do not think she realized how wounded I felt. She was falling in love with Dante, and as I am sure you are well aware, we are blind when Venus casts her spell."

"Wow. We actually have a lot in common. I felt the same way about my sister when she started dating someone seriously, not too long before she died. I felt like she'd forgotten about me, and her boyfriend was now the person she looked up to when it used to be me," Pia says softly.

"So you understand only too well, then."

Pia nods her head. "I'm sorry. Please go on."

"Not long after Giuliana stopped taking me with her to the pharmacy, Dante came to our house one Sunday for dinner. I will never forget that day. He looked the most handsome that I had ever seen him. And he was a true gentleman. He brought for Giuliana a bouquet of white and violet daisies tied with an ivory ribbon. From that moment on, Giuliana fell in love with daisies, and Dante showered her with them. He brought for my mother pastries from the best bakery in town, and for my father, he brought a box of fine cigars. He even gave me a gift of a giant swirl lollipop. But instead of being happy that he had included me in his thoughtfulness, I was enraged. For only children received lollipops. I almost cried in front of him when he handed me the gift. I thanked him and went to my room where I threw the lollipop at the wall, shattering it into little pieces."

"I can just picture a smaller version of you throwing a tantrum." Pia laughs. I join her and hold my side from laughing so hard.

"My temper has always gotten the better of me, even as a child. Anyway, Dante had come to dinner to ask my father's permission to court Giuliana. My father granted it, and they were together every weekend and a few nights during the week when my mother chaperoned them for an evening *passeggiata* or stroll as you Americans call it. Giuliana was so happy. She would tell me about their dates and how Dante would take her to see the newest cinema or buy her a gelato at the bar in town. I would go to bed and cry myself quietly to sleep since Giuliana and I shared a bedroom. I prayed to God every night and asked him to hurry up and make me grow so that I would capture Dante's eyes. My prayers were answered three years later when I was discovered by a movie scout while I was at the beach."

"Did it also take three years for your curves to show up?" Pia asks me.

"I began menstruating six months after Giuliana and Dante started dating seriously, and my breasts started growing. It was not until shortly after I turned fifteen that my body took a much more dramatic appearance. But Dante still did not notice me.

"Once my village heard that I was going to be in a movie, everyone started paying attention to me, including Dante. Now every time he came to see Giuliana, he also brought a bouquet for me. Only mine contained jasmines instead of daisies. To show Dante how much I appreciated his flowers, I began wearing jasmine perfume, which only encouraged him to bring me more bouquets."

"Giuliana must have been jealous," Pia says.

"Not at first. Sweet soul that she had always been, she acted very well about it, thanking Dante for being so kind and considerate toward her younger sister. But soon, there was no denying that Dante was losing his interest in poor Giuli." I stop as tears fall down my face.

"Instead of taking Giuliana out for their *passeggiatas*, Dante just wanted to stay in our home and talk to me about the making of my first movie. On a few occasions, Giuliana became quite persistent that they go for a walk. But what did Dante do? He invited me to join them every time. And I always accepted. I could see how our actions were killing Giuliana on the inside, but Dante and I still openly flirted with each other. All of Giuliana's efforts to lure her boyfriend back failed miserably. One night, I overheard Giuliana crying to my mother. I was shocked, for she was telling our mother that Dante was taken with me. Giuliana became hysterical and said it was not right. She was the older sister, and as such, it was her turn to fall in love and get married first. I was still young and would have plenty of suitors once my movie came out and made me famous. Giuliana never had any doubts that I would make it as a movie star. She was the only one who truly believed in me, probably because she knew when I set my sights on something I wanted terribly, I almost always got it. Our mother consoled her and told her Dante, like everyone else in our village, was just fascinated with me because I had been discovered. She assured Giuliana that there was nothing going on between Dante and me, and that he would be her husband if that was what she wanted.

"But a month later, Dante ended his relationship with Giuliana. He told her the truth: that he had feelings for me and while he did not mean to hurt Giuliana, he could not ignore the powerful emotions he had developed. I was hiding behind a tree in the park where Dante had decided to break my sister's heart. He had told me how and where he would do it. I could not resist witnessing, which was insane, but I suppose I needed to hear for myself that Dante would really end it with Giuliana. I have never given my trust easily, and I would not believe he would truly leave her unless I heard it for myself. Giuliana laughed after Dante proclaimed his desire for me. I will never forget that laugh. It was ugly and did not sound at all like the gentle sister I had grown up with.

"She told Dante, 'You are a stupid fool. Francesca already has an army of suitors. Listen to me, Dante, and listen well. Francesca will leave you once she gets bored. She is going to be a famous movie star. She will have no use for a simple man like you—the son of a local pharmacist. Francesca will never love you. The only person Francesca loves is herself.'

"I ran out from my hiding place behind the tree and told Giuliana that was not true. I told her I had been in love with Dante since I first met him. I cried and said I never meant to hurt her and hoped she could forgive me one day. Giuliana slapped my face so hard that I lost my balance and almost fell, but Dante steadied me. Giuliana then said, 'You are not my sister,' and ran away. She avoided me as much as possible after that, which was easy to do since I was traveling back and forth to Rome to shoot my first movie, *La Sposa Pazza*.

"A year later, *La Sposa Pazza* was released. Of course you know how successful the movie was and how it instantly made me rich and famous. I bought my family a lavish home in Taormina, which became my primary residence ten years ago when I dropped out of the spotlight. My agent insisted that I needed to leave my parents' home and move to Rome immediately so that I would be closer to the Cinecittà movie studios. He had managed to sign me up for two more movies after *La Sposa Pazza*'s success. It was no longer feasible for me to live in Sicily and travel back and forth to Rome so much. Besides, I could not take Giuliana's icy treatment of me any longer. My parents did not like the idea of a young woman living alone in Rome, but what could they do? I was supplying them with a steady source of income, and they no longer had to worry about their finances. So I bought a villa in Rome that happened to be across the street from Mussolini's old residence, Villa Torlonia."

"Signora Tesca and Lorenzo's home was actually your home?" Pia asks me.

"Yes. I will get to that later in my story. I continued to see Dante. He would come up to Rome whenever he could get away from the pharmacy, which was not often. I do not think his father approved of his seeing a movie star who was also quickly becoming the country's sex symbol. I loved showing him Rome. He made me very happy, but I loved the attention I was receiving from the public more. Many suitors were knocking on my door. Mario Scarpone, who was my leading man in my first film, *La Sposa Pazza,* was courting me fervently. The paparazzi had snapped several photos of us together at various social affairs. The rumors were soon flying that we were involved."

"Were you yet?" Pia looked directly into my eyes.

"At first, I kept Mario at a distance. I told him I loved Dante. But Mario broke me down eventually. I missed Dante terribly and only seeing him a few times a month, if even that, was taking its toll on me. I did not have intimate relations with Mario until after

Dante and I were finished, but we did share a few kisses. I am not proud of that, and to this day I regret my foolish behavior."

"Dante found out about Mario," Pia says.

"Of course. He had seen what the gossip mags were saying about us, and he asked me if we were involved. When he asked me, I was not involved yet with Mario. I know that does not excuse me from withholding the truth about my having kissed Mario. But I just could not bear to hurt Dante. And naturally, I still had feelings for him. I was not ready to let him go even though I knew I should. My refusal to be honest with Dante backfired, and instead he had to find out about Mario and me by walking in on us in a heated embrace." I dab at the corners of my eyes again. Remembering all of this is too painful. I sigh and continue.

"Dante yelled at me and called me every horrible insult. I had never heard him swear before. I begged him not to leave me and to let me explain. I tried to tell him what I had with Mario was nothing. Instead of looking upset, Mario seemed amused. He lit a cigarette and smirked as he watched Dante and me. I should have remembered that when that godforsaken *cretino* proposed and I accepted. Well, at least I did not marry him. Anyway, Dante told me that Giuliana had been right about me all along. He asked that I never contact him again.

"A few weeks later, Dante went to Giuliana and begged her forgiveness. Giuliana had never stopped loving Dante even though he betrayed her. I always thought it was interesting how she could forgive Dante when for all those years she could not bring herself to forgive me. But then again, there is much more to the story, as you will soon learn.

"Six months after Giuliana and Dante began dating again, they got married. My mother called to tell me. I was happy for Giuliana since Dante was rightfully hers to begin with, but I was also devastated. I cried so hard. A part of me truly thought I would marry Dante someday when I was ready. But who was I fooling? My love of acting and fame was stronger than my love for Dante and my desire to get married. Besides, now that I look back I can admit I was ashamed of Dante and where he came from. He was a village boy who worked in his father's small pharmacy. In Messina, he was someone, but in Rome, he stood out. I cringed when I read in the papers Dante described as my 'girlhood crush' and the 'simple boy with the sex symbol girlfriend.' The reporters were mocking him, and I knew everyone was wondering what an emerging movie star wanted with a village boy.

"My betrayal of Giuliana had created a rift between my parents and me. They still spoke to me, but I could hear the disappointment in their voices whenever we talked and the few times we saw each other after I moved to Rome. I kept my distance as much as possible, for seeing my parents only reminded me of Giuliana and how I had hurt her.

"Although I was not invited to their wedding, I still sent a lavish gift to my sister and Dante. But it is for the best that I was not invited. For if I had been, I would have had to make an excuse as to why I could not attend."

"You couldn't bear to watch your first love marry someone else," Pia says with much sadness in her voice. I am surprised she is not disgusted by my actions and actually seems to have pity for me. But there is time. She has not heard the entire ugly story yet.

"True. But that is not the reason why I would not have attended." I get up and take the bottle of sambuca that I left on the kitchen counter earlier. I pour myself a shot and gulp it down before resuming.

"Francesca, you don't need to tell me all of this. I can see how painful bringing up these memories is for you."

"I am all right. The reason I could not attend their wedding is that I was six months pregnant with Dante's child. Only my agent knew. When I could not hide the pregnancy any longer, I went to hide out at a convent in the Italian Alps. My agent told the press I was taking a much needed vacation. If the media had found out the truth, it would have caused a scandal in those days and my career would have been over. I gave birth to the baby at the convent. Then, I paid the nuns generously to raise the baby, and I made sure to send them payments every month. Leaving my baby was the hardest thing I have ever had to do."

"I'm so sorry, Francesca. I can't even begin to imagine the loss you felt."

I nod my head and continue.

"When I returned to Rome, I resumed where I had left off with Mario Scarpone."

"Didn't he wonder why you suddenly took a vacation? Didn't he try to say he'd come with you?"

"I am sure Mario was happy I would be away so he could enjoy his other girlfriends without risking my finding out."

"You didn't care that he was seeing other women while he was with you?"

"Not in the sense that he was cheating on me and I felt betrayed. You have to remember, Pia, I was never in love with him. Dante still had my heart. I cared more about not being made to look like a fool, and Mario was doing exactly that. When the reporters got wind of Mario's other women, they dragged my name into it and made it sound like we were all having an orgy. I almost killed him with my bare hands when that story broke. Mario swore he was through with the other women and only wanted me. I did not believe him. But then he spent every waking hour either calling me or showing up at my home. I was so depressed over losing Dante and my baby that I tried to convince myself I could have feelings for Mario and have a normal marriage with him. So when he proposed to me after I returned to Rome, I accepted. I broke off the engagement when I finally came to my senses and realized I could not bear to marry a man I was not in love with.

"A month later, I was in Taormina, Sicily, where my latest film was being shot. Giuliana and Dante had been married now for nine months. Giuliana got pregnant immediately after the wedding, and they had a baby girl named Ana. Apparently, they heard I was in town, and Dante suggested to Giuliana that they invite me to their house so that I could meet my new niece. Dante felt that he was to blame for my estrangement from Giuliana. He wanted us to make peace and put the past behind us. I do not think Giuliana was ready to forgive me, but I think she felt that if she could ease Dante's burden of guilt then she would do it. Giuliana would have done anything for Dante.

"I was shocked to receive the invitation, but I was happy that my sister was ready to have me back in her life. And I wanted to meet my niece. I was not sure how I would feel once I saw Dante living a happily married life with a woman other than me. And naturally, I knew seeing their baby would be especially painful for me since I had given up my own child with Dante. But I wanted Giuliana and Dante's forgiveness so badly that I knew I had to go. To this day, I regret having visited them.

"Giuliana was upstairs giving Ana a bath when I arrived. Dante let me in. I asked him if we could step out into the courtyard for a few minutes because I wanted to talk to him in private. Dante looked nervous, but agreed to my request. I began by telling him I was sorry for hurting him and Giuliana. Then I told him about my baby. Dante asked me who the father was. When I told him that he was the father, he did not believe me. He asked me how I could be so sure since I had also been seeing Mario Scarpone. I told him I had not slept with Mario Scarpone while I was still with Dante. He did not believe me. I pulled out of my purse a recent photo that the nuns had sent me of my baby and showed it to Dante. When he saw the photo, he let out an anguished cry, and a moment later, he grabbed his head. He fell to his knees as he let out another ear-piercing scream.

"I asked him what was the matter, but he just kept screaming in agony. Then he collapsed and blacked out. I was holding Dante's face and begging him to wake up. Giuliana came running toward Dante and pushed me away from him, yelling at me, 'What have you done to him?'

"I cried and told her I had not done anything. She screamed at me to call the ambulance. I ran inside and did so. When I returned, Giuliana was still hugging Dante's body to her, stroking his hair and kissing his forehead. She then asked me again what I had said to him, and she admitted that she had been on her way to the courtyard, where she could hear our heated whispers. Obviously, something I said must have brought on Dante's attack. I was saved by the arrival of the paramedics. They strapped Dante to a gurney and rolled him into the ambulance. He still had not gained consciousness. Giuliana wanted to ride in the ambulance with him, but realized Ana would be alone. I immediately told her I would watch Ana. I could tell Giuliana was reluctant to leave me alone with her baby, but with no other alternative, she agreed.

"After the ambulance left, I called my parents to tell them what had happened. They rushed to the hospital to be with Giuliana. My mother called an hour later to tell me that Dante had suffered from a brain aneurysm and had died. They would be escorting Giuliana home from the hospital.

"I hung up the phone and cried hysterically, feeling it was all my fault since I had told Dante about our baby and had insisted he believe he was the father. When Dante saw the photo of our baby, it was such a shock to him. My baby looked just like Dante. I had seen photos of him as a child, and there was no questioning the resemblance."

"So Dante knew in that moment without a doubt that he was the father."

"Yes, Pia. I am sure he was also thinking of what this would do to Giuliana when she learned. He knew it would have been too much for her to bear just as it had proven too much for him. The doctors told my family that the aneurysm had been present for years and would have eventually burst, and that exceptional stress could have caused it to rupture at any time. So you see why I felt guilty." I pause, needing a moment before I go on with my story.

"Francesca, I can understand your guilt, but the aneurysm would have burst eventually even if you had never told Dante about his son. You can't blame yourself for his death."

"As I get older, I have resigned myself to this fact, but it does not hurt any less that he died after hearing my revelation. And when I was alone with Ana while I waited for my parents to bring Giuliana home from the hospital, I felt guilty that now this baby would grow up without her father. And once again, I had taken away the love of my sister's life.

"When Giuliana and my parents finally arrived back at her home, my sister looked as if all the blood had drained from her face. She did not even seem to see me. I kept my distance from Giuli until the funeral. And even at the funeral, I did not stay by my sister's side. As soon as the funeral was over, I left.

"A year later, my mother called to tell me that Ana had caught pneumonia and died. So now Giuliana had not only lost her husband but her daughter as well. I was utterly devastated.

"I decided to visit Giuliana nine months after Ana had died. Giuliana was not only shocked to see me but the toddler boy who was by my side. I asked her if we could come in for a few minutes. Giuliana let us in. Once we were seated, she asked me who the boy was. I introduced him as Lorenzo."

"Oh my God," Pia whispers, placing her hand over her mouth. Tears roll down my face. I hold my forehead in my hands, feeling as if I am going to completely lose all control.

"Lorenzo is your son, not Giuliana's?"

I nod my head, unable to look into Pia's face.

"Lorenzo doesn't know, does he?"

I shake my head no.

"After I introduced Lorenzo to Giuliana, he looked up and into her eyes for the first time since they had met. He was tired from the long trip and had been rubbing his eyes and glancing down at the floor, so Giuliana had not gotten a good look at him. But once their eyes met, she dropped the glass of water she was holding and gasped. She knew immediately, just as Dante had, that Lorenzo was his son. Lorenzo has Dante's eyes as well as the same mole on the right side of his chin. Giuliana asked me, 'Is he?' and I told her he was indeed Dante's son.

"I placed Lorenzo down on the couch so he could take a nap. I then took Giuliana by the arm and led her into the kitchen so we could talk privately. Giuliana was dazed with shock. Once we sat down at the table, clarity began to set into my sister's mind. She asked me if I had told Dante the day he died about Lorenzo. I told her I had and how he had not believed me until I showed him Lorenzo's photo. I told her that I later realized it was foolish for me to have told Dante the way I did. I also admitted to her that my motives had been selfish. I had hoped that once Dante knew about Lorenzo he would return to me. I told her I had not been thinking right, but my last sentence seemed to fall on deaf ears. Giuliana became very upset and asked me how I could have expected Dante to leave her and baby Ana. Giuliana asked me, 'How could you have been so heartless, Francesca?'

"I told her I knew that I had sinned greatly and did not expect her to ever forgive me, but I wanted her to finally know the truth behind Dante's death. I then told her that I wanted her to raise Lorenzo instead of the nuns. Giuliana could not believe what I was saying. She asked me if I were insane. I told her I was absolutely serious. She then asked me why I had given Lorenzo to the nuns only to now give him up once again. I told her that having a baby when Lorenzo arrived would have destroyed my movie career. I was not ready to give up being an actress. I also reminded her of the scandal that would have ensued since I was a single mother.

"Giuliana asked me to quit my career so that I could raise my own son. I smiled sadly and told her, 'Acting is my greatest love.' Can you believe I actually told her that?"

Pia is crying silently. She reaches over and places her hand over mine. I sigh deeply and continue with my story.

"I pleaded with Giuliana to take Lorenzo so that he could be raised by family rather than strangers. I told her I would not have been a good mother anyway. Giuliana expressed that she did not think that was true. Even after all that I did to her she was still able to see some hope for me. But I remained firm in my conviction that I wanted my sister to be Lorenzo's mother. Giuliana got up and walked over to Lorenzo, who was now sound asleep on her couch. She said aloud, 'Even with his eyes shut, he is the spitting image of Dante.'

"I am sure she was also thinking of the baby she had lost and how alone she was without a husband and daughter. In that moment, I could see that Giuliana already loved Lorenzo. She told me she would raise him. I told her that Lorenzo did not know that I was his mother, and I asked her never to tell him. It would be easier that way for everyone. Giuliana agreed. I also explained to her that I had told Lorenzo we were going to meet his mother. Since Lorenzo was so young and had only known the nuns as caretakers, he did not know really what a mother was. I knew he would adjust well, and I was grateful that he was so young since that would help ease the transition even more.

"After that day, I did not see Giuliana again until I went to Astoria. I sent her money every month for Lorenzo's care. Giuliana was kind enough to send me letters and give me updates on Lorenzo. She even included photos of Lorenzo as he grew up. But she would never ask me how I was or reveal anything about her own life to me. Though I knew she still had not forgiven me, she managed to show some compassion by telling me how Lorenzo was doing.

"Thirty-four years after I gave up my son to Giuliana, I received a letter from Lorenzo, asking me to fly to New York because of a 'delicate matter,' as he put it. He did not want to reveal the news of Giuliana's fatal illness in a letter, but wanted to do it in person. He did say I could call if I insisted on knowing why he wanted me to visit right away, but I knew something was very wrong with Giuliana. I could feel it. So I wasted no time and booked the next flight out of Sicily."

"I thought Lorenzo was away on a research trip?" Pia asks.

"Yes, he was, but he had a summer break so he planned on flying to Astoria so that he could meet with me. But when I landed in New York, Carlo, Giuliana's butler, was waiting for me instead. Carlo told me Lorenzo had not been able to leave Rome after all because his best friend's mother had died suddenly. So he asked Carlo to give me the news before I arrived at the house. He did not want me to be shocked when I saw Giuliana's frail state.

"Of course when Carlo told me, I asked him to drive me immediately to Astoria. All I could think of was that I needed to be by her side and that I might have lost the opportunity to repair our relationship before she died. I also hoped that once Lorenzo returned, we could build our relationship even if it were just in aunt and nephew roles. So now you know why I came to Astoria and why Giuliana and I had been estranged all those years."

"I don't know what to say, Francesca. I'm stunned. And Lorenzo still does not know the truth? You did not tell him after Giuliana died?"

"No. This is what has been weighing on my mind so heavily. On her deathbed, Giuliana asked me to tell him the truth. I promised I would, but I have not done so yet. I am terrified. He will surely hate me and deservedly so. He will hate me for having given him up and for hurting his mother not once but twice. He might even blame me for his father's death. I have changed, Pia. I cannot tell you how many times I have regretted over the years giving my son up. That was my greatest mistake. I chose myself and my need to become a star over my own child. If I could do it all over again, I would choose him. But it is too late now. When I saw the photos of Lorenzo that Giuliana sent me, I ached terribly. How I wished so many times to have a relationship with him as mother and son. We did become closer as we took care of Giuliana in her final days. So, what do you think of me now, Pia?"

Pia sighs. "We all make mistakes, Francesca, and you were young. You can't keep punishing yourself. You need to move forward, and it sounds like Giuliana wanted you to do the same by finally revealing the truth to Lorenzo. Will you tell him?"

"Yes, I know I must even if there is a good risk he will hate me." I laugh. "First my sister despised me; now it will be my son. But it is the right thing to do and my sister's last request. How can I not honor a dying woman's wish?"

"When do you think you will break the news to Lorenzo?"

"He is supposed to come over in the morning. I will do it then. Pia, can you please just do one favor for me?"

"Of course."

"Please be there for my son in the coming days. He will need the support of a good friend, and I know he respects you very much."

"I will do my best, Francesca."

"Thank you, Pia. You are a fine young woman."

Pia gets up and hugs me.

"You're a good woman, too. Francesca, you've never let yourself believe that. It's time you also forgave yourself."

"Thank you. But all I care about is forgiveness from my son."

# 27

# Pia

Though I went to bed so late after Francesca narrated her stunning revelation, I made sure to wake up early and plan to leave before Lorenzo arrives. I don't think I could look at him without giving away that something was wrong. Lorenzo and I were supposed to start our sightseeing tour today, but I doubt he'll be in the mood to play my guide after he receives the shock of his life.

Hoping to slip out quietly, I'm about to open the door when Francesca calls out to me.

"Where are you going so early, Pia?"

"Francesca, you're up."

"I barely slept, as you can imagine."

I nod my head. "I was just heading over to the Campo de' Fiori. I heard it's best to get there early before the swarms of people arrive."

"*Sì. È vero.*" Francesca glances at the miniature grandfather clock that sits on top of the table in the foyer. It's almost eight o'clock.

"Lorenzo should be here by nine. I asked him to come earlier so we could have breakfast together." Francesca looks off to the side. Her eyes are bloodshot from lack of sleep and crying.

"Yes, you mentioned to me last night that he'd be here for breakfast."

"Ah! No wonder you are up so early. You want to avoid the storm." Francesca manages a slight smile.

"No. I just wanted to give you privacy. Besides, I have been dying to see the Campo early in the morning." This is true, but I can't help feeling Francesca doesn't believe me.

"Will you be returning after the Campo?"

"I was going to visit a few sights I had on my list. I'll probably be out most of the day."

Francesca reaches into the pocket of her robe and takes out a cell phone.

"Please take this. I know I am asking a lot of you, Pia, but if Lorenzo would like to talk to you after our discussion, I want you to be available for him. I am so worried about how he will take this. Is it all right if I tell him you are expecting his call? You were supposed to begin your sightseeing with him today, correct?"

I feel awkward. But how am I supposed to refuse a request like this? I was hoping to escape Lorenzo for today. Somehow I doubt he'll want to see anyone, let alone me, after the bombshell his mother is going to drop on him. But Francesca has a point. If he does remember our plans, he might wonder why I ditched him.

"That's fine." I take the cell phone from Francesca and put it in my purse.

"You are a dear friend. I do not know how I can repay you."

"There's no need. As you say, we are friends." I walk over to Francesca and give her a quick, light hug. When I pull away, her face is slightly flushed. I think this is the first time I've seen her embarrassed.

"*Ciao*. Enjoy the Campo." Francesca walks toward the kitchen.

Descending the steps of Francesca's apartment, I pretend this is my home in Rome. This is a little game I love to play whenever I visit another city or country. I imagine I am someone else. Today, I am a Roman citizen, and my morning ritual is to go to the Campo de' Fiori to buy my fresh produce for the day's meal. Of course, Italian cuisine requires only the freshest ingredients.

As I approach the Campo de' Fiori, most of the stalls are set up with only a few stragglers still filling their bins with fruits and vegetables. A few of the vendors are chatting and sipping espressos. The Campo de' Fiori or Field of Flowers was once a meadow and is one of Rome's biggest open-air markets. The Campo has existed since medieval times. Cardinals and noblemen along with foreigners and fishmongers visited the market. The sculpture of philosopher Giordano Bruno, who was burned at the stake for heresy in 1600, stands in the center of the Campo piazza where many executions were performed. The piazza was also surrounded by inns for pilgrims and travelers during the medieval era. Today, the Campo remains just as vibrant as it was centuries ago. In the evening, after the merchants have folded up their stalls, the Campo becomes a thriving nightlife spot in Rome. Popular restaurants and cafés dot the area. In addition, Renaissance palaces such as the Palazzo Farnese and Palazzo Spada lie nearby. Maybe I'll go to one of the palaces after I'm done at the Campo.

Seemingly out of nowhere, throngs of tourists and locals soon fill the open-air market. Instead of Campo de' Fiori, the market should be called Campo de' Gioielli or Field of Gems, since the gleaming multicolored array of locally grown produce resembles sparkling jewels. Glistening onyx-colored eggplants . . . bulbous pearls of scallions . . . shiny emerald-hued peppers . . . ruby-red raspberries . . . coral-toned cherries. . . . The market is a culinary treasure trove. All of my senses are engaged by the stunning collection of produce and the vendors calling out their specialties and the fresh scent of the produce along with the aromas coming from the cafés and restaurants that are preparing their midday entrees.

Since I don't plan on returning to Francesca's apartment until late in the day, I don't want to load myself with heavy produce. So I opt to buy just a few fruits that I can eat as I stroll through the Campo. Summer fruit has always been my weakness. I purchase a few nectarines, cherries, and blackberries. I'm overwhelmed by their intense succulence.

After I'm done eating my breakfast of fruit, I head over to one of the numerous stand-up bars, where I buy a quick cappuccino. The *cornetti* or croissants are calling to me so I splurge on one as well. I don't feel too guilty since all I've had to eat is fruit. As I soon discover, the Italian version of croissants is different from their French counterparts. *Cornetti* are more cake-like and less flaky than French croissants. They're also less buttery and slightly sweeter with an orange marmalade glaze on top.

Completely satisfied and full, I leave the Campo de' Fiori and head over to the Palazzo Spada. Though the Palazzo Farnese is the more famous and elaborate of the two palaces, I learned from my guidebook that in order to reserve tickets, one has to e-mail or write a letter as much as four months in advance. So the Palazzo Spada will have to do. I'm interested in seeing their collection of Old Master paintings as well as its famed trompe l'oeil garden gallery.

After paying five euros for my admission ticket, I enter the Palazzo Spada. The Old Master paintings do not disappoint. My two favorites are Andrea del Sarto's *Visitation* and Titian's *Musician*. I take my time admiring the paintings. Inevitably, my mind drifts to Gregory. He could be done by now with his paintings for his second show. If only he were here with me. I want to share with him the feelings of awe that these paintings are inspiring in me. Suddenly, I regret canceling my international cell phone plan. Tears fill my eyes. What am I thinking? The guy cheated on me, and I'm still harboring fantasies of his joining me here in Rome. I feel stupid to admit that I've imagined him dropping everything in New York and surprising me here, begging me to take him back. Francesca's words from last night haunt me. "You will probably never hear from him again."

I should be glad if that's the case. Then why do I feel sad when I think that I'll never see or talk to Gregory again?

I'm shaken out of my reverie by Francesca's phone, which belts out a loud Beethoven melody. The guards in the palazzo give me annoyed glances. I quickly answer the phone, doing my best to keep my voice low.

"Pia?"

"Lorenzo." I don't mean for my voice to come out with such a tone full of dread, but I can't help it.

"Francesca told me she gave you her cell so that I could reach you. I'm sorry. I know we were supposed to meet a couple of hours ago."

"That's okay. Lorenzo, I'm fine on my own today. I'm actually at the Palazzo Spada right now. We can reschedule our plans for to-morrow—or even another day."

"It's okay, Pia. You don't have to pretend. Francesca told me that she confided in you about everything."

"Oh. I'm really sorry, Lorenzo. I don't know what else to say. I'm sure this must all be a huge shock."

"Yes, to put it mildly. But I'll be fine. I still would like to see you."

"Are you sure? I'd understand if you needed time to yourself to . . . to sort through everything. Really."

"To be quite honest, Pia, I could use the company—unless you already made plans on your own."

"No, no. That's fine. Why don't you meet me in front of the Palazzo Spada?"

"That's perfect since I have tickets for the Palazzo Farnese."

"You were able to get tickets? I thought you had to write and request them up to four months in advance?"

"Normally you do, but I'm good friends with the palace's chief curator."

"Wow! I'm impressed."

Lorenzo laughs. "I take it then you would love to go?"

"Absolutely. But only if you're up to it."

"I need the distraction, Pia. I have never been one to wallow in misery, though I suppose this set of circumstances warrants it."

Lorenzo's voice finally sounds somber. He's doing his best to mask his pain. My heart goes out to him. I can't even begin to fathom all that he must be feeling.

"I'm here if you want to talk about it, Lorenzo."

"Thank you, Pia. I appreciate that. Just do me a favor and let's not talk about it until we've had some wine or at least cocktails during happy hour."

He plans on being with me the whole day? I thought we were just going to visit a sight or two. But I remain mum.

"Your wish is my command."

"I'll meet you in front of Palazzo Spada shortly. I'm already walking over."

"See you soon, Lorenzo." I hang up the phone and make my way toward the palace's exit.

It's close to one p.m. and my stomach is growling. Trying to ignore my hunger pangs, I think about Lorenzo. I'm still amazed by his strength and that he wants to see me. If it were me, I'd be brooding home alone. After Erica died, I shunned all of my friends and just kept to myself. I regret now having pushed them away. A few really wanted to be there for me, but I was too absorbed in my grief to deal with anyone.

"Pia?"

I look up to see Lorenzo staring at me with concern written all over his face. It should be the other way around. His eyes appear more serious than usual, but other than that, he seems okay.

"Hi." I lean forward to kiss him on the cheek. He hugs me, much to my surprise, and doesn't let go. I return his hug. Obviously, he's not the rock of strength he was making himself out to be over the phone.

"Lorenzo, I am so very sorry."

"Thank you, Pia. I'm wavering between anger and hurt. I'm angry at my mother and Francesca for keeping such a secret from me all these years. I'm also hurt that my mother never felt like she could confide in me about this." Lorenzo shakes his head. "I'm the most mad that my mother had to die without my knowing the truth."

"How is Francesca?"

"She's a wreck. I blew up at her. I didn't mean to, but I was livid."

"Understandably so."

"On the walk over here, I already regretted yelling at her. She was young when she was pregnant with me, and I don't blame her for giving me away."

"So you're not hurt that your own biological mother chose to give you up not once but twice?"

Lorenzo shrugs his shoulders and glances at a few crumbs that someone has thrown to the pigeons flocking the street. "I'm disappointed that I wasn't enough for her. She chose her career over me after all. But I think I'm more disappointed in my mother—or rather my aunt. God, do I stop calling mother the woman I knew my whole life and start calling the woman who has essentially been a stranger in my life my mother instead?" Lorenzo places his forehead in his hands.

"Let's go get something to eat or even just a drink." I place my hand on Lorenzo's arm. He takes my hand and kisses it, much to my surprise.

"You're an angel, Pia Santore." Lorenzo smiles at me. I shyly return the smile, but glance away.

"Yes, let's get something to eat. I never had breakfast. Francesca could've at least waited until after I ate to spill the news." Lorenzo lets out a boisterous laugh, causing several pedestrians to look our way. He's being snide of course.

"You know, Lorenzo, it's not too late. We can forget about the Palazzo Farnese. Maybe you should go home and get some rest."

"If I didn't know any better, Pia, I'd think you're trying to blow me off." Lorenzo winks at me.

"That's not it at all! I'm just amazed that you even are trying to go about as if nothing out of the ordinary has happened today. I wouldn't have handled it this way."

"As I said earlier, I'd rather try and keep myself occupied. If I don't, I might just kill *La Sposa Pazza*. Ahhh! The absurdity! Who would've ever thought my mother is none other than the famous Crazy Bride. She's crazy, all right. I'll give her that."

I feel sorry for Francesca. Although I can understand Lorenzo's anger toward Francesca, she is still his mother. She was young and in love. Unfortunately, when you combine youth and passion, good sense is often thrown out the window. No wonder Francesca called off all her engagements. She'd been pining away for Dante. How sad that she couldn't find love with someone else. And now her son, the only family she has left, probably wants nothing to do with her ever. I want to ask Lorenzo if he sees himself having a relationship with Francesca down the road, after he's come to terms with everything. But I know now is not the right time. He's experiencing too many emotions that need to be sorted out.

"Let's eat at Ar Galletto. It's quite popular and close by."

"Okay. I am starving so the thought of walking around forever to find a restaurant wouldn't have sat well with my stomach."

Ar Galletto is just a few feet away from the Palazzo Farnese. Since most of the patrons have already arrived for *la seconda colazione* or midday meal, there isn't a line and we're seated immediately. Fortunately, one last table is available outside. I can see why this restaurant is so popular. Dining al fresco affords diners with an amazing view of the Palazzo Farnese. The beautiful fountains and the majestic architecture of the Palazzo Farnese create a gorgeous backdrop.

I decide to order a typical Roman dish—Carciofi alla Giudia or twice-fried artichokes. The artichokes are stuffed with sprigs of mint and garlic and are then braised. Deep frying them twice creates a very tender artichoke heart. And I've never seen in America artichokes as large as the ones in Rome.

Lorenzo opts for the Penne Arrabbiata, which features a spicy tomato sauce. We order a bottle of Cabernet Sauvignon. We're both famished and eat most of our meal in silence. After we're done, Lorenzo orders two shots of sambuca. I order one as well. Lorenzo raises his glass and says, "To living happy in La Città Eterna."

I clink his glass, but I think it's a rather odd toast to make given the news he received today. Then again, I'm sure he's being sarcastic. As I sip my sambuca, I can't help noticing most of the women in the restaurant are glancing in Lorenzo's direction. There never has been any doubt that he is attractive, but now that I see the effect he's having on all of these women in the restaurant, I take closer notice. Today, he's wearing jeans that hang slightly lower than his waist. His burnt-orange fitted T-shirt shows off his well-defined biceps and enhances his deeply tanned skin. He leans back in his chair, taking in the view of the Palazzo Farnese. I'm sure his mind must be on Francesca and Signora Tesca. His lips are slightly apart and have a rose blush to them. I can't believe I didn't see it before, but he *is* Francesca's son. He's every bit as gorgeous as she is. He must sense that I'm staring at him, for his eyes meet mine. And for the first time since I've met him, they're an intense emerald green, just like Francesca's. I can't stop looking at him. His lips curl slightly upward, and he reaches over the table and holds my hand. I don't pull back, but I finally take my gaze away from his. My heart is racing, and suddenly I remember the kiss we shared the night of Gregory's show.

Lorenzo downs his second shot of sambuca and says, "Ready for the Palazzo Farnese?"

I nod my head, but don't dare meet his eyes this time. He continues holding my hand as he takes out his wallet with the other hand, flips the wallet open, and manages to pull out a few euro notes, tossing them on the table. He stands up, finally releasing my hand, but comes over and helps me out of my chair.

As we walk the few steps over to the Palazzo Farnese, I cross my arms across my chest. Though I can't deny I like the way my hand felt in Lorenzo's, I'm confused. Yes, I'll admit now there has been a strong current of attraction since the first day I ran into him at the Mussolini Mansion, but I don't think I have the energy to get involved with someone so soon after my breakup with Gregory.

The Palazzo Farnese is breathtaking to say the least. To think I almost missed out on seeing its interiors.

"I've seen most of the palaces in Rome, and this one is definitely the most beautiful Renaissance palazzo in the city," Lorenzo says.

"I believe it." My eyes can't stop circling all around the stunning architecture.

Lorenzo gives me a brief history of the Palazzo Farnese, which is most known for the exquisite Baroque ceiling in its Galleria Carracci. The friezes and the main window over the piazza were designed by Michelangelo, as well as part of the courtyard and the lovely arch over Via Giulia at the back of the palace. After we take in the astounding Galleria Carracci, we head into the Salon of Hercules. I'm fascinated by its heady opulence.

"The Palazzo Farnese is now home to the French Embassy." Lorenzo gives me facts every now and then.

I take several photos with my cell phone camera.

"Can you please take a photo of us?" Lorenzo asks a young American woman. He takes my cell phone and hands it to her. She looks every bit as captivated by him as the women in the restaurant earlier. Lorenzo flashes a deep smile that makes her absolutely blush. He then runs over to me and places his arm around my shoulders. I do my best to look relaxed and smile, but every time he touches me, my pulse races.

"Are you okay, Pia? You look a bit pale."

"I'm just tired. I didn't get much sleep last night."

"I know what will make you feel better. Gelato!"

Lorenzo says "gelato" like a gushing school boy. I can't help but laugh.

"Have you had gelato at any of the *gelaterie* by the Pantheon? They're the best in Rome."

"No, I haven't been by the Pantheon yet, but it's one of my must-see sights."

"Perfect. After we take our gelato break, we can go into the Pantheon."

Lorenzo's mood seems lighter already. I'm glad he decided to keep his plans with me. I'm having a good time even if his intimate gestures have rattled me a bit.

We arrive near the Pantheon. Several *gelaterie* greet us.

"So we have Giolitti, which has been known for its gelato for years and for a time was considered the best in Rome. Della Palma, which is quite popular with tourists for it serves one hundred flavors."

"One hundred?"

"Yes."

"And I thought Baskin Robbins with thirty-one flavors offered a lot of choices."

"My personal favorite is Cremeria Monteforte, which has won several awards."

"Wait! There's a gelato contest?"

"Of course! Gelato comes second next to the church in sacredness in Italy."

I laugh. "I'm sure they're all stupendous. You can choose."

"No, this is your first time in Italy. I insist you choose."

"Hmmm. This is going to be tough. What about that place, Fiocco di Neve?" I point with my index finger. "Do you not recommend that *gelateria?*"

"The gelato is good there also, but they're more known for their coffee *granite*. We can go there for breakfast tomorrow if you like."

"Breakfast?" I can't conceal my surprise.

"I guess you forgot that we were supposed to spend this week, and possibly next, together exploring Rome." Lorenzo smiles.

"No, I didn't forget, but I do remember I had reserved just this week to take a break from writing your mother's autobiography. I never said I'd also take next week off." I suddenly realize I've called Francesca his mother. Placing my hand over my mouth, I say, "Sorry."

"No need to apologize. She is after all my mother. But I'm not quite ready to begin calling her that."

"Of course. I understand. I'm sorry."

Lorenzo waves his hand as if to say "don't worry about it."

"So it's decided, breakfast tomorrow morning at Fiocco di Neve. I think tomorrow we should go to the Vatican and Castel Sant'Angelo. We definitely want to get to the Vatican as soon as they open or else it'll be a mob scene worse than rush hour on the New York City subways."

"Sounds good." I decide to give up fighting Lorenzo. It's obvious he has no intention of changing our plans to see Rome together. I'm actually feeling less self-absorbed knowing that I'm helping to keep him occupied after his learning the truth about his parentage.

"So which *gelateria* do you want to go to?"

"Oh, right. Hmmm." I mull over the choices. I'm tempted to go to Della Palma just to see the one hundred flavors, but I don't want to appear like the typical tourist since it's popular with them. I decide to go with Lorenzo's favorite Cremeria Monteforte, especially since it's won several awards.

There's a line inside, but it's not too long.

"You chose well, Pia. If we had gone to Della Palma, we never would've gotten out of there."

"Why didn't you tell me that?"

"If you really wanted to go there, I wouldn't have denied your wish. Like I said, this is your first time in Italy. Whatever you want, you shall have."

"Wow! Okay. *Grazie molto!*"

"*Mio piacere.* My pleasure. Now, let me know if you need help translating the flavors or if you want a recommendation."

I look at the list of flavors. Except for *"cioccolato,"* *"vaniglia,"* and *"pistacchio,"* I can't figure out what the other flavors are.

"What's '*nocciola*'?" I ask Lorenzo.

"Hazelnut. That's my favorite."

"And *'fragola'*?"

"Strawberry."

I don't want to ask Lorenzo what every flavor is so I opt to go with his favorite *"nocciola."*

Lorenzo orders *"stracciatella"* or chocolate chip, as he tells me.

"I thought '*nocciola*' was your favorite?"

"It is, but I like to experiment."

I taste my *nocciola* gelato. "Yummy!"

"Heavenly, right?" Lorenzo laughs.

*"Si, molto!"*

"Wow! The power of gelato never ceases to amaze. You're speaking in Italian."

"I'm picking up a few words here and there."

"Your mother never spoke to you in Italian? She's from Italy, right?"

"Yes, but since my father didn't know much Italian, she felt she had to speak English most of the time. I do know a few words that I have heard her and my aunt say repeatedly, but that's about it. Being here is making me want to take lessons."

"You should. What better place to take Italian lessons than in Italy?!"

"Oh, I didn't mean while I'm here. I meant when I go back home to California."

"Why shouldn't you take a lesson here? It'll be fun. I have a good friend who offers private lessons. I'm sure she can fit you into her schedule."

"That's okay. I appreciate the thought, Lorenzo, but I have my hands full as it is between interviewing Francesca and working on her autobiography. I'll be heading back to New York in a few weeks. There's no sense in starting lessons here even if I had the time."

"Why don't you extend your stay then?"

"I can't. I also have to finish up the article I am writing for *Profile*. My editor gave me an extension when he heard that Francesca wanted me to join her in Italy and begin working on her autobiography. He knew I could get more information for the article and even talk about her home and life here in Rome."

Lorenzo lets out a long sigh. "Okay. I won't try right now, but know that I'll keep trying to change your mind every few days. Trust me, Rome will work her charm on you, and the more time you spend here, the harder it will be to leave." Lorenzo smiles mischievously.

My heart skips a beat for I've already begun falling for the Eternal City, and I can see how the more time I walk along her cobblestone streets, the harder it will be to stick to my guns.

We finish our gelato and walk over to the Pantheon, which is on the left side of Cremeria Monteforte. I stop to take a photo before we head inside.

"The Pantheon is considered to be one of the wonders of the ancient world, and it is the best preserved monument of ancient Rome. It used to be a pagan temple."

"It's beautiful. I can't wait to see what its interior looks like."

"Pia, I hope you don't find it presumptuous of me when I give you the historical facts of the landmarks we visit. It's just that I know Rome so well because I did some of my post graduate studies here."

"No, I don't mind. It saves me the money of having to hire a tour guide." I elbow Lorenzo playfully.

"I knew it. You're using me. I feel so wounded." Lorenzo feigns a pained expression and places his hands over his heart. I laugh.

"How long were you studying here?"

"Two semesters."

"You spent all that time in Rome and you never met Francesca? Didn't you find that odd? I mean, we know now why she kept her distance from you, but I would think you would've tried to see your aunt, who you knew lived here."

"Remember, Francesca was already living in Sicily at this point."

"That's right. I almost forgot. But still, she kept her apartment in Rome; I'm sure she must have traveled up here on occasion. And even if she didn't, Sicily is just an hour away from Rome by plane. She could have easily flown up to finally meet you in person."

"I did call to tell her I wanted to meet her in person. But she told me she had to respect her sister's wishes. Apparently, my mother had made it clear to her at some point that she wanted Francesca to keep her distance from me."

"And you didn't question that?"

"I just thought their hostility toward each other was so strong that my mother didn't want me to have anything to do with Francesca. I was disappointed, naturally. There was nothing I could do about it, so I just let it be." Lorenzo shrugs his shoulders. The somber look his eyes held earlier is back, and I regret bringing up the subject.

We enter the circular structure of the Pantheon. I don't want to ruin it for Lorenzo by telling him that I actually read up on this architectural marvel and already know some of its history. I can tell he enjoys giving me his little lectures. So I pretend not to know any of what Lorenzo tells me.

"The Pantheon was rebuilt by the Roman emperor Hadrian around AD 120, and it is on the site of an earlier pantheon that was erected by the emperor Augustus's general Agrippa. I'm sure you noticed the inscription on the outside of the temple at the top?"

"Yes, I do remember seeing the word 'Agrippa,' but of course I don't know what the inscription says since it's in Latin."

"It says that Agrippa was the builder of the Pantheon. When Hadrian rebuilt the temple, he decided to keep the original inscription. That threw historians off for centuries until around 1892 when a French architect was able to discern that all of the bricks used dated from Hadrian's era."

"That's so fascinating!" My awe is genuine here since I didn't know the fact about the confusion over the bricks.

I stare up at the ceiling, where there is an opening right in the center of the Pantheon's dome.

"That's the oculus. Isn't it amazing?" Lorenzo stares up with me, and for a few moments, neither of us says anything as we watch the blue sky and clouds that the view of the oculus affords us.

Once we get our fill, Lorenzo continues his lecture. "Would you believe the oculus was the temple's only source of light in ancient times?"

"Well, that explains why they decided to have an opening in the dome." I can't help what I'm about to do next; even though I know it's wrong, I go for it. "I wonder if the opening was intended for more than providing light. I could see the architect or even Hadrian himself having a symbolic reason for having this opening."

"Pia, you're absolutely brilliant! Yes, the oculus was also meant to represent God or Heaven's all-seeing eye." Lorenzo looks at me with new admiration.

Secretly, I feel a tad bit guilty that I played this little game. Of course, I knew of the oculus's symbolism from the reading I'd done. I just wanted to show Lorenzo that I'm smart. Then again, why should I care that he knows I have a brain?

We walk over to where the tomb of the famous Renaissance

painter Raphael lies. I take a photo, thinking Gregory will want to see this since Raphael was one of his favorites of the Old Masters. But as soon as the thought enters my mind, I remember we're no longer together. I close my eyes, trying to force out the pain that I'm feeling. Lorenzo is behind me so I hope he doesn't notice, but he does.

"Pia, are you not feeling well?"

I shake my head no, but I hold up my hand, trying to let him know it's nothing. I'm about to say so, but I can't. I open my eyes, and the tears come sliding down.

Lorenzo, ever the gentleman, produces a tissue from his jeans pocket.

"It's clean."

"Thank you," I manage to whisper. I wipe my eyes, but it's no use. I just keep crying silently. A few German tourists are standing near me, talking animatedly and pointing to Raphael's tomb as they begin snapping photos with their cameras. It isn't until they see I'm not getting out of their way that they notice I'm crying. Their fascination with the tomb is then replaced by their fascination with the American girl who's sobbing. I turn around and walk over to the tomb of two nineteenth-century Italian kings: Vittorio Emanuele II and Umberto I.

I feel hands on my shoulders—Lorenzo's. His touch is welcome right now. I shouldn't have lost it on him. He's the one who should be having a meltdown after learning the truth of his parentage.

"What do you say we get out of here and go for a walk? Huh?"

I nod my head and let Lorenzo lead me out of the Pantheon. We continue walking hand in hand once we're outside. The sun is getting lower in the sky. I glance at my watch and can't believe it's a little after six p.m. I was enjoying myself so much that I hadn't looked at the time once since we met.

Lorenzo somehow finds a quiet side street. Then again, he not only lived here as a student, but he's come to Rome many times, since he and Signora Tesca own a home here. He stops and pulls out a pack of cigarettes and matches from his shirt pocket. Placing a cigarette between his lips, Lorenzo lights it then offers one to me.

I shake my head and say, "I don't smoke."

"Neither do I, but when you've had a day like today, it merits a smoke. Oh, wait. I didn't mean the entire day. I just meant my morning after Francesca told me she's really my mommy. The rest of the day has been great. I can't begin to tell you how much you've kept my mind off things, Pia."

"I knew what you meant. Don't sweat it. I have to thank you as well for keeping my mind off Gregory." Even just saying his name hurts. I turn around and pace back and forth, waiting for Lorenzo to finish his cigarette.

"He's why you cried back there?"

"I'm sorry. I shouldn't have done that to you and in public of all places! Those German tourists were gawking at me like I was a freak." I manage a light laugh.

"Tourists," Lorenzo says with obvious disgust in his tone.

"Hey! I'm a tourist right now, too."

"Trust me. You're not like the majority of tourists."

"Why don't you like tourists?"

"It's nothing personal. It's just that when you live in a city as populated as Rome, they crowd the streets even more. And they move so slowly! I know they're taking in the sights and aren't rushing off to work like the residents, but it still drives me insane."

"Do you consider yourself more Italian than American since you were born here and didn't go to the U.S. until you were of school age?"

"You've been doing your homework on me, I see!"

"Signora Tesca mentioned it to me one of the times I was at the house, waiting for Francesca."

"Yes, she loves to keep everyone waiting, even her own son. When I blew up at her this morning, I was also mad because she didn't tell me the truth as soon as my mother died."

"She was griev—" Lorenzo stops me with his hand.

"Grieving, I know. Whatever. My mother's been dead now for a few weeks. She could've told me by now."

"Lorenzo, I'm not on anyone's side, and I know it's hard for you to do this right now, but try to place yourself in her shoes. You were both mourning the loss of your mother. And Francesca probably didn't want to add to that grief the explosive news that she is really your mother. She was terribly afraid, too. That's why she confided in me last night."

Lorenzo takes a long drag off his cigarette before flicking it into the street. He exhales long and slowly before meeting my eyes. "You're right. My head knows that, but my heart is still raging. But enough about me. We were talking about you and Gregory. What exactly happened between the two of you? If you don't want to talk about it, I understand."

"I guess I should talk about it. But I'm embarrassed."

"You have nothing to be ashamed of, especially with me."

"I'm almost certain he cheated on me."

"Almost?"

"I showed up at his place a few weeks ago. He didn't hear the bell, and the front door was open so I let myself in. When I got upstairs, he was in his studio, painting, and he wasn't wearing a shirt. That bitch art columnist at *Profile,* Madeline Drabinski, was hanging over him and whispering into his ear. They then giggled. That was all the proof I needed."

"I take it he swore he wasn't cheating?"

"How do you know that?"

"I'm a guy."

"Are you speaking from personal experience?"

"Look, Pia, you said 'almost certain,' and then the scene you just described doesn't have them actually doing the dirty deed. I'm merely guessing that maybe he didn't cheat on you. That's all." Lorenzo shrugs his shoulders and takes out another cigarette.

For some reason, I'm not loving his reaction to what I've told him. But I don't want to upset him any more than he's already been today, so I refrain from saying anything about this.

"You don't think he did?"

"It doesn't matter what I think. I wasn't the one dating him."

"Just humor me, Lorenzo, and tell me what you think."

"I don't know, Pia. Honestly. I have no idea, and I don't know Gregory. You could be right that they were sleeping together. He felt comfortable enough with her to paint half nude. Then again, some guys don't care about baring their chests to anyone, especially when it's hot. Then, there's whatever she whispered to him followed by their giggling, which could suggest some dirty joke shared between them."

"Gee, thanks, Lorenzo. I thought you were going to make me feel better."

"Pia, I'm not going to gloss over the truth just to make you feel better. If I did that right now, you would only feel better for the moment. You broke up with him. It's going to hurt. That I can speak of from personal experience. I guess what I've been trying to say is that it's hard to say whether Gregory cheated on you based on what you saw."

"What is your gut telling you? Everyone has a feeling one way or the other. And don't say that you don't know Gregory and you weren't there, blah, blah, blah. Just tell me what your first instinct was when I told you."

"My first thought was that the bastard was guilty."

"So why are you even playing devil's advocate and making me think that maybe he didn't cheat?"

"I don't know. Well, I do know. I guess it's because you didn't actually see them in the act. But yes, I'm sorry to say I have to agree with your assessment of the situation when you first came upon them."

I'm getting really annoyed with Lorenzo, and I don't know if I'm going to be able to hide it much longer.

"Lorenzo, can we please drop this and just go get a drink and some appetizers?"

"Of course. Look, I'm sorry if I upset you." Lorenzo places his arm around my shoulders as we walk.

"I'm fine. Let's just have a good time, okay? That's what we both need anyway, right?"

"I say we both get stupid drunk tonight."

I laugh, not expecting those words to come out of his mouth.

"When in Rome, what's that famous saying?" I ask.

" 'When in Rome, do as the Romans do.' I guess you're implying that Romans do nothing but get drunk?" Lorenzo raises his eyebrows.

"No! I forgot what the saying was. I thought for a moment it was, 'When in Rome, let your worries slide,' or something like that."

"Well, the ancient Romans are known for their Bacchanalian orgies in which they drank lots of wine in honor of Bacchus, the god of wine. Modern Romans do like to party, so maybe the proverb is right for this occasion after all."

"Most people in the world like to party now and again, even workaholics like me. So, shall we head off to the nearest bar, then?"

"I'll lead the way."

Lorenzo keeps his arm around my shoulders as he guides me to our next destination. I push our conversation from my thoughts. As usual, I'm overanalyzing. I need to forget about Gregory while I'm in Rome and clear my head. After all, I am supposed to be on vacation and relaxing. And who better to emulate than Italians? After all, they've made relaxing an art form.

# ❧ 28 ❧

# Francesca

The stillness inside the church of Santa Maria della Vittoria is a much-welcome balm after Rome's busy streets. Its sumptuously decorated, candlelit interior adds to the serene atmosphere. I always feel comforted when I come here. But today is different from my other visits. I am waiting to make my confession.

Though my apartment is in the Navona district, I always love to venture over to the Repubblica district to visit my favorite church in Rome. The area itself leaves much to be desired, especially near the modern Termini train station. But Santa Maria della Vittoria church is worth the trip. Edgardo came alone today. My other bodyguards have fallen ill with food poisoning. If you ask me, I think they drank too much last night and have hangovers. *Disgraziati,* I mentally curse them. Remembering I am in church, I quickly ask God for forgiveness.

Edgardo gives me my privacy and waits for me, seated in the last pew of the church. I am wearing my best mantilla made from artisan lace that I purchased on a trip to Venice's lagoon island of Burano not long after I had become famous. In Italy, many older women still choose to wear mantillas over their heads in church, even though it is no longer a requirement as it was when I was younger. However, shoulders and legs must still be covered. I cannot tell you how many times I see tourists wearing shorts turned away at the entrances of the city's churches.

For six months, I will be in *lutto*—wearing black to show that I am in mourning for a loved one. From head to toe, I am clothed in black. My simple black dress has short sleeves, and my sheer black stockings are embroidered with an intricate rosebud design. My Laura Biagiotti eyeglasses have a large, square-shaped frame and are tinted a pale rose, helping to disguise my features. My black lace mantilla also conceals my identity. Beneath it, my hair is pulled up into a severe bun. I hate covering my luxuriant locks. They were meant to be seen. Also, all my fine lines and wrinkles that have formed on my forehead are exposed when my hair is swept off my face. But I must not risk being recognized in church, the one place I cannot tolerate being disturbed.

I will be in mourning for six months. Part of me feels guilty that I am not doing *il lutto* for a full year, but even that custom has been falling out of favor in Italy. My poor mother once wore black for three years straight after both of her parents died within a year of each other, and then my father's mother died just a couple of months before she was due to stop her mourning. One might think that a famous actress who wears nothing but the finest designer couture would shun *il lutto*. But instead of looking at it as a cross to bear, I am comforted that I can do this small act for Giuliana.

The most famous feature in Santa Maria della Vittoria is Bernini's brilliant and astonishing sculpture of *The Ecstasy of Saint Theresa*. It sits in the church's Cornaro Chapel, which was designed by Bernini to look like a theater. For me, it is one of the best examples of Baroque art. The chapel's benefactor was Cardinal Federico Cornaro. Bernini even designed an audience for this miniature theater by sculpting members of the Cornaro family seated in boxes as they watch the drama unfolding—St. Theresa's ecstasy of divine love.

Every time I visit this church, I am completely mesmerized by this work that shows St. Theresa lying on a cloud. Her head is thrown back and her eyes are shut as she is in the midst of her rapture. An angel stands above her, and he is holding an arrow, preparing to pierce the saint's body for a second time. Shards of heavenly light made from bronze rain down on the saint and angel, creating a stunning iridescent backdrop.

For some reason whenever I come here, I am moved to tears when I admire this masterpiece. But today, I am also crying for my son. I have let him down by giving him up all those years ago and choosing to keep the truth from him for so long. While Lorenzo might not be ready to forgive me, I need to feel pardoned. That is why I am here.

Finally, it is my turn to enter the confessional. A man exits the confessional and stops when he sees me. For a moment, I am afraid he recognizes me, but he merely scans my body from my chest down to my legs and then whispers, *"Hai un corpo stupendo."*

I scowl and whisper in reply, *"Porco schifoso."*

He smiles and shrugs his shoulders, indifferent to my anger. I can still feel his eyes lingering on me and taking in my backside as I enter the confession booth. To think even in Italy, one of the most sacred countries in the world, you can encounter a filthy pervert like that who has the audacity to tell me in church that I have a gorgeous body.

Kneeling down behind the panel that separates the sinner from the priest, I make the sign of the cross and say, *"Nel nome del Padre, del Figlio, e dello Spirito Santo. Perdonami, Padre."*

In Italian, the priest asks me, "How long has it been since your last confession?"

I answer, "I am afraid to say about forty years."

"What is important is that you are here now."

"I have lied and coveted material wealth."

"*Sì.* What else?"

"I am afraid to say, Padre, I had marital relations before marriage."

"How about during marriage?"

"I have never taken the sacrament of marriage, Padre."

"Ah. And you said your last confession was forty years ago?"

"*Sì,* Padre." No doubt he is doing the math and thinking, *She is quite old to never have married.*

"May I ask, *signorina,* why you have never taken the sacrament of marriage? Did you not find any suitable men who could become your husband?"

I am taken aback for a moment. My anger is beginning to simmer.

"I mean no disrespect, Padre, but do you really need to know the answer to that question?"

"Ahh, no, no, of course not. Please go on with your confession."

"I . . . I . . . betrayed my sister."

"How so?"

"I seduced and stole her boyfriend when we were teenagers."

"You were young. I am sure God will forgive you."

"I did not stop desiring him even after we broke up and he returned to my sister and wed her."

"*Thou shalt not covet your neighbor's wife.* Or in this case husband. Yes, you broke that commandment. Did you have relations with him while he was married to your sister?"

"No. At least I can say no to that. But I did go to him after they were married to tell him I wanted him back and that I had had a child with him as well—a child I gave up for adoption. That is perhaps my greatest sin, giving up my own son."

"It is not a sin to give up a child for adoption. You ensured the child would be raised by parents who could do so since you were not able to, correct?"

"I did ensure the child had a good home. But I would have been able to provide financially for him. I was a coward and afraid of what everyone would say about my being a single mother. I chose my career as well, knowing a baby would put an end to it."

"What do you do?"

"I would rather not say, Padre."

"As you wish. You have punished yourself enough for giving up your child, but I assure you it will not be looked upon as a sin by God."

"How can God forgive me if my own son does not?"

"You have been reunited with him?"

"Yes."

"Be patient. And place your trust in our heavenly Father. Surrender to His will and whatever plans He has for your destiny. Are there any other sins you wish to confess, my child?"

"No, Padre."

"For your repentance, pray fifty Hail Marys, ten Our Fathers, and find a worthy charity to devote some time to."

"Excuse me, Padre, but that seems like a lot considering you told me my sin was not really a sin and the sin of taking my sister's boyfriend could be forgiven since I was just a young girl."

"Do not question me, *signora*."

"*Signorina*."

"Excuse me, *signora*."

"It is *signorina!* As I told you, I have never been married."

"Ah! That is correct. I am sorry, *signorina*. Now if there is not anything else, you may leave."

"You have not blessed me yet, Father!" My voice rises. I am ready to reach over the panel that separates us and thrash this priest over the head with my purse. I do not care that he is a man of God.

"Please bow your head. *Nel nome del Padre, del Figlio, e dello Spirito Santo. Dio, perdona questa donna.*"

I close my eyes as the priest blesses me and asks God to forgive me, but it is difficult to listen to his words. My blood is boiling. Volunteer at a charity? I cannot do that. He does not know who I am or else he would never give me such a preposterous repentance. I would be mobbed. But I know I must do something worthy besides praying all those Hail Marys and Our Fathers. I will have to give it some thought.

Once the priest finishes his benediction, I wish him a nice day and exit the confessional. Edgardo is waiting for me.

"I thought you would never come out of there. I know you have a lot to ask forgiveness for, but Lord!" Edgardo lets out a low whistle.

"*Basta!* Enough! And do not use the name of the Lord in vain. We are in His house."

"All I said was L—"

"I said enough."

We exit the church. I keep my head down lest anyone recognize me. We walk to my car, which is double-parked outside the church. My driver is waiting. As I am about to get into the back, I hear, "Francesca! Wait!"

I have been recognized! But when I turn around, I am stunned.

"Rocco? What are you doing here?"

"Yes, what are you doing here, Mr. Vecchio? That's 'old' in Italian, isn't it?"

I look up at Edgardo, shocked by his rude comment. Brave soul that Rocco is, he merely smiles at Edgardo and says, "Yes, that is correct.

"Francesca, you look beautiful as always, but I can see the ache of losing Giuliana is still fresh for you." Rocco embraces me. I merely kiss him on both cheeks and thank him. While I am a sex symbol, I have never been comfortable with open displays of affection. Besides, Edgardo has the meanest expression on his face right now. I can only imagine what he would do if I were daring enough to kiss Rocco on the lips in public.

"I am happy to see you, Rocco, but you should have called first."

"I am sorry. I had to come to Italy to purchase jewelry for my store, and I thought since I was here, I would surprise you. I know how much you love to be surprised." Rocco winks at me. I can feel myself blushing.

"We need to get going, Francesca, before you are recognized." Edgardo takes my elbow and begins leading me to my car.

I pull free and say to Rocco, "Please join me. We can catch up at my apartment. By the way, how did you know I would be here, or is meeting you a coincidence?"

Rocco smiles. "I wish I could say it was destiny. How romantic that would be—here in Rome and then we meet by chance, ah?"

This man knows how to get to me. I giggle softly like a schoolgirl who has been noticed by a boy for the first time. Edgardo scowls at me.

"I stopped by your apartment and your housekeeper told me you were here."

"We'll be sure to fire her when we return," Edgardo states flatly.

"We will not fire Maria. She has been with me since I moved to Rome." Now it's my turn to scowl at Edgardo.

"Since when do you have a problem firing people?" Edgardo shoots back. I am embarrassed that he has said this in front of Rocco, but I immediately realize that was Edgardo's intention—

humiliation in front of the man who worships me so that Rocco will see my flaws and drop me.

"*Si*, Edgardo. Remember that. *Anyone* can be replaced. Now if you will excuse Rocco and me, I need to talk to him." I return my attention to Rocco, who seems amused by my exchange with Edgardo. Edgardo steps into the passenger seat of my car and slams the door shut with all his brute force.

"Whew! I don't think you want to make your bodyguard mad. There's no telling what he'll do." Rocco shakes his head.

"I am sorry you had to witness that. He is very good at what he does. But he forgets his place sometimes, I am afraid to say."

"I think it's more than that, Francesca. I think he has the hots for you."

"Please!" I wave dismissively and give a laugh so false that I fear Rocco will see through to my acting. I have always suspected Edgardo is attracted to me, but I will not admit it to Rocco. He must feel like he is the *only* man in my life.

"I'm serious, Francesca. He's jealous of me. You think I didn't get that crack he made about my name meaning 'old' in Italian? I know he's also still mad at me over sneaking you out of your sister's house for our nights on the town."

"Do not trouble yourself over Edgardo. He is a big boy. So, will you ride back with me to my apartment? We will have dinner together."

"Sure. But I have to tell you something first, Francesca."

"Is everything all right?"

"Yes. I want to be completely honest with you. While it is true that I always come to Italy in the summer to buy more jewelry for my business, I originally was planning on sending my associate to make the trip this year. But I wanted to see you. I've missed you terribly since you've left. I was hoping that maybe we could take in some of the Roman sights together and just relax a bit. But I understand if you're not feeling up to it, being that you lost your sister a few weeks ago."

I am touched by Rocco's sincerity and candidness. Tears fill my eyes. I quickly blink them back and hope Rocco cannot see through my tinted glasses. What is the matter with me? Ever since Giuliana died, I cry over anything.

"Hey! It's okay. If you don't want to see my ugly mug again, I'll get on the next flight back to New York."

I laugh. I know Rocco is only joking.

"I can use a shoulder to cry on, Rocco. I have been upset by more than Giuliana's death. Look, Rocco. I am going to be honest with you as well since you have been so gracious and open with me. You need to know all about Francesca Donata, and I am warning you, a lot of it is ugly. After you hear my story, I will understand if you never want to see me again."

"It's going to take a lot to chase me away, Francesca. Besides, you're not the only one with a few skeletons in your closet."

"I doubt that, Rocco. I doubt it very much."

# ❧ 29 ❧

# Pia

I'm walking through the famous halls of the Sistine Chapel, and like the rest of the tourists, my head is bent back as I take in the magnificent ceiling where Michelangelo painted nine scenes from the Bible's Book of Genesis. While I am in awe, I'm also overwhelmed. Lorenzo and I don't talk, reluctant to break our focus.

Suddenly, the crowd of tourists completely stops walking. As I get closer, I see why. They're all dazzled by the *Creation of Adam*. Goosebumps quickly dot my arms like raindrops pelleting a street. There is so much beauty and strength in all of the frescoes, but viewing this majestic scene in which God's finger meets Adam's as He creates him moves me. And there it is again—I am wishing Gregory could be here, sharing this moment with me. I look down to the marble floors beneath and shut my eyes tightly, attempting to physically shut him out.

"Pia, are you okay?" Lorenzo takes me by the wrist and excuses himself as he ushers me through the crowd.

"I'm fine, Lorenzo."

"You probably just need some air."

"No, really. I'm fine. I was upset, but I am feeling well. Don't rush on my account. I'd like to finish walking slowly through the Chapel."

"All right, but please, Pia, don't feel like you have to do so on my account. I have been here several times, so we can leave when-ever you're ready."

"You've been here before yet you looked just as moved as I was when we were staring at the ceiling."

"It never ceases to astound me that one person was able to paint all of this while lying on his back on a scaffold. And it's beyond per-fect."

I nod my head. "I'd always heard people say how you can't truly appreciate the Sistine Chapel until you've seen it in person, and now I see why."

We continue strolling through the rest of the Chapel in silence. Once we exit, Lorenzo suggests we get refreshments at the Vati-can's café. We make our way to the café. Lorenzo orders an espresso for himself and an Orangina soda for me. I decide to quickly engage Lorenzo in talking about himself before he can ask what upset me earlier.

"Have you spoken to Francesca since she revealed to you that she's your mother?"

"I called her last night after I got home. I apologized for blow-ing up at her and told her that I understood her actions, but I asked her to give me time. I told her I want her in my life, but that we need to take baby steps. She was relieved to hear what I had to say, of course."

"That was very generous of you."

"It was the truth." Lorenzo shrugs his shoulders.

"But there's still some anger, isn't there?" I ask gently.

"Yes, but it's simmering down. Francesca is the only family I now have, Pia." Lorenzo looks off.

"I'm glad you're not making the same mistake your mother made and that you have decided to forgive Francesca now rather than make her wait three decades."

"Well, my mother was extremely hurt and devastated after los-ing my father, the love of her life. Then she loses their child only to find out later that her sister had had a baby with her husband."

"It was before your father and Giuliana got back together. It's not like he cheated on her with Francesca while they were mar-ried."

"True, but of all the people for him to have a child with, it had to be her sister, who had already stolen him from her. And then to hear Francesca admit that she had wanted him back—I can't even begin to understand my mother's anger or how much she was hurt."

"I'm sorry, Lorenzo. I didn't mean to make it sound as if Giuliana had no reason to be mad at Francesca. It's just sad that they couldn't have made up years ago rather than right before she died."

"Yes. Well, I suppose what's really important is that they did patch things up before she died. Although I didn't know exactly why they hadn't been talking, I knew my mother was pained by her estrangement with her sister. That's also why I wrote to Francesca and insisted she fly to New York immediately."

I place my hand over Lorenzo's. "You're a good son."

Lorenzo latches onto my hand and with his free one he strokes my cheek. His eyes meet mine, and this time, I don't glance away. I feel closer to him after just the past two days that we've spent together exploring Rome. And before I can stop it, Lorenzo leans in and kisses me. I should pull away, but I don't want to. Lorenzo's expert kiss leaves me longing for more, but unlike the night of Gregory's show, this one is much shorter. The café is getting more crowded with tourists, and we don't want to give them another show.

"Pia, I'm going to speak candidly. After losing my mother and finding out the truth about Francesca, I don't want to waste time like they did. I like you, Pia—a lot. And I'd like to see where we can take this relationship. That is, of course, if you're interested. I realize you're still dealing with your breakup from Gregory, and I don't want to rush you. But I know I can make you happy."

I'm speechless. Though it's no secret that Lorenzo and I have had chemistry since we first met, I didn't think his feelings for me were more than just a physical attraction.

"I'm flattered, Lorenzo. And while I can't deny there is a strong attraction between us, how can you be so sure of your feelings for me? We've known each other only a short time."

"I've seen enough to know you possess all of the traits I've always wanted in a partner. Look, I probably shouldn't be jumping to that stage right now and scaring you off. We can take it slowly and just date and enjoy each other's company. I'll let you set the pace. If and when you think you're ready to take it to the next level, it's your call."

"Thank you for being so open with me, Lorenzo. Now it's my turn to be honest with you. I'm not sure I'm ready to date anyone just yet—even casually. I do have a good time with you, and having you as my unofficial tour guide is taking my mind off . . . off things." I can't even say Gregory's name, but I don't need to. Lorenzo knows the "things" I'm referring to.

"I'm happy to hear you've been having fun with me and that it's helping you. Okay, no pressure." Lorenzo raises his palms. "Forget we even had this conversation. Let's just continue to hang out and see where this goes. How does that sound?"

"I guess that's fine. I don't want to mislead you, Lorenzo. You've already been through so much lately."

"And so have you, Pia."

"It's not the same."

"Don't diminish your experiences."

"You know what I mean, Lorenzo."

"Okay, fine. Enough with the heavy talk. So do you agree that we concentrate from here on out on having a blast in Rome?"

"How can I say no to that?" I laugh.

"Good! Now there's just one other small matter. You need to take a second week off of working on Francesca's autobiography. We're already in the middle of this week, and there's still so much more I want to show you in Rome."

"I can still work part of the day and go sightseeing with you for the other half of the day."

"You forget, Pia. This isn't New York, where people do nothing but work. Shops and businesses close for their siestas in the middle of the afternoon and don't reopen until evening. We run the risk of many places being closed if you work in the morning and save your sightseeing for the afternoon."

"I'll switch it then. We can go exploring in the morning, and I'll work in the afternoon."

"Just one additional week, Pia. Come on! How often will you come to Rome after this?"

I'm tempted. The emotional drain of my breakup with Gregory

has taken its toll both physically and mentally. What's the harm in another week?

"Before I give you my answer, I'm wondering why it matters that I give up my afternoons, since as you say most places will be closed for their siestas. What would we do then?"

"Trust me. I have that all planned." Lorenzo smiles mischievously. "So what do you say?"

"Okay. I'm yours for another week."

Another week has turned into an additional week and one after that, so that I have now been in Rome for almost six weeks. We are nearing the end of September, and I'm enjoying the Eternal City in the autumn as much as I did in the final days of summer.

Lorenzo and Francesca teamed up in doing their best to convince me to stay longer. Colin called to tell me that Francesca herself had contacted him and asked him to grant me a second extension on handing in the article. She told Colin that because of the recent death of her sister she had not been feeling well and had not been able to finish up our last interview for the article. She also assured Colin that the article would reveal a side to her that no one had ever seen before. Colin told her to take her time. What he didn't know is that I was already done with the article. Though Lorenzo has been keeping me busy touring Rome by day, I have been able to write a few nights a week. I was thinking of sending the article to Colin about two weeks ago, but then Francesca informed me that she had been able to get an additional extension for me. I couldn't send the article to Colin or he'd know Francesca had lied to him. And now that I've won Francesca's admiration and respect, I'm not about to risk falling out of her good graces.

The past few weeks have spun by in a flash. Lorenzo was right that I needed more time to relax. After our second week sightseeing, I felt reenergized and inspired again to return to my writing in the evenings. I've even started writing Francesca's autobiography. While I'll have to interview her again at some point, I have enough from our sessions for the *Profile* article as well as from her revelation of her past for the beginning of the autobiography. Of course, the book won't reveal that Francesca is really Lorenzo's mother and that she had stolen her sister's boyfriend, but I was able to use some of what she'd told me about her childhood with Giuliana when they were close. Since there has been interest in her relationship with the sister no one knew she had, readers will be curious about their childhood together. I just haven't figured out yet how I will explain their long estrangement. But I'm not going to worry about that for now.

As for Lorenzo, I finally stopped fighting our attraction. We've been seeing each other for the past month. True to his word, he hasn't been rushing me, but the past few days I've sensed an urgency in him, which is making me slightly nervous. Neither of us has discussed yet what's going to happen when I return to California. I can't help feeling like I'm making the same mistake I made with Gregory all over again, since I had avoided that discussion with him as well. Part of me wants to just have a good time as Lorenzo encouraged me to do that day in the café at the Vatican. But I know he wants more. After all, the guy told me I have everything he wants in a partner. He's just agreed to treat what we have casually so that I won't go running.

I haven't even allowed myself when I'm alone to truly examine how I feel about Lorenzo. I've had an amazing time with him in Rome, and he's managed to keep me distracted from Gregory. The pain over losing Gregory aches less every day. And helping Lorenzo come to terms with the truth about his parentage has brought us closer. He's also confided in me about losing his mother, and I've started to tell him more about Erica.

Today, he's asked me to get dressed to the nines. That's all he's told me. I decide to wear the royal-blue sheath dress that Francesca had Angelica alter for me. I've taken Zia's advice finally and have been wearing my eyeglasses less. It's been so hot in Rome, and the glasses reflect the sun's light, adding to the shine on my face. I tried doing my best, but after the first day without my glasses and hardly being able to see more than five feet in front of me, Lorenzo took me to an optical shop where they fitted me with a pair of contact lenses. He insisted on paying for them. Then again, he's insisted on paying for *everything*. I hate to admit this, but I've been dazzled by all the money that he and Francesca have. Lorenzo has not shied away from spoiling me, whether it's paying for my elaborate meals in five-star restaurants or buying flowers for me every day at the Campo de' Fiori.

I'm finishing braiding my hair to the side. Unlike Zia, Lorenzo loves that I wear my braids and ponytails over my shoulder as opposed to letting them hang down the middle of my back. He's taken to playfully tugging my braid, which still manages to make me blush like a schoolgirl.

"*Molta bellissima!* Pia, you look gorgeous in that dress!" Francesca walks in and sizes me up from head to toe. "May I make a suggestion?" Francesca opens her eyes wide in an innocent, imploring way. Something tells me I'm not going to like her suggestion.

"Of course."

Francesca walks over to me, takes my braid, and coils it around the base of my skull. She reaches over to my dresser and flips open a small crystal box holding hairpins. She fastens the braid securely to my head.

"*Perfetta!* Take a look." She grabs the handheld silver mirror on the dresser and holds it up in front of me. I hate to admit that she's right, but she is. The coiled, braided bun looks classic and elegant with my sheath.

"*Grazie,* Francesca."

"Anytime. I am so happy you and Lorenzo are together. He is absolutely glowing and so are you!"

Since Lorenzo and I broke the news to Francesca that we are seeing each other, not a day has gone by that she doesn't utter how thrilled she is that we're dating. We waited two weeks before telling her, but I could tell she knew. She always made sure to excuse herself when Lorenzo was dropping me off so that we'd be alone and he could kiss me.

"Thank you, Francesca."

"I have a little confession to make. I have secretly hoped that he would fall in love with you."

"Really?"

"Yes. Why do you sound so surprised?"

"I don't know."

"Pia, I could not hope for a better woman for my son."

"I don't think Lorenzo is in love with me. We've only been seeing each other casually for a month. It's not like we're boyfriend and girlfriend."

"Yet. It is only a matter of time. And as for Lorenzo's being in love with you, of course he is. I know you tend to follow your head before your heart, but I can assure you this is the ideal match."

"Francesca, I'm flattered that you think so highly of me, but please, don't get your hopes up. A lot can happen. Lorenzo and I have agreed to take it slowly."

"Bah!" Francesca waves her hand dismissively in my direction. "You need to trust your feelings more and not analyze so much. If it feels good, go for it. Do you like being with him?"

"Yes, but—"

"But nothing. He is completely yours, unlike Gregory, who had his attentions divided."

I wince at the mention of Gregory, and Francesca notices.

"I am sorry to bring him up. It is because of me that the two of you even met."

"Well, it wasn't exactly because of you. I had met him outside Giuliana's house."

"Yes, but you were there hoping to see me. You cannot deny it."

I remain silent. My irritation is growing. I haven't been frustrated with Francesca since our interviews in Astoria. I'm also annoyed that she had to bring up Gregory, whom I've managed to keep mostly out of my thoughts. I say mostly because I still haven't managed to stop having the occasional dream about him.

The doorbell rings, saving me.

"It must be Lorenzo."

"I need to use the restroom. Please tell him I'll be out in five minutes."

"Of course. If it were me, I would make him wait longer." Francesca winks before she leaves my room.

I close the door and sit on my bed. I lied about having to use the bathroom. I just want a few minutes to myself.

Suddenly, I don't feel like going out. Though I've had a great time with Lorenzo, all the sightseeing is beginning to wear me out. Except for the few nights a week that Lorenzo has agreed to let me stay home to work on my writing, I haven't had much time alone. And even on the nights I'm home, Francesca is always here and often drops in to chat for a few minutes. I had hoped that with Rocco's arrival, she'd be too preoccupied with him. But as usual, she's playing her games and insists on only seeing Rocco a few times a week. I roll my eyes.

I'm tempted to tell Lorenzo I don't feel well, but I don't want to lie to him. He's had enough lies in his life. I think about what Francesca said about Lorenzo's being in love with me. Is he? I know Lorenzo cares about me, but I hadn't imagined that he could be falling for me already. We haven't even made love yet—not that he hasn't tried, but I've told him it's too soon. The past week was tense between us because we marked one month since we began seeing each other, and in Lorenzo's eyes that was a milestone. He asked me if I was ready several times last week. Maybe that's part of my hesitation in going out with him today. I do have feelings for Lorenzo, but I don't want to make the same mistakes I made with Gregory. If Lorenzo truly loves me and wants to be with me, he'll wait.

Sighing, I get up and examine myself one last time in the mirror before heading out to the living room.

"Pia, I was about to come searching for you myself." Lorenzo comes over and gives me his customary kiss on both cheeks. For some reason, it irks me today. We're dating now. He can just give me a quick kiss on the lips.

"So, where are you two headed today? Or is it a surprise again, Lorenzo?" Francesca asks.

"Of course. I wouldn't have it any other way." Lorenzo grins at me.

"You are definitely my son." Francesca laughs and gives Lorenzo a quick hug. I can't help but notice his eyes narrow a bit at Francesca's comment. He's still adjusting to thinking of her as his mother.

We say good-bye to Francesca and head out.

"You look gorgeous, Pia. I was having a hard time keeping my eyes off you in front of Francesca."

"Thank you, Lorenzo. You look great as always."

Lorenzo suddenly grabs my hand, pulling me into him as he begins kissing me. His free hand snakes around my waist to my back. He presses me up against him. I return his kiss. Usually, his expert kisses completely unravel me, but today I'm having a difficult time being as passionate as he is.

"Sorry. I couldn't help myself." Lorenzo wipes my lipstick that has smeared onto his mouth with the back of his hand.

I can't help but laugh at his comment. Lorenzo puts his arm around me and we walk that way. A few men glance my way and don't hide the fact that they're checking me out in my body-hugging sheath. I glance nervously at Lorenzo, but he has a smirk on his face as if he's enjoying the attention his woman is receiving. I would've preferred a little jealousy on his part, but I guess I can't fault the guy for being proud of me.

"Let's go into this shop." Lorenzo leads me into a Prada shop. "See anything you like?"

"Yes, a few, but they're too expensive."

"Go ahead and pick one handbag—or even two—that you like. It's my treat."

"Oh, I couldn't, Lorenzo."

"Why not? You are my girlfriend."

"We haven't actually talked about that yet, Lorenzo."

"Well, we're talking about it now. Pia, as you know, I have been very patient and have been taking this slowly. But I think it's time we lay all our cards out on the table."

"Right here?"

"No one's listening to us. It's fine. Pia, I'm going to be honest with you again. What are you so afraid of?"

"I'm not afraid of anything." I play with the handles of a taupe satchel.

"Don't lie to me."

"I've never lied to you, Lorenzo."

"You're doing it now, Pia."

Sighing, I cross my arms over my chest. "Okay, I'm sorry. I am afraid. I'm afraid you're going to meet someone else you like more than me and . . ." I let my voice trail off.

"And cheat on you the way Gregory did?"

I nod my head.

"Pia, what he did to you was horrible, but I'm not him. You need to have a little trust, and you need to start living."

"What's that supposed to mean—'start living'?" I can't disguise my annoyance.

Lorenzo takes my hands in his.

"Again, I'm going to be direct with you, Pia, risking that you're not going to like what I have to say, but you need to hear it. How much longer are you going to punish yourself for your sister's death?"

My heart starts beating rapidly. I murmur softly, "I'm not punishing myself."

"Yes, you are. By pushing me away and insisting you need to take our relationship slowly, you're not giving yourself permission to fully be with me. It's as if you think you don't deserve happiness and love."

My chest feels constricted. Gregory's words from the day we broke up echo through my mind: *"You run away whenever there's conflict, Pia. Whenever things get too difficult for you, you escape."*

I close my eyes, willing my heart rate to slow down. He was right. Gregory was right that I always run when a situation gets too difficult, just as Lorenzo is right that I've been punishing myself for Erica's death—for not being able to save my sister . . . for being alive. The tears come furiously.

"It should have been me," I whisper. "I'm the older one. It should have been me."

"Oh, Pia." Lorenzo pulls me to his chest. A saleslady comes up to us and asks him if I'm all right. Lorenzo doesn't answer her as he ushers me outside.

"I'm sorry, Pia. I shouldn't have had that discussion with you in there."

"It's okay," I mutter through my tears. "You had no idea I was going to fall apart."

"I'm glad you fell apart."

"Geez! Thanks!" I manage to let out a soft laugh.

"I just mean that you needed to let yourself fully feel what you've been carrying on the inside since Erica died."

"I know what you meant. And you were right. I have been punishing myself. And I've been afraid that you're going to hurt me the way Gregory did. I'm sorry. I haven't been very fair toward you.

But if you give me a second chance, I think I'm ready to be your girlfriend."

"Are you sure? I know I've just put you on the spot."

"I'm positive." And to prove it, I give Lorenzo the longest kiss I've ever given him.

Finally, he pulls away. "So you'll let me spoil you as a man should do for his woman?"

"Oh, okay, if you insist."

"That's the spirit!" Lorenzo laughs.

Two hours later, Lorenzo's hands are full of shopping bags from many of the designer shops on Via Condotti. From handbags to beautiful clothes and leather shoes, he's going all out on treating me. I'll have to buy a new piece of luggage just to be able to take all of his gifts back home to California. Just when I think we're done, he says, "One last place. I promise."

He walks briskly ahead of me and enters the jewelry shop that has the necklace I was admiring earlier. I follow him inside. The saleswoman hasn't noticed me behind him and is all but drooling over Lorenzo.

*"Si, un attimo."* The saleslady asks him to wait as she walks over to the shop's display window.

She returns with the necklace that stopped me in my tracks when we were outside.

"Please, place it on her," Lorenzo instructs the saleswoman. She looks disappointed to see he's taken and that I'll be receiving that exquisite piece of jewelry.

The saleswoman places the necklace around my neck. The necklace is eighteen-carat yellow gold and plunges into a V in the center. It's both understated and striking.

"You have good taste, Pia. It really complements you." Lorenzo's eyes are glowing. Francesca told me earlier that he's been glowing, but I hadn't really noticed before. But it's completely evident to me now.

"Thank you. I love it."

"Please wrap it up—unless you'd like to keep it on?"

Normally, I don't like to draw attention to myself, but I can't bear to take the necklace off just yet. And as Lorenzo pointed out to me, I need to start living.

"Yes, I'd like to keep it on. But please still include the box in a bag."

The saleswoman nods her head toward me, but I see the envy in her eyes. She is wishing she were me.

"Maybe we should pick something up for Francesca? She's going to feel left out." I smile at Lorenzo as he drapes his arm around my shoulders.

"I want only you to feel special tonight," he whispers in my ear.

Today, Lorenzo and I are headed to the Via Appia Antica, also known as the Appian Way. While there, we also plan on visiting the Roman catacombs. I have been dying to go since I first arrived. Via Appia Antica was built in 312 BC. Here, one can truly envision ancient Rome. The road was extended eventually in 190 BC to the Benevento, and to the Taranto and Brindisi ports, linking it to Rome's expanding empire in the East. The Church of Domine Quo Vadis is built on the spot where tradition states the apostle Peter was visited by the vision of Christ, who implored him not to escape Rome, but to return and face his persecutors.

A week has passed since I agreed to be Lorenzo's official girlfriend. Lorenzo has been surprising me every day that we've spent together exploring the Eternal City, so today, I've decided to turn the tables on him. I've packed a picnic for us to enjoy. Francesca had mentioned to me that there are beautiful, grassy fields where many people like to picnic along the Via Appia Antica. She told me it's one of the best spots in Rome for a picnic, especially a romantic one.

I woke up early yesterday morning and headed to one of the many open-air markets in the city to buy my ingredients for a muffuletta. I prepared it as soon as I returned home from shopping. A muffuletta is a sandwich that originated at the famous Central Market in the French Quarter of New Orleans. The store's founder, Salvatore Lupo, a Sicilian immigrant, invented the sandwich to make it easier for the Sicilian farmers who sold their produce at the local farmers market to eat their lunch, which usually consisted of various deli meats, cheese, olive salad, and Italian bread. The farmers would eat the foods separately and all balanced on their knees while they sat on crates or barrels. Salvatore suggested they place all of the ingredients in the round Italian bread. And the muffuletta was born. My father had been to New Orleans when he was a teenager and immediately fell in love with the sandwich. He taught me and Erica how to make a muffuletta, and we always made one for our family outings at the beach.

Muffulettas are typically made with round Italian bread. Layers of *prosciutto,* salami, *capicollo,* ham, provolone cheese, and either *giardiniera* or a combination of marinated artichoke hearts, sundried tomatoes, roasted red peppers, and olive paste can be used. You can also choose which of the deli meats you want to add as well as which cheese. I like to make mine with *prosciutto, capicollo,* provolone cheese, marinated artichoke hearts, sundried tomatoes, green Sicilian olives, and roasted red peppers. I also like to add slices of plum tomatoes as well as either fresh basil or parsley leaves.

The round loaf of bread is cut in half, and each half is drizzled with extra virgin olive oil. It helps to remove some of the bread crumb filling before adding your ingredients. After I've layered the meats and the other ingredients on one half of the loaf, I place the other half of the bread on top and wrap the entire muffuletta in wax paper. Three heavy plates are then placed on top. If you haven't thought ahead of time to make the muffuletta, you can leave the plates on for a minimum of fifteen minutes. But the muffuletta comes out best if you can let the ingredients settle for twenty-four hours. I made mine yesterday so that the ingredients in the muffuletta have time to settle. I can't wait to try it, especially with the fresh Italian cold cuts! Next to gelato, my favorite foods to eat in Italy are the deli meats. My favorites are *prosciutto, mortadella,* and *capicollo.* I also go crazy for *provoleta,* or provolone cheese, which can be bought mild or sharp. Since I have a lot of salt in my ingredients for the muffuletta I've made for our picnic, I decided to opt for a mild *provoleta.* I've also packed figs, grapes, and two bottles of red wine in our picnic basket.

I glance at my watch. It's nine a.m. Lorenzo should have been here by now. As if reading my thoughts, the phone rings. This has to be him.

*"Pronto."*

"Pia, it's me. I'm sorry, but a good friend of mine has had a car accident and is in the hospital."

"I'm so sorry. How seriously hurt is he?"

"He's lucky. He escaped with just whiplash and a few cuts and bruises. But he's going to need someone to drive him home after he's discharged."

"I'm glad he's not more seriously hurt."

"Thank you, Pia. I won't be able to meet you until later this afternoon. But I don't want you to wait for me to eat. Just go ahead, and I'll call you after I've dropped him off at home."

"Well, this was supposed to be a surprise, but I had packed a picnic for us to have at the Via Appia Antica before we headed over to the catacombs."

"I'm really sorry. Why don't you go ahead and enjoy the day. It's gorgeous outside. I'll do my best to hurry and meet you as soon as I can."

"Of course. Don't worry about it. Go be with your friend. I'll call you later to see how he is, and I'll save some food for you since I'm sure you'll be starving by the time you're done."

"Thanks again. I'd better get going. Talk to you later. *Ciao.*"

*"Ciao."* I hang up the phone. My spirits plummet. I was really looking forward to surprising him. I suppose Lorenzo is right. I should still take advantage of the beautiful day and have my picnic. I can even bring my laptop and work on Francesca's autobiography while I wait for Lorenzo to join me.

I make sure all of the contents of my picnic are in my basket, and then I pack up my laptop. I'm alone in the apartment this morning. Francesca left quite early with Rocco. She didn't mention what they had planned, and I know better than to ask her too many questions. Like me, Rocco has also extended his stay here.

I make my way to the foyer when something swishes past me, and out of my peripheral vision, I see a flurry of white race by.

Mewsette!

Francesca couldn't bear to leave her back in Astoria even though

Giuliana's household staff is still in the Mussolini Mansion. Once in Rome, Francesca decided to adopt the cat.

A series of "meows" escapes from Mewsette as if she's begging to go out with me.

"Sorry, Mewsette. You're not a dog, and even if Francesca had a leash for you, she'd kill me if she knew I took you without her blessing." I bend over and pet Mewsette on the head. That seems to subdue her. She sits down and watches me unlock the door and let myself out.

I exit Francesca's apartment out onto the street and begin making my way toward the bus stop. I get no farther than two steps when I hear, "Pia!"

I freeze in my tracks, and my heart stops beating. It can't be. I turn around slowly.

"Gregory?"

I open my eyes wider, still not believing I'm seeing correctly. But it's really him.

"Hey, Pia." He smiles nervously.

"What . . . What are you doing here?"

"I'm sorry. I would have called, but I was afraid you wouldn't agree to see me. I know this is a shock, but I really need to talk to you."

A mixture of nausea and dread fills my stomach. He looks thinner since I last saw him two months ago. His hair is cut differently, too. He's now sporting a crew cut. His eyes look red and tired. But he is still as handsome as ever.

"I don't know, Gregory."

"Pia, if you won't listen to me in person, then I'll write everything I have to say in a letter. It'll take me forever, and I'm certain you'll have questions that you'll want answered right away. Please. Can I walk with you?"

My curiosity has been piqued. But what could he have to say that would elicit questions from me?

"Okay. But just to the bus stop. I'm going to Via Appia Antica."

We begin walking. Neither of us says anything for a good two minutes. Finally, Gregory breaks the silence.

"Can I carry something?"

I'm about to protest, but my laptop is already causing my shoulder to ache. I hand him my laptop bag. "Thanks."

"No problem. I'm sorry. I see you have a picnic prepared. I won't keep you long if you're meeting anyone."

I shake my head. "No, I'll be by myself for a little while. My friend got held up."

Gregory nods his head. We get to the bus stop and wait. No one else is at the bus stand. I must've just missed the bus.

"The Via Appia Antica is beautiful. I still remember it from when my family and I lived here."

"I haven't been there yet. I'm also planning on visiting the catacombs after I eat."

"You'll love them. I saw them as a kid. They definitely spooked me then." Gregory smiles, but I don't return his smile.

"When did you arrive in Rome?" I ask him.

"Around eight this morning."

"And you came straight here?"

"Yeah. I haven't even booked a hotel yet."

I frown. Whatever it is he needs to talk to me about must be serious if it couldn't wait for him to get settled first.

"You look great, Pia. I see this trip has agreed with you."

"It's just the tan." I shrug my shoulders and don't meet his gaze.

"How do you like Rome?"

"I love it."

"I figured you would."

I nod. Another couple of minutes of awkward silence elapse before I ask him, "How did your second art show go?"

"Not bad. More people attended the first one. The gallery owner said a lot of people were away for vacation in August so that's why there was a low turnout."

"No more shows coming up?"

"Not until the end of October. Since I didn't sell most of my paintings at the second show, I won't have to kill myself. I might just do two new paintings."

"So you have a bit of a break now."

"Yes. But even if I didn't, I would've still come to Rome. I've missed you a lot, Pia. I could hardly paint those first two weeks after you left. You were all I thought about."

I refuse to fall for his words, and instead ask, "How's Madeline?"

"That's part of what I need to talk to you about."

I shut my eyes for a second. He's finally going to come clean about their affair. He could've done this over the phone or in an e-mail. Then again, I'd told him the last time we talked not to call anymore.

"Gregory, we don't need to rehash what happened. You don't owe me an explanation."

"Yes, I do. You need to hear the truth, Pia."

The bus pulls up at the curb.

"Pia, I'm sorry. I know you have plans, and I just dropped in on you suddenly, but please give me some more time—at least until I tell you what I came here for. Can I ride with you to Via Appia Antica?"

I hesitate. "Okay."

We climb the stairs up to the bus. Before I insert my ticket, I ask Gregory, "I take it you haven't yet purchased a bus pass since you only arrived a few hours ago?"

"Oh, that's right. I forgot that you have to buy tickets ahead of time for the bus."

"I'll get your fare." I insert my bus ticket into the reader twice.

"Thanks. I'll pay you back." Gregory takes his wallet out of his pocket, but I push it away and my fingers graze against his skin. The contact sends tiny jolts of electricity through my body. He must feel it, too, since his gaze meets mine. I look away and start to head to the back of the bus, where I spot a few empty seats. I sit down next to an open window. The air in the bus is already quite stuffy. Gregory sits down next to me.

I want to hurry up and get this over with.

"So, we were talking about Madeline and how she's part of the reason why you're here."

"Pia, I know you thought that Madeline and I were having an affair. Again, I never had an affair with her. I never cheated on you with anyone. In hindsight, I can see how we must've looked when you showed up at my place. I guess I was hurt that you would even entertain the idea that I would betray you like that. It hurt that you didn't trust me."

He's good. I'll give him that. He's turning the tables to make me feel like I was wrong in thinking that he cheated on me. I'm tempted to lash out, but I decide to be patient and hear his whole "explanation"—if that's what he wants to call it.

"The truth is, Pia, you were partially right."

"Oh?"

"You were right that Madeline was interested in me and was trying to get me to sleep with her. But again, I swear I never did. I know this is going to be hard for you to believe at first, but I'm just going to cut to the chase. Francesca bribed Madeline to seduce me."

"What? I don't believe you." I start laughing.

"Pia, it's true."

"You really will think of anything, I swear, Gregory." I shake my head. "That's crazy! Why would Francesca do that?"

"I thought the same thing, too, when Madeline confessed to me, and I asked what Francesca's motives were. She said that Francesca wanted to break up you and me so you'd be available for her nephew, Lorenzo."

The blood drains from my face. Though it's so hot on the bus, I feel cold. Suddenly, Francesca's words come back to me. *"I have secretly hoped that he would fall in love with you. . . . I could not hope for a better woman for my son."*

Gregory continues. "I still had a hard time believing it—until Madeline played a tape for me. When she was at Signora Tesca's house to interview Francesca about her visit to Astoria as well as Giuliana's vast art collection, she forgot to turn off her recorder when they were done. There's no question the voice on the tape is Francesca's. She bribed Madeline not only to seduce me, but also to pay off an art dealer to discover me."

"Nathan Horowitz?"

"Yeah," Gregory says in a pained voice.

"I'm sorry, Gregory, but I'm really having a hard time with this. Why would Francesca want you to be discovered so badly that she'd bribe Nate?"

"I have the tape here. I knew you'd have a hard time believing me." Gregory pulls out of his backpack a mini recorder.

"I'm not saying I don't believe you, Gregory, but I don't trust

Madeline. You don't have to play the tape for me." I place my hand over his before he can push the "play" button on the recorder.

Gregory covers my hand with his. I want to wrest it free, but for some reason I don't.

"Pia, I'm positive this is Francesca. And I'm sure you would agree with me if you listened to it. I know you've become close to her and this is hard for you to hear. But I don't want there to be any doubt in your mind that this is Francesca. Can I play the tape?" Gregory looks into my eyes. I nod my head.

He removes his hand from on top of mine, and I pull it back onto my lap. He starts the recorder and raises the volume. I don't have to worry about the other passengers hearing since the traffic noise coming from the street is quite loud.

*"Madeline, I will pay you $25,000 to seduce Gregory and sleep with him. And I will pay you another $25,000 to use to bribe Nathan Horowitz to discover Gregory. Once Gregory is preoccupied with fame, he will be too busy for Pia. And once he sleeps with you, that will seal the end of their relationship."*

"That's enough. I don't want to hear any more." Gregory stops the recorder. I can't believe Francesca would go to such lengths to break up Gregory and me. I was actually starting to feel like I could understand her, especially after she opened up to me about her past. I've been a fool.

"Why did Madeline fess up?" I ask Gregory.

"She claimed that it was the right thing to do, but I didn't believe her. My guess is that something must've happened between Madeline and Francesca. This was probably Madeline's way of getting back at her."

"Yeah, I can totally see that, Gregory."

"I still have a hard time wrapping my head around why Francesca took such extreme measures to try and pave the road between you and Lorenzo. Granted, he is Francesca's nephew, but she hadn't even met him until she came to Astoria. It's not like they were close. She never even breathed a word about him to me."

I hesitate. What's the matter with me? It's ridiculous that I still feel some sense of loyalty to the woman who intentionally set out to destroy my life. My anger returns. Although I had promised Francesca that I wouldn't tell her secret to anyone, Gregory needs to know the entire truth.

"Actually, Gregory, Lorenzo isn't Francesca's nephew. He's her son."

"What?"

"It's true. She told me not long after I came to Rome. He was part of the reason why she was estranged from Signora Tesca."

I fill Gregory in on the whole story with Francesca, Signora Tesca, and their love for Dante, Lorenzo's father. By the end of the story, we've reached the stop for Via Appia Antica. I glance at my watch. Lorenzo is probably still tied up with his friend. Gregory gets up and follows me off the bus. I guess he's forgotten that he was supposed to just be with me during our bus trip. But I know our discussion isn't over, so I don't object to his getting off with me. Once we descend, we make our way toward the picnic grounds. Gregory looks lost in thought and doesn't seem to be paying much attention to where we're going.

"Okay, now that makes more sense, why she wanted to set up her son, but why you? I mean, don't get me wrong. I already know what a fantastic woman you are." Gregory looks at me with that look he's always given me, and suddenly, I know. He's always loved me, long before I even knew I loved him. But I've ruined it all.

"Francesca told me she's come to admire me and she couldn't think of a better woman for Lorenzo."

"Wait a second. She's told you this already. So—" Gregory's voice trails off as we both realize what I've just said. I completely wasn't thinking. Tears fill his eyes. I hate myself. I hate myself for not believing in his love for me, for not trusting him, for hurting him now.

"I'm sorry, Gregory," I say through choked sobs. "I really did think you cheated on me with Madeline. I missed you terribly, too, the first few weeks I was here. Lorenzo kept me distracted by taking me sightseeing, and I kept him preoccupied after he learned the truth about Francesca's being his mother."

"How long have you two been seeing each other?"

"A little over a month, but I've only agreed to see him more seriously in the past week."

"Gee. *That* makes me feel better."

"I'm sorry, Gregory."

We reach the picnic grounds, but I don't want to sit down even though I feel drained from all that I've just learned. My head is spinning. How could Francesca do this to us? And she claimed she cared about Gregory. She only cares about herself.

"So what are you going to do now that you know the truth?"

"I'll have to confront Francesca, of course, and I can't stay with her anymore. I'll probably book the next flight back to California."

"I meant what are you going to do about Lorenzo?"

"I don't know. He's going to be so upset to hear about what Francesca did. First, the woman he thinks is his mother dies, then he learns that his aunt is really his mother and gave him up for adoption, not once but twice. And on top of that, she bribed someone to make it easier for him and me to get together. He'll never want to talk to her again."

"Pia, you're avoiding the question. You know what I'm asking. Are you still going to continue to see Lorenzo?"

I look at Gregory then glance away.

"I can't think about this right now. It's too much. Everything you've just laid on me. I've hurt you. I don't want to hurt someone else again. Lorenzo's already been through so much."

"So have I, Pia. I lost the love of my life, and all because of a crazy actress's meddling. And to think, I agreed to paint her portrait out of a sense of obligation and respect toward her. From day one, Pia, your instincts about Francesca were right on target. I just wish you had trusted me more instead of believing so readily that I had cheated on you." Gregory curls his hands into fists and turns his back toward me. I hear him exhale deeply.

"There was more to it than just my thinking you were unfaithful, Gregory. You were right when you told me that day that I was running and that I was afraid of fully committing to you. I was afraid of losing you the way I lost Erica. I was also worried because ever since you were discovered, you had so little time for me. I thought that would be the norm, and I couldn't deal with it."

"You didn't give me much of a chance, Pia. I know I should have made more time for you, and I was planning on it, but I guess that doesn't matter now. I'm too late. And so much for my being 'discovered.' " Gregory makes quotation marks with his fingers when he says "discovered."

"The only reason I was discovered is that Madeline bribed Nathan. No wonder there was a low turnout at my second show. I wouldn't be surprised if Madeline was also mad that I had rejected her, and she made sure her friends from the art world didn't show up. I don't know what I was thinking."

"Gregory, stop that. You are talented. Even if Madeline and Nathan persuaded their friends to come to your show, they didn't pay them off to buy your paintings."

"As far as I know." Gregory lets out an exasperated laugh.

"Come on, Gregory. You can't let this make you insecure. I've always believed in you as an artist, and I still do."

"But you don't believe in us anymore, do you?"

I turn my head to the side, taking in the beautiful cypress and pine trees that line the Via Appia Antica. Fragments of tombs and statues are strewn across the fields, and in the background, the Alban hills make for a stunning panorama. Francesca was right. This is a romantic place to have a picnic. But here I am, breaking up with Gregory a second time.

"Pia, I know you still care about me. Don't go back to California. My return ticket is for the day after tomorrow. Come back with me to New York. Let's start all over."

"I do care about you, Gregory, but that doesn't mean that we should get back together. I also care about Lorenzo. I'm sorry, but I can't give you an answer now. My mind is still reeling from all that you've told me. I need to think."

"Okay. I'll be staying at the Hotel Trevi, right by the Trevi Fountain." Gregory takes out a Post-it pad from his backpack and jots down the hotel's name.

I take the Post-it and place it in my purse.

"I'll get going. I know you have plans."

I can tell by the way Gregory says this that he's figured out my plans are with Lorenzo. The hurt that was in his eyes earlier when he learned we were dating is back.

"Oh! I almost forgot your laptop bag. Here you go. Will you be all right carrying that back by yourself?"

"Yes, thanks. My picnic basket will be emptier after I eat so I'll be fine."

"I guess bye for now."

"Bye."

Gregory heads back in the direction of the bus stop. I watch him for a little while. He's staring down at the ground while he walks; both of his hands are in his pockets. Finally, I turn around and walk. I don't pay attention to where I'm going. I just keep walking. But soon the weight of the picnic basket and my laptop bag are too much. I stop. No one is around. I've strayed quite far from the picnic grounds. I take out of my picnic basket a bed sheet and lay it on the ground. I sit down and take out one of the bottles of wine I brought. I'm extremely thirsty and realize I should've also packed water. After opening the wine bottle, I fill the plastic cup I brought and down it in one huge gulp. I pour another cup. Instead of unwrapping the muffuletta, I just take one of the figs and eat that. My stomach has been doing somersaults since I saw Gregory. The thought of eating something heavier repulses me right now. I can barely even eat the fig.

Taking in a few deep breaths, I realize this is the first time I've been alone outdoors in weeks. Lorenzo has been by my side almost every day since we started our sightseeing excursions. And when he was busy, Francesca would take me out to eat or to go shopping. I close my eyes and enjoy the serenity here. But it doesn't last. My cell phone rings. About two weeks ago, I reinstated the international plan and had my cell phone activated. It was easier for when Lorenzo wasn't picking me up at Francesca's, and we were meeting in some crowded part of Rome. My cell phone screen shows Lorenzo's name.

"Hey." My voice sounds flat.

"Pia, I'm finally leaving my friend's apartment now. I'll hop into a cab and meet you at the Via Appia Antica. I should be there within the hour, depending on traffic, since everyone is leaving work now for their midday meals."

"That's fine. Take your time. I haven't even begun eating."

"Really? I thought you were going to eat without me. What have you been doing all this time?"

"I've just been walking around and enjoying the scenery. I

couldn't wait to open the wine. I got thirsty and forgot to bring water. But don't worry, there's still plenty of wine for you."

"I wasn't worried. I have yet to see you drunk!" Lorenzo laughs.

"Well, I'll see you soon. *Ciao!*" I can't get off the phone soon enough.

"I can't wait!" Lorenzo says before he hangs up.

Fortunately, Lorenzo was out on the street so I'm certain with all the background noise he wasn't able to detect my less-than-enthusiastic responses. Part of me was hoping that he would've still been held up with his friend at the hospital. I should have canceled on him, but then he'd know something wasn't right. I just want some more time alone before I tell him what Gregory told me. Perhaps it can wait until tomorrow. Maybe for one more afternoon, I can pretend everything is fine.

And on that last thought, I pour another cup of wine. Lorenzo might finally get to see me drunk after all.

By the time Lorenzo arrived, I had a good buzz going. He found it amusing, and it made it easier for me to joke. He wasn't able to tell that something was bothering me. He loved the muffuletta, and I ate some before all my drinking made me sick. After eating, we headed over to the catacombs.

The Roman catacombs lie underneath the Via Appia Antica, along either side. They date as far back as the second century. Many examples of early Christian art from before AD 400 can be found in the catacombs. Jewish art is also present. Lorenzo tells me there are at least forty catacombs, and some have been discovered only in recent decades. Ancient Romans were adhering to the laws of their day that required the dead to be buried underground and far from the city's perimeters. It was long believed that the creation of the catacombs stemmed from Christian persecution. But historians later discovered the underground cemeteries came about because of Rome's edicts. Since a large number of saints were buried in the catacombs, they also became shrines and were popular for pilgrimages.

We decide to visit first the Catacombs of San Callisto, which is the oldest and best preserved of the catacombs. Many popes are buried here as well as martyrs, along with other Christians. Named for deacon Calixtus, who was appointed by the pope in the third century to supervise the cemetery, the Catacombs of San Callisto became the official cemetery of the Church of Rome.

Luckily for Lorenzo's quick thinking, he asked the friar at the entrance to the catacomb if we could leave our picnic basket and my laptop with him. Normally, I'd be nervous about leaving my laptop with a total stranger, but the fact that he's a man of the cloth allays my anxieties. Lorenzo informs me that there will be more friars who act as guides inside the Catacombs of San Callisto. The guided tour is included with the admission price.

As we enter the narrow passageway of the Catacombs of San Callisto, I'm glad I didn't take the picnic basket and my laptop. A friar soon greets us in English. As he begins our tour, he tells us that these catacombs stretch out on four different levels. He goes on to explain that the rooms and passageways are made out of volcanic tufa. The dead were laid in niches, also known as loculi, which could hold two or three bodies.

The air is cool, as you would expect it to be beneath the ground, but the narrow passageways can make one feel claustrophobic. The air smells like a combination of sulphur and dirt. We enter a gallery with Early Christian frescoes. I'm amazed that I'm looking at artwork that dates back centuries, and it almost manages to make me forget Gregory's visit. I haven't decided yet if I will tell Lorenzo this afternoon that Gregory is in Rome or if I will wait until tomorrow. I know the longer I put off telling him, the harder it will be. There's also the issue with Francesca. I don't think I can put on an act like I'm doing with Lorenzo and wait to have my confrontation with her.

We move on to the Crypt of the Popes, where many of the first popes were buried. It is one of the most ancient areas in the catacombs, along with the Crypt of Santa Cecilia, which we're making our way over to now. I'm disappointed to learn from our friar guide that Santa Cecilia's body no longer rests in this crypt. After her body was discovered in the Catacombs of San Callisto in AD 820, her remains were moved to the church named in honor of her in Trastevere, which is the site where she was martyred.

After we visit the Catacombs of San Callisto, we head over to the Catacombs of Domitilla, the largest in Rome. Once we're done exploring these catacombs, we decide to go back above ground and visit the Church of Domine Quo Vadis, where Christ appeared to Peter. As soon as we enter, I go and sit down in one of the pews.

"Tired, huh?" Lorenzo joins me.

"It's been a long day."

"Is everything all right, Pia?"

"Why do you ask?"

"You just don't seem yourself, and then drinking all of that wine before I even got here and before you ate. That's not like you."

"Something happened today. I'm still rattled, and I wasn't sure if I wanted to tell you this afternoon or tomorrow. But I might as well tell you now. Gregory is here."

"In Rome?"

"Yes. I ran into him when I was leaving Francesca's. He told me he had to talk to me and was quite insistent."

"Where is he now?"

"He's staying at one of the hotels by the Trevi Fountain."

"What did he want?"

"This is going to be a shock, Lorenzo. He told me that Madeline Drabinski confessed to him that Francesca bribed her to try and sleep with him so that I'd break up with him to pave the way for you and me."

"That's preposterous! Boy, I guess the guy will do anything to get you back." Lorenzo's voice rises, causing a few people who are kneeling in front of us in prayer to cast stern glances in his direction.

"Let's go outside so we can talk more easily," he whispers.

The frankincense of the church along with all the wine I had to drink earlier is making me feel woozy. As soon as we step outside, I take a few deep breaths. We walk slowly along the Appian Way.

"Francesca really did bribe Madeline, Lorenzo. Madeline had it all on tape. Gregory played it for me, and there's no mistaking Francesca's voice. She also had Madeline bribe Nathan Horowitz to discover Gregory, again, so that he'd be too busy for me and that would create a wedge between us."

"I see Francesca hasn't learned from her past mistakes. She's wrecking people's lives again just as she did with my parents all those years ago." Lorenzo pinches the corners of his eyes shut and lets out a long sigh.

"I'm sorry to have to break this to you after everything you've been through recently."

"So you said she bribed Madeline to 'try and sleep with Gregory.' Does that mean he's still professing to you he didn't?"

I nod my head.

"You believe him now, however."

"Lorenzo, you said it yourself that I didn't actually catch Gregory and Madeline in the act of making love. And now with this revelation, everything makes sense."

"How so?"

"Gregory couldn't understand why Francesca would go to such lengths in hopes of you and me dating. But that was before he knew that you're her son. She also admitted to me just the other day that she'd secretly hoped we would get together. She told me she's come to respect and admire me and couldn't think of a better woman for you. She was manipulating all of us, Lorenzo. I'm sure as your mother she thought she was doing what was best for her son."

"I'm sure, just the way she thought it was best to have nuns raise me and then give me to her sister so that her acting career wouldn't be jeopardized." Lorenzo's voice sounds very bitter.

"The more I think about it, the more it becomes clear. She was also trying to convince me shortly after I arrived here that Gregory wasn't the type to commit; she said as long as she'd known him, he had gotten bored easily. She also assured me I would never see him again."

"I'm sorry on her behalf, Pia. I know I'm not the one who should be apologizing, but unfortunately, I am related to her."

"More than anything else, I'm disappointed in her. I was really beginning to grow fond of her."

"Don't lose sleep over her. She's not worth it."

"Does this mean you're not going to try and forge a relationship with her, Lorenzo?"

"I can't trust her. And besides, I have my own life, and so does she. Maybe if I had been younger when I found out the truth, but then again, I would've been more susceptible to her manipulative ways then. No, I think it's better I cut all ties with her."

Though I'm mad at Francesca, I can't help feeling sad that

Lorenzo won't try to have some sort of relationship with her. She is after all his mother.

"So I take it Gregory wants you back."

I can't look at Lorenzo. I should say something, but I can't.

Suddenly, Lorenzo stops and picks my chin up with his hands, forcing me to meet his gaze. I start sobbing. He hugs me to him.

"Shhh. It's okay. I've always known, Pia, you weren't crazy about me the way you are about him."

"I did—I do—care about you. I don't want to hurt you," I cry into his chest.

"I know you don't, Pia. But I also want you to do what will make you happy. Your staying with me to avoid hurting me doesn't help either of us, now does it?"

"You've been nothing but kind and generous with me. I'll never forget that."

"Good. I want you to only have the best memories of me."

His being so magnanimous toward me just makes me cry even harder.

"Listen to me. I'm going to hail a cab to take you back to the Trevi Fountain. Go to Gregory. Don't waste any more time. And don't worry about me. I'll be fine."

"We can share a cab." I can't believe I've just said that, but I feel horrible leaving him alone.

"Pia, I'll be fine."

I nod my head. We walk toward the entrance of the Via Appia Antica. Lorenzo holds my hand. A few empty cabs line the curb. He walks over to one of them, tells the driver my destination, and pays him.

"No, Lorenzo. I can't let you do that."

"Please, Pia. Let me do this last thing for you."

I know it's no use arguing. I'd just make an already awkward moment worse.

I hug him, and he hugs me back. He whispers into my ear, "Be happy."

And with that he walks briskly away, never turning back once.

# ❧ 30 ❧

# Francesca

My favorite time of the day in Rome is just as the sun is setting. This is when I usually like to take my *passeggiata*. Tonight I want to walk by the Colosseum, so Edgardo and I drive over since it is quite far from my apartment. We park and then take our stroll. The sun casts long shadows over the Colosseum. Closing my eyes, I hear the shouts from the spectators of long ago when gladiators fought. As many as fifty thousand spectators sat in this massive amphitheater. All the history that surrounds Rome is what I love about her so much.

Rocco could not join me tonight. He had a business dinner. I have come to appreciate his companionship these past few weeks. And dare I say it? My feelings for him have grown. It has been so long since I felt this way for a man, probably not since Dante. But this is different. After I told him the other night the truth about Lorenzo's being my son and what I had done to Giuliana, he took my hands in his and told me it was all right. He truly cares about me.

My days in Rome are coming to a close. Soon, Pia will be done with our interviews for my autobiography, and it will be time for me to return to my villa in Taormina, Sicily. And of course, Rocco will return to New York and his jewelry shop. I never met a man who loves jewels almost as much as I do. But in his case, he loves selling them, while I love acquiring them.

I know I will miss him when he returns home. But I have come to accept that I simply do not have luck when it comes to love. Maybe that was my price for fame and a wonderful acting career.

Sighing, I walk away from the Colosseum. I glance over my shoulder and see Edgardo keeping his distance behind me. This is the closest I can get to being alone outdoors. Edgardo lightly nods his head in my direction. I return the nod then turn around.

The thought of losing Rocco is not all that is making me sad tonight. Lorenzo and I will part ways as well. He has agreed to come visit me in Sicily for the holidays. I know I cannot press him for more of a relationship. He has spent his whole life without me, and I see now not much will change. But I am grateful that he finally knows the truth and has not shunned me altogether.

Edgardo joins me as we approach my car. The Colosseum is quite far from my apartment in Piazza Navona. He holds the door open for me before getting behind the steering wheel. My driver has left for his vacation, so Edgardo is doing double duty as my chauffeur. Thankfully, he leaves me to my thoughts as we ride back to my apartment in silence.

Once home, I head straight for the kitchen and make my favorite nonalcoholic drink. I pour Pellegrino water into a tall glass. Slicing a few cucumbers and strawberries, I throw them in with the Pellegrino. I also squeeze half a cup of lemon juice into my glass. If I am out of lemons, I then use limes or oranges. Sometimes, depending on my mood, I finish off the beverage with a few sprigs of mint.

I kick off my shoes and walk out onto the balcony. I am startled to see Pia leaning over the balcony's railing, gazing at Piazza Navona.

"Pia, I thought you would have still been out with Lorenzo."

"My plans changed."

She does not turn around when she says this. Something is wrong; I can sense it.

"Did you and Lorenzo have a fight?"

Finally, she turns around. Her eyes are red, and her mascara is smeared.

"Not really. I need to talk to you, Francesca."

"Of course. Let me make you one of these drinks." I turn to go, but Pia stops me.

"I don't need a drink."

"All right." I sit down on one of the chairs that accompany a dinette table on the terrace. Pia remains standing. She crosses her arms over her chest and then looks at me with the most hostile expression.

"I know what you did, Francesca."

My pulse begins to race. "What are you talking about, Pia?"

"I know how you bribed Madeline to seduce Gregory."

I swallow hard. "I see." I take a sip of my drink, hoping the raised glass conceals the flush that has spread over my face. Standing up, I walk over to the railing. As dusk approaches, the lights begin to come on around the city. Though it is a mild night, I feel a chill. I have made a mess of everything. Regret washes over me. I turn back around and look directly into Pia's eyes.

"I had my reasons," I say.

"So, you're not going to deny it?"

"I am many things, Pia, but I am not a coward."

"I also know how you paid Madeline to bribe Nathan Horowitz so he would discover Gregory. I know you wanted to break up Gregory and me so that I'd be free for Lorenzo." Pia claps her hands. "*Brava, La Sposa Pazza* gives another Oscar award–winning performance, probably the best of her life."

"Pia, please let me explain."

"Nothing you say can make me change my mind about your actions. I thought we had become friends. I actually started to think that the world had misjudged you and been harsh in their criticism, especially when they labeled you a bitch. But they were right. If only I had stuck by my initial thoughts and never trusted you, I would have been spared becoming another one of your victims. Instead, you made me doubt Gregory, the one person who truly loved me."

"Pia, your doubting Gregory was not solely my fault. You had your own reservations about the relationship. You were insecure in his feelings for you."

"That's true, but your convincing Madeline to try and seduce him only made me more insecure. How could you do that to me? I didn't do anything to you." Pia is crying.

"I am sorry. Honestly, I meant what I told you a few weeks ago that I did not think you and Gregory made a good match. I thought I was acting in your best interest and Lorenzo's. As his mother, I did not want him making the same mistakes in love that I had made in my life."

"Do you know how warped that sounds? How about trusting Lorenzo to make his own choices in life, whether they turn out to be mistakes or not. You profess to have acted out of interest in what was best for Lorenzo and me, but you were just doing what you have always done best—manipulate. You did it with your sister and Dante, and now you were trying to do it again."

"How did you find out about this? Did Madeline call you?"

"No. Gregory is here in Rome. He told me everything this morning."

"And Lorenzo? Does he know?"

Pia nods her head. A fresh round of tears erupts from her eyes. "We are no longer together."

Hmmm. How convenient, I cannot help but think. Her old lover comes running to Rome to save the day, and she dumps Lorenzo without a second thought, ruining all of my carefully made plans. And now she has the nerve to act like everything is my fault? Of course, Pia cannot see it my way or understand. She is not a mother who will sacrifice herself for the happiness and welfare of her children. Someday, she will understand. And someday, my anger toward her will also lessen. But right now, I am feeling a mother's fury over her son's being hurt.

"So you are going to run back to Gregory. You just used my son to forget about your old boyfriend and to have a companion in Rome."

"I did not use your son! You were all but begging me to let him take me sightseeing. I care about Lorenzo. He was the one to break it off."

"Naturally. He can tell you still have feelings for another man. He is not going to play second fiddle or wait for you to come around only to break his heart eventually."

"He is honorable, unlike you. He wants me to be happy above all else, and if that means letting me go, then that is what he felt he needed to do."

Though I have given up on trying to convince Pia to see I was only doing what I thought was best for my son, I am losing the energy to continue being mean toward her. I have always resorted to acting the "bitch," as the media has called me, when I feel cornered. And Pia has most certainly cornered me. I do not want her to see that I am dying on the inside. For once again, I have hurt those I love. Old age is making me soft.

Standing up, I deliver my last blow before I lose all emotional control.

"I suppose I was wrong about you, Pia. My son deserves a better woman than you." And with that I quickly walk back inside, heading toward my bedroom.

Edgardo looks up from the couch, where he is seated watching TV. Tears race down my face. Edgardo begins to rise, but I hold my hand up, imploring him to back off. As I enter my bedroom, I notice Pia's luggage is standing outside the door to her room down the corridor. Of course she is leaving. There is no way she could or would stay here now after everything.

Slamming my bedroom door shut behind me, I walk to my bed and collapse. I have always sensed that I was meant to be alone, but now that reality is ringing truer than ever. I do not know why I keep alienating the ones I love by my manipulative behavior. When I was younger, I could blame it on my youth. But I am older now and should have learned from my past mistakes. Perhaps I do not know how to be any other way? I have become accustomed to being alone and not depending on others—that is, except for the adoration of my fans. Maybe that is why I did not always feel so compelled to hold on to the affection of those closest to me? I had the love of thousands of admirers, and sadly, that was what I craved most. The love of strangers was enough for me when it should have been the love of my family and friends who had proven their loyalty to me.

These last few months, I was finally making deeper connections: Giuliana, Lorenzo, Pia. But I have thrown it all away. The only one left is Rocco, and soon enough, he, too, will want nothing to do with me. Although he did not care about what I had done to Giuliana and Dante all those years ago, he cannot be that understanding forever. I am sure he will discover some other part of my character that he finds repulsive and unforgivable, probably when he learns what I did to Pia and Gregory, not to mention my own son. I should have stayed in Sicily and never gone to Astoria. If I had, I would not have hurt them or be suffering the pain I am in now. With this last thought, I curl into a ball and cry myself to sleep.

# ❧ 31 ❧

# Pia

The taxi is driving through the cobblestone streets of Piazza Navona, taking me to the Hotel Trevi, where Gregory is staying. In the weeks since I've arrived in Rome, this is the first time that I feel I am truly seeing her. I let my eyes linger on the famous landmarks we pass—Fontana dei Quattro Fiumi, Palazzo Pamphilj, Palazzo Madama, Colonna di Marco Aurelio—and my heart races in anticipation of seeing Gregory.

As I left Francesca's apartment, Edgardo had offered to drive me to where I was going. I could tell he felt bad for me. He must have overheard some, if not all, of my argument with Francesca. I thanked him, but told him I had called a cab already.

Though Francesca had the last word in our argument, I don't care. Her controlling nature demands that she always have the last word in any matter. I am sad that our friendship is over, but more than anything, I'm hurt by her actions. Besides, I suspected she wouldn't give me the chance to tell her everything I wanted to express. So I had written a letter as soon as I arrived at her place after leaving Lorenzo. In it, I told her that after what had happened I could not finish writing her autobiography. I did not want to go straight to Gregory's hotel because I wanted to pack my belongings and confront Francesca. I didn't want that ugliness hanging over me. When I see Gregory, I just want to focus on us.

The cab driver pulls up in front of the Hotel Trevi. After I tip him generously, he offers to take my luggage up to the hotel's lobby, but I tell him I'll be fine. Gregory is expecting me. I called him earlier to let him know that I wanted to talk. I was afraid that maybe he'd changed his mind and would leave Rome without telling me. There I go again letting my insecurity get the better of me.

If I had stayed at a hotel instead of staying at Francesca's home, I would have chosen the Hotel Trevi. I had read about it in my guidebook on the flight over from New York. Once a sixteenth-century *palazzo,* the Hotel Trevi is just steps away from the Trevi Fountain. It is also near the Spanish Steps and Via Veneto.

I approach Gregory's room on the second floor. Before I knock, I pull out my compact, ensuring my makeup is in place. Taking a deep breath, I knock on the door. Gregory doesn't even ask who it is, and within a second of my knocking, he's opened the door.

"Hey!"

Though Gregory is doing his best to sound nonchalant, I detect a hint of nerves in his voice as well as in his eyes.

"Hi."

"Come in—unless you'd feel more comfortable talking in the lobby or we could even go outside."

"No, that's okay. Here is fine. It might be too noisy outside anyway. Now that most of the Romans are back from their vacations, it's even noisier than it's been the past few weeks."

"True."

Gregory steps back and motions with his hand for me to enter his room. I can't help noticing his face turn serious when he sees my luggage.

"Are you leaving Rome today?" He points to my luggage.

"I'll get to that in a moment."

"Okay. Would you like something to drink? I don't have anything here, but I can call down for room service. Coffee, beer?"

"No, I'm fine. But thanks."

I sit down on the chair that's at the desk in the corner. The room is decorated tastefully with modern furniture and accents.

"The rooms are really nice here."

"Yeah, I like them. I wasn't expecting the modern furnishings. I figured they would have a Renaissance or more Roman feel to them, know what I mean?"

I nod my head. Gregory sits on the edge of the bed. He looks to either side of the room as if he's taking it in for the first time.

"So, I confronted Francesca a little while ago."

"How did it go?"

"Not well, of course."

"Did she try to deny it?"

"No, she didn't. She was proud to tell me that she might be many things but not a coward."

"Naturally." Gregory grins.

"She did try to explain to me that she honestly always thought you and I were not a good match for each other."

"She said that?" Gregory frowns. He curls his hands into fists.

"Francesca had also said this to me weeks ago when she was trying to console me over our relationship's ending. She brought it up again to try and make it seem like her bribes were meant to protect me since we weren't right for each other. She also used the whole 'I was doing what I thought was best for my son.' But I let her have it."

"I'm sure you did." Gregory laughs. "I wish I had been there."

"Well, she didn't let me rejoice in my triumph over her—if you can call it that—for long. In fact, the discussion was quite short. She went from trying to get me to understand to being a bitch. Francesca accused me of using her son, and then she said she was wrong about me and that Lorenzo deserves a better woman than me. She stormed off after that. And I left her apartment."

"The spoiled diva threw a tantrum instead of owning up to her sins."

"Well, she did own up to them in her own way, and she did apologize."

"But it was a halfhearted attempt."

"I know." I can't disguise the sadness in my voice.

"I'm sorry, Pia. I know you were beginning to grow fond of her."

"I'm disappointed in her. That's all. And once again, she's hurt those closest to her—Lorenzo." My voice trails off as I remember how sad he looked when I left him at the Via Appia Antica.

"Did you tell him?"

I nod my head. I can't talk at the moment. Having seen Lorenzo in pain and knowing I was the cause of it is too much for me to bear.

"Take your time. Do you want to use the bathroom?"

I shake my head no. Gregory gets up and walks over to the window, giving me time to compose myself.

"I hurt him so bad, Gregory."

Gregory turns around, surprise registering on his face.

"You were just delivering the news to him, Pia. You're not the one who used him and manipulated his life. Francesca's all guilty there."

"You don't understand, Gregory. He let me go."

"He let you go?"

"Lorenzo could tell I was still in love with you, but I didn't want to break his heart. He told me that even when we were together, he knew I still had feelings for you. He said that because he truly cares about me he wants me to be happy." I start sobbing, feeling guilty all over again.

Gregory comes to my side and rubs my back.

"Shhh! It's okay. You're a good person. But you know staying with him would have done more harm in the end, right? He would've always sensed you weren't giving yourself fully to him, and you wouldn't have been happy."

"I know. I just feel so bad. He's a good person, too, and has been through so much, especially lately."

Gregory leaves my side and goes to the bathroom. He comes back with a few tissues and hands them to me.

"Thanks." I blow my nose.

We're both quiet for a while. I'm still amazed at how patient Gregory has always been. Instead of urging me to go on, he just waits until I'm ready to do so.

"I left Francesca a letter and told her I couldn't continue working on her autobiography."

"How do you feel about that? I know how excited you were when she gave you that opportunity."

"I don't care. Gregory, being in Rome has made me realize a lot about myself. I accused you of being so focused on your painting once you were discovered, but I wasn't that different. That day at your apartment when I thought you and Madeline were together, I wasn't lying when I told you that I had used you to score an interview with Francesca. There is some truth to that. I'm sorry. I feel really horrible about it now. But I was also attracted to you. I was drawn to you from that first night when I met you in front of Signora Tesca's house. Yet I also knew that you would be my ticket for gaining access to Francesca. I was quite opportunistic. Now, I don't even care about my writing career or where it will go."

"Thank you for your honesty, Pia. I admit it. When you told me that day at my place that you had used me to get to Francesca, it stung. But I knew anger was making you say those words, too. I don't blame you for hoping I could help you get an interview with Francesca. I just see that as your being motivated and going after what you want in life. I commend you for it. So stop beating yourself up about it."

"Someone has to. You're not beating me up. Lorenzo didn't beat me up."

"It's because we care about you, and we know you're not a calculating person."

"Rome has also made me see that I need to go back home to California and fully deal with losing my sister. I never talked to a counselor or anyone about it until I met you. I don't want to run anymore as I've been doing, as you pointed out to me in New York."

"I'm sorry about that, Pia."

"No, I'm glad you told me that, because it was true. When I left California, I didn't know if I ever wanted to return. But these past few weeks, I have finally been missing it and my family. While I grew to love Astoria and being with my aunt, my true home is the West Coast. And interning at *Profile* made me all the more aware that I'm not cut out to work for a cutthroat magazine. Manhattan is great, don't get me wrong, but I could never see myself living there."

"So you've already decided you're definitely going back to California?" Gregory is seated on the bed again, but this time he's on the side, facing away from me.

"Yes, I have decided to return home."

"I guess Lorenzo was wrong when he thought you were still in love with me."

"I am still in love with you."

Gregory looks up at me.

"Then why have you chosen to go back to California?"

"I was hoping that somehow I could convince you to spend some time with me on my home turf. You know I could take you around, like you did with me in Long Island City and Manhattan. Show you more of who I am and where I come from. And then maybe we can figure out what's next."

As I say all of this, I keep my head turned away from Gregory. I've grabbed the pen on the desk and have been doodling aimlessly. I'm so absorbed and frightened of Gregory's reaction that I haven't noticed he's left the bed and is standing behind me until I feel his arms cross my chest. As I close my eyes, tears escape once again, but this time they're tears of relief. For I know without Gregory's speaking what his answer is.

I rise from my chair. Gregory turns me around to face him and kisses me, softly at first, then urgently. I start laughing, and so does he, but I also see that he's crying, too.

"Please forgive me for not trusting you and for running away from you," I say as I hold Gregory's face in my hands and look into his eyes.

"Only if you swear to never do that again."

"I swear."

"I love you, Pia. I've never loved anyone the way I love you."

"I know. I'm sorry it took me so long to believe it. I love you, too. I never stopped loving you."

"So I guess I'll be booking the next flight to California."

"Actually, I was hoping that we could stay a few more days in Rome. I can't tell you how many times I wished you were with me when I was visiting the sites."

"That's a great idea."

"I guess it's okay if I stay here in your room, then?"

"Do you even have to ask?"

I giggle as Gregory lifts me in his arms and drops me on his bed. We make love over and over again until I notice the sun has set and it's dark outside. Gregory soon falls asleep beside me. I stare at him for a long time, making sure this is real. A flash of light from the window catches my attention. I walk over and look out. Fireworks are going off over the Trevi Fountain, which is all lit up. I can't decide if I like the view of the fountain more in the day or at night. Suddenly, I remember the three wishes I made at the Trevi Fountain shortly after arriving in Rome. I wished that I would return to Rome, see my sister Erica someday in heaven, and see Gregory again. I didn't even care in that moment that I thought he had cheated on me or if we would ever get together again. I just knew I wanted to see him at least one more time. Maybe part of me did always know deep down that he hadn't betrayed me. I was too afraid of the powerful feelings I had for him and that, like Erica, I'd lose him, too.

Before I leave the window, I send another wish out toward the Trevi Fountain. This time, I wish that nothing ever separates us again.

# EPILOGUE

## Pia

*Dear Pia,*
*Congratulations on the* Profile *article! Colin*
*Cohen sent me copies of the issue. I was very pleased*
*with the article. Thank you so much for honoring*
*your word and not revealing the personal details of*
*Lorenzo's true parentage in the piece. I wanted to*
*also thank you for casting me in such a positive light,*
*especially after what transpired between us.*

*Once again, Pia, I am truly sorry for the pain I*
*caused you and Gregory. Lorenzo is not talking to*
*me, but I have only myself to blame for that. I hope*
*that one day you both can forgive me, and I am*
*being sincere now when I say that I did admire and*
*respect you. I still do. That last day in Rome, I did*
*not mean what I said to you about my son deserving*
*a better woman. I was ashamed over my actions, and*
*I did what I often do, I lashed out unjustly.*

*There are two possessions of mine I wanted you*
*to have. One is enclosed in this package, and the*
*other Gregory will be delivering himself. He had no*
*idea I would be giving you this other possession. But*
*I thought it fitting if he delivered it himself. You'll*
*understand why when you see it. I hope you enjoy*

> *both gifts, and I wish you the happiness that seems*
> *to have always eluded my own life. I have only*
> *learned recently what it truly is like to be happy.*
> *Francesca*

Six months have passed since I left Rome. After spending three months with me in California, Gregory decided to make the move to California permanent. We're renting an apartment right on the beach in Carlsbad. Gregory found a new art dealer to work with, and he'll be having shows both in New York and L.A.

I've been in therapy since returning home, and I finally feel like I'm starting to heal from losing Erica. The beach doesn't haunt me anymore. Instead, I choose to remember all the happy times I shared with Erica and my family growing up on the beach. My mother is doing better, too. We all are. I could tell my family was happy to hear that I had decided to come back home. Now I can't believe I even entertained thoughts of moving to New York for good. And to put a lid on any doubts that might have resurfaced, when I was taking my walk along the beach early this morning, I spotted a seal. Of course I was immediately taken back to when Erica and I were children and had taken such pleasure at seeing the seals. I knew this was a sign that I'd made the right choice.

Zia has agreed to visit us in the summer. She's finally going to take a vacation and close the shop for the entire month of August. Mom said Zia's never taken a vacation in the twenty-three years she's owned her bakery. Gregory and I are planning on spending Christmas in New York later this year. Connie and Lou got engaged while we were in Rome, and Gregory is going to be Lou's best man. Zia told me that Connie is going to be wearing the knock-off of the gown that Francesca Donata wore in *La Sposa Pazza*—the same gown I was admiring that day shortly after I'd arrived in Astoria. I'm a bit surprised since I pictured Connie in a more daring, alternative wedding dress. But I guess when it comes to a bride's special day, many girls still long just to be the traditional princess in white.

With that last thought, I look at the gift that was enclosed in Francesca's package along with her letter. It's the beautiful jeweled hair comb Francesca was wearing when we had lunch at Trattoria

L'incontro in Astoria. She must've noticed how I was constantly eyeing the comb while we were eating. I take the comb out of its velvet-lined case and insert it into the side of my hair. It looks dazzling, but thankfully, I don't feel any different wearing a former prized possession of Francesca Donata's. Though I let go of my anger toward Francesca months ago, I don't want to keep the comb. Taking it out of my hair, I decide to send it instead to Olivia DeLuca. I'll even suggest to her in my note that she may want to give it to Connie as her "borrowed" item to wear on her wedding day. It'll be perfect since Connie will be wearing the knockoff of the gown Francesca wore in her film, and now she'll have a piece of jewelry that actually belonged to her. I'm sure Olivia won't want to give the comb to Connie permanently. She's still just as obsessed with Francesca.

"I'm home!" Gregory shouts as he stumbles through the door with a large wrapped board.

"Hey! You'll never guess who I heard from." I run over and kiss him. Gregory lowers the bulky item he's carrying.

"Francesca."

"How did you know?"

"She called me last week when I was in New York and asked me to deliver this to you. She also told me you'd be receiving a letter and package from her today."

"And you're only telling me this now?"

"You'll see why I waited when you open it up."

"So you know what this is?"

Gregory turns his back toward me so that I can't read his expression.

"Secrets! I thought we swore to tell the truth above all."

"Hey! I'm not lying about anything. Just open this already. I killed myself getting this up here."

I rip open the brown paper covering the board and gasp when I see my own face staring back at me.

"My nude portrait! I don't understand."

"After you got upset with me, on the night of my first show, I had decided I wasn't going to sell it anymore. But that was before I knew that someone had already paid cash for it earlier in the night, during the show. Nathan Horowitz wouldn't tell me who the buyer was, and he insisted he couldn't get the painting back. He said that would ruin my reputation as an artist, and I'd be finished, not to mention that his name as a dealer would get run through the muck as well. I was going to tell you, but then we got into our fight and broke up."

"And you haven't thought to tell me since we got back together?"

"You hadn't brought up the painting, and honestly, it escaped my mind. I've been so focused on moving here and building our life together. I guess the couple of times I thought about it, I was afraid it was going to bring up mixed feelings for you. I'm sorry. When Francesca called me last week, I almost hung up on her, but not before I gave her a piece of my mind for breaking us up. She begged me not to hang up and told me she had something important to tell me about you. Of course, she hooked me. Francesca revealed that she was the buyer of your portrait. She said she really wanted you to have it. So she had asked Signora Tesca's butler Carlo to give me the painting. Francesca had never gotten around to having it shipped to her home in Italy. She even instructed Carlo to give me a check for shipping the painting to California. I asked her why she bought the painting if now she was giving it away. Francesca said the look in your eyes in your portrait reminded her of a time in her life when she had that same expression. She immediately fell in love with the painting and wanted also to help me out as a new artist, but didn't want me to know she was the buyer. Francesca said she no longer needs the painting to remind her of that time in her life because she's recaptured that feeling."

"She's so weird." I shake my head.

"Are you ready for what she told me next?"

"I'm afraid to ask."

"Let me show you since I guess you haven't been out today."

Gregory pulls out a magazine from one of the pockets in his cargo pants and hands it to me. It's a copy of *Starstruck,* a trashy tabloid. The headline screams, *"CRAZY BRIDE FINALLY TIES THE KNOT!"*

"And you believe this?"

"Francesca told me herself before I even saw the tabloids in the supermarket. Not long after we left Rome, Rocco proposed to her. They got married in the Italian Alps."

"I'm shocked! I mean, I know Rocco was crazy about her, but I'm shocked that Francesca finally went through with a wedding. And I can't believe she's managed to keep it a secret for six months, not to mention that you were able to keep it from me for a week!"

"That's only because I was dying to surprise you with your painting. If I had told you I found out she and Rocco got hitched, you would've wanted to know how I had learned. And I couldn't say I'd spoken to Francesca without your getting suspicious. I'm sure the rest of the world is as shocked as you are over her recent nuptials. Anyway, that's what she must've been alluding to when she said she no longer needed the portrait of you to remind her of a time when she had that look. Your portrait must've reminded her of when she was young and in love with Lorenzo's father Dante. As you said, she never really forgot him—until Rocco. Who would think that a down-to-earth small businessman from Astoria would finally be the one to get *La Sposa Pazza* to the altar?"

I remember the last lines in Francesca's letter about how she only recently discovered what it's like to be truly happy. Even when she was with Dante, she was never really content. She'd been too addicted to fame to give it up and be with the man she loved.

I had felt sad to read in her letter that Lorenzo is no longer talking to her. Of course, that came as no surprise to me, but it still saddens me to think they were reunited only to be separated again. I haven't heard from Lorenzo since the day we broke up. Connie told me she has seen him at Signora Tesca's house a few times, and he seemed fine. Someday, I hope he finds in his life the love I have found.

"Gregory, I'm going to send Francesca a note thanking her for her gifts, especially the painting. I'm also going to tell her that I no longer harbor any ill feelings. And I'm going to send her a gift of my own." I can't help but smirk.

"You're not."

"Why not? I think she'll be honored in a way."

I walk over to my desk and pick up a magazine. A month after I moved back to California, I decided to make my dream of starting my own magazine a reality. That's what I always really wanted. And after my experiences at *Profile* and with Francesca, I decided I never wanted to work with another celebrity again. Gregory has helped me tremendously, and I received a grant to help with the funding.

The magazine targets career-minded young women. Gregory and I came up with the title together—*Signorina!*

"Do you think Francesca will be sad when she sees your magazine's title since her marital status has now changed?"

Gregory walks over and stands behind me as he places his chin on my shoulder and wraps his arms around my waist. I look up into his face and give him a quick kiss on the lips before saying, "Oh, I'm sure in Francesca's mind, she'll always be '*signorina.*' "

# RECIPES FOR *CARISSIMA*

### *Biscotti d'Anise* (Anise Cookies)

1½ cups all-purpose flour
½ teaspoon baking powder
¼ teaspoon salt
8 tablespoons (1 stick)
   unsalted butter, softened

½ cup sugar
2 large eggs, at room temperature
2 teaspoons anise extract
1 cup lightly toasted walnuts,
   coarsely chopped (optional)

Preheat the oven to 350°F. Butter and flour a large baking sheet. Combine the flour, baking powder, and salt.

In the large bowl of an electric mixer, beat the butter until light and creamy. Beat in the sugar until fluffy. Beat in the eggs one at a time. Beat in the anise extract. On low speed, beat in the flour mixture until combined. Stir in the nuts if using them.

Shape the dough into two 12- by 1½-inch logs on the prepared baking sheet. Smooth the sides with a rubber spatula. Bake for 20 minutes, or until the logs are lightly browned and firm when pressed lightly in the center. Remove from the oven but do not turn it off. Let the logs cool for 10 minutes.

Slide the logs onto a cutting board and cut diagonally into ½-inch-thick slices. Stand the biscotti on the baking sheet. Bake for 10 minutes, or until the cookies are lightly toasted. Transfer to wire racks to cool.

## *Muffuletta* (Submarine-style Sandwich)

1 large round Italian bread
Extra virgin olive oil
Olive paste
Sundried tomatoes
3-4 plum tomatoes, sliced
1 tablespoon capers
2 tablespoons marinated
    artichoke hearts

1 tablespoon fresh parsley
4 or 5 scallions
Ground black pepper to taste
¼ pound sliced prosciutto
Block of fontina or any other
    sharp cheese of your liking,
    sliced thin

Cut loaf of Italian bread in half. Scoop out the excess bread crumbs from both halves. Place top half aside.

Drizzle extra virgin olive oil on bottom half of the loaf of bread.

Spread olive paste on bottom half of loaf.

Add sundried tomatoes.

Add the plum tomato slices, followed by the capers, artichoke hearts, parsley, and scallions.

Add the black pepper.

Lastly, add the slices of prosciutto and fontina cheese.

Drizzle extra virgin olive oil on top half of loaf. Place top half on top of bottom half of loaf that has all the ingredients.

Wrap muffuletta tightly with wax paper.

Place three dinner plates on top of wrapped muffuletta and place in the refrigerator overnight if time allows. If time does not allow, then let the plates rest on top of the muffuletta for at least 15 minutes.

## *Ravioli Fritti* (Fried Pastry Ravioli)

### SHELL

4 cups flour                    1 tablespoon sugar
2 eggs                          1 cup warm water
3 tablespoons vegetable oil

### FILLING

3 pounds ricotta                1 egg yolk
2 cups sugar (taste for         1–2 teaspoons cinnamon
  desired sweetness)              (taste for desired sweetness)

### ADDITIONAL INGREDIENTS

2 egg yolks beaten with         ¾ cup vegetable oil
  1 teaspoon water, for         Confectioners' sugar
  egg wash

Dust a large, flat, clean surface with flour. Then pour 4 cups of flour and form a small hill with your hands. With the end of a wooden spoon, dig a small hole in the center of the flour.

Crack your eggs, dropping them into the hole of the flour hill. Then pour oil, sugar, and water into the hole.

Knead dough. If dough is tough, add more water. Only add 1 teaspoon of water at a time. Knead the dough again until the consistency is smooth. If not smooth, repeat, adding 1 teaspoon of water and kneading the dough.

Mix all of the above ingredients for the filling in a large mixing bowl.

Roll out the dough you made above with a rolling pin. The sheet of dough should be about ½ inch thick.

Place about 1 tablespoon of filling onto a corner of the rolled out dough. Using a pastry cutter, cut around the dough. Be sure to leave about an inch from where you placed the filling to the edge of the dough so that the filling doesn't leak out when frying the raviolis.

Carefully fold over the dough, covering the filling in the center. If it seems like you might have placed too much filling in the center of the ravioli shell, then scoop some of it out. You'll know if you placed too much when you fold over the dough and the filling spreads to the edge of the shell. Repeat process until all of your raviolis are made.

With a fork's prongs, press the edges of the raviolis to seal them shut.

Carefully separate the yolks from 2 eggs into a small bowl. Beat the yolks. Stir 1 teaspoon of water into the yolks to create an egg wash.

With a pastry brush, lightly brush the egg wash onto the raviolis.

Add ¾ cup of vegetable oil to a skillet. Turn heat up to medium. Let oil heat for about 1 minute.

Carefully drop the raviolis into the skillet. Watch them closely and turn them over with a spatula after about 1–2 minutes. Fry until each side of the raviolis is golden brown.

Place fried raviolis onto a large plate lined with paper towels to absorb the excess oil.

Once raviolis have cooled, dust with confectioners' sugar.

Once raviolis are cooled, they can be served. Any leftover raviolis should be covered with plastic wrap and placed in the refrigerator.

### *Riso Nero di Pasqua* (Black Easter Rice Pudding)

1⅛ pounds short grain rice
1 quart milk
¼ teaspoon salt
3½ cups sugar
1 teaspoon vanilla
1 pound unsweetened
   cocoa powder
1½ teaspoons orange zest

1 pound roughly chopped
   almonds
1½ tablespoons triple sec or
   orange liqueur
¼ pound semisweet
   chocolate, crumbled
Ground cinnamon

Place rice in a large pot. Add the milk, salt, sugar, and vanilla, and stir. Cook according to rice package directions. When the rice is almost cooked, lower temperature to a simmer, and stir in the cocoa, little by little. Then stir in the grated orange zest. Keep stirring. Be careful that the rice doesn't overcook or stick to the bottom of the pot.

Remove the pot from the heat and stir in the chopped almonds. Let the rice cool for about 15 minutes. Then stir in the orange liqueur and semisweet chocolate.

Scoop rice pudding into small dessert bowls. Sprinkle cinnamon generously on top of rice pudding. Can serve either once pudding has completely cooled or can chill in refrigerator and serve later.

## *Spiedini di Vitello* (Skewers of Breaded Veal)

1 pound veal cutlets
½–1cup extra virgin olive oil
½–¾ pounds seasoned Italian bread crumbs
½–¾ cup Pecorino Romano cheese

Ground black pepper
1 tablespoon minced parsley
Skewers (If using wooden skewers, soak them in water for an hour beforehand.)

Set your oven to the broil setting. Pound veal cutlets with a meat mallet until they're a nice, thin consistency. Be careful not to over pound them. You don't want the veal to be too thin.

Cut veal cutlets into long strips, about a half-inch wide.

Pour olive oil into a shallow dish. Set aside.

Mix bread crumbs, Romano cheese, black pepper, and parsley together in a shallow dish. Set aside.

Dip veal strips into the extra virgin olive oil. Then dip both sides of the veal strips into the bread crumbs mixture.

Roll one end of each of the veal strips all the way to the other end. Carefully slide them onto the skewers. You should be able to fit about 5 veal strips onto each skewer, depending on how thick your meat is and how long your skewers are.

Place the veal skewers under the broiler.

After about 4–5 minutes, turn the skewers over. Broil the other side for another 4–5 minutes. Keep a close watch on the skewers so as not to burn them.

**The recipe for *Biscotti d'Anise* was adapted from the cookbook *La Dolce Vita*. The recipe for *Muffuletta* was adapted from *The Martha Stewart Cooking Show*. All the other recipes I received from my family. *Spiedini di Vitello* and *Ravioli Fritti* were my grandmother's recipes, which she passed down to my mother, who then passed them down to me. *Riso Nero di Pasqua* was passed down to me from my father, but instead of making it for Easter, he made it for Christmas. For more recipes, special reading group features, and blog posts, please visit www.RosannaChiofalo.com.**

**Please turn the page for a very special
Q&A with the author!**

**How do you pronounce your name?**

KEY-OH-FAH-LO.

**What inspired you to write a novel in which one of the protagonists was a silver-screen star?**

My brilliant editor, John Scognamiglio, and I brainstormed on the storyline for *Carissima*. He thought it would be cool to have a sort of Italian *The Devil Wears Prada* subject in which a young ingénue clashes with a diva actress. I loved the idea! I wanted to continue the story of Signora Tesca, who was a secondary character in *Bella Fortuna*. I felt she was intriguing and had secrets and I wanted to explore her story more deeply in the second novel. So I thought, what if she were related to a famous Italian silver-screen star who suddenly comes to the working-class neighborhood of Astoria, New York, much to the surprise and pleasure of the residents.

**You show us the relationship between Pia and her sister, Erica, when she was alive and between Francesca and Giuliana. Why did you choose to focus on sisters? Do you have a sister and are you close?**

Yes, I have a sister. Her name is Angela. She is older than me, and we are five years apart. When I was very young, we were close and were always by each other's side. But as I got older, we started to fight more, as many siblings do. However, once we became adults, we became close again. I've always been fascinated with relationships between siblings, and I knew I wanted to focus on sisters in my second novel. Ironically, a few months before I started writing *Carissima*, a childhood friend of mine died quite unexpectedly. She was my sister's age and had been very good friends with her when they were teenagers and into their twenties. And when I was a child, I looked up to her as another older sister. I'm also very good friends with the younger sister of my friend who passed away. This only convinced me even more that I wanted to focus on sisters in my second novel. I also wanted to show two different relationships with sisters. Pia was always close to her sister, but then she loses her. Francesca was once close to her sister, but then they have a huge falling out and don't talk for decades, only to be reunited later in life. I wanted to illustrate how different some sibling relationships can be from others and how they can influence the people we become.

**In *Carissima*, the residents of Astoria go crazy when they hear Francesca Donata is in town and when they see her. Do you have a similar obsession with celebrities? And who is your favorite movie star or celebrity?**

I've never been particularly starstruck by celebrities, not to the point where I must read the gossip mags or follow their every move. Also, as a New Yorker, I do see celebrities walking the streets of Manhattan quite frequently. New Yorkers, for some reason, don't get fazed by famous people as much as other Americans. However, there are a few luminaries whom I do find quite intriguing. I don't really have a favorite movie star, but the ones who have fascinated me are Princess Grace, Gina Lollobrigida, Claudia Cardinale, Raquel Welch, Marilyn Monroe, Elizabeth Taylor, Meryl Streep, James Dean, Robert De Niro, and Daniel Day-Lewis. I do have a favorite celebrity who's not an actor—Bono, the singer of the Irish rock band U2. I've always been moved by his lyrics and his unwavering passion and commitment to human rights.

**There have been many movies made about Rome. Do you have a favorite one?**

I love *Three Coins in the Fountain,* and you're probably going to laugh, but ever since I saw *Gidget Goes to Rome* as a child, that's been a favorite of mine as well. I also enjoyed very much Woody Allen's *To Rome with Love.* The city looked absolutely stunning in it!

**I take it you made a wish when you were in Rome and visited the Trevi Fountain. If so, do you remember what your wish was, and did it come true yet?**

Yes, of course, I visited the Trevi Fountain and made the famous coin toss and a wish. That's a must, if you go to Rome! But sadly, I don't remember what my wish was. I guess I'll have to go back and make a wish that I'll never forget! One custom I didn't know about when I visited Rome is that there is a certain way you are supposed to toss the coins into the Trevi Fountain, as Pia learns when she is in Rome. Perhaps that is why I don't remember my wish, since I didn't throw the coins the proper way!

**In both *Bella Fortuna* and *Carissima*, you chose Astoria, Queens, New York as one of the settings. Is this because you are a native of Queens and have a special affinity for it? Or do you have another motive for choosing Queens as the setting in your novels?**

Naturally I do have a special affinity for Queens, especially Astoria, where I was born and grew up; however, I also wanted to set my novels in Queens because whenever New York City is featured in books or movies, Manhattan is usually the borough that is chosen. While I love Manhattan, I wanted readers, particularly non–New Yorkers, to get a flavor of what the rest of New York City is like.

**Now that you are a published author, has it changed you in any way? Has it helped you understand how some people can either change for the better or, in some cases, like Francesca's and Gregory's, for the worse when they reach their dreams? And what is the best part about becoming a published author?**

I think becoming a published author has given me a thicker skin. As writers, we tend to isolate ourselves and are very protective of our writing. Once we decide to try and get our work published, we must expose ourselves and our writing. Having grown up as the child of Italian immigrants, my mother strove to always make a good impression and avoid at all costs making a bad impression, or *fare la brutta figura,* as it's known in Italian and which Francesca talks about in *Carissima*. *La brutta figura* is very much an integral fiber of Italian culture, and it's definitely worn off on me. But after deciding to seek publication for my first novel, I knew that sharing my writing with the world was important to me, especially if I wanted to grow as a writer. In terms of helping me understand how some people can change for the better or worse when they reach their goals in life, I guess I can see how you can get consumed by all the attention you receive when people share their enthusiasm for you and your work. However, I've always been a very down-to-earth person, and even at a young age, I knew who I was. I know that will never change, especially since for me, writing is as much about making a personal connection with my readers as it is about fulfilling my childhood dream of becoming a novelist. The best part about becoming a published author is without a doubt hearing from my readers and having them tell me that they were able to re-late to my characters or certain aspects of my book. I have been very moved by readers who have also told me that reading about Italian American characters and their culture has helped them to reconnect with their heritage as well as helped them to relive some of their own special family memories.

# CARISSIMA

## Rosanna Chiofalo

## ABOUT THIS GUIDE

The suggested questions are included to enhance
your group's reading of Rosanna Chiofalo's
*Carissima*!

# DISCUSSION QUESTIONS

1. Why do you think Francesca is obsessed with being adored by her public? Why do you think the neighbors in Astoria are so fascinated by Francesca, besides the obvious reason of her being a star?

2. Do you think Signora Tesca was justified in holding a grudge against Francesca for all those years? How much do you think jealousy played a part in her refusal to talk to Francesca for so long?

3. How was Pia's relationship with her late sister Erica different than Francesca's relationship with her sister? How have both of these women been influenced by their sisters?

4. Compare and contrast Pia and Francesca. How are their dreams and goals similar? How are they different?

5. We first meet Signora Tesca in *Bella Fortuna*. What were your first impressions of her in *Bella Fortuna*? Did your impressions change when you encountered her again in *Carissima*? If so, how? The same question for Antoniella. How have your initial impressions about her changed from the first book to this one?

6. Francesca is infatuated with jewelry almost as much as she is with being loved by her fans. Why do you think she loves jewelry so much? Of the gifts that Rocco gives her, which was your favorite?

7. Do you feel that Gregory's sudden discovery as an artist goes to his head? Why do you think many people become more self-absorbed when they find fame and/or success in their lives?

8. Do you feel sorry for Francesca in the beginning of the novel when you learn that her five engagements never resulted in marriage? How has her decision to remain single shaped the person she's become? Do you feel sorry for her toward the end of the novel? Do you think she's grown?

9. Francesca chooses to wear *il lutto,* the dress for mourning, after her sister dies. This custom has been losing popularity in Italy over the years. What do you think of it? Were you surprised that a glamorous star like Francesca chose to honor this decades-old Italian custom?

10. How has Pia's trip to Rome changed her? Do you think she would have had the same insights if she had not gone to Rome?

# GREAT BOOKS, GREAT SAVINGS!

When You Visit Our Website:
## www.kensingtonbooks.com
You Can Save Money Off The Retail Price
Of Any Book You Purchase!

- **All Your Favorite Kensington Authors**
- **New Releases & Timeless Classics**
- **Overnight Shipping Available**
- **eBooks Available For Many Titles**
- **All Major Credit Cards Accepted**

Visit Us Today To Start Saving!
## www.kensingtonbooks.com

All Orders Are Subject To Availability.
Shipping and Handling Charges Apply.
Offers and Prices Subject To Change Without Notice.